BINDING BLOOD

BERONIKA KERES

IMMORTAL
WOODS BOOKS

Cover design by www.trifbookdesign.com

This is a work of fiction. Names, characters, places, and incidents either are the products of the author's imagination or are used fictitiously. Any resemblance to actual persons, living or dead, businesses, companies, events, or locales is entirely coincidental. The publisher and author acknowledges the trademark status and trademark ownership of all trademarks, service marks and word marks mentioned in this book.

ISBN 978-1-7771514-6-1 (paperback)
ISBN 978-1-7771514-7-8 (hardcover)
ISBN 978-1-7771514-5-4 (ebook)

CONTENT WARNING

Binding Blood is a new adult fantasy thriller that contains strong language, violence, sexual content, mentions of sexual violence, and subject matters best suited for mature readers.

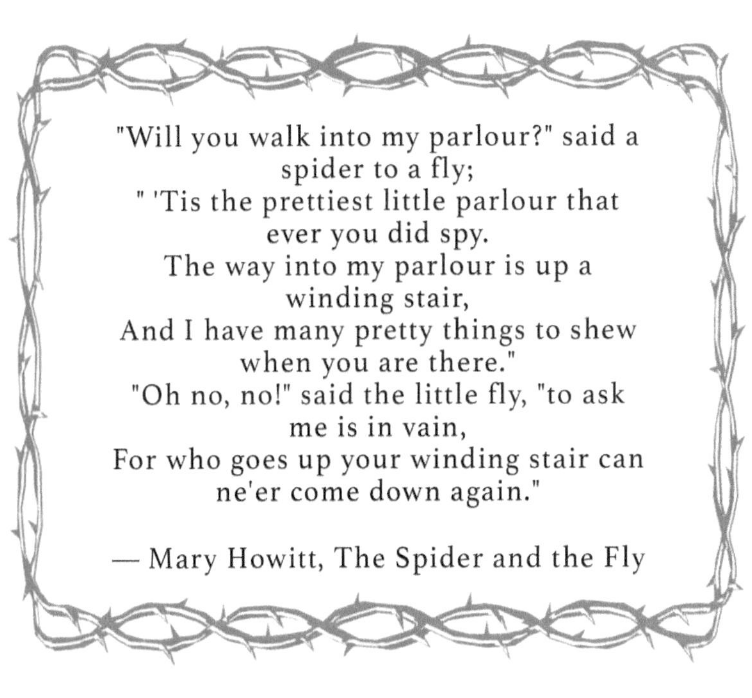
"Will you walk into my parlour?" said a
spider to a fly;
" 'Tis the prettiest little parlour that
ever you did spy.
The way into my parlour is up a
winding stair,
And I have many pretty things to shew
when you are there."
"Oh no, no!" said the little fly, "to ask
me is in vain,
For who goes up your winding stair can
ne'er come down again."

— Mary Howitt, The Spider and the Fly

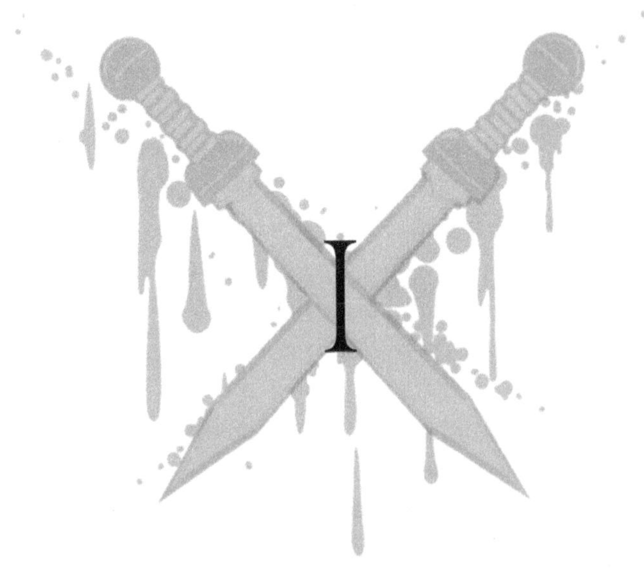

The inevitable lurks on as I sit on the bathroom floor next to Denendrius's body, my finger jammed against a pulseless vein in his wrist. Though I cannot be unshakably sure he will wake since not a breath has passed through him in the last half hour, I swear I can feel it in my bones that he will.

Denendrius deserves a permanent death. He deserves to remain a cold corpse, unable to harm anyone else ever again. He doesn't deserve breath when he took it from so many others. His death would set the balance back. I'd never have to be afraid again.

His death is what *I* deserve. It's what countless other girls deserve.

But it's not what I want.

It's not what I *need*. His suffering is what I need. I need him to remember, and want to see the pleading look in his begging eyes that should surely come when he understands what I'll be able to do to him now that he cannot hide behind immortality. Even if he doesn't admit it aloud, will he regret *everything*?

Alive and wishing he wasn't.

That would make things right.

I thump my head back against the bathroom cupboard, Denendrius remaining where he fell unconscious on the age-stained white linoleum floor after Agatha had the cure for vampirism forced down his throat. Fewer moments of hesitation and he wouldn't have forgotten, wouldn't need to be alive to remember. It would've been much easier if I'd gone through with killing him a few minutes earlier. But his last thoughts—his confusion—couldn't have been not knowing who I am and what he did.

That is not something I deserve. It's unfair.

Rayonne must sense my plotting as she wanders to the doorway of the bathroom to peer down at me from beneath her black bangs. Carefully, she says, "You understand that if he wakes, he must go to Romania, right?"

Does she understand it will be her against Denendrius and me? She really can't expect me to forfeit Denendrius's retribution.

I grit my teeth and clear my throat against the pulsing pain from Denendrius's attempt to strangle me while I was working up the courage to kill him. "Do you really think you can *take him* from me? If he wakes up and remembers me, I'm killing him."

She crosses her arms. "No. This is bigger than you, Marianna. I understand you want him dead—and I agree you deserve that—but it changes nothing. Viorel wants him after he wreaked havoc on so many clans, so Viorel gets him. Unless you'd rather enrage a powerful vampire like him, because I'd rather not."

"Let Viorel be pissed," I snap. What do I care about the feelings of some vampire? "It's not my problem."

"It'll be your problem when he kills you," she says simply. "And I doubt it would be quick. Denendrius kidnapped and killed hundreds of Darklings and Children of Stars, so Viorel's going to be pissed if he doesn't get his revenge. Many of them were clan leaders, Marianna. He's not going to let this go."

I give Denendrius's body a lethal glare. "*I need to see him die. I need to know for a fact he's gone so I can go back to my life.*"

She fishes her cell phone from a hidden pocket in her black skirt and flips it open. "I understand the thought, but that's impossible. This is out of your hands now." She taps her fingers against a few buttons and tucks the phone under her mass of silky black curls to rest it against her ear. "I've got to make some calls."

I sit alone with him as Rayonne paces from the room and down the hall of Denendrius's apartment, the previous day and tonight playing over in my pounding head. Sarah's admission—that Denendrius has been assaulting her as a twisted way of getting back at me—still has my stomach roiling. The ache in my legs remains from running away from school afterward in my last-ditch effort to avoid Denendrius turning me and kidnapping me, taking me to Italy to steal children and raise them together in the villa he bought us.

I can't believe I thought for even a moment that running off could work out for me, and I suppose I should consider myself lucky Denendrius tracked me down after Rayonne and those vampires nabbed me. What would have happened if he didn't show up? I used so much energy running around Lorimer while trying to hide and think of a plan that there's no way I could have fought any of them off even if I had managed to escape the chair they'd tied me to.

Despite her being gone for a handful of minutes, there's no conversation aside from the disgruntled one she has with herself under her breath.

Rayonne grimaces as she returns and fixes her long black skirt. She sits on the floor across from me. Lips twitching with the emotion of whatever thoughts spin in her mind, she stares

off into space for a few minutes before saying, "Marianna . . .
I've got a problem."

My face scrunches with a scowl. "Is it my problem?"

Her nose lifts, upper lip curling. "It's about to be. Viorel's
men aren't answering my calls. Their numbers are disconnected, one already reassigned to some human. They switch
them every few years, but—" Slowly, her jaw lowers with whatever realization she has. "They must have picked up new ones
before Agatha turned me . . . and she must not have passed
them on to me so I couldn't tattle on her . . ." She hunches. "I
rarely called them myself. They always preferred to speak with
Agatha since she led us." She hangs her head and pushes out a
deep breath. "They won't know to come looking either if the
last update she gave them was that we found him in Lorimer,
right before she turned me back. I doubt she'll tell them about
this, or she'll have to explain what she did to me too."

"Maybe they blocked you for turning on Agatha and
helping me and Denendrius escape?" I spitball.

Her head snaps up, and she meets me with hostile brown
eyes. "Blocked their connection to the person with Denendrius? Unlikely."

My triumphant grin splays from one cheek to the other. "I
guess Denendrius isn't going to Romania after all?"

Her red lips purse, and her chest rises and falls so fast that I
can hear the breath as it passes in and out of her nose. "This is
as bad for you as it is for me, Marianna. I can't get in touch with
Viorel's men, which means we're stuck with Denendrius and
have to deal with Agatha when she inevitably hunts us down.
She will kill *both of us* and take Denendrius. That means I have
to go speak to my friends at Estrella de Sangre and put the
word out that I have Denendrius and I need Viorel's men to
come collect him."

I shake my head in confusion. "Why is there a 'we' in this?
Thank you for saving me from Agatha and all, and I'm sorry he

destroyed your life, but I still have the pieces of a life to pick up. I'll be killing him as soon as he remembers. Viorel is not my fucking problem."

She gapes at me. "I'm sorry, but are you being purposefully obtuse? You killing Denendrius is not happening. I am talking about the most powerful and terrifying vampire known to man. Killing Denendrius is practically an act of suicide. This means you cannot go back to your normal life. That's how this becomes your problem as well."

My scowl is so deep that my forehead hurts. "You—" My hands curl into fists in my lap. "You told me I would be free after."

Her eyes avoid mine, and she picks at the black polish covering her thumbnail. "That was before Agatha was going to kill you, before she lost her entire team. When all there was left to do was load him up and call him in. Aside from us now having to draw mass attention to ourselves, she will do the same while she looks for more vampires to help her retrieve him." She takes a deep breath and shakes her head. "Once vampires catch wind Denendrius is human, they'll be flocking to Lorimer, hoping to capture him to collect whatever bounty they know of. Things might get noisy, and we'll be in the middle of it all. Even when Denendrius is dealt with, if someone other than Viorel gets him, nobody is going to be eager to declare it and risk having the attention on them. Which means if you stick around here you're as good as dead."

"No. There's got to be a way I can go back to my life—"

"There isn't. In fact, you're the whole reason we found him as fast as we did. It took us five years—until last year—to discover he'd taken up residency in Lorimer. And when you came into his life full-time, his entire behavioral pattern changed. He got sloppy. I spotted him for the first time in decades by accident in a *diner*. That is the last place I would have looked for him. You have to understand how entwined your life is with his here."

"Then I'll move somewhere else!" I can use Denendrius's money and the fake identification he got for me. "I'll start a new life."

Her serious eyes bore into mine. "No, Marianna. Life as you knew it before Denendrius is *over*. Whether or not you like it, the vampire world sees you as Denendrius's. I wouldn't put it past someone to hunt you down based on that fact alone. He's done a lot of evil things to many people. They'll be looking to get revenge in any way they can, especially once they find out Denendrius won't be able to protect you."

My skin burns. I suck in a deep breath and scream against clenched teeth while booting Denendrius's dead leg half a dozen times.

"Marianna, stop!" she demands. "I'm sorry things didn't go the way they were supposed to, but I have a plan that could work."

I push the heels of my hands into my eye sockets, causing colorful stars to explode behind my eyelids. "Is it a better plan than a fucked-up game of vampire telephone?"

"As crazy as it sounds, it'll probably work. It's only been a year since our last update—which sounds like a long time, I know. But to vampires, it's merely a blip. That means they're likely somewhere close enough to overhear. Vampires *talk*. I'm sure this will be dealt with quickly." A little grin plays at the corner of her lips. "And perhaps if I tell them how much help you've been . . . you'll get half the reward."

Lowering my hands, I cautiously eye her smiling face. "The reward? If it's not killing Denendrius, I'm not interested."

Her back straightens, her grin growing. "Well, I'm getting a place in Viorel's castle once I turn him in, right? If I vouch for you, say you're half the reason I found him, I bet they'll let you come too. I've heard Viorel is as generous as he is brutal, and he'll be so ecstatic to have Denendrius after centuries of searching he probably won't question making you part of the clan."

My heart hammers as I try to imagine myself in a castle, but the only good I can think that would come of it would be knowing Denendrius is locked away and being tortured and I won't be killed for my act of revenge. Would they let me watch? Would they let me *torture him*? "I don't know. How would I belong in a place full of vampires?"

Her lips twist. "I'm not completely sure, to be honest. Better than what you've got going on here. I haven't been there yet, of course, but I've heard plenty about the place through the grapevine. Despite all the vampires, humans *do* live there. Mostly the human families of vampires, or children who have been sucked into the world, but I don't see why you couldn't find a place amongst all that. Or perhaps they could turn you."

My heartbeat spikes. "I don't want to be a vampire." The words choke me.

She sneers at me like I've said something ridiculous and borderline offensive. "How come?"

I give the thought some real consideration and try to imagine myself as a vampire *without* Denendrius being in that equation. The idea of it when he wanted to turn me was terrifying, but if I don't have to worry about him? I could do *anything* I want. "I-I don't know." There's already too much to think about right now, never mind that.

She sighs. "Still, I don't see why coming as a human would be a problem."

I shrug and stare at the yellow glow on the ceiling from the dim light, not wanting to say anything more in case she tries to push the topic. "Wait a second." My brow furrows. "Two vampires Denendrius killed—Alaire and Edmond— mentioned how I was spotted at a restaurant with Denendrius. Was it you who reported that?"

Rayonne frowns. "I didn't realize they died."

I cock a brow. "You knew them?"

"*Of* them. They were loosely connected to Viorel. Stayed with his clan and introduced some new tech in the nineties, I think. I tipped them off through their forum post in case things went awry with Agatha. Figured she'd probably try to kill me to cover up turning me back." She turns sideways and leans against the off-white wall across from the bathtub. "Damn. I don't know how we thought we had a chance if he killed them."

"Yeah." The wanted write-up had warned Children of Stars to steer clear of him. Obviously, it was for a good reason, even if they had the cure to their advantage.

Another realization pops into my mind. Alaire and Edmond talked about taking me somewhere safe to live. Could they have meant Viorel's castle? I may not know tons about the vampire world, but I can't imagine there would be many clans accepting human members.

I groan and close my eyes, trying to detach myself from the idea of a vampire-free future. It hurts that Rayonne is right. Even if I went on with my life without vampires interfering, how could I truly enjoy it? I'd be wary of every dark corner, constantly looking over my shoulder expecting someone to kill me. It would be ten times the fear of having Venganza Roja wanting to kill me. Perhaps trying to get into Viorel's castle is my best bet. If Alaire and Edmond thought I could go . . . then maybe her offer isn't so crazy.

Could it really be any worse than death—possibly prolonged torture—at the hands of spiteful vampires?

Maybe it's time to give up on my dream of a normal life. My past has been nothing but abnormal. Why do I think my future has any chance of being different?

I release a defeated sigh and open my eyes. "If you help me get into Viorel's castle—make a case for me keeping my humanity and for a little torture—then I won't kill Denendrius."

Her grin returns. "Deal."

I assess Denendrius's body. He looks no different, and when I press my fingers to his wrist, there's still no pulse. "This is all assuming he wakes up. If he doesn't wake up, do we forfeit everything?"

"No, Viorel must know the risks of using the cure if he passed it along to us. We got him, so they must still recognize our efforts. We can't control the outcome." She grunts as she stands. "Besides, only a few more hours before rigor mortis sets in if he's truly dead. We'll know soon either way."

I cock a brow. "Then what? Off to Estrella de Sangre? Like Blood Star? Is that an underground blood club?"

"Yes, for Children of Stars. Word will travel fast from there, which is both good and bad because more than Viorel's men will hear. But that's a risk we have to take."

"Can't you call Viorel himself if his men aren't answering?"

Her laugh is sharp. "Nobody speaks to Viorel outside of the castle. Everything goes through his men. I was merely lucky enough to be at a bar at the same time as them and Agatha to overhear Denendrius's name and insert myself."

"And you still stuck with her after she turned you back? She seemed like a real bitch to work with."

Rayonne rubs her forehead like she's trying to ward off a headache. "I have had little purpose aside from revenge, Marianna. Until she turned me human, I cared more about avenging my son and husband than I cared about how poorly she treated us. Besides, I can't imagine how I would have had a better chance to find him. We only knew he was in Lorimer because Laura's old clan told her they overheard his friend call him by his name at a casino."

"Ugh. Well, we could wait for her to come for us, then snatch her cell phone," I suggest. "We could stake her too and let Viorel's men pull it out and punish her when we explain what she did to you."

She scratches her head. "That is extremely risky. But it could work. Let's hope Viorel's men catch wind of things before it comes to that. She still has to track us down here."

II

Blood cakes my skin, so I brave the shower despite Denendrius being unconscious on the bathroom floor. I can't help but glance around the curtain every few seconds to check if he's awake. I would have preferred to shower with him out of the room, but moving him proved impossible, even with Rayonne's help.

Rayonne pops her head through the cracked door, her black-shadowed eyes closed to give me privacy. "So, there's absolutely no food here and I have eaten nothing but half a cookie in three days. How do you feel about me running to the store quick to grab food and garlic? The sun's about to come up, so it should be safe."

I roll my eyes and dip my hair under the hot stream of water, bubbles running down me. "At least wait until I'm dressed so I don't have to fight him naked if he wakes up."

She fights a smile. "Fair. I doubt he'll be awake soon, anyway. Any grocery requests? I bet he'll be famished upon waking like I was. I ate an entire precooked rotisserie chicken—oh, I'll pick one of those up too."

I frown when I try to remember what I ate last. The emptiness of my stomach isn't demanding to be filled. "Anything, I guess. Strawberry milk."

Rayonne turns away. "Got it."

Water beads down my legs and arms when I step out of the bathroom with a towel wrapped around me. I navigate around the bloodstains on the hallway carpet, past the bedroom on the right, and turn left past the eighties-style kitchen and toward the dining area across from the living room. Rayonne stands from her place on the black leather couch when I come into the living room.

"Oh—"

"My clothes are in one of those boxes," I clarify, nodding my chin toward the stack in the far corner—between the empty black ladder bookshelves on the farthest wall, and the entertainment stand across from the couch on another—that Denendrius had packed to bring to Italy with us before I fled.

"I'll leave you to dress. I've got to grab my suitcase from the car and change anyway."

I scowl at the stack of boxes, and when the apartment door closes behind Rayonne, I open the closest one, unloading a hot breath when I find Denendrius's clothes. I kick that box aside and open the one beneath it, discovering girl clothes in shopping bags I've never seen before. My curiosity makes me drag the box to the couch with one hand while I hold my towel in place with the other.

I grab the bottom of a bag and pull it upside down, soft baby-blue fabric spilling over the other neatly arranged bags.

"Oh, what the fuck." I hold it in front of me, towel tucked under my armpits.

It's the pants of an expensive velour tracksuit. It wouldn't be so alarming if I hadn't fawned over the same one two months prior to meeting Denendrius, when Jenna, Daina, Camille and I went if-I-were-rich window shopping. Daina dreamed of us getting matching ones in different colors: pink for Camille, purple for her, peach for Jenna, and baby blue for me.

I pull them on after a pair of underwear, the gentle fabric silky compared to my usual old jeans. They're my size and would fit perfectly if I hadn't dropped a handful of pounds over the past few weeks. I rip the tag off the waist and throw it back in the box.

While placing the matching velour jacket aside for when I find a shirt to put underneath it, I wonder why Denendrius didn't give them to me and instead packed them up. I pull out another shopping bag from a teen store my friends and I visited on the same day. My hands sweat when I hold a pair of designer jeans and some plain but brand-name tank tops I tried on that day too. I yank a white tank top on before the jacket.

I know I should throw the clothes out since he bought them for me. But they're so expensive . . . and is it such a big deal if he might not remember enough to benefit from me wearing them?

I throw that headache of a thought process to the back of my mind and continue rooting through the box. When I find a blue velvet jewelry box at the bottom, I know exactly why he hid the gifts instead of giving them to me. In the box, underneath a receipt for four thousand dollars dated to the day I met him in the mall, sits a necklace covered entirely in white diamonds.

He must not have thought I deserved them since I broke my promise to remember him after he kidnapped me from Enchanted Land for twelve days when I was five. Clearly, he went out of his way to hide the extent of our knowing one another, especially with him giving me as little information as possible. Was he hoping I'd remember on my own? Or did he think I didn't deserve to know if I couldn't recall it myself and fought even the little truths he gave up?

I pack the necklace up, drop it into the bottom of the box, and throw it all back into the corner of the room.

My heart skips a beat when the apartment door crashes open into the old fridge, and I step out of the living room in time to see Rayonne hauling in a large antique suitcase. With both hands in a death grip on the handle, she grunts and swings it forward out of the doorway, dinging the wall past the little closet.

"He'll never know," I reassure her while she inspects the damage and cringes. "Maybe think about getting a suitcase from this era. One with wheels if you're going to pack it full of bricks?"

She snickers. "It was *much* lighter when I had immortal strength."

After Rayonne changes in the bedroom—into a dress as black and lacy as before—she pulls the strap of a deep velvet purse over her shoulder and climbs into a heavy-looking pair of leather boots. The first bit of sunlight sneaks into the apartment through the gray slats of the blinds covering the large patio doors behind us and creates a striped pattern of sunlight and shadows. Rays glint off the metal legs of the chairs around the small table, the only furniture in the bare dining area.

"You trust I won't kill him?" I'd be nervous to leave him alone with her.

She straightens and grabs the knob. "I trust you don't want Viorel to skin you. Wound him—nonlethally—if you have to. I know it's probably not best if I go, but we *absolutely* need garlic to protect ourselves." She pauses and taps her bottom lip in thought. "If he wakes up, you need to pretend to be his friend—girlfriend—whatever. I know you hate his guts, but he can't know. He needs to think we're his friends and we are protecting him from something bad and are there to help him remember."

"Should we not tie him up?"

"And deal with him *how* in this apartment if we get stuck with him for a week? He's stronger than both of us, and I am not risking overdosing him with sedatives." Her pale skin loses even more color at the thought.

"Fine, I'll be his . . . *friend*." I almost choke on the word. It'll hurt to be nice, but it's the easiest way. And if he remembers, I'll have to bust his kneecaps.

The corner of her lip lifts for a friendly half-smile. "I left my number on a scrap of paper on the counter. Call me if anything happens. I'll rush back," Rayonne says before trying to shut the door behind her.

"Wait—" I rush down the hall to the bathroom and fish Denendrius's wallet out of his jeans before running back to her. I pull out a handful of bills and hold them out. "Can you pick up some booze?"

Her upper lip curls back in judgement, but she takes the money. "It's a terrible idea to get drunk in our position."

"I won't get drunk. I want to take the edge off. *Especially* if I'm about to play friendly with my abuser."

She tucks the money in her purse. "Understandable. I'll grab cigarettes too."

With that, she's out the door.

I can't think of anything else to do but pace around the apartment. I'm in limbo again, merely waiting for the universe to decide what to do with Denendrius. What if he wakes up and remembers? What will we do with him while we scramble to contact Viorel's people? How will we control him, stop him from calling his friend to turn him back like he had planned before passing out? Tying him up and sedating him would be one solution even if Rayonne thinks it's dangerous, but if we have to move him? Run from other vampires? We'd be screwed, never mind the hell he would give us knowing we plan on handing him over to Viorel.

But if he doesn't remember, how the hell do I make him? And how do I time it—not that I can—with when we hand him over? Because surely his memories of me will return with his fury. But at least if he doesn't remember, I can trick him. I can get him to trust us. He won't know our plan until we hand him over. And I guess he doesn't *need to* remember before Viorel's men get him. If I can go to the castle too, him remembering while he's stuck in a cell is good enough for me. As long as he remembers and suffers for it.

My head spins. "Ugh." I lean against the kitchen counter, a headache creeping into my skull.

I want this to be over already.

Denendrius's phone rings from the bathroom, rattling against the linoleum behind the toilet, where it landed during our struggle. My heart plummets into my empty stomach and I take tentative steps down the hall, hands clammy at my sides. The ringing stops when I enter the bathroom. I climb over Denendrius and scoop up his phone. When the screen lights up again, shaking and blaring in my hands, a chill wafts through my bones.

Sergei Calling

I gulp. Denendrius's Russian friend was supposed to fly us to Italy today. He must be waiting. Will he come to the apartment if I ignore his calls? Does he know our address? I realize the only way to know the extent of the dilemma is to answer and convince him to keep waiting until I can figure something out.

I take a deep breath. It shouldn't be a problem. If I could lie to cops when I was in Red Revenge, surely I can convince him of something.

When I accept the call and place the phone to my ear, a deep and middle-aged voice rambles in annoyed Russian.

I clear my throat. "H-hello?"

Unfortunately, Sergei isn't a cop. My stomach twists and I'd rather be answering a call from the DEA than a vampire who must be as terrifying as Denendrius to be friends with him.

"Marianna?" His confusion is obvious.

"Uh—yeah—"

"Where's Denendrius?" he asks, a frustrated edge to his voice.

My hand is slick on the phone. "I don't know. He was agitated this morning and left me the phone and walked out. He told me if you called to tell you he'd be back later." I stare down at Denendrius's body and wonder what would happen if he woke up right now to this.

Sergei grumbles in Russian. "When he returns, you tell that bastard I went back to the hotel. You both meet me here tonight and we all go to the hangar together."

What would Sergei do if he knew what was really going on?

"I'll tell him you called."

There's a long pause. "Are you okay, Marianna? How about you tell me your address and I can send a cab to collect you. We can wait for him together here. I'm unable to leave the room now, but there's complimentary breakfast downstairs and the pool is opening soon. Leave a note."

The genuine concern in his question throws me for a loop, but I'm glad he doesn't know where we are. "Why wouldn't I be okay?" I ask carefully, not sure what to make of his offer, though I definitely won't be accepting it.

"Denendrius has been upset lately, *da*? We both know how he is in his moods. But if he left you with the phone, he must not want to hear from me right now. Knowing him like this, he might not be back tonight, and the place you are in is packed already. Maybe you need a different atmosphere to relax and eat right now. He won't be mad you left."

I'm careful with my choice of words. "No, it's okay. I'll stay here. Thanks, though."

"You would be safe here, Marianna. Denendrius and I are different in ways, you understand? We are great friends and I do anything for him, but we don't share all the same . . . *interests.*"

My lips twist, and my stomach tightens. What kind of friendship do they have then? Does he want to take advantage of me being alone and is lying about not being a pig like Denendrius did to get my guard down? Or is he trying to monitor me for Denendrius's sake?

"I'll stay here, but, um . . . how did you and Den meet?" I ask, unable to help my curiosity while also trying to dig for more information on how crazy Sergei could be. What kind of person will I have to deal with when Denendrius inevitably doesn't call him back?

"Oh, has he never spoken of me?" There's a layer of disappointment in his words.

"Not really. He was kind of . . . resistant to talk about his life."

He's hesitant as he says, "He is my maker. I was a pilot in the Soviet Union in the Second World War. The Germans shot my Yak-9 out of the sky and Denendrius was close enough to rescue and turn me. I am indebted to him."

My eyes narrow. That's what they built their friendship on? Does Denendrius hold his life over his head, or is Sergei so grateful to be alive that he's happy to be his buddy? "Oh."

His tired sigh is loud in my ear. "Well, I must sleep. I can answer all your questions later. Call and wake me if you change your mind."

I give Denendrius's calf a tap with my big toe. He's still limp, flesh squishy. "Okay."

After ending the call, I slip the phone into the pocket of my sweater and scowl down at Denendrius. "Goddamn it. He's going to come looking for you, isn't he?"

III

I snatch the scrap paper off the counter and sprawl out on the couch, texting Rayonne a simple greeting so she'll have a way to contact me too. Then, I check the rest of Denendrius's messages and call history. There's no history—not even from his friend—other than texts and calls from my smashed phone. He must have deleted everything.

When I return to the home screen, the photo app catches my attention and I'm overtaken by nausea. My fingers tingle and I lose feeling in them when I force myself to press it. I can't breathe when the screen turns black before the gallery opens.

Thankfully, a quick glance shows nothing resembling the kinds of sick videos he made with his camcorder. I find multiple photos of his Mustang instead. In one, he's holding a black rectangular object that's clearly a tracking device from the image of a car on it. The next photo is of the tracking device's serial number. After that, there's a few photos of expensive houses with For Sale signs in the yards. If I had kept my promise to remember him, would he have moved us into one of them? He had said if things went the way they were supposed to with us, we would have moved if I didn't want to live in the apartment.

My tenth-grade school photo from last year appears under my fingertips next, and a little gasp escapes my mouth. *I don't even have a copy.* My foster mom at the time hated it, and would not waste money on photos when I "couldn't even bother to smile," and demanded I do retakes. I refused, so the school was stuck with using it for the yearbook. It's not like I look angry or even sad, only neutral. I put effort into getting ready that day too. My sandy hair was perfectly straight, I wore the blue blouse my foster dad had bought me despite it being too formal for my liking, and I went as far as covering the bags under my eyes with foundation. I attempted a small smile, but it didn't translate. I didn't bother with photos this school year.

Another swipe across the screen shows the same photo, but it's brightened and someone has expertly photoshopped the ugly blue backdrop white. Another swipe, and I'm looking at it on an Italian passport, a dark hand holding it open to show that my name is Maria Romano. My birthday is the same, except for the year, where he's made me eighteen. The same school picture appears on two driver's licenses, one issued in Italy with the same information as the Italian passport, and one issued in California under the name Marianna Sovetta, but I'm twenty-one. There's two birth certificates matching their corresponding sets. I was born in the city of Rome on the Italian set; Anaheim for the California set.

As much as I hate the reason my false identities exist, I'm glad they do. I'll be able to get to Romania without issue now, or start a life somewhere else if needed. Plus, he's made me old enough to buy alcohol and cigarettes. Now, I only have to figure out where he hid them so I can actually leave.

The next dozen photos take my breath again. They're of diary pages, signed off by *Sarah*.

The dates of them vary—all written before our truce—and share common themes. Sarah hated me and was intensely jealous of my parental neglect and interpreted it as freedom she didn't have around her cop father's strictness, and she was sick of hearing about how much CJ liked me. Apparently, CJ was going to dance with her as a friend at the school dance if I didn't show up. When I did, she had her friends jump me, which CJ demanded an apology for before he'd speak to her again. As soon as she heard I had a boyfriend, she planned on seducing him so she could prove to herself and CJ she was better than me.

Nowadays, it's hard to be mad about the mean things she wrote considering Denendrius beat CJ to death at her house party and proceeded to torment her. Did Denendrius plan on showing me in hopes I'd hate her more?

I snoop through the rest of the phone, trying to clear my head of her thoughts. There are no browser tabs open, but when I bring up the search history—which hasn't been wiped —surprisingly—I find odd searches. Not odd because of *what* he searched, but when. I thought he bought our phones at the mall, but if that's true, how is there a search for restaurants from the day before our first date? For flower arrangement deliveries on *Valentine's Day*?

"What the hell," I whisper in astonishment. Did this fucker lie for the sake of lying? "*I don't have a phone, my ass.*"

What did he do, pretend he bought himself a phone when he bought me one? Then, I think of how we didn't really set my phone up. He took it straight out of the box and opened it before putting his number in. He disappeared for quite a while . . . did he set mine up before I found him on the bench? Except, even if that's true, he pulled his phone out of its own box.

He didn't get his phone when we were shopping, I bet—he got it *back*.

Because clearly he had it before our first date, and I had no evidence to suggest he was lying when he told me he didn't have a phone. Where did it go for the past few weeks? Did he buy one for me and give them both to someone—mine to bug, track, and relay information back to his like I was worried about? When he disappeared at the mall, was it because he was retrieving them from someone?

Could Denendrius have listened in whenever I had the phone on me? Would he have been able to see all my calls and texts?

I rip through my memories, trying to think of anything bad I might have said or done when the phone was with me. I can't think of anything too awful.

My eyes burn with exhaustion, and a headache forms deep in my skull. The adrenaline coursing through me wards away any ability to sleep. I put the phone on the counter next to his wallet and go back to pacing the apartment in deep thought, only stopping to throw the bloodstained blanket and sheets into the washing machine and attempt—with partial success— to scrub the blood from the carpet.

When I check on Denendrius, he's in the same shape as he was when he fell unconscious. Still no heartbeat, that I can feel by touch at least, and though his skin isn't warm, it's not becoming stiff with death. Aside from the lack of a clear heartbeat, visible breathing, and the fact that his brown eyes are wide open, there's no sign he's past the point of no return. If I didn't know any better, I'd assume he died mere moments ago, not *hours*.

He's going to wake up. It's just a matter of whether he remembers. But since he didn't remember me before passing out, I'm not counting on it when he wakes.

I scramble down the hall when it sounds like someone is kicking the door, and a quick peek through the peephole shows Rayonne. I hold it open for her as she hauls in bags of groceries dangling from her arms and gripped in her fists.

"You could have asked for my help." I close the door behind her.

She offers a breathless grunt.

"We have a third source of potential vampire trouble, by the way." I lean against the wall between the hall and living room as she comes in.

She rests the bags on the floor and pulls her arms from the handles. "*Heavens.* I left for three hours. What did you do?"

I help her lift the bags onto the counter and start unpacking, opening one of the cheap walnut-stained cabinet doors overhead. "Blame Denendrius. His BFF called looking for him. Denendrius arranged for him to help kidnap me to Italy."

"Great." She pulls a tall stack of paper plates out of a grocery bag. "And who is this best friend we have to worry about?"

"Some Russian pilot from World War Two that Denendrius saved. I don't know how big of a problem he's going to be. But he said he'd do anything for him. He'll probably come looking when he doesn't hear back. He doesn't know where we are at least."

"Care to share any good news?" she grumbles.

I perk up a little as I unwrap my bottle of whiskey and set it aside. "Denendrius is definitely not dead. Either rigor mortis is taking its sweet time, or he's going to wake up."

Her shoulders lower as she exhales and smiles, setting a box of drinking glasses on the counter. "Great." She raises a brow at me in warning. "If he remembers nothing, we need to gain his trust. So don't . . . you know . . . start beating him or something."

I stop unpacking and cross my arms. "I won't. I've thought about this. You can trust me. If Romania is my best bet, I won't screw this up."

Rayonne's smile is soft, though it doesn't meet her eyes.

"Okay—and I know you want him to remember. Trust me, I do too, but . . . I don't know. He might not. Be prepared for that."

I swallow. "Well, if I'm going to Romania, then he has years to remember me. Maybe it'll be easier if he doesn't remember me right away, especially since we need that trust."

She offers a solemn nod.

I think about what Alaire and Edmond said, that sometimes their memories *never* return. My heart beats out of control. "You think he'll remember *eventually*, right?"

Rayonne turns to the fridge with pursed lips and piles some bagged vegetables on a wire shelf. "I have no idea, Marianna. But I hope so."

Pulling a jug of milk from a bag, I hand it to her and she sets it beside the veggies. "But *he has to.*" If the universe gives a single shit about me, he will. This month, in a year . . . I need him to know. If I can't forget what he did to me, neither can he.

She closes the fridge. "Either way, he'll pay."

"When you turned back human, did you forget your vampire years?" I ask her. If she did, they must have come back quickly.

Her lips twist like she's thinking hard about something as she stands. "Not exactly. Strangely, I can't remember much of my human ones since she turned me back. I recall the big things, and much of the year before I was turned, but everything else is hazy. I'm not even sure if they'll come back when I turn again, but I can hope."

My heart sinks, my hands slowing as I unpack fresh fish. "Maybe because you're a Child of Stars and he's a Darkling? It probably affects you differently. He has almost two thousand years of memories, so something *has* to come back, right?"

I think back to what Alaire and Edmond told me about the two kinds, and what I learned when Denendrius took me to that abandoned house and showed me the Child of Stars he was holding captive. If being a Darkling is a much more intense experience than being a Child of Stars since the changes are more dramatic—with a transformation so long and violent it makes you hallucinate and convulse, gives you godlike speed and strength, as well as powerful hypnotism instead of other special abilities like Children of Stars sometimes get—it would make sense that turning back would be just as intense.

"Perhaps. Vampirism improves your ability to remember things, so something must happen physiologically when that's reversed. As much as it hurts, his memories might have been destroyed when his DNA was practically torn apart. And hell, for all I know, it might make a difference which vampire the doses came from." She pauses. "Agatha used the backup vial on me—they gave us two, in case Denendrius stopped us from using the first on him—but I have no way of knowing if they both came from the same vampire."

I ball the empty grocery bag up and stuff it in another. "From what Alaire and Edmond told me, it doesn't sound like anybody knows much about the cure."

She scoffs and leans back down to tackle another bag. "*A cure.* Such a strange thing to call it, as if being a vampire is some sort of affliction you can be healed from with *special* Children of Stars blood. They should call it what it is: poison. Truly, all it does is unravel whatever DNA change occurred to leave a mess behind. At worst, it kills you. Personally, I've always thought of it as a rare defensive ability considering only Children of Stars are born with it in their blood. If it's supposed to cure vampirism, then it doesn't make much sense that I'd still be dealing with a vampire's biggest struggle: thirst."

As if we have the same thought in sync, we both gasp, our heads snapping toward the hall.

"How bad are your cravings, would you say?"

She winces. "I dream about feeding every night. And the human blood I get at the club never satisfies, of course, but the action alleviates some tension, though it's nothing like when I was a vampire. I've taken up smoking to deal with the cravings, actually."

The hair stands on the back of my neck, a chill rushing over me. "And you've only been a vampire since the Victorian era . . ." She nods, seeming to know exactly where I'm going with this. "And he's almost two thousand years old . . . and already had a serious issue with thirst. Above average for a vampire, I think. He had a taste for *vampire* blood too . . ."

She bites down on her bottom lip, eyes flickering back to me. "This could be bad."

"Yeah. Let's hope his experience with turning back and cravings are different from yours."

We continue to unpack the groceries in tense silence, my worries gnawing at me so deeply that I resort to pouring myself a glass of whiskey in hopes to flush them out. Rayonne puts two precooked rotisserie chickens in the oven to keep them warm while I grab the last bag to empty. It's full of garlic cloves, a couple spray bottles, and more kitchenware.

"Protection from Children of Stars. We'll spray it around the doors and windows to keep them from entering," Rayonne explains. "I know Denendrius said he already did it, but we shouldn't trust that. We'll have to hope Darklings don't show up too, or we're basically helpless since garlic will be no physical barrier to them. Oh, and we'll need weapons. I brought a stake in with my suitcase, but everything else is still at the house we were staying at with Agatha."

My brows shoot up, hand tightening on my glass of whiskey. "We should go there and ambush her. Force her to give us Viorel's contact numbers, though maybe we should just kill her instead of staking her."

With so much new danger, I want Denendrius dealt with *quickly* now.

There's no humor in Rayonne's laugh. "I already told you, killing her is *not* a problem I want. Once Viorel sees she did *this* to me, she'll pay. Besides, she's tight-lipped and I highly doubt she'll go back to the house. We need to find a contact on our own and be ready when she—or anyone else—comes after us."

"You should check your car for a tracking device then," I suggest, thinking of the one Denendrius photographed. "Denendrius found one on his, so clearly someone was trying to track him."

She leans against the counter and yawns. "I do every time I drive. Also, that was me. I don't know why we thought putting one on his car would work. I placed it after spotting you two at the mall, but it went dead before it even left the lot."

"Hm." I take a sip, a warm burn splashing over my tongue and down to my stomach. I try to remember if he messed around with the car when we got back to it. He dropped his keys before we got back in, which was odd, but he also disappeared for a bit while Carol and I were shopping. If he left to get our phones off someone, did he find the tracking device then?

Why hadn't he said anything to me either about vampires being after him again? He even left me alone with Carol hours later. "How did you find me in that alley, anyway?"

Rayonne pours herself a cup of whiskey while saying, "I figured out where you went to school and checked every day, hoping our paths would cross, or I could follow him from there. Usually, I was unlucky, except yesterday. I saw him waiting for you, and he eventually got out and walked halfway across the road before turning around and driving away pissed off. I followed him to the convenience store, but I double-checked the directions he got—said I was your best friend looking for you and the man they spoke to was after you—and they gave me a vastly different answer. Said you hopped in a yellow cab and went the opposite direction. It didn't take me long to catch up, and since I was alone during the day, I had to follow you until nightfall. I lost track of you at one point, but once I called for help, the vampires of the group walked around until they caught your scent and tracked you to the alley of that church."

So they had lied for me when he asked. I can't help my flicker of a smile. "You didn't think to intercept me and get my help?"

She shrugs. "You were blood marked, Marianna. We have no way of knowing how deep that was. For all I know, you could have attacked me for trying to help."

"I guess. It doesn't matter now, anyway." *Was* blood marked. I take a relieved breath and another warm sip. I suppose it makes sense that Denendrius turning back would sever that tie. Alaire said it could be overwritten or removed with a vampire's death. Does this count as a vampire dying?

Rayonne and I navigate the kitchen with clumsy steps and tired minds, both of us too nervous about the multitude of things waiting to risk a nap. My protests don't stop Rayonne from trying to mother me, telling me every time I almost drop something to go lie down.

"Can't, I have to move the sheets to the dryer," I fuss, pressing the flat side of a butcher knife on a few garlic cloves, a bottle half full of water open and waiting to be made into garlic spray. "Besides, I don't want to be asleep when he wakes up."

She yawns again and lowers the heat under the broccoli and red peppers she's frying on the burner. "I'll be awake. Nap on the couch?"

"Why don't you?" I shove the crushed pieces of garlic into the spray bottle and screw the head on. The water is murky when I shake it. "You're probably tired too."

"I'm already cooking."

I start on more garlic cloves for another spray bottle. "We should have ordered a pizza."

"No. We need good food. We will not function properly on minimal sleep *and* greasy food."

"Can't argue with that, I guess." The garlic fumes only make it harder to keep my heavy eyes open. "That's it, I'm tapping out." I wash my hands, toss the sheets in the dryer, and haul my ass to the couch. "But I'm not sleeping." I watch her cook, trying to figure out how old she is as she pushes the veggies around in the pan. Older than me, I decide, but definitely under thirty. It's hard to tell with all the dark makeup.

I'm jolted awake when Rayonne nudges me, a plate of veggies and chicken held out.

"Eat, then go back to sleep," she says.

I take the plate. "Damn it. I tried. I should check on him."

"I did a minute ago. He's still unconscious." She sits on the couch next to me and flicks the television on.

I rub my eyes, then grab my fork and dig in. After the first few bites of juicy peppers, broccoli, and chicken, I'm glad she took it upon herself to cook.

"Is it good? I might have added too much spice. I dropped the shaker in the pan. My taste buds are a little off these days, so I'm not sure."

"I couldn't tell."

She stops chewing to give me a small smile.

I remember my manners. "Oh, thanks for cooking."

"No problem."

My chewing slows with a nagging in my gut and I stab my fork into my chicken and bite my cheek. Sighing, I set my plate on the carpet. "I'm going to see if there's any change in him," I mumble while pushing myself off the couch.

"Okay." She takes another bite of her chicken, eyes trained on the TV as she searches for a show.

I'm halfway between the bedroom and bathroom when Denendrius steps into the hallway, his brown eyes wide with terror and landing on me.

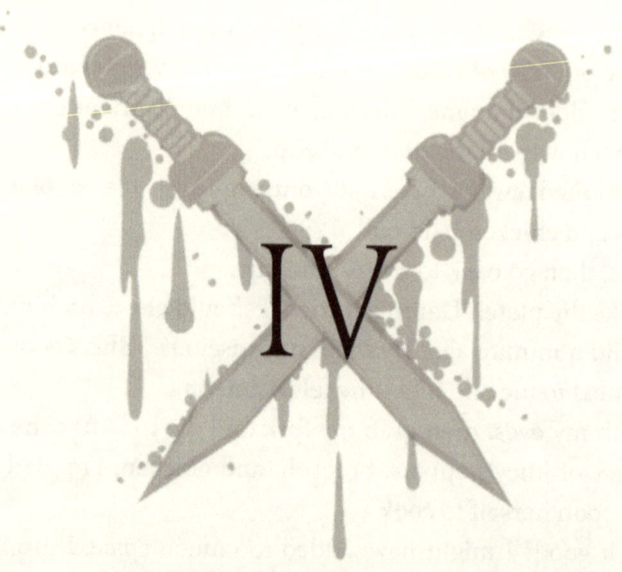

IV

I'm shocked back into wakefulness, a fresh surge of adrenaline ripping through me, my heartbeat slamming against my ribs.

"Oh fuck," I breathe. Jumping backward, my hands come up in defense.

He lifts a bloodstained hand, index finger over his lips to shush me.

My heart launches into my throat. "Do—do you remember me?"

His eyes turn suspicious of me, his gaze tight as he says something low in warning.

Something definitely not English.

I take a step back. "Denendrius . . . ?"

There's a commotion in the living room as Rayonne scrambles off the couch, her steps frantic against the carpet.

Denendrius shouts something short in what I can only assume based on his origins is Latin, and the next thing I can process is his arm hooking around my waist and swinging me into the bedroom. The door slams shut as he drops me. I leap to my feet and rush to the far wall, standing flat against it.

"Marianna!" Rayonne hollers.

As soon as she gets the door cracked, he slams his palm against it while she fights for it to open. I wait for him to lock it as he directs half-panicked shouts between me and her, but he doesn't even reach for the knob. Instead, he motions between the door, me, and the room with a flat hand, like he's demanding to be told where he is and who we are.

"Stop trying to get in!" I tell her. "He doesn't remember me —anything—and he's freaking out! Don't come in until I say so. Let me calm him down, I know him—"

But I don't know him, do I? If he's reverted to whoever he was before he turned, then I have no idea who he is.

How terrified of him should I be?

"Denendrius, it's me. Do you remember me?" My words come out like a plea. "It's Marianna."

Has he lost *all* his memories? Or is it possible a handful remain, scattered across his mind without context? What's the last thing he remembers? Being human in ancient Rome? Beyond his transformation? Does he remember me straddling him with a knife mere moments before he passed out?

Denendrius's wild eyes meet mine, and a sense of clarity relaxes some of the tension in his face and shoulders. His voice is smooth when he slows his words down—sweet—though his accent is strange. Through his tangle of words, one pops out at me from his question.

"Marciana?"

My brows twitch together. "Marianna . . . my name's *Mari-anna*." Who's Marciana?

His eyes wander dizzily over my face. He closes them, and they roll around against the back of his lids before he opens them again. He blinks hard a few times and says my name while looking me up and down.

My throat dries, but I nod. "Yes . . ."

What does he remember?

Denendrius is nonplussed, a blank look in his eyes as he stares at me with parted lips.

My brow furrows. If he remembers me, why isn't he mad?

"Oh shit." My expression falls.

He thinks I'm Mariana, doesn't he? If he's speaking Latin, he probably thinks he's in Rome. Of course his mind would go to that girl.

"I'm not grown-up Mariana. I'm Marianna *Cortez*," I say desperately. How the fuck do I explain this to him?

Denendrius's brown eyes narrow, his head tilting slightly. When his gouged hand comes up toward my head, I gasp and lift my arms to cover my face before I've considered his intentions fully.

A surprised exhale falls from his mouth, the sickliness of his brown eyes adopting a dull glimmer as he takes my hand in his. The strangeness of his warm skin makes the hairs on my arm stand up as he marvels at the promise ring, more foreign words rushing past his lips along with my name—though I'm not sure if he's talking about me or *her*.

I pull my hand out of his grip and lean harder into the wall. "*Cortez. Marianna Cortez.*"

His lips are parted dumbly, the bewilderment and confusion fighting for space on his face.

"Cortez," I repeat back to him, tapping my chest. "I'm not her."

"Marciana?" he asks again with another rush of words, a hint of frustration creeping into his voice.

I shake my head madly as I shrug, confusion tight on my face. "I don't know what you're trying to ask me."

"I think he said *mater*," Rayonne says from the other side of the door. "Mother?"

My mind whirs. "Are you asking if I'm Mariana's mother? Or if she's *my* mother?"

He inhales sharply and thinks to himself, eyes wandering over me.

"I don't know how to explain your own obsessive craziness to you. I probably share some of the same features as her . . . but I'm not *her*," I say, the shakiness of my voice making me grit my teeth when I'm done speaking.

"Cortez," he mumbles as he squints at me. He tries the name out again. "Cortez . . ."

I nod and motion to myself again. "Yes. *Cortez*."

Does it sound familiar to him?

Denendrius appears no less confused—though hopefully it's for a different reason now—as he mulls me over for a painful minute while mouthing my last name.

He swallows, gears turning as he looks over the scratches on the back of his hand. My breath catches when he touches the bruising on my neck—that matches his hands—and grabs my hand again. He scrutinizes the remaining blood under my nails before his eyes flicker to mine, and he asks a question I can't understand. It's clear from the reservation on his face that he knows something violent happened between us he can't remember.

I swallow my anger, my eyes burning with tears that attempt to flow out of me with my fury. I want to shake him and scream at him. *How dare you forget! How dare you feel even a glint of remorse for what you did to me when—if you remembered—you'd make me pay worse?*

With a wary gaze, he carefully lifts my left hand again. I stiffen. Like he's trying to propose a truce, or apologize for the fact that he did something awful, he flattens my palm against his chest.

His heartbeat rages on behind my palm and he looks at me with wide, yet wondering eyes, like he's trying hard to remember me. Like he *knows* he should remember me and that I'm not *her*.

His words sound so painfully genuine. Like they're some sort of apology.

The feel of his heartbeat mixed with the softness of his soft *brown eyes* makes my vision blur with tears, and I grit my teeth to hold back the sharp words I'm ready to snarl. The warmth of him . . . with the *coldness* of who he truly is, is so conflicting it's sick.

It's all *sick*.

I can't stand seeing him breathing . . . with a *heartbeat*. A soulless monster like him should not be capable of having a heart that can beat so strongly. He's too human for what he truly is.

I feel like I'm in a nightmare, the exhaustion running through me, twisting up my rational thoughts like a noose. If it weren't for Rayonne's quiet reminder we need him to trust us, I'd tell him—show him, if he didn't understand—*exactly* how I feel. He wouldn't have to be confused anymore.

When he brushes an escapee tear from my cheek, I rip my hand out from under his and ball my fists at my sides. "Don't!" I bark, yanking my face away, my teeth chattering with fury.

I can't help my cry—the whimper that escapes me—when he takes my face in his hands. His eyes bore into mine, his foreign words slow and desperate.

I squeeze my eyes closed. It's possible I'm more terrified of him now than when he remembered me. At least when he had his memories, he knew why he didn't want to kill me.

"I don't know," I whisper, blinking away tears. His skin is so hot against my cheeks it burns. "I don't understand you."

His stare travels down to the sleeves of his leather jacket, down his body to his sandals, and to the carpet beneath him. Eyes jerking back up to mine, he drops his hands before swiftly stepping away. His chest heaves as he gazes around the room, as he understands that the unfamiliarity of me and this place is stranger than he knows.

"Jesus, don't have a panic attack," I say, rubbing the tears away from my bottom lashes.

He sits on the bed and rests his head in his hands, inhaling deeply in timed intervals. He straightens and sets his palms on his lap, staring straight ahead as he loosens his shoulders and practices breathing. I can't help but wonder if he used to do this before going into battle. Yet waking up in a type of clothes or room you've never seen before, with people you don't know, speaking a language you've never heard before, must be far more terrifying than a man with a weapon.

When he looks up at me, the confusion and terror remains in his eyes, but his expression is unnervingly impassive, like he's hiding the fact he's barely holding back from a complete meltdown.

I suppose I have a way to answer one of his questions—sort of. "Rayonne, can you bring me his wallet from the counter?"

Rayonne winces as she enters the bedroom a few moments later, leather wallet gripped in her hand. She takes a relieved breath when there's no sign he knows who she is and hands the wallet to me.

I saw the photo Denendrius took of us—in my old room at Pam's house—in his wallet when I was giving money to Rayonne. I remove it from where it's neatly folded in a card slot. Carefully—knowing that he's technically never seen a photograph before—I hold my breath as I sit beside him on the bed and hold it out.

He jerks when he sees it, his hand shaking as he takes it from me. His words waver as he runs his fingers over the glossy image.

"It's a photograph," I say. I tap my finger against it and enunciate the word. "*Photograph*."

He stumbles over the word as he tries to repeat it, his unsure eyes flickering between me and the picture. He points out his black eyes and whispers something before staring up into the empty air with a tight gaze. I can tell he's trying to remember something—or *knows* something already that gives the situation he's in now some sense—and is trying to connect the pieces.

When he stares into the empty air, his lips part for shallow breaths as his eyebrows scrunch. I think he understands what black eyes mean, and that he became a monster of sorts. I wonder if he understands what the extent of his condition was. Did they believe in vampires in ancient Rome?

He asks me something, pointing to where I am in the photograph. He then drags his finger under his eye like a mock tear, his lips in a firm line. My sadness is clear in the picture. My lip twitches and I want to slap him for pointing it out.

Flipping the photo over, he studies the writing on the back. My name and Denendrius's are inked in black with his perfect writing, scrawled beside a heart. He peers closely at it with a tilted head. It doesn't seem like he recognizes his own name, so I offer some help by sounding out our names as I tap my index finger on the letters. When I pull my hand away, he presses his thumb against each letter in my name like he's counting them.

"Hm." Clearing his throat, he folds the picture—a crease between us—and hands it back to me.

Surely he must understand now I'm not her.

I slide it back into his wallet and instinctively hold it out for him to take. He stares at it but doesn't move to take it, his timed breaths still so far from calm. I sigh and set it aside on the bed.

His wild eyes meet mine and he speaks again, enunciating his words carefully and slowly, as if that might help me understand.

I shake my head and shrug. "Denendrius . . . I have no idea what you're saying . . ."

Denendrius frowns. "Ah—"

"*Sanguis!*" Rayonne exclaims. "Blood. *Sanguis* means blood. I'm fairly certain that's what he said."

He looks back at her and smiles. "*Sanguis.*" He tilts his head and presses his index and middle finger against his jugular, words tumbling from his lips again.

I scratch my forehead. "What—Marianus?"

When he responds, I only catch Mariana's name.

"*Pater,*" Rayonne says, thankfully picking up another word. "Father."

I rise and cross my arms. "Mariana's father? *Marianus?* What are you talking about, Denendrius?" What does Mariana's father have to do with him being bitten?

"So, he remembers being turned," Rayonne says.

My throat dries, my heartbeat pounding so fast I feel woozy. "By Mariana's . . . *father*? That can't be right."

Rayonne shrugs. "That sounds like what he's saying."

"That is *not* the story I got. He told me he was stalking a woman, and when he couldn't control his urge to kill her, he followed her home. He was supposedly in the middle of cutting her up when the chick's husband came home and killed him in revenge. Apparently, he dragged himself to the forest." But knowing now that Mariana's father is the one who killed Denendrius isn't an easy piece to fit into the puzzle of his first story. If the woman's husband killed him, does that make the woman Marciana? How could that be if he was asking me about her?

Rayonne's head jerks and her eyes narrow. "Pfft. It's a physical impossibility that he dragged himself anywhere, never mind a forest. Do you know Rome's layout? It was massive. There are no forests close enough for someone in his condition to get to. I don't know where he lived, but it would have taken him hours alone to get through the city. There's no way he did that in the middle of a transformation. Maybe he was dumped there and thinks he got there himself if he was hallucinating as much as he would have been."

I grit my teeth. Why would he lie? Was it because he didn't want to bring up Mariana earlier in fear of scaring me off? Did it have to do with the fact that her father was responsible for his vampirism and it caused some sort of sadness or anger he didn't want to deal with? Was he worried I would see him as weak, that someone as strong as him was so easily overtaken by another man? Could he have lied in an attempt to scare me? To make me think he was a monster beyond his immortality so I wouldn't even try to fight him?

"What happened, then?" Why did Mariana's father kill him? How did things go from marriage planning to Denendrius being turned?

She shrugs. "So he lied to you when he was a vampire, and obviously can't remember his lies."

My fists curl. I knew his transformation story reeked of bullshit. Why did he lie? What *else* did he lie about? "We need to figure out a way to communicate with him. Because, clearly, I know nothing real about him, and I feel like this could go bad quickly."

"I don't even know where to start with translations, Marianna. Latin is a dead language, and the only words I know are basic ones I unintentionally picked up over the decades."

I bite my bottom lip as I think. "Books won't be good enough. And I don't think the internet is a smart option either. Online translators are hardly accurate for modern languages, never mind Latin. Maybe we could find a forum with people who know Latin, but we'll have to hope for a response in time and trust they know what they're talking about and aren't fucking with us. Then there's the issue of posting whatever we can get Denendrius to write to the internet. Who knows what we'd be putting out into the world if we don't know what he's written. Last thing we need is vampires stumbling upon it and figuring out that Denendrius is human without his memories and vulnerable. It's risky enough that we have to talk about it at some club."

"True." Rayonne taps her foot. "So then, what?"

I straighten. "Wait, maybe we could talk to my history teacher. That's safer than a stranger with unknown connections. He mentioned in class last year that he was once studying to do more, and he's already met Denendrius and nothing came of it. I don't have any other ideas."

"Your history teacher? You want to drag another human into this?" She gapes at me.

I lift my nose. "Let's hear your ideas."

"Can he even translate Latin?" Rayonne mashes her lips together.

I shrug. "I can ask. If he can't, maybe he can point us in the right direction. We don't have time for trial-and-error right now. Besides, I'm not getting my ass beat over an inadequate translation."

"Fine. Let's give it a shot."

With my cheek caught between my teeth, my eyes turn back to Denendrius. His head is back in his hands, his breathing labored. I flinch when his head comes up, and he shakes his leather jacket off, throwing it aside like it's a nuisance.

When he looks between Rayonne and me, I think he's about to say something before he abruptly rises and wanders from the bedroom. I follow him to the hall and to where he stops before the kitchen.

Nervous eyes locking with mine, he touches his head and says a word that, after I mull it over for a few seconds, sounds a lot like *memory*.

I pull in a deep breath and motion to the apartment, then him and me. "This is ours." I'd rather not call the apartment mine, but aside from the reality that he forced me to live here, I want him to think I have a right to be here so he doesn't question it. Though, I suppose the ring on my finger automatically leaves him with a lot of assumptions.

Maybe it's for the best if he thinks we're married. Maybe he'll believe there's already some sort of *trust* between us, even if we wouldn't have married for love in his time.

I recognize one Spanish-like word from the question he asks the tense air as he looks around. "Familia?"

"Y-your family?" I swallow. My eyes dart to Rayonne. "Yeah, he definitely doesn't remember being a vampire, just being turned."

"How do you know?"

I swallow. "Because if he's asking about his family, he clearly doesn't remember killing them."

Her eyes widen. "What?"

"Yeah—"

Denendrius faces me, clearly expecting an answer. All I do is shrug with my hands up and offer a sympathetic frown. To be fair, I don't technically know what happened to them. Who's to say he was telling me the truth about that?

His chest lifts with a breath, but he doesn't exhale as he wanders toward the sunlight spilling through the slats of the balcony blinds. The color drains from his face when he gazes outside. Eyes locked on the expanse of busy road and beaten buildings, skyscrapers in the distance—which must seem futuristic to him—he pushes the slats aside despite the resistance they give. He doesn't even look when he feels around behind himself and takes a chair from the table. He turns it around and sits on it crookedly. Then, he exhales, puts his elbows against his thighs, and holds his head as he takes it all in.

Rayonne and I share a worried glance before inching closer to him. Minutes pass without him moving, though every once in a while, he whispers something.

What does he think of it all? Does he think he lost his

mind? That he time traveled? If the last thing he remembers is being turned, what does he make of that? Does he truly understand that it was *him*? Or does he think he fell into some sort of mental sleep and that a demon controlled him?

"This is terrifying," Rayonne whispers beside me. "Do you think he's going to lose it and attack us?"

I huff. "I damn sure hope not."

"One of us should . . . I don't know . . . see if he's okay. It might help."

I swallow. "I will. He thinks I'm his wife."

Instead of going straight to him, I make a detour into the kitchen and make up a plate of chicken and vegetables for him. I carry it with a fork to where he sits unmoving and pull another chair out.

"You'll be okay," I tell him, trying to decipher his face—which is blank aside from a tense line between his brows. "But you better cope with this, because this is easy compared to what's waiting for you."

"*Marianna*," Rayonne hisses from the couch. "We have to be careful what we say. Last thing we need is him understanding English before he can remember how to speak it. Who knows how his memories will return, if they do?"

I grimace. Good point.

Balancing his plate in one hand, I give his thigh a gentle pat with the other to get his attention. His eyes snap to mine, then lower to where my hand rests on his leg.

I yank my hand away and hold the food out to him. "Hungry?"

Denendrius takes the plate and sets it on his lap but stares at the plastic fork when I offer it. After too many seconds of holding my hand awkwardly in the air, I put it on the table on the way to grab my food from where I left it by the couch.

I'd much rather eat on the couch away from him, but I sit back at his side and take a bite of broccoli. He pulls meat off the chicken bones with his fingers, somehow being neat as he eats with his hands. He scrutinizes the plate as he eats, scowling when it bends under his grip and tears a little at the edge.

Seeing him do something so normal and human like eating is . . . uncanny. With the color back in his face and the brown in his eyes, it's almost hard to imagine that this is the same body that once needed human blood to survive.

He catches me watching. "Hm?"

"Fork?" I point to mine.

He shakes his head and resumes eating.

We're quiet as we eat, the three of us exchanging a mix of curious and nervous glances. Despite his build and the tense air around him, there's something about him that's significantly less threatening than when he was a vampire. Perhaps it's only the difference in his eyes—soft brown versus murderous black—and his human motions. It could also be because he's on his best behavior. I suppose if I woke up with no memories, in a foreign place, with a bunch of strangers that were likely the only ones who could help me, I'd play nice too.

From the corner of my eye, I catch Rayonne squinting at me. "Did I hear through the door correctly, that he thought you were a *different* Marianna? What's all that about?"

I nod. "He told me about some little girl he was arranging to marry when she grew up."

"All this because you share the same name as someone from his past?" She bites her bottom lip, and the pity in her eyes makes me look away.

My eyes burn, but I inhale sharply and straighten in my chair. "Seems that way. I'm assuming I look like her mom or something, since he never actually met her."

"Christ," she whispers to herself.

When I glance back at Denendrius, his gaze tightens on me like he knows we're talking about him.

"*What?*" I snap, giving him a sour scowl that demands his explanation.

He motions at me, then at his neck, but in the same spot as the gang tattoo—the red double Rs outlined in black—below my ear. When he asks me a question, one word sounds suspiciously close to *criminal.*

My brows shoot up, only to furrow when he releases a nervous laugh and looks over his bare arms and under his shirt.

I put my plate aside and yank the cell phone from my pocket.

"Tattoos in ancient Rome," I say while typing it out in the search bar. My eyes widen when I'm immediately given the answer. "In ancient Rome, tattoos were used to mark slaves and criminals."

I lower my phone and glower at Denendrius, who misses the look on my face since he stares horrified at the phone in my hand. I shove it back in my pocket, and his gaze shoots back up to mine.

"This is going to be a rough change for you, I can see it already." I flip my hair back over my shoulder so he can see the tattoo better. "It's art. For my *familia.*" Not technically my family anymore, but it's not worth figuring out how to explain all that to him.

From the way his nose crinkles, it's clear he doesn't get it.

I huff and roll my eyes at him. No wonder he made comments about hating my tattoo when he was a vampire, though maybe his opinion about tattoos changed over the years but he didn't like the gang connection to mine.

Denendrius sets his empty plate on the table behind us and touches the back of my left hand—with focus on my ring— with his, his greasy fingers curled inward to avoid touching me. He gives me a sheepish smile and an indifferent shrug, before saying something that sounds consoling.

"Are you trying to tell me it's probably okay since you're

married to me and I have it? Or . . . something like that?" I offer a slight smile, not sure what to make of the entire exchange, but also not wanting him to press further.

He glances around the apartment expectantly before grumbling something and picking up his plate to carry with him to the kitchen sink. He stares at the taps—making me think they must have had some kind of them in Rome—before deciding to try the cold one to rinse his hands.

"Marianna—" He jerks a little when he sees I'm already staring at him.

"Hm?"

He points at the plate and makes a washing motion, an inquisitive brow raised.

"Are you asking me if *I'm* going to wash it, or if there's a slave who is going to come wash it for you?" I tongue my cheek.

He looks to Rayonne like maybe she's the one with the responsibility. She scoffs and crosses her arms.

Denendrius must understand that he's made an offensive mistake as he bares his teeth in embarrassment and tells her something that's probably some sort of apology.

Not knowing how else to explain who she is to us, I motion to her and say, "*Rayonne . . . familia.*"

"Ah."

"And it's a paper plate," I grumble. "It gets thrown out."

I snatch one of the grocery bags that was stuffed under the sink after unloading, and hook it on the handle of a bottom cupboard. His head tilts when I throw our plates in the bag, but when I point to the package of them on the counter, he must understand as he frowns and grumbles something.

"You should get a go bag ready," Rayonne says while disposing of her plate. "One for him too. If we're attacked here, we'll have to get out quickly."

"We need to go pick up Denendrius's car too. I'd feel much safer using his Mustang than your beater. It's faster, and yours looks like it's ready to break down, which is super inconvenient if we're trying to escape Agatha."

Her nose scrunches, like I've offended her, but that she knows I'm right. "Fine. Good thing he told us where he parked it. How about you start on the go bags? I'm going to call my friend at the club and prep him since I'll be bringing two humans along tonight. It's probably better if I step out though …" Her eyes flicker to Denendrius.

My heart rockets into the base of my throat. "Vampire club *tonight*?"

After a beat of laughter, she says, "Scared?"

I glower. "I'm not exactly thrilled."

"I know. But I need more weapons and to talk to some people in person who might help."

"As long as nobody tries to drink my blood, then fine."

She ignores my comment and instead asks, "Do you think your history teacher will hang around before school hours on Monday? We should see him ASAP."

I rub my eyes, the long list of tasks making me painfully aware of my exhaustion. "Yeah, probably."

V

Denendrius tries to see into the hallway as Rayonne leaves, eyes narrow with scrutiny as the apartment building sounds leak in. When she shuts the door behind her, the sound of a man's low conversation echoing somewhere in the stairwell disappears with the distant rap music.

He blinks, lips parted in shock, and looks back at me. His words are full of disbelief when he motions to the door. I'm not sure what he's on about until his eyes rake over the apartment as he sneers.

"Yeah, it's no patrician villa, but you picked it."

He crosses his arms and paces around while I hunt down my backpack or duffel bag to pack. I find both between the wall and the boxes while Denendrius studies everything from the paint on the walls to the bed in the bedroom.

Hauling them to the couch, I unzip and find them already packed. Denendrius has a couple outfits in a black duffel bag, while he stuffed my backpack with the clothes Carol bought me, along with my toiletries.

"Marianna."

I look up and find Denendrius in nothing but his boxers and holding a glass half-full of water. He asks me a question, and all I know is it has something to do with the water in his hand.

My eyes widen. "What the hell are you doing?" My lip curls as I look him over, trying to figure out what he could want.

When he repeats himself, he says it slow like he thinks I'm stupid.

I deadpan. "You better remember how to speak English pretty fucking soon here because I'm not dealing with your attitude. You're getting way too comfortable too quickly for someone in your position."

He exhales a frustrated sound and spins back around, disappearing down the hallway.

My eyes roll back.

I make a mental list of what else to add to my bag, finding my fake identification at the top. I'll have to swipe the cash in Denendrius's glove compartment as well, but I'm not sure if that will be enough. Where's the rest of his money, anyway? I have my doubts it's in a bank account.

How much cash do I need at the castle? Do I need money at all? Will they expect me to . . . *work* . . . somehow? Will they provide everything for me? If they even allow me to come, what the hell am I supposed to do with myself?

The bath turns on, loud enough that I can tell he left the door open. At least he figured out the taps himself.

Roughly, I zip my backpack up and throw it and the duffel bag against the wall between the hallway and living room.

What could Rayonne possibly be telling her friend that's taking so long?

When she returns with a bag from the convenience store a few blocks down, I figure out the holdup but swallow my complaints when I see that it's full of energy drinks and cold brew coffees, a pad of lined paper tucked behind them all.

"Sorry," she starts, the jars and cans rattling as she hoists the bag onto the counter. "We need to drive without crashing, and now we're prepared to speak with your teacher. I snagged the last pad of paper, but they were out of pens. Luckily I found one that works properly in my car."

"Good call. Stay away from the bathroom, by the way. He's in the tub with the door open." I swipe an orange-flavored energy drink as she piles them in the fridge. My finger aches when I open the can, though the cold taste of it splashing over my tongue when I take a long gulp makes up for it.

She picks a coffee for herself, then slumps on the couch and cracks it open. "We'll leave when he's out then, I guess."

"I'll get him to write when we get back." I flop down next to her, the twitching muscles in my legs begging me for a break.

Rayonne sets her drink between her thighs and pulls the strap of her purse over her head. She unwedges a pack of cigarettes from the various items inside. "What's the general opinion on smoking in the apartment?"

"Vampire Denendrius would have a meltdown if you smoked in here. I won't care if you share." But first, I search the apartment for smoke detectors and wonder what Denendrius's reason was for ripping the only one off the hallway ceiling. There's nothing but the wires and base left dangling.

A mischievous smile appears on her lips when I plop back down beside her, and she plucks a slim cigarette from the white pack and places it between her lips to light it. White smoke billows from her mouth as she passes the lighter and a cigarette to me. I place my own between my lips and light it.

I feel numb to the first drag. The menthol hits my throat and I have the unusual urge to cough like I sucked in cold air the wrong way. My nose feels raw when smoke spurts out my nostrils as I choke and clear my throat. There's no nicotine rush, no release of stress or calmness, even with the next two and three inhales.

When I pull the cigarette from my lips to exhale, there's no desire to put it back. It feels odd between my fingers—like an old habit that I'm no longer acquainted with—and not only because I rarely smoke slim cigarettes. I feel . . . indifferent now. Maybe even a little burdened that I asked for one, and that it now burns and wastes in my hand.

So weird.

A few days have passed since I last smoked, and as I think them over, I can't recall having a single cigarette craving. Has it merely been too chaotic for me to think about smoking? Or have those cravings—like the itch to indulge in drugs—waned with my addiction to Denendrius's blood?

But if he's human now, would that still affect me? When a blood mark goes away, does it take all the changes with it? Or even with that connection severed, is the damage still done to my system, the progression merely halted?

It wouldn't be the worst to never crave drugs again if the side effects linger, especially since the severity of his mark didn't get too extreme. I could still run. But cigarettes . . . I stare at the one in my hand and frown. I already miss craving them.

I hold it out to Rayonne, who cocks a brow at me. "What?"

"I suddenly don't like cigarettes," I say, exhaling a heavy breath as I lick my fingers and pinch it out. From my dry and raw throat and the odd taste on my tongue, it's like my body doesn't either.

She lowers her cigarette. "That's odd . . ."

"Right?" I hand her my cigarette.

She shoves it back in the box. "Denendrius didn't like when you smoked?"

I shake my head. "*Hated it.*"

"I don't think that's a coincidence."

Rubbing my nose, I try to relieve some of the itchiness of it.

"Earlier, you said I *was* blood marked. I'm not anymore since he's human, right?"

Her lips purse in thought. "I meant you were blood marked at the time, not that you aren't anymore." She takes a short drag. "I actually don't know how him turning human affects the mark. I don't know of any other time where a situation like this has happened."

I groan and sink back into the cool leather of the couch.

"Logically, it would make sense that you're no longer marked. It's a vampire thing, and he's no longer a vampire."

"Craving blood is also a vampire thing, and you still have that issue," I counter.

She scratches the side of her face while cringing. "Yes, you have a point there."

The sound of draining water spills into our silence. I sip at my energy drink and try to think of what I can say to convince Mr. Derek to help us. Everything sounds insane in my mind.

"Did you, like, pick up smoking one day for fun when you turned back human?" I ask, trying to figure out her reasoning.

She sighs, a streak of white rushing between her lips. "I heard they suppress hunger in humans, so I thought I'd try them. They help with the blood cravings, believe it or not."

"Not worried about coughing up your lungs one day?" I tease.

Her laugh sprays out with smoke. "No, I don't plan on staying human long enough for that."

"Are blood cravings the worst part of being human again?" I can't help but wonder what other problems Denendrius's sudden return to humanity could create.

"No. The worst is how disconnected I feel from myself, from my life with Alessander."

When Denendrius calls my name, I apologize and stand, knowing exactly what he wants. I rummage through his box of clothes, grabbing a pair of jeans, a plain green shirt, and a pair of boxers before carrying them down the hall. I close my eyes so I don't catch him naked, and toss them. He grunts at the same time I hear them collide with something, so I assume I hit him.

"Get dressed, Denendrius." I only open my eyes when I'm turned around.

He finds us back in the living room, dressed, with his hair untied. It looks strange loose at his shoulders, the curls and waves of his medium-brown hair looking dark and silky wet.

Denendrius poses a disgruntled question while pulling up the sleeve of his T-shirt to expose the shallow wound where I sliced him. He makes a wrapping motion.

I stand and scrutinize the wound. It could use some stitches and bandaging, but it's not a bloody mess anymore.

"I have a first aid kit in the car," Rayonne says before I think of my own solution. "Let's go."

I nudge him toward the door. "Come on, we'll fix it in a minute."

With a garlic spray bottle shoved into each of the two cup compartments of my backpack, I carry it and the duffel bag out of the apartment. Rayonne leaves everything but her stake, purse, and drink behind, convinced we'll make it back to the apartment without issue. At least if she's wrong, I'll have some belongings. I'm not the one with extra bags in her car.

Denendrius tries to take both bags from me at the top of the stairs, and we play a short game of tug-of-war. His smirk the entire time only adds to the temperature of my boiling blood. It's clear he's trying to prove he's a *big strong man* and that he thinks I'm being stubborn.

"I am fully capable," I snap, one hard pull yanking the handles from his loose grip.

He laughs at me as we climb down the stairs.

"Glad you think my desire for independence is amusing," I shout back over my shoulder.

My frown deepens with each step, my face a full scowl by the time I turn onto the next flight of stairs. Even though he's stopped laughing, I can feel the grin emanating off him. When I glance back at him on the second flight of stairs from the main level, he wipes his smile off his face.

"For someone who's probably in shock, you sure have a lot of audacity," I accuse.

He doesn't retort, of course.

When we reach the main level and amble outside into the crisp morning air, there's not an ounce of humor on his face. We barely step off the concrete before Denendrius stumbles back and grabs at his chest.

"You better not be having a heart attack," I growl.

His eyes dart over the unkept houses and apartment complexes across the street, his chest lifting with quick breaths. After a deep inhale, any trace of panic leaves his face, and he adopts that same eerie composure that he did in the bedroom.

I swallow. "All right. To the car then."

He catches up to me, and we meet Rayonne at her purple car. She digs around in the trunk, pulling out a red first aid kit and handing it to me before slipping into the driver's seat.

I open the back door of the car. He watches the vehicles rush by on the road past the parking lot, staring between the car and them.

"Come on, get in. You'll be fine," I complain.

He climbs into the back seat and scoots behind the passenger seat to make space for me. After slamming the door, I reach across him, pull the seat belt, and buckle him in.

"I'm not having you die in a car accident of all things," I explain.

Rayonne starts the car and reverses out of the parking spot.

Once I'm buckled in, I zip open the first aid kit and rummage around until I have a few butterfly bandages and a sterilization wipe. I lift his sleeve as we turn onto the main road. He offers me a glance before the world beyond the window steals his attention.

He's lucky he was wearing his leather jacket when I stabbed him, or he might have had more than a deep gouge on the side of his shoulder. Because of the bulk of the leather, my aim wasn't even accurate enough to get any of his muscle like I had hoped. That's probably for the best now. I'll need him in fighting condition if we get attacked by Agatha.

I tear open the sterilization wipe and clean the wound, scrutinizing his face for any reaction that it stings. He's perfectly composed, even when I pinch the wound closed and stick the butterfly bandages to him.

"There, fixed. Can't do anything for your face and hands, though." I hold back a grin as I look over the scratch marks. I hope it still hurts.

Denendrius is rigid for most of the ride, mumbling to himself and occasionally drawing close to the window. He acts like he's on another planet. I suppose it must seem like he is. He occasionally points things out to me like I've never seen them before—or maybe he wants an explanation—but I don't muster up more than a pursed-lip nod.

Rayonne and I don't hold a conversation over our forty-minute drive either. There's something uneasy in the air we share. By the way Rayonne scrutinizes cars and roads, peering into neighboring ones when we stop next to them at lights, I can tell that unsettling feeling has nothing to do with us but with vampires. We might not have to worry about Children of Stars and most Darklings, but there's probably the occasional ones like Denendrius, and Alaire and Edmond, who wander during the day.

We locate Denendrius's car—exactly where he said it would be—in heavily graffitied industrial part of town, parked behind a sketchy auto repair shop.

White tufts of clouds float through the blue sky, the back of the shop cast in a shadow as we park behind his car.

"I'll take Denendrius and the Mustang," I say, holding my hand out for the keys. "You have them, right? Because I don't."

She grumbles as she digs through her purse. "Aha!" They jingle as she pulls them out from an interior pocket and hands them to me.

"We'll meet back at the apartment?" she asks, like she suspects I might flee.

"Yep. See you there." I shove the door open and step out, gravel crunching under my shoes, the heavy smell of oil and gasoline thick in the air.

Denendrius grunts as he crawls across the back seat after me, like he isn't even aware there's another option to exit.

I slam the car door and pull in a deep breath, able to feel my heartbeat in my temples. My arms and legs are heavy with exhaustion when I circle the Mustang and get Denendrius in the passenger seat. Then I do a quick check for tracking devices that might've been placed while the car was parked.

Despite how my body feels, there's a bright alertness to my mind, though tiredness remains around the edges of my reality, ready to seep in at any moment. I can't help but grin at the fact that I get to drive Denendrius's most prized possession, but I'm a little nervous my reaction time is likely impaired.

I rub my dry eyes and dip behind the wheel, the cool leather soothing to my aching body. Denendrius figures out his seat belt while I buckle myself in, then he tinkers with the buttons on the dashboard, eyes wide when the radio comes on.

"Stop, you're going to fuck something up." I shove his hand away and turn the radio off. "You have literally no idea what any of those buttons do and have no concept of technology. How do you know one of those buttons won't eject us?"

He ignores me and presses the button that turned the radio on again, an amazed smile creeping onto his face as he messes with the dials, switching between songs and adjusting the volume.

My brain burns with anger, but I grit my teeth and tilt the wheel lower. "Whatever, man. Do whatever you want, like always."

Feet far from reaching the pedals, I grope around the seat for a button or lever.

When I find and push the button on the side of the seat to bring it forward, it moves a couple inches before jamming against something. Grumbling, I shove my hand under the seat and my fingertips slide against the cool grip of my handgun. Cursing, I pull it out and turn it over in my hands to make sure he hasn't broken it before checking the clip. Out of the fifteen bullets my Beretta M9 can hold, eleven of them are missing, and I find one in the chamber.

My gaze swings to Denendrius. "Who the hell did you kill with my gun?" I shove the clip back in and it clicks. "You didn't even put the safety back on. I could have shot myself digging around under there."

Knowing Denendrius wouldn't consider leaving DNA evidence, I'm glad Red Revenge taught me never to load my gun with bare hands. If I hadn't taken precautions, how many bullets with my fingerprints would the police be uncovering right now in whichever victims he shot?

Denendrius reaches out a curious hand—that I dodge—to touch it.

"No, you'll turn this car into a coffin. I don't feel like getting shot today so you can learn what a gun is."

Rayonne honks her horn, giving me an impatient *what gives* gesture, hands jerking in the air.

I grumble and shove the gun back under the seat before starting the engine.

Denendrius returns to fiddling with the radio and the

sound of static fills the car while I pull out of the parking lot behind Rayonne.

With no identification or legal registration, I use extreme caution. Slowing for yellow lights instead of slamming on the gas is agony, and without speeding, it takes forever to get back to the apartment.

My heart skips along as the smooth pavement passes under the Mustang's wheels, and for one nostalgic moment, I yearn for the days when my brothers and I would jack cars and race them through the dead of night.

Denendrius tires of the radio and moves around in his seat, peering into the back before touching the soft ceiling and finding the visor mirror, where he prods at the marks on his face.

When he glances at me before shutting the visor, I give him a look that could cut and say, "You deserved that, if you were wondering."

He exhales a heavy breath, eyes latching on the scenery and jumping from building to car and whatever else catches his attention. The only time he pauses his pondering is to tie his hair back again now that it's dry.

When I park in his usual spot at the apartment, I kick him out of the passenger seat to stand with Rayonne—who waits against the Mustang—so I can get to the glove compartment. With my backpack unzipped on my lap, I stuff the few bundles of cash into it, as well as the numerous fake identifications he has. I leave the buck knife but take my gun. I don't find the IDs he got for me, so I search the console before gritting my teeth and wracking my brain.

I reach under the passenger seat, and my fingers land on silky paper. When I pull it out, a lump lodges itself in my throat at the sight of the thick, card-sized gift wrapped in shiny red paper.

"What is it?" Rayonne asks, as if I can see through the damn paper.

I tear open the gift and find exactly what I was expecting: all the fake identifications Denendrius had photos of in his phone. "IDs he had made for me."

What was he planning? To tell me he had a surprise and to reach under the seat? What the hell.

"Oh, perfect. We should have no problem getting you to the castle then, if they look real."

"Trust me, they're good fakes." Denendrius may be a bastard, but he's not an imbecile.

Denendrius tries to get a look at them, but I shove them in my bag.

We head back up to the apartment, and Rayonne throws her purse on the counter while I shut the door behind me.

"I desperately need sleep before we head out tonight. Let's get him writing, then we should use the remainder of the day to rest so we have some strength if we get attacked."

"Yeah, this energy drink really isn't helping. I'm so tired I want to puke." I drink the last drop and set it by the sink before grabbing the large notepad and pen.

I nudge Denendrius toward the table and pull back a metal chair for myself. It clangs against the table legs before I flop down in it and pull the blue cap off the cheap plastic pen.

He sits down in another beside me, a crease between his brows as I slide the paper in front of him and hold out the pen.

Though he takes the pen, it hovers above the page as his eyes wander across the table and to the counter behind me like he's looking for something.

"Oh—" I feel stupid for a second. "You're looking for ink, aren't you?"

He doesn't resist as I take the pen and paper back, and I make sure he's watching as I write Denendrius's first name between two blue lines.

Denendrius makes an astonished noise. When I hand it back, he looks it over before resting his hand against the pad.

As he sets pen to paper, a wary eye flickering between me and the first blank page, I can only hope he understands the assignment and isn't going to write down nonsense. Though, if our positions were swapped, I'd be filling the pages with questions without needing to be asked to.

Rayonne stands at my side, gripping the back of the chair, while we watch Denendrius write.

As the pen slowly makes its way across the page, I'm surprised to find his writing is still tidy, but it's different and not nearly as elegant as when he was a vampire. I can't make out all the letters, though they're not connected, and there doesn't appear to be any differentiation in uppercase or lowercase, punctuation, or spacing between his words either.

Incredulous, I say, "How could anyone possibly read that?"

"This is going to be harder than I thought," Rayonne complains.

After two full pages, Denendrius pushes the paper and pen back to me, a nervous flicker in his eye that conflicts with the little optimistic smile on his lips.

A headache dances around the edges of my skull as I attempt to distinguish even a single word. I set the paper on the counter, and say, "Yeah, let's just sleep now."

Rayonne taps her bottom lip in thought and stares at Denendrius. "What do we do about him? Should we sleep in shifts?"

I groan. "I'll lock him in the bedroom with me and maybe he'll be tired enough to nap too. You take the couch."

"Works for me." She trudges to the living room and flops down on the couch.

"Nap," I tell him, pointing toward the bedroom before folding my hands under the side of my face and mocking sleep.

From his nod and the way his face relaxes, he must be more

tired than he's letting on. Would he have woken up exhausted after all that, like he woke up hungry?

He follows me to the bedroom, and I curse when my eyes land on the unmade bed. I can't hide my anger—Denendrius standing out of my way—when I charge to the closet at the end of the hall for the blanket and sheets. I make it up quickly, my arms feeling like noodles by the time I'm done.

I lock the door after us. It'll give me a chance to wake up in case he escapes. Hopefully, he'll make a lot of noise trying to figure out how to open it.

He touches the faded bloodstains on the blanket before sighing and pulling them aside. Denendrius crawls into my space on the bed and I step forward to stop him.

"You sleep on the other side—" I bite my tongue. Why does it matter?

Denendrius's head tilts at me as he crawls under the covers. I swallow and round the bed, crawling onto his side. With my face nestled in his pillow, I note that it still smells earthy like him, of woods and pine. It reminds me he's still somewhere in the man rolling over to face me.

His warm hand finds my left one under the blanket and he takes it to rest with his on the crack between our pillows. His thumb moves the ring on my finger, his lips a firm line. I wince before his other hand even makes it to my face. He brushes his fingers across my bruised skin.

It's difficult not to think about all the times he's struck me, how saying the wrong thing would have his hands circling my throat or his knuckles pounding my skin.

Eyes empty, he says something before his hands retreat. I don't respond. Instead, I cautiously watch his eyes as they wander over the room before closing, a line appearing in his forehead as he takes a deep breath and rests his palms on his stomach.

I'm thankful when he rolls away from me, and that he's big enough to block the reflection of us in the mirror.

When I finally fall asleep, my slumber is short-lived. I wake to Denendrius's deep and terrified scream, my eyes flying open in time to catch his hard elbow slamming into my jaw as I sit up.

VI

I hold my pulsing jaw, convinced he's trying to hurt me until he leaps off the bed, his legs tangling in the blanket and bringing him to the floor where he lands in a patch of afternoon sunlight.

He twists himself into a sitting position, his back against the mirror. His wails are bone-deep, making my heart hammer so fast I swear it could rip out of my chest. I expect a breath to break his hysterics, but he covers his face with his hands as he cries, his whole body shaking.

Rayonne pounds on the door as I jump off the bed.

"Are you okay?" she hollers.

"I'm fine! Not sure about him."

Denendrius's wails seem endless as I carefully make my way toward him, each step feeling fatal. He lifts his head out of his hands, eyes wide, more white than brown showing, his terror so loud the pulsing in my temples turns painful.

"Denendrius?" I squat beside him since there isn't enough space between him and the bed to stand.

I hold my breath as I reach out to touch him. A gasp cuts through his sobs when my fingers contact his bare arm. Goose bumps rise under the pads of my fingers, and even though he dips out from under my touch, the way he gazes through me telling me he isn't present.

"Marianna?" Rayonne asks carefully from the other side of the door.

The muscles in my legs protest when I stand from my squat. "I think reality finally caught up to him and he snapped."

His trembling worsens, his upper body rocking as he mumbles and moans, his haunted eyes unblinking on his hands.

I open the door for Rayonne.

"What's wrong with him?" she asks after taking one look at him.

"He snapped."

Her brow furrows in thought when his mumbling becomes a little more coherent.

"He's talking about *blood* again," she says. "I think he's remembering something. I think he's having a full-blown flashback."

I catch it the next time the Latin word leaves his mouth, and though I can't understand the rest of his sentence, his reaction has me filling in the pieces.

"There's so much blood."

The thought makes my mind circle around a memory of my time in Venganza Roja, the last time I saw someone hunched over and wailing like this.

A few weeks after I joined the gang at eleven, they called Diego and me into the basement of the gang house after school. The older members had an old white man chained to the support beams by his wrists, his navy blue suit torn and bloody. We were told to choose how he died because he owed us forty grand and couldn't pay up. The man had taken the money he was supposed to clean for us and lost it when he'd tried to double it at a casino.

Unfortunately, Diego decided that was the time to gain a conscience. He was too brave for a fifteen-year-old boy and didn't think of the consequences when he stood up to Carlos, our leader. I was told to sit down and pay attention as they handed Diego a machete. Once they forced him to start hacking, they didn't let him stop.

I still remember the stench that filled the basement. The man's blood smelled almost sweet, overpowering the stench of shit and piss. I wasn't allowed to look away from our lesson.

Carlos had to pull him off the sliced-and-diced corpse. He was in a trance and clearly couldn't stop on his own. When he finally saw the blood, the ripped and dismembered masses of flesh, he screamed. It was like a switch, and he became an echo of what he had done.

He kept screaming the same phrase repeatedly in Spanish. *"Blood! Blood! There's so much blood!"*

Carlos and another member rushed him to the floor, stuffing his red bandana in his mouth. He didn't fight them, and it wasn't enough for his screams to stop.

It took stuffing him full of drugs to quiet him, but that wasn't enough to bring him back. He was too far gone for their lesson to be of any value. And all I learned was that I should fear my family as much as the rest of the street feared them.

The smell of that man's death followed me for months, but Diego's screams followed me for years.

It must have followed him too, because a week later, I heard Diego shot himself in the bedroom of his foster home.

Nobody knew why he did it but me and the gang. Diego had been a good kid looking in the wrong places for somewhere to belong.

I never thought I could hear screams more soul-crushing

than his, and I never thought Denendrius would be the person to prove me wrong.

Which poses the question, what did he do that could be horrifying enough to elicit such a response from a man like Denendrius?

He still doesn't acknowledge our presence, continuing to mumble the same word and phrase, moaning as tears rim his eyes and spill over.

Squatting back down next to him, I whisper, "What the hell did you do, Denendrius? What are you remembering?"

He shakes so hard I'm worried he'll shatter the mirrored closet door behind him.

As much as I want to yell at him to snap out of it, to get over it like he told me when I had my panic attack, I run my shaky hand up and down his arm. Attacking him won't help to get him trust us. "You're okay," I murmur. Even if he can't understand me, maybe the comforting tone of my voice will help. "It's not real."

His breath slowly steadies with the stroke of my hand until his breathing is even and all that's left is a few tears rolling down his cheeks.

I swallow when he looks up, bloodshot eyes meeting mine. My mind hangs on to a few of his careful words. *"Familia . . . Adelia . . ."*

My hand shakes as I draw it back. "Adelia?" I look at Rayonne, who still stands cautious at the door. "That's his sister."

Something uneasy swims in my stomach, and I stand. "I think he remembered killing his entire family. He told me he tried to turn his mother and sisters but they died, and he waited for his dad and snapped his neck and buried them."

She blows a breath between her lips. "Sounds like a lot of self-control for a newborn." She thinks for a moment. "From what I've seen, thirst is far more consuming for a Darkling than a Child of Stars. I accidentally killed tons of people in the beginning. Alessander had to pull me off victims. I call bullshit that he knew how the transformation worked since his maker apparently dumped him, never mind that he had enough self-control his first night to change them."

"Yeah." I cross my arms, my leg bouncing.

"What's wrong?" she asks.

I place the problem. "He shouldn't be reacting this way. I didn't even think he could cry actual tears."

She steps into the room and leans a lace-covered shoulder against the black dresser. "What do you mean?"

Rubbing the back of my neck, I say, "He was practically gloating when he told me he killed them. Denendrius said he didn't care when they died, only that it confused him. How can he go from indifferent to this?"

Rayonne is hesitant as she says, "He was rich, wasn't he? How many people did he kill?"

"I don't know. There probably would have been slaves in that house too . . ." Did he kill *everyone* in that house? How many? If he went in there crazed and bloodthirsty, it's hard to imagine that *anyone* would have made it out alive.

I slowly look back to Denendrius, unsure of what to make of the man who whimpers and pleads into his hands.

"So, he didn't try to change them," I breathe. "He just . . . massacred them."

"Jesus Christ," Rayonne mumbles, running her long black-painted nails through her curls.

My perception of Denendrius twists. Is this why he lied about what happened? Because he couldn't come to terms with what he had done? Did he want to create the image from the start that he was born vicious and soulless? So then what? He threw his hands up after messing up and decided it was either go hard or go home on being a piece of shit?

I can't blame him for not telling me the truth. I'm glad he

didn't, because I might have been angry enough to use it against him.

It makes sense now why he said the things he did when I was slumped over Jenna's body in the alley after he killed her and made it look like a suicide. How he told me everyone I love will die one day, how it will be my fault, and there will be nothing I can do, how I need to stop caring. Was he speaking from experience? Did he have to force himself to stop caring? Did he tell the same lie about his family's demise to himself until he believed it?

"Let's hope this is the worst of his memories," I say.

"Marianna . . ." He reaches up a hand to me, the other planted on the floor.

I unload a heavy breath and help him up. He crawls back into bed, face buried in his pillow.

"If he's okay now, I'm going back to my nap," she says.

"Same."

She closes the door behind her, and I relock it. Denendrius mumbles something to me and wipes his eyes before fixing the blankets and pulling them back from my side.

I'm nervous to crawl back into bed with him, my jaw still tender, but I lay my head down and study him.

His sudden change in emotion conjures up flashes of dreams when I inevitably fall back asleep. I dream of Denendrius waking up alone in a dark patch of trees, pained with thirst with nobody to explain what happened or what he is. In my dream, he finds his way home in search of comfort from his family. Adelia greets him, the rest of his family close behind. When she goes to hug him, he can't help but rip into her throat. After blood and shrill screams, I see him sitting in a candlelit room with over a dozen torn corpses strewn around him.

The memory of his screams slips into my dream and jolts me awake. Denendrius lies in his spot beside me, the blanket pulled up to our shoulders. I don't recall pulling the blanket up or letting him stretch his arm around my waist. When I throw it off me, his brown eyes momentarily peek from under red eyelids.

I watch him until his breathing changes, convincing me he has fallen back asleep.

His emotional state almost makes me hate him more. Where was his guilt—his remorse—when he was hurting me?

I wake with the moon, a pounding headache in my temples from getting elbowed in the face. It feels like I was only asleep for a handful of hours.

I sneak out of bed, creep out of the room, and follow the bathroom light down the hall.

Rayonne stands at the bathroom counter with freshly washed hair as she applies a new coat of foundation to her clean face. Her age isn't any easier to tell even without all the black.

"How old are you?" I ask as I grab my brush from the other side of her pile of cosmetics.

"Twenty-three." She lifts a liquid eyeliner brush to her top lash line, intense focus shaping her face as she draws a black wing over maroon eyeshadow.

So I was close. "Ah. When are we expected at Estrella de Sangre?"

Rayonne checks the time on her phone. It's ten o'clock. "Midnight or one. I have time to cook food."

"Dude, let's order a damn pizza this time," I say.

She focuses on drawing a wing on her other eye. "Fine."

I finish brushing out my hair and move on to snooping through her packed makeup bag. I'm not even sure what some items are for.

"You can borrow something, if you'd like," Rayonne says, rolling a tube of mascara between her palms.

I purse my lips. "I never really learned how to do makeup. Not the stuff you're doing, at least."

Too bad my drawing skills aren't transferable to my face.

"Do something simple, or I can help," she offers.

I study her as she applies the mascara, thinking about how Denendrius insulted me over such a tiny amount of makeup on our first date.

When she's done with the mascara, I apply some as well before giving myself a small smile in the mirror. He'd be so annoyed. I find my foundation and slather it on over the bruises on my neck and face to appear presentable.

"By the way," Rayonne starts, "don't mention Denendrius's name when we're there. This clan is pretty docile and won't want to get involved in something like that, so they'll probably ignore the issue if anyone recognized it, but there are visiting vampires who might take issue. He's human now, so it's unlikely anyone will connect the pieces, especially since his face isn't well known, but his name might cause some problems."

"Got it."

I leave her to get ready while I order pizza in the kitchen. When I'm done, I smooth out the wrinkles in my baby-blue tracksuit and crack open another energy drink.

Our pizzas—a large cheese, and a large pepperoni—arrive twenty minutes later. Denendrius wakes and eats almost a whole one by himself, acting like it's the most interesting thing he's ever eaten.

Once we're all full of pizza and caffeine, we soak the trim of the doorway and windows, then the apartment entrances, with more garlic—which is likely overkill since Denendrius would have kept up with that—and head out with a gun in my hand and a stake in Rayonne's.

After almost an hour of driving and following Rayonne's

directions into a commercial part in the city's north, I pull into an alley and park. I shiver when I climb off the heated seat and into the brisk air. Denendrius is at my side as we walk, following Rayonne's lead.

She guides us out of the alley and through the empty street. The lack of life—despite it being after midnight—is odd. There's nobody shuffling around in alleys, yelling into the darkness, or zipping around on stolen bikes. It's safe . . . which only makes me search the shadows more, like there's some hidden danger waiting.

There's hesitancy in my steps when she takes us to the metro tracks. I can't help but think of the metro security, even though I know they're not around in this part of town unless they're called, unlike in the west and south, where they get called so often there's no point in them leaving.

Still, I'm antsy as we follow alongside them on the gravel for a couple minutes until we reach the mouth of a tunnel, where they continue underground.

My steps pause. "I feel like this is a really prime area to get murdered by vampires, Rayonne."

It's bright enough that I can make out the way her eyes roll back into her skull. "It's a quick walk, we'll be fine."

I grab Denendrius's hand so he doesn't wander onto the tracks or run away into the dark.

"Fuck, fine," I grumble. "Are there cameras in there?"

"No." She retrieves a tiny flashlight out of her purse as we step into the concrete tunnel, the crunch of gravel under our feet and our hushed voices echoing against the gray walls the deeper we go.

After what feels like ten minutes, a beaten green door appears under her flashlight, the beams reflecting off the high voltage warning signs screwed to it. The lock is missing from the metal latch, which Rayonne uses to open the heavy door since there's no handle.

We step into a musty darkness, heavier than the one in the tunnel. The room is cramped for the three of us, a layer of dust and dirt on the concrete floor, another door to our right.

Rayonne knocks on it casually. My heart hammers, my grip tight on Denendrius's hand.

"We won't meet Agatha here?" I ask.

She laughs. "God, no—the clan here loathes her."

The door creaks when it opens, revealing a dim yellow light glowing over the head of a vampire with a dozen facial piercings and burning red eyes. He holds the door open for us and we scurry in, the only place to go being a long stretch of graffiti-covered concrete steps.

I pull in a deep breath, but it's not enough to put out the heat of my nerves.

VII

The vampire follows at a distance behind us, and I check over my shoulder a handful of times.

I can feel bass when we near the bottom of the steps, and we approach two smooth steel doors, the words *DARKLINGS PISS OFF* spray-painted across them in red.

My beat of laughter bounces off the wall, and the vampire behind me snickers.

"Does it work?" I can't imagine it would do more than piss them off.

The vampire says, "Sometimes. Depending on why they're here."

"Why do they have a problem with Darklings, anyway?" I ask Rayonne. "Is that a normal thing between Darklings and Children of Stars?"

Rayonne answers, "Estrella de Sangre is basically half fetish club. Vampires get willing blood, humans get their fantasies tickled. They've had issues with Darklings coming in and taking things too far with some of the humans and ruining their fun. But outside of them, there's not much concern about mingling together. Still, I don't see many clans that have both Darklings and Children of Stars in them. All the Darklings often group in small families or pair off. It's far more common for Children of Stars to be a part of a large clan of multiple families. Perhaps it's because of the massive population differ-ence, the different lifestyle needs, or simply because it's safer for Children of Stars to stick together."

"Makes sense," is all I say.

We reach the bottom of the stairs and walk toward the steel doors.

Rayonne pushes one open and says, "Welcome to Estrella de Sangre."

I feel oddly at ease as soon as I step in, and a quick look at Denendrius's calm face tells me he must feel similarly.

Loud industrial music plays. Red velvet drapes cover some of the gray concrete walls, and there's a wrought-iron bar with a mirror countertop on the far left end of the room, the wall behind it a mirror too. It reflects the group of vampires playing around a pool table. I suspect the bar serves blood despite the massive amount of alcohol on display.

Large rugs with red-and-orange designs cover high-traffic areas of the long room. Aside from a few mannequin lamps and neon signs, the lighting is all bare bulbs. A handful of vampires lounge in boisterous conversation with seemingly happy humans, some half-naked and trailing in and out of one of the many green doors around.

There's no proper place to dance, so I suppose it's not the type of *club* I had initially thought.

"Wow. This is pretty sweet." As long as none of the vampires expect me to take part in any type of exchange.

"I'm glad you think so," a guy says with an accent that I'm unable to identify as anything more specific than British.

We turn and a lanky guy who's wearing a sheer mesh tank

top and torn black jeans with worn patches slips through the dark to greet us from a side room, his dark brown eyes rimmed with smudged black eyeliner. I pin him at around twenty.

"Hey, Ziggy," Rayonne greets him.

Ziggy's grin is perfect. "All right. Welcome, welcome," he says, gaze alternating between us.

"Cool, so—" Rayonne's words fall away when Ziggy holds a hand up.

Ziggy's eyes fly to me. He releases a strangled chuckle as he sweeps an untamed strand of bleach-blond hair—the rest of his half-grown-out Mohawk black and unstyled—from his eye with one finger that pokes from the end of his leather fingerless glove. "Your master knows you're here, right?" He bares his teeth like a nervous dog. "I really don't feel like being murdered tonight by any Darklings."

I'm aghast, and my jaw lowers. "My *master*?"

His eyes flicker between Rayonne and me before he leans in a little closer to me. "You know you're blood marked, right? I could smell it the moment you walked in."

My heart sinks to my heels. I suppose the cure isn't enough to break that bond. "Oh."

Rayonne nods her head pointedly at Denendrius.

Ziggy lets out a laugh so sharp that I lean away from him and scowl. "A human? My gosh you're funny," he says. "But really."

"Yes, really," I snap, wondering how well she prepped him.

His lips pinch, and he lifts his dark brows while looking to Rayonne for answers.

She sighs and in a low voice says, "This is the man I was telling you about on the phone."

"I was expecting him to look much different." His eyes sparkle as they wander over Denendrius. Ziggy grabs hold of his hand with both of his and gives it an enthusiastic shake, his smile wide. "Well, I've heard so much about you! From the rumors, you're truly awful." His grin grows so large it's preposterous. "It's so wonderful to get to meet you. I don't meet infamous vampires very often. Usually, they're dealt with much quicker than you."

Denendrius holds a polite smile, the confusion in his eyes obvious as he looks at me for help.

"He doesn't speak English," I tell Ziggy.

Ziggy finally releases Denendrius's hands and wipes them together while grimacing. "Oh, well, that's probably for the best. As I said, I don't want to be murdered tonight."

Rayonne takes a step away from us and says to Ziggy, "Do you mind keeping an eye on them still? I have to talk to Ahana."

"It'll be my pleasure. She's back in the flat." He smiles and looks back at me. "Care for a drink?"

I wrinkle my nose. "Of what? Not blood, I hope."

He matches my attitude. "No, of nasty, foul alcohol."

Our smirks come in unison.

"What's your poison?" he asks, motioning with black-painted fingers for me to follow him.

We move past curious—yet seemingly friendly—vampires and toward the bar at the back. I study faces as various shades of eyes trail over us, trying to figure out if anyone here recognizes Denendrius. If they do, they either hide their reaction or don't care enough to have one.

"What's it cost?" I wonder as we approach the bar. My eyes scan the rows of alcohol on the back wall, but the dim light bouncing off the mirrors makes it hard to read any labels.

Chuckling, he says, "Absolutely nothing." There's pep in his step as he wanders around to the other side of the bar while softly headbanging to the music. He stops in front of an old sticker-covered fridge. "We've got no official bartender, so help yourself as long as you promise not to make a mess."

Denendrius is still silent, right behind me as I step up onto the little platform behind the bar and scrutinize the shelf.

"Or you could try this," Ziggy says, turning from the fridge with a glass bottle full of pink liquid. "It's a vodka drink. It tastes like soda and candy and used to be my favorite when I was human, so I highly recommend it."

I shrug and hold my hand out. "Sure."

With his thumb, he pops the bottle cap off. It bounces against the floor and he kicks it under the wrought-iron shelf of alcohol while passing it to me.

I take a sip, a bubbly and overly sweet cream soda pouring down my throat. It's like liquid sugar and covers the taste of vodka well.

"Yummy?" Ziggy grabs a blood bag from the fridge and a crystal wineglass from a shelf under the bar. He tears the blood bag open with his teeth and pours it out.

"Definitely. Can you drink? I know Darklings can't."

He shakes his head as he pops the glass into a microwave under another section of the bar. "No, but enough humans filter through here. I like to be an excellent host for my guests." He winks at me. "You feel at ease?"

I catch the insinuation in his crooked grin and ask, "Is that why I feel so calm? Like I come here all the time? Are you doing that?"

He gives me an innocent shrug. "Perhaps. I'm focusing most of my energy on your master. He was alarmingly agitated."

"Can you manipulate other emotions?" I wonder before taking another sip.

It's ironic someone as eccentric and energetic as Ziggy has a calming ability.

"Nah."

"Oh." My eyes sweep the room when someone's bright laughter catches my attention. I count at least seven girls and guys total who are clearly human from their tattoos, flushed cheeks, and bite marks. "Hm. Do a lot of humans come in here?"

"We've got our own familiars—you know, marked ones like you that come and go if they don't live with us—plus the humans belonging to whichever vampires pass through here . . ." He jerks his chin at me. "Well, and then there are the vampire fetishists who want to be drank from . . . amongst other things."

"Oh. Rayonne . . . mentioned something like that." I can't think of a better response. "So, a lot of you are a clan that live here?"

He nods, taking his glass from the microwave when it beeps. "Yes. We've got quite the underground setup; this is just the main entertainment area. We restrict the rest to the clan. It's like a big flat with loads of rooms."

"Ah—"

"Marianna." Denendrius nudges me and I whip around.

He grins and excitedly references a bottle of wine in hand, particularly the image of grapes on it.

My brows lift. "It's called *wine*."

"Ah! Wine?" It sounds funny coming off his tongue.

"Wine," I enunciate.

He tries the word out a few more times as he smiles and steps around me and grabs a crystal glass. Bringing it to the sink, he fills it with a bit of water before pouring his wine into it. Then, he says something to me before taking a sip.

"Oh." This must be normal then, if he expected me to know what the hell he wanted with his glass of water earlier.

Denendrius turns to Ziggy, and once he has his attention, he motions to the bottle of wine in hand and to the door.

Ziggy peers at me. "He wants to take it with him?"

"That's what I got from that too."

Ziggy's laugh comes out strangled. "Well, I'm not about to tell *him* no." He grabs another bottle off the shelf and sets it down. "There, take an extra and remember my kindness to you in the future. Fair?"

Denendrius gives him a grateful grin.

"So, does he still crave human blood like Rayonne does? I'm so curious about how similar their conditions are now," Ziggy asks before taking a sip of blood. His eyes burn red as it touches his tongue, and when he swallows and licks his lips clean with a sigh, I notice his fangs.

I try my best not to look disgusted. "If he does, it hasn't come up yet."

"Let's hope he doesn't. She's really quite frustrated. Don't tell her, but I'd much rather stand in the sun than be human again. Seems like a nightmare."

"So I've heard." Alaire and Edmond shared similar thoughts.

We follow Ziggy back to an empty lounging room, the music and voices now hushed.

"I wouldn't worry about that blood mark either," Ziggy says as he sits backward on the chair belonging to a little black table against the wall. The crystal glass of blood dangles loosely in his fingers. "As soon as you're a vampire, it'll be ancient history."

I scowl as I flop down on a green velvet couch in the middle of the room facing him, Denendrius plopping down beside me. "Who says I'm going to be a vampire?"

He pushes the hair from his face. "Will you not? Rayonne told me she's taking you to Romania. You're fairly at ease here, even without my intervention."

"I probably won't *have* to be a vampire." I rub my thumb against the label of the glass bottle, but the clear sticker doesn't budge under my nail.

"Hm. Well, what do I know about it anyway? I don't understand why you wouldn't want to be immortal given the opportunity though," he teases.

The vivid return of memories? Having no purpose in my life . . . but *eternally*?

"Is it the blood drinking?" He pushes his stained bottom lip out in a pout.

"Well—"

"Because when you turn, your concern with that will as well. You'll be no more concerned than you are now with what you eat. The circle of life is extended to vampires, Marianna. The blood will taste more divine than anything, and you won't feel bad for taking it any more than you do for the life you survive off now."

I roll my eyes. "Why would I want to turn if I'm going to be okay with torturing and murdering people?"

His eyes widen. "Torturing? Goodness gracious, no. I hunt and kill, that's it. You only play with your food if they deserve it, or you're deranged and like the taste of all that adrenaline . . ." His eyes flicker to Denendrius. "Besides, how many farmers chase their cows down and beat the piss out of them before putting them on the chopping block? Taking life is all the same, in the end. You can dislike mistreatment, be thankful, and acknowledge that the animal gave its life for you, but lions don't starve because they feel bad for gazelles. Hunger is hunger, and humans—and some vampires—seem to be the only ones who ever question it."

"Right . . . but many people have families and aspirations— don't you feel bad for ending that?"

He frowns. "Do animals not have families and a desire to live? I am at nature's mercy and I accept that."

I sigh, hating that his argument makes sense. "I guess."

Ziggy fights a smile. "Yet, I enjoy it to some extent. Violence in the right situation is very freeing. I can see you as a vampire who *loves* to hunt and kill. You may have a sweet face, but that hard look in your eye and the resting bitch face tell another story. I can imagine you hunting down wicked humans and taking out all your frustrations on them. Then you would never have to think past the love of blood if you deemed them unworthy of life." He gives in to his grin. "Actually, I know a few girls you would get on with. They got to a ring of traffickers before the police could and brought them to their clan . . . from what I heard, they had a *torturous* party."

I can't help my smile. It *would* be nice to hunt and kill wicked men like those girls. Maybe immortality wouldn't be so bad if I was a vigilante vampire. It would give me a sense of purpose too. But I'm still not completely convinced. Once I turn —cure or not—there's no true way to undo the decision.

"I could deal with that lifestyle if it came to it," I decide, if it was that or nothingness.

Ziggy takes a long sip of blood from his glass and gives me a red-toothed grin. "I hardly know you, Marianna, but I can feel that you are *destined* to be a vampire. You have that"—he feels at the air with his fingers—"air about you. There's a certain darkness to you that gives me vampire vibes. You would make a perfect vampire girl."

My cheeks burn at the way his admiring gaze holds mine. "You think so?"

He raises his glass to me. "Absolutely." After another sip, he says, "And if the castle isn't for you, you might find a home in my clan. Or I could call those girls up and see if they have space for another angry soul."

"I'll keep that in mind." I mull over his words a little longer and ask, "But why wouldn't the castle be for me?"

His lips twist, like maybe he's considering whether he said the wrong thing. "I'm sure it's a perfectly fine place. Rayonne trusts the word of others on that. But it has its restrictions, for the sake of secrecy. You can't have hundreds of vampires coming and going as they please, you understand? I had a nomadic friend, years back, who left because he tired of scheduling his leaves to and fro, and they expected him to rely on the castle's blood supply rather than go out and hunt on his own whenever he was thirsty. He felt so confined there."

"That doesn't sound too bad, actually. I'm in foster care and have to move from family to family and house to house all the time. It would be nice to stay in one place with the same people and have it feel like home." A castle is an enormous place. I doubt it would feel like being confined, like I was in my bedroom when I was little. I don't want to be nomadic right now—I want a stable home.

"How interesting. You're in foster care? How does that all work with . . .?" He juts his jaw at Denendrius. "Tell me more about yourself." He blinks rapidly, like he's trying to flutter his eyelashes at me as he sets his chin on the back of the metal chair. "I'm all ears."

I scratch my neck and shrug. "I don't know."

His head pops back up. "You don't know? You have a human master and you're trying to tell me you have nothing noteworthy about yourself to discuss?"

What could I tell him, a *stranger*? A diluted version of the truth? "Yeah." Saying nothing is better than expending energy on fake friendly banter.

"Bollocks," he spits, taking a long swig of blood. "Come on, vomit it out of you. All the ugliness, I want to hear it. You're in the world of vampires, we're all long sick of chitchat. Now come on, feed my curiosity."

I merely sigh and shake my head while sinking deeper into the soft velvet of the couch.

When he rolls his eyes at me, a smile teases at his lips. He mimics my sigh and sets the crystal glass on the table behind him. "All right, all right. I'll be hospitable and go first." He crosses his arms over the back of his chair. "I was born in Venezuela as"—he drops his voice while adopting a Spanish accent—"Eduardo Gonzalo Hernandez." He laughs and returns to his regular voice. "My parents immigrated to London when I was a baby, and I grew up in a regular middle-class household. I had wonderful grades through school and had many friends when I collided with the alternative scene in the eighties. But I ruined it all when I was nineteen. I got my girlfriend pregnant when she sabotaged her birth control, got kicked out by my parents when I wouldn't marry her and go to rehab. I ended up sleeping on couches, drinking, partying, frequenting clubs, and succumbing to my cocaine addiction." He squints in thought, then smirks.

My eyes widen at the breeziness of his overshared words. "Wow."

He waves my concern away. "It's all an intoxicated blur." He points out a tall and pale raven-haired guy wearing a black satin shirt with embroidered roses and red lace on the sleeves. He's at one of the pool tables across the club. "My lovely Lance over there found me one night after I had a heart attack in a club bathroom. We'd been eyeing one another all night but had been waiting for the other to make the first move. He gave me the quickest and most painful rehabilitation I've ever had, and I inherited his ability to calm others. He's the complete opposite to me with his tranquility. It makes us a balanced couple."

He stares fondly at him, and Lance looks over his shoulder, a smile playing at the corners of his lips. "I'll love him forever for that." He sighs and his excitement returns. "When I woke up, he slapped me across my face, told me I wasted all my human potential and that I'd better *be a good vampire*. Then, we went back to partying! Honestly, the parties are much better now."

I'm not sure what to say other than, "Sounds like a wild ride."

Cocaine . . . yeah, makes sense.

"Oh, it was. I throw wicked parties now." He bats his eyelashes again. "You'd find out if you ever joined us. Ask Rayonne, she's had tons of fun chasing parties with Lance and me."

I can't help the bright laughter that bubbles out of me at the thought of all three of them living it up. "When did you meet Rayonne?"

He claps his hands together once and grins as he reaches behind himself and takes another sip of blood before saying, "Late eighties. About three months after Lance turned me. She frequented all the underground vampire clubs with us until she got caught up in all this Agatha bullshit."

I scratch my cheek. "Where—"

He leaps into a crouch on his chair and shakes his head at me. "I will take no more questions until you've had your turn."

I groan. "Right."

He twirls his finger in a *go on* motion. "Go on, don't be shy. We're practically friends now."

Did he only tell me his entire life story so I'd feel obligated to share mine? I sigh and offer a crumb of information that he'll be able to relate to. "I was"—or am?—"a drug addict too. Heroin. I overdosed, but he healed me."

He grimaces, teeth bared. "Oh my. I could never. Needles terrified me as a human. But I'm glad you found your way through that."

I shrug. "Never had a chance to develop a fear of them."

"Well, tell me more," he presses with a tickled smile.

I'm thankful when Rayonne interrupts, an unfamiliar duffel bag in hand.

"Hey, Ziggy, I'm going to take them back home now."

I frown and swish my drink around. "I'm not even done with my drink yet. We've been here for like an hour. Can't we hang out for a few more hours?"

If everyone here hates Agatha, wouldn't it be wise to stay a little longer?

Ziggy scoffs at her and stands. "You're leaving me so soon? Marianna and I were having such a pleasant conversation."

Rayonne scratches her head, bag swinging in her fist. "I

know, but we have to go. I'll be back anyway and won't leave the city without saying bye."

"Hold on now," Ziggy tells her with feigned annoyance. He scampers over, wedging himself against my side and the wooden arm of the couch. "Hi."

"Hey . . .?" My heart pounds, resistance against the breaths in my chest at the feel of his body pressed alongside mine. I swallow against my tight throat, intimidated despite how cute he is.

"May I have your phone, please?" He's so close that the scent of blood and faint patchouli wafts off him and fills my nostrils. He holds his open hand over my lap. "I want to text myself so I have your number."

Rayonne stretches her groan as she taps her foot. "Don't you and Lance already share four other familiars, Ziggy?"

"Pish posh. Don't be jealous," he says to her before smiling down at me with a gleam in his red eyes. "Sorry, I don't mean to make you nervy."

I'm acutely aware of the calmness that floods through to my extremities and dials my heartbeat back a notch. I know I shouldn't hand the phone over so easily, but I'm far too comfortable to protest as I place it in his hand.

Ziggy's giddy—legs bouncing—as he adds himself as a contact and sends himself a smiley face. His pocket vibrates against my hip as he sets my phone in my lap. "There."

I slip it back into my jacket pocket, a laugh bubbling up my throat. "Thanks?"

"You're welcome." He gently pokes my knee before clasping his hands together in his lap. "Now you all may ditch me, I suppose."

When I look to Rayonne, she gives me a tight-lipped smile and jerks her head toward the door.

I chug the rest of my drink. "*Fine*, let's go. Nice meeting you, Ziggy."

"It was lovely meeting you as well, Marianna." He pouts at Rayonne as we leave.

"What the hell was that about?" I click my seat belt on. Denendrius sits with his bottles of wine in the passenger seat since I'm not fond of having him behind me, where he could easily strangle me.

Rayonne starts the Mustang and pulls forward out of the alley. "Your blood mark was making a group of visitors nervous. They were convinced some Darkling was going to come looking for you, and I really didn't want to get into it with all of them and risk their questions. It's easier if we leave. I don't want to be the reason Ziggy loses guests."

"Isn't Ziggy the clan leader? He seemed pretty intent on my staying," I growl.

She turns onto the road. "Yeah, but he's a people pleaser, especially with newcomers. I don't want him arguing with his clan over a situation I created."

My hands curl into fists in my lap. "This is stupid. I wanted this mark *gone*. Now what the hell do I do? I don't want to be connected to him when—well, you know!" When we go to Romania.

I can only hope that if Denendrius starts understanding English, he doesn't remember the plan we have for him.

I throw my head back against the seat. I'm back to my only two options: his death, or another vampire overwriting his mark. But I don't want him to die yet. He deserves years of torture first. Who do I get to overwrite this blood mark, then? Can I even trust some vampire not to tinker with my head?

Under her breath, Rayonne grumbles, "At least you probably can't kill him."

"Oh, *please continue*."

She flicks the turn signal on and heaves out an agitated breath. "You're marked, Marianna. Eventually, it turns into an automatic barrier to killing your master. You get some wiggle room in the beginning as your body tries and fails to fight . . . but eventually . . ." She clicks her tongue. "What's the point in a mindless blood slave if they can murder you whenever they'd like?"

I shake my head in utter disbelief but then think about how much I struggled to pull the trigger on him despite really wanting to. "Shit." She's right. "At least it's paused and won't get worse, right?"

"Right." There's something in her light tone that makes the hair stand up on my arms, like she's only telling me what I want to hear.

I pull in a breath and try to breathe out more blood mark thoughts. "Aside from that, did you get any leads on how to contact Viorel's men?"

She shakes her head as she turns a corner. "No, but Ahana and Ziggy will both throw out some hooks and will pay extra attention to anyone passing through. We have a big bag of weapons now, which is as important since Agatha is probably going to try killing us."

Denendrius groans in pain before I can say anything. There's sweat in his hairline, and he's sickly pale.

"You're going to puke, aren't you?" I say.

As soon as he makes a heaving noise, Rayonne pulls over on the side of the road and he jumps out of the car, puking against the brick wall of a closed business.

"Hurry!" I holler, the urgency in my voice clear in any language. "Unless you want to get murked out here."

He swats at the air like he wants me to shut up, his other hand holding himself up against the wall as he retches. After about thirty heart-pounding seconds, he spits and drops himself back in the passenger seat.

As soon as we're back in the apartment, he's on his hands and knees puking into the toilet. I leave him there with a glass of diluted wine and heat myself up some more pizza.

"Do you think we have food poisoning?" I sit next to Rayonne on the couch, the sound of Denendrius retching echoing from the bathroom.

Her face scrunches in disgust as she looks at the pizza in my hand. "If you think that, why are you still eating pizza?"

I shrug. "I already had some. Aren't I going to be sick either way?"

She shakes her head at me, the judgment clear.

"When do you think we're going to have to deal with Agatha?" I take a bite.

"She has to find us here first. Maybe we'll get lucky and get in contact with Viorel's people first."

Too bad I don't have a lucky streak.

Denendrius retreats to the bedroom after he's done puking his brains out, sliding the blanket over his head and blocking out the world. Even when I crawl back into bed—body still begging for sleep after going so long without a proper rest—he doesn't even remove the blanket to look at me. When I wake up with a confused start in the middle of the afternoon, he's still lying under the blanket. I get so worried that I poke my head under too, which is when he cracks an eye open to look at me before squeezing them shut again.

Is he trying to will himself back to Rome? Or could reality be hitting him so hard he's trying to hide from it?

My head spins with a hundred incoherent thoughts as I climb out of bed and tread to the bathroom. When I check on Rayonne, she's fast asleep on the couch, the remnants of a home-cooked meal spread over the kitchen counter.

I find leftover baked macaroni in the fridge and help myself to some after I clean the kitchen.

My thoughts come in line as I slump down at the table and

eat. I consider Ziggy's offers a little more but decide I'm going to try my best to stay human. Maybe I can find some kind of normal at the castle if other humans can.

I stifle a laugh. Yeah, because vampires and a castle totally go hand in hand with *normal.*

Once Rayonne wakes, we try to learn some Latin. After three hours of videos that don't bring us to any helpful level of understanding for speaking or decoding Denendrius's block of words, we tap out with aching brains.

When she watches a romance movie—no mental energy left inside us for productive conversation—I slip back to the bedroom and binge random videos on the phone after looking through Denendrius's music search history. He has an odd combination of classical music, World War Two era songs, and heavy metal and rock. When the phone dies, I put it on the charger and crash.

VIII

Denendrius's uncontrolled breathing invades my thoughts as I park in his usual spot across from West James High and climb out of the Mustang into the crisp morning air. His eyes dart across the building, landing on me when I mesh my fingers together with his to stop him from freaking out and running off. I'm surprised at the heat of his palm again and almost drop his hand.

"It's okay," I say, forcing a calmness to my voice that I hope he picks up on. "You can trust me." He can't, but he doesn't need to know yet.

Nausea bubbles in my stomach, and I hope it's only the rising temperature, energy drinks, and exhaustion and that we all didn't get food poisoning.

We dart across the street and dip into the school foyer. My heart clenches when I see the security guard on his cell phone —back to us—beyond the entrance doors and through into the office. Carefully, I push open the door and we dart past the office and staircase and down the first corridor. Thankfully, it's too early for them to expect any shenanigans, but I don't want them to know I'm here since I have two nonstudents with me.

Pinpointing Mr. Derek's classroom halfway down the hall—door open, light on—I grip Denendrius's hand tighter and drag him along. My history teacher is at his desk at the front of the empty room when we slip inside, head snapping up from a stack of papers as I shut and lock the classroom door behind us.

"Whoa! Hey!" His chair flies back into the chalkboard as he leaps from it. Eyes locked on Denendrius, he lifts a defensive hand in front of himself as he picks up his landline phone in the other. As my teacher shouts alarmed warnings, I drop Denendrius's hand, scramble across the classroom, and jam my finger down on the end call button.

"Mr. Derek, he won't hurt you—"

He tries to yank the phone base out from under my hand. "Like hell. Last time he threatened to—"

"Stop! Listen to me." I disconnect the phone line and toss it toward the shelves.

Mr. Derek falls into silence, eyes wide as Denendrius approaches the desk. The confusion and distrust for my teacher is clear on his face, and I wonder what he must think. Is there any possibility he remembers threatening Mr. Derek when he retrieved my phone and ring?

His wide eyes tighten, concern appearing as lines in his forehead as his brows pull together while studying Denendrius and me. "What happened to you, Marianna? The other day they saw you running off school property like you were being chased, and you show up this morning looking like you've been beaten half to death. Did he do this to you—"

Folding my arms, I say, "I'm okay, but that's not what I'm here to talk about. I need help with some translations and stuff on ancient civilizations—"

"Please tell me you didn't bring your boyfriend to convince me to let you retake your quiz." He stares at me.

Scowling, I snap back with, "*No.* Jesus, let's chill out for a minute so I can attempt to explain this shit."

He sighs and plants his palms on his desk, leaning over to inhale deeply. "All right."

I swallow and pull the folded pages with Denendrius's writing from my pocket. "You can translate Latin, right?"

His eyes narrow. "To an extent. I studied it when I was getting my degree. Why?"

Grimacing, I hold out the papers. "Can you translate this?"

Mr. Derek straightens and crosses his arms. "Why?"

My gaze shifts from him to Rayonne and back. "Uh—"

"I need a good reason," he presses.

Maybe we should have taken our chances finding a professor and paying them to translate without question.

Rayonne speaks from a few desks behind me, the impatience clear in her voice. "He's Roman. He woke up speaking Latin and not remembering anything from the past two thousand years. You're currently our safest option for translation."

I suppose we're not worrying about keeping secrets safe.

Mr. Derek's breath audibly stops. He gapes blankly at Rayonne. "Excuse me?"

"He was born in 58 AD," I add.

His eyes flicker between the three of us, his expression deadpan.

Trying to get the ball rolling, I set the papers on his desk—Denendrius twitching at my side—and say, "Will you at least look at them?"

He's incredulous, head shaking slightly as he looks between us.

I turn to Denendrius and motion with my hand from my mouth for him to speak to my teacher, hoping to convince him quickly.

With wary eyes, Denendrius's voice comes out slow as he says, "*Salve...?*"

Mr. Derek scowls. "That's supposed to convince me? A basic 'hello'?"

"You can speak Latin?" Rayonne asks as she joins me at his desk.

His suspicious eyes shift from Denendrius to her. "Not nearly as much as I can read it. I studied some Greek and Latin in college, and I spent some time with historians in Italy. I was going to do more than teach, but . . ." He stares at Denendrius and rattles off some very English-sounding Latin to him.

Denendrius turns his head to stare down at me, and for a moment I think he looks completely insulted from the way his lip draws back.

"Are you sure you know Latin?" I rub my eyes when the fluorescent lights flicker overhead.

Mr. Derek sighs and repeats something.

Finally, he must say something that clicks with Denendrius, as he relaxes and rambles off a long and excited string of Latin. Mr. Derek's eyes widen, and Denendrius breaks off speaking when it's clear that my teacher can't truly understand him.

"That was interesting," Mr. Derek says. "I don't know what he said."

"Do you believe us now?" A hopeful smile creeps across my lips.

Mr. Derek titters. "Absolutely not. But I'm impressed at your dedication to . . . whatever this is. What else can you tell me about him, since you've taken a sudden interest in this history unit? If you want extra credit, you can always come in at lunch —without them—and write a short essay."

My scowl is heavy. "This isn't about school. I need your help, or some books or something if you absolutely refuse—"

Denendrius leaves my side and wanders toward the other end of the classroom, eyes locked on the large poster of the

Colosseum ruins that I've had the pleasure of looking at for the past three years. He gapes at it and the color drains from his face as his unsteady breath returns.

"He was a gladiator," I whisper to offer a bit of context. "A dimachaerus."

Nobody says anything as he lifts his shaky fingers up to the glossy image to touch it. He yanks his hand back like it zapped him.

Almost two thousand years gone and unaccounted for. So much has changed beyond recognition. I don't know how the confusion and horror hasn't driven him past the point of no return. Though, I suppose there's still time for that.

When he stumbles away from it, he wavers and collides into a desk, sending it sliding a few feet into the aisle. Denendrius's desperate eyes meet mine, and the emotion makes him look so unfamiliar that my stomach winds around itself.

"Marianna . . ." Mr. Derek sighs. "I have to ask. Are there drugs involved in this? Your eyes look a little . . ."

I grit my teeth and spin back around. "*No.* I haven't slept properly, and I'm hyped up on caffeine."

"Okay." It doesn't sound like he believes me.

"So, you won't help us?" I demand. "I could really use some translation help since I'm walking on eggshells around here. I don't want my ass beat over a culture clash."

He shakes his head. "No, I'm sorry. I'm honestly not really sure what's going on here. You're welcome to go to the library and look through their books, or flip through mine—*here*—if you're wanting to do extra credit work. I am more than happy to allow you to make up for your grades."

"I told you. This isn't about my grades." What else could I divulge that won't risk my ass but will also convince him to just do a translation? It's not like I can drop the vampire bomb on him here. "He's really from ancient Rome. You heard his Latin. Just look at the papers, you'll see."

When he releases a beat of nervous laughter, I grit my teeth. "Marianna, what little you've told me is completely unbelievable. With enough practice, I'm sure anyone could fake a little Latin and copy from the internet. And frankly, I want him nowhere near here. You're welcome to stay and discuss school with me, but I want him—and your other friend here—*off school grounds*. If I see him again, I'm calling campus security and the cops."

"Is there anything I can do to convince you?" I turn to Rayonne, hoping she has ideas to offer, but she merely looks between the three of us while mashing her black lips together.

Useless.

He sits back at his desk and nods toward the door. "I have dozens of assignments to grade."

"Ugh." I grab the papers and Denendrius, dragging my feet from the classroom and into the empty hallway. Denendrius trails at my side with Rayonne following behind us.

We take a few steps before the sight of Sarah leaving a classroom a few doors down and turning toward us stops me in my tracks. Thinking of Denendrius beside me and how he raped her, my stomach flips.

Sarah freezes as she lifts her head, her eyes widening when they land on Denendrius. Her lips part for a horrified gasp and her zipper binder collides with the floor. She looks like she's about to scream.

I scramble for something to say, some way to explain why I've brought her attacker into school. "Sarah—"

Her eyes dart to me, then back to Denendrius, before she twists and bolts down the hall.

"Fuck." I glance at Rayonne before I leave Denendrius's side. "Take him back to the car. I'll meet you there."

I dash down the hall, snagging Sarah's binder while I follow the squeak of her sneakers around the corner and through the closing bathroom door. She disappears into the accessible stall at the end, and I hold my arm up as I try to enter, expecting her to slam the door on me. She leaves it open and doesn't protest when I step inside to find her standing rigid against the white concrete wall with her face red and eyes teeming with tears.

"Sarah, I'm sorry—"

"Why is he here?" she sobs, her entire body shaking as she speaks. "Does he know I told you? Is he following behind you? What's he gonna—"

"You're safe—"

Sarah gasps for breath between incoherent questions. Her knees buckle and she slides down the wall until she's sitting. She covers her face with her hands and pulls her knees up as she sobs while trying to squeeze out more words.

I crouch in front of her, my eyes stinging. Is this how I looked to her mere days ago when I had my breakdown at school before trying to run away? The terrified hopelessness returns to me and I swallow a lump.

"He's never going to hurt you again," I whisper. I lift a hand, but I'm not sure how to comfort her, so it hangs above her knee as thin tears trail down my cheeks. "Sarah, I promise he'll never hurt you again."

She looks up when I sniffle and takes a deep breath, furiously wiping the tears from her blue eyes. "What did he do to you?" she squeaks, her index finger poking out of her hoodie sleeve to reference the bruising around my throat. "What happened? Did you try to leave him?"

I wipe my cheeks and try to sum up reality as truthfully as I can without dragging her into it all. "Yes, but—he found me."

"*I'm sorry*," she cries, her face twisting as more tears barrel down her cheeks. "I shouldn't have said anything to you about what he did, but . . . I needed to tell you—"

I shake my head. "No, no, it's not your fault, Sarah. None of this is your fault."

She inhales a deep breath and squeezes her eyes shut, but the tears keep falling.

"You never have to worry about him again." I hope she'll believe me.

Her sobs return. "That doesn't make me feel better," she blubbers. "I know that means he's getting what he wants from you if he doesn't need me anymore."

"Don't worry about me."

She wipes more tears. "How can I not? It looks like he tried to strangle you. He beat CJ to death. He told me that he's made other girls disappear so I wouldn't tell . . ."

I'm almost surprised he went with fear over hypnotism.

"I can't explain it in a way you'll understand or accept, but *I promise* I'm okay and that you will be too." I'm dizzy at the fact that once I'm gone—even if I'm safe—she will think the worst. How could she not?

"Okay," she squeaks.

I think of Denendrius and Rayonne alone in the car waiting for me and a dozen things that could go wrong while I'm in here run through my mind.

Despite everything that was once between us, I want to stay and be here for her, so I feel like a bitch when I say, "I'm sorry, but I have to go. You should talk to the counselor. Liz is actually really helpful, okay? I promise it's safe to get some counseling. He's waiting outside for me though—"

"Don't go!" She grabs my hand before I can even stand, her grip making my bones ache. "You can't. He'll hurt you for following me, won't he?"

If he were still a vampire, he would have kicked the door in by now, if I could step away from his side. "No, he won't. I'll be fine."

Her face twists in frustration at my words, but the expression quickly crumbles. "No, you won't be okay, Marianna. We both know that." Her eyes lift to mine, desperate. "Let's tell my dad together—"

My brow furrows. "He doesn't know? But your dog—"

"Dad thought it was a break-in—that it was personal to him —and I let him believe it. I didn't want Den to hurt him too . . . but you need to come with me and tell him. He'll protect us, and it'd be you and me against him even when Dad's on duty. Dad will arrest him, and with two of us he'll definitely go to jail and get a longer sentence—"

I shake my head. "I can't."

"Why not?" she pleads.

"I just . . ." I swallow a glob of emotion. "I can't leave him, Sarah. I can't."

Her eyes wander over my face, her eyes so full of hopelessness I want to look away. "Why, Marianna?"

I gulp. "I'll get hurt. Really bad." It's not a lie. I'll probably have to leave Lorimer, even if it's not for Romania. She'll know something has happened to me, and that it's related to Denendrius, even if she doesn't know exactly how.

"Then don't leave," she insists, her grip relentless.

But when I gently shake my hand free from hers, she doesn't fight me. "I have to."

"But—" Sarah's eyes are wild with panic.

I stand and wrap my arms around my stomach. "You're safe now," I say one last time. "Okay? *I promise.* None of this is your fault, so don't worry about me."

She leaps to her feet and I jerk in surprise when she wraps her arms around me. My initial reaction is to pull away, but I stop myself. I twist one of my arms out from where it's trapped between us and wrap it around her thin waist. My lip shakes when I feel her cold tear against my cheek.

"I'm sorry," she whispers. "I'm sorry we haven't gotten along. But I'm so scared for you."

Swallowing a lump, I nod. "I'm sorry too." I hate how it took

Denendrius harming us both to get us on the same side, but at least we're past it, no matter the reason.

We break apart, and she slumps back on the floor.

"Be careful," she whispers as I turn to leave.

"I'll be okay." I look over my shoulder and offer an unconvincing smile.

IX

I climb into the driver's seat after I've let Rayonne and Denendrius in.

"You really couldn't help at all with that?" I growl at her as she buckles up behind me.

"What was I supposed to say? We sounded nutty. I'm not really sure how we thought that could go any other way."

I grit my teeth and punch the horn. "Goddamn it!"

Gently, she says, "We'll be okay without his help. I called the college while you were still inside, and there's a Latin professor teaching. Let's drive up there and see if we can speak with him."

Leaning my head back against the headrest, I groan. "Fine."

I'm hopeful as I drive across the city to the rich north, thinking it might be better to get a Latin professor than Mr. Derek anyway. But my spirit is swiftly squashed.

We're on the University of Lorimer campus for barely five minutes when security starts trailing us. Not wanting to risk finding out why—knowing it likely has something to do with

Denendrius and the car—I keep my speed and head for the nearest exit.

"There goes that fucking plan," I snarl while taking the closest exit, the security car stopping as we leave the property.

She grumbles to herself before saying, "We've got all day, so let's try to teach him some basic English instead. Stop by the bookstore."

"Ugh, fine."

If only I could find more of Denendrius's money. Maybe I could pay Mr. Derek to work with us, even if he thinks we're all on drugs.

I drive us to a bookstore on the east, middle-class side of town, and we stock up on various English learning books, a Latin dictionary, the only two books they had on ancient Rome, and a few notepads.

"I don't know if I want him learning English," I decide as we pile back into the car.

"Why not? He needs to understand enough not to die if we get attacked. How can we tell him to fight or run if he doesn't know what that means?" Rayonne says as she buckles into the back seat.

I jam the key in the ignition. "I don't know, I think our method of interpretive hand motions and expressions is working fine."

"That doesn't work in the dark while we're under attack, Marianna."

"And what if learning English triggers a bunch of memories?" I counter while I start the car after glancing at Denendrius, who buckles himself in beside me.

"We can't *stop* him from remembering if he's going to. But either way, he's going to pick up on some English by being around it. It's easier if we speed up that process so he's more than quiet and useless. He can pull some weight until, you know . . ."

"Yeah, I guess."

Once we're back at the apartment, Denendrius pours himself a cup of diluted wine from a pitcher he premixed earlier and sits down on the couch with Rayonne and some picture word books—that are technically for children—to go over the alphabet. That lesson is over swiftly, and she's moving on to teaching him basic words like *no, yes, stop.*

No is the most important word for him to learn.

While she does that, I take the notepad and work on drawing a more specialized picture dictionary. I sketch a vampire, stake, gun, a dude being killed, and their accompanying English words, along with a handful of other images that might be useful since the baby books have nothing of the like.

"He's picking this up fast," Rayonne notes from the couch.

I look up from my drawings. "Think his memories are helping him out?"

She shrugs. "Our alphabets aren't *that* different, so maybe that's why. But I don't see how we're going to teach him more than basic words and sentences. It'd be nice if we can either get your teacher to help us before something gets lost in translation, or he remembers English, if nothing else yet."

He's going to be *so* goddamn annoying when he can speak English again. Every bit of my will to play nice is going to be tested, I know it.

"I've been trying to think of ways to convince my teacher, and aside from money, I'm drawing a blank. Maybe we really don't need his help at all, and him refusing to entertain us was the world's way of stopping a big mistake."

She bites at her bottom lip. "I don't know, Marianna. Some proper translations from someone who knows what they're doing would benefit us. As of now, he has *basically no idea* what's going on. He's only going to be okay with not having answers for so long. He'll get frustrated for various reasons and possibly violent."

As if on cue, Denendrius grumbles something and drops the book he's holding in her lap. He rises and cracks his back before wandering over and plunking down in the chair across from me. His nose scrunches when he looks over the images.

When I try to teach him the words I've written under their corresponding images, he grunts and waves his hand dismissively at them before leaning back in his chair and crossing his arms.

I shove them across the table so they're in front of him. "This is *important*." I go over the words anyway, point at the picture of a guy being stabbed, and enunciate each letter in the word *kill*.

He yawns. Does he not understand we're being hunted? What does he think? That we're all chilling together at his place while we help him recover from being a vampire?

"Got it, Rayonne. I'll think of something super convincing."

She lets out a spiritless breath and flips through the pages. "Something like this is how I taught my son, Thomas, to read."

"I'm sorry you lost your little boy," I whisper, piling my hands in my lap. "I want to say that I can't believe he killed a child, but I guess he's capable of anything."

She picks at the hem of her shirt. "He wasn't so little when he died. Thomas was fifteen. We planned on turning him after a few more years, but he died protecting the house. He was a brave boy, thinking he could kill . . ." Her eyes trail to Denendrius and she sniffs. "He was very brave."

My nod is succinct. "Yes, he would have to be incredibly brave to even think of taking a vampire on."

She wipes at her eyes and stands, hurrying to the kitchen like she's trying to outrun her tears. "Hungry? I'll cook something up. We should see if we can get more sleep. It's probably best we stay awake at night and sleep during the day so we can be awake in case Viorel's men—or Agatha—come looking."

With how sleep-deprived I've been, I'm pretty sure I could sleep for two full days still. "Are you sure you're up to cooking?"

The pan clatters on the stove. "Yes. Cooking always makes me feel better. It takes all the attention away from whatever is on my mind. I used to cook for my entire family after my mother passed when I was . . . hmm. I can't quite remember now, but I was fourteen or fifteen."

"Did you cook for a big family?" I ask, lending a hand with the distraction.

Through the space between the bottom of the cupboard and counter, I watch her dig through the fridge. "Our family was as big as any other back then. I had three brothers and four sisters, plus my father. My mother died with her youngest, and I was the oldest, so I took on all her duties around the house. I was lucky to have a fair father though. Even with all the work he did in the fields, he helped me with what he could."

I scowl. "Well, they were his kids, so you shouldn't have had to do anything. I hated being a parent to my foster siblings in the last home I was in."

My lips twist. In hindsight, my problems were far simpler than now. Extremely rough, but simpler. I wish I could go back to taking care of Samantha and Charlie, because at least I wouldn't have to wonder how they're doing.

She sets veggies down on the counter, peeking through the space and smiling softly. "It was the best thing for my family for me to step up. It was difficult, but I'm still glad I could do it. I would have done anything for my family back then. Even at twenty-three, the only reason I stopped helping raise my siblings was because I died. I may have missed out on a lot when I was human, but my vampire years made up for it."

"That's good then." I smile, but a pang of jealousy rips through me.

I wish I knew what that kind of familial love felt like. What all did she give up for their sake? I can't imagine what it would be like to have a family love you—and you them—so much that you would do something like that. Even with Red Revenge, we weren't that type of family. We were dysfunctional, and our loyalty was founded on fear and a desperate need for belonging. Between juvenile detention and my criminal record, I gave up pieces of my life for them. But unlike Rayonne, I regret being a part of it.

"Do you want help?" I ask as she rinses potatoes.

"I'm okay." There's a bit of cheer back in her voice.

I prop my elbow up on the table and drop my chin in my palm, eyeing Denendrius as he looks over the papers across from me, mouthing the words on them.

The TV calls to me, so I abandon Denendrius at the table and flop down on the couch. A commercial for cars comes on, and Denendrius's head jerks up. His brow furrows as he stands and wanders over, eyes locked on it.

He stands a few feet from it, completely in my damn way, and squats so he's staring right into it.

"Dude, seriously?" I press the guide button and he leans away in surprise when it pops up. "Move."

He pokes the screen as he stands, then yanks his finger back at the TV fuzz. "Hm."

I slap the space on the couch next to me. "Sit."

He remembers that one from Rayonne's lesson, as he smiles and plops down next to me, releasing a grunt as he does.

I point at it, clearly enunciating, "Television."

He repeats the word a few times, then his slitted eyes alternate between the remote in my hand and the screen. His face relaxes, and he grins at how I control it.

I put a mixed martial arts show on and it only takes him a few minutes to become absorbed in the fighting, shouting enthusiastic Latin as the two men beat the snot out of each other.

We have tilapia and mashed potatoes for dinner. I only get a chance to eat after a quick potato lesson, since apparently Denendrius has never seen one before. He also critiques how Rayonne cooked the fish, but we ignore him since we can't understand more than his tone. Eventually, he shuts up and finishes eating it.

Denendrius resists going back to bed when the time comes, even after I do my best to explain why we're sleeping during the day instead of night. So I lock him in the room with me and his learning materials and pass out.

It's hard to stay asleep with him awake next to me. I rotate in and out of terrified dreams, waking to check on him every twenty minutes. I worry about him suffocating me with a pillow, even dreaming he's remembered all along and is waiting to kill me when I least expect it to keep me on edge.

My eyes flutter open at some point, and I see he's passed out beside me. I fall into a deeper sleep and don't wake until Rayonne's exclamation pulls me from the deep.

"You scared the shit out of me!" Rayonne hollers from the living room.

I launch out of bed, eyes landing on the cracked door that I completely slept through him figuring out how to unlock. I scramble out of the room and find Denendrius at the table in the fading evening light, scowling between Rayonne and me as he eats plain bread and drinks his wine.

"Sleep," he commands, motioning back at the couch with irritated motions.

She crosses her arms. "It's *night* now."

He glances over his shoulder at the sunset beyond the blind slats.

I rub my eyes. "I didn't even hear him leave the room. My bad."

"It's fine," she grumbles, hauling herself to the kitchen, where she grabs a cold brew coffee from the fridge. She holds an energy drink out to me. "Want?"

I stumble a few steps forward and take it. "Thanks."

We take sips of our drinks, staring at Denendrius as he dips his bread in his wine before eating it.

"This is super weird," I note before another sip. "Him. He's too . . . normal. Except he's also the farthest thing from normal right now."

She nods. "Last time I woke up to his face, the room *was on fire.*"

"Damn. I bet once he gets more comfortable, he'll be back to his usual self. He probably shit-talks us already, we just can't understand it." It's weird he hasn't tried to start any fights with me, but I'm sure there's a ticking bomb in him. Perhaps he'll get sick of my tone when I'm annoyed and lash out.

I take a sip of my drink and choke—energy drink spraying everywhere—when a deafening alarm fills the building hallway and spills into the apartment.

My heart slams against my rib cage and Rayonne and I spin, facing one another while Denendrius looks between us with wide eyes and hands clamped over his ears.

"Fire alarm?" Rayonne and I yell while cringing against the noise.

I race to the front door. "Think someone pulled it to be an asshole?" I shout at her. "Or do you think this is related to us being here?"

Rayonne stares at me with white-rimmed eyes, her chest lifting and falling with her short breaths. I read her thoughts on her face, and they're solidified by coughing and shouting in the stairwell.

We're being smoked out.

Rayonne yanks a revolver out of the weapon bag and shoves it into my hand.

"Wooden bullets!" she hollers as I secure it in the back of my jeans. "Run straight for the Mustang."

She throws Denendrius a stake as he hops out of his chair and he catches it with one hand. I get him to hide it in the waist of his pants before I throw my backpack on and grab Denendrius's duffel bag—which I let him snatch from me this time—and we rush out the door and down the first flight of stairs.

All I can hope is that whoever has come for us—Agatha or otherwise—doesn't meet us at the door. Because we're being driven out of the apartment, I rule out a Darkling attack.

A thick layer of gray smoke clings to the air on the third floor, irritating my eyes and lungs as I skip stairs on the way down. The smoke clears a bit on the second floor, and on the first there's nothing yet but the smell. I grab Rayonne's wrist as we reach the front door, eyeing the group of people gathering in the parking lot. A group that vampires could hide in, while also making it hard to back out and drive anywhere.

"We need to go over our plan, right now," I tell her. "I'm driving the Mustang. You climb between the seats and into the back. As soon as we shut the doors, I'm driving off." I ready the keys in my hand, finger hovering over the unlock button.

"If it's Agatha—" Her eyes focus behind me as Denendrius's duffel bag thuds against the floor beside me. "Where the hell are you going!"

I spin. Denendrius races back up the stairs.

"Get back here!" I shriek as I chase after him, all the way back up to the apartment door.

He yanks on the door handle, his Latin vehement as he shouts demands over the alarm.

I swing my arm back toward the stairs. "Come on! The building is on fire!"

Denendrius practically snarls at me, his brown eyes hard and filled with a fury so familiar that it sends a chill through me. It freezes me long enough that I don't react when he plucks the key ring out of my hand. He picks through the keys and it feels like the heat of his anger radiates off him.

"Marianna!" Rayonne calls from the stairs below.

He turns back to me, shaking the key ring at me and jostling the door in its frame.

There's a warning in Denendrius's voice. "Marianna . . ."

I forget the rest of the surrounding danger, my breath stuck in my throat as I take the key ring with a shaky hand and unlock the apartment door for him. All I can think about is the soreness of my bruised throat and what happens when that look flashes in his eyes.

He shoves the door open before I've got the key fully out, disappearing down the apartment hallway as Rayonne appears at my side.

"We need to get out!" She jogs into the apartment after him, the handle of his duffel bag in her fist.

The apartment stinks like smoke already, my throat itching as I watch Rayonne try to get Denendrius to pay attention to her. He ignores her, hands running up and down the bare hallway wall, a look on his face like he's trying to recall something.

"Denendrius!" I snap.

He looks back at me, then motions to the wall and utters words of disbelief.

"What about the fucking wall is more important than not being burned to death?" I point at the front door. "Move your ass!"

Even if he could speak English, from his narrow eyes and gritted teeth, I'm not sure he knows what he's looking for.

"Come on!" Rayonne grabs his arm, and he relents.

We race back down the stairs, bracing ourselves for the worst as we pass the garlic barrier of the building door and head into the loud crowd that's gathered in the parking lot.

My eyes scan the excited crowd as we weave through it, but I don't see anyone that should cause immediate concern.

I manage a breath when we make it to the Mustang. After I unlock the door, I toss my bag in the back and keep watch around us as Rayonne scrambles into her seat, Denendrius dropping into the passenger seat and slamming the door as he has a coughing fit. I slip behind the wheel, shut and lock the door, and jam the key in the ignition.

My ears ring in the silence of the car. "I'm honestly concerned with the fact we *didn't* get attacked on the way to the car." I lay on the horn as I back up, a handful of people scurrying out of my way.

"We're not safe yet," Rayonne says while rubbing her ears.

"Well, we've got weapons and garlic. If we can get somewhere safe, we should be fine," I decide as I turn into the road from the lot. As long as she doesn't have an army. "Unless . . . what are the chances we're overly paranoid and one of the many apartments full of drugs finally caught fire?"

"The timing is too perfect."

I shoot daggers at a yellow light as I fly beneath it. "Yeah, I know. Where should we go?"

"Pick somewhere, and don't say it aloud."

A brown sedan pulls up behind us, close enough that the lights shine through the car and reflect in the rearview mirror. My eyes narrow. I turn right when I have the option.

They turn right too.

My heart pounds and I adjust my grip on the wheel, making another right after three blocks.

They turn right behind me.

"We're being followed," I announce.

"I already assumed we were."

I bite at my lip in thought. "How good is a Child of Stars' hearing?"

"As good as a Darkling's."

Shit.

My eyes search the road for suspicious cars. "And what are the chances Agatha found more vampires to join her?"

"I don't know. She's a treacherous bitch, so an alliance with her is asking a lot. Especially since it'll be spreading like wildfire from the club that she forced me to turn back. I bet she'll have her own bounty on her head as soon as they catch wind of that one, so I doubt very many want to get caught up in that." Rayonne purses her lips.

"I hope you're right."

"If I wasn't, she probably would have had us attacked in the parking lot before we could even get to our car instead of following behind us . . ." Rayonne coughs.

"She doesn't have any special abilities, right?" If she does, clearly none of them helped her at the warehouse when we stole Denendrius from her.

"Only the power of being a super-bitch."

The horn blares behind us, and I cackle.

Rayonne smirks. "Yep, that's her. I had one though, which I think was her main reason for turning me back. I was very influential . . . *almost* like hypnotism. I always wondered if my power was the foundation for Darkling mind control."

"You believe the eugenics theory for Darklings too?" I hit the gas when we get to a yellow light and fly through it. Agatha runs the red to keep up.

"Oh, definitely. And if you were to learn about you-know-who, you'd think so too."

I lock my question concerning Viorel away for later, not wanting to say his name too many times around Denendrius in case he spontaneously remembers our plan for him. "What could you do?"

"I could *think things* at people. Little suggestions or my demands. I had others tell me it was almost like having an intrusive thought or an unexplained gut feeling when I would do that. You could resist it, of course, unlike hypnotism, but it still worked wonders."

"Sound like Agatha was super jelly of you."

The horn sounds again, one long and annoyingly loud droning noise.

I don't want to get cocky with our chances, so I decide to lose her. I speed up, passing in and out of cars, turning corners until she's several vehicles behind us . . . and then no longer in sight.

"You know her. Think she's got something planned?" The dryness of my throat makes me cough, and I wish we could stop for a drink.

"I'm not sure if her plan was to follow us in the car until she figured out her next move, or if she's got an actual plan. She's desperate, so . . . I'm honestly not sure what to expect now that she doesn't have a team to throw out ideas and do the legwork." Rayonne picks at the black polish on her nail, the sound grating on my nerves. "She must not have given an update if they haven't swooped in yet to fix her mistakes."

My brows draw together as I pull up to a red light, eyes scanning the busy streets. "Wait . . . what actual value did she provide?"

"She's just another vessel for vengeance. Agatha found *his* men somehow. She wants to be part of their clan so bad. I guess they said she had to earn her place, that she provided no value to them on her own, so she was one of the many given the task of capturing Denendrius. It was only me and her back then, so they gave us blood since my involvement gave us a foot up."

I scowl at the road. "That's a tall order. Finding him is one thing, but actually trapping him and delivering him . . . it's like they expected her to fail."

"Perhaps. The only reason they gave us blood is because so many attempts to capture him as an immortal have failed." She hisses in pain, then the nail polish picking stops.

"And you're *absolutely sure* they'll let you in? And me?" I know she keeps saying it, but how confident is she it'll work out for me as well? She really has no way of promising me anything.

"Yes, Marianna. I've fulfilled my part already. Now, I'm merely going above and beyond. I'm sure they'll meet my requests—bringing you along—considering everything Agatha did to me and how I'm fixing everything." She smiles at me in the rearview mirror.

Well, if she says so. It's not like I have many other options to put my hope into.

I mull over what Agatha's plan could be while I drive, trying to figure out why she let us get to the car instead of attacking us in the parking lot. She's a vampire . . . she could have injured Denendrius enough to haul him away if she got a jump on us. She could have hidden behind the car, broken *into* the car, and waited there even. Instead, she let us get away.

It hits me.

"Oh, shit!" I pull into a gas station and park under the lights. "*We're* stupid!"

I kick the door open and immediately drop to my hands and knees, groping around underneath for a tracker. After a few minutes of wriggling on the ground, my body half jammed under the car, Rayonne joins me.

"I should have grabbed the mirror from my trunk." Rayonne stares at the dirt on her hands.

"Yeah." I wince and strain while reaching as far as I can under the car, running my hand against the undercarriage. I hold my breath as my hand collides with plastic, only exhaling when it doesn't hurt. "I think I found it."

I swear when I grip the rectangular box and give it a yank. It comes off the undercarriage and I shimmy out from under the car.

"So she was following us so we'd assume that was her method and forget about the GPS. She probably hoped we'd think we're safe once we lost her," Rayonne says.

"Well, her plan worked for a bit." I stand and set the black tracker down on the concrete wheel stop. Maybe after watching us sit here for a while, she'll come check and find us long gone. For a moment I consider sticking the GPS under someone else's car to throw her off, but she'd probably kill them out of spite when she caught up.

"I'm still nervous about what she's got planned," Rayonne says hoarsely.

I wipe my dirty palms on my pants and create black streaks. Even after giving my hair a shake, it feels like I bathed in dirt. I choke back a cough before saying, "At least we found it *before* we parked somewhere and let our guard down."

The window rolls down, and Denendrius pokes his head out and clears his throat, about to say something before he's overtaken by dry coughs.

"Drink?" I ask, hoping he remembers the word from his lesson.

He clears his throat again and squints at me for a moment. "Ah." He nods. "Drink."

Rayonne and I hop back in the car and stop at a different gas station. I fill the gas tank so we can go as far as possible without stopping again if need be, while she pays inside and loads up on sandwiches, snacks, and drinks.

I get back in the car, the air now swelling with a sickly combination of dirt, smoke, gas, and cheap food. "I know a motel we can stay at. Also, I call dibs on the shower."

We arrive fifteen minutes later. It's a dingy motel, half the letters on the sign dead, the other half flickering so fast from malfunction it's only a matter of time before the owner catches a lawsuit. Regardless, I'm sure they'll accept cash, and it's a good chance to test out my identification, with a lower risk of having the cops called on me.

"Do you want me to get us a room?" Rayonne asks, plastic bags rustling as she slips her arm through the handles and lifts them off the seat.

"Wait for me in the car, I want to test my identification." I'm cautious as I climb out of the car with my backpack. With my California ID in hand, my eyes rake over the shadows of the parking lot.

Denendrius catches up with my brisk steps as I near the brightly lit front office. A man stands behind the counter, no friendliness on his face as he watches us approach through the large window.

He gives us a gruff greeting as we enter, and I immediately

set my fake driver's license on the counter. "Can I get a room with . . . two beds, I guess?"

A lump forms in my throat as he takes the plastic card off the counter and scrutinizes it. But if there's one thing I trust, it's Denendrius's ability to pull a fast one on people. He wouldn't risk taking a hostage across the planet, through borders, with a crap fake.

The guy smiles at me. "California, huh? Must have been a long drive."

I adjust my backpack on my shoulders. "Yeah, it was."

The rest of the check-in goes smoothly. I get my card back without question, and he accepts my cash before handing two keys to me for room twelve.

We join Rayonne back at the car and park in front of our room before loading Denendrius's arms up with the remaining bags.

I unlock the teal door and flick the light on. "Hey, it's actually not too bad."

The room is a modest size, with two queen beds—salmon-pink bedding—facing the doorway against dark wood paneling. There's a TV on the left side of the room and a table in front of the window. A small counter with a mini fridge beneath it is on the right, a closed yellow door to what I assume is the bathroom before it.

I enter and leave my sneakers on, despite the thin red carpeting. The room looks well cleaned at a glance—though severely outdated.

"Let's get the doorway and window scrubbed with garlic right away, then we'll get cleaned up," Rayonne instructs.

Denendrius watches us with serious scrutiny as Rayonne and I each take a bottle of garlic spray and an entry point. With a cloth taken from the counter, I climb on the table and spray garlic around the edges of the window trim, using the fabric to smear it consistently while Rayonne does the same to the doorway.

Upon finishing, I remove the gun from my pants and hide it under a pillow on the bed closest to the window. Then I take a peek through the bag of weapons and grin when I pick up a pistol crossbow and load it with a thin wooden stake.

"Sick," I whisper to myself, looking over the black weapon. Perhaps I'll reach for this in the night if we get attacked instead of my gun, so I don't blow my eardrums.

"There," Rayonne says as she stands. "We should be safe now."

"I have dibs on the shower," I remind Rayonne when it looks like she's going to head that way.

The door swings open, Agatha grinning and leaning in the doorway with a pistol in hand. She cringes against the air, the skin around her eyes reddening—presumably from the garlic fumes.

I jump backward and ready the crossbow, aiming it at her. "Where the fuck did you come from? How'd you even get in here?"

She shrugs. "Easy. I followed you and picked the lock when I overheard what room you were staying in."

Rayonne wields her stake. "How? We dumped the GPS."

She sneers at us. "How dumb do you two think I am? Give me some credit. I swapped cars when you started dodging me, then followed you to the gas station, and then here."

"Well, congrats. You're literally trapped in here now, smarty-pants," I spit.

She flicks her gaze over her shoulder into the bathroom. "That's okay, I'll leave out that window after killing both of you."

Having never used a crossbow before, I do my best to aim it at her chest. "How do you plan on doing that?"

Denendrius stands beside me, gaze swinging between the three of us as he grips a stake of his own.

"How do you plan on explaining killing me to Viorel's men?" Rayonne inquires. "Because if it weren't for that issue, I would have killed *you* already."

Agatha flips her blond braid over her shoulder. "I already explained it all to them. I called them the moment you three rushed out of there and told them you stole a vial of blood for yourself, turned back, and stole Denendrius from me to give him to someone offering you money so you could take it and start a human life again."

Rayonne's jaw falls open. "You liar. My God, you jealous *bitch*. They'd be here dealing with us if that were true. Not you, *alone*."

Agatha gives her a disdainful smile. "I told you to kiss your immortality goodbye if you betrayed me. You get what you deserve."

I shake the crossbow. "Shut up, Agatha. My arm is getting tired. What's your plan now? Because I'm ready to unload one of these on you. You already missed your chance to snipe us from the bathroom."

Rayonne shoots me a warning glance and I roll my eyes.

"I'm going to take Denendrius, of course."

Denendrius bristles beside me at the sound of his name, and he takes a step toward Agatha, his eyes locked on her.

"Are they here in Lorimer?" Rayonne asks.

Agatha shrugs. "Maybe they're on their way. Maybe they'll come once I can confirm he's human and that I have him."

"So you don't waste their time and put them at risk, right?" Rayonne smiles.

She grits her teeth and bares her fangs. "They're coming, okay?"

I purse my lips. "Hm. Okay, well, I haven't seen that bathroom window, but I'm going to take a wild guess and assume it's going to be a struggle to get Denendrius out of it on your own. So, what's your plan there?"

She does a double-take. "What? I'm going to shove him through the door after you two are dead and climb out the window."

I rock back and forth on my heels, the muscles in my arms burning. "Hmm . . . okay, so how are you going to do that? Because there's three of us, and one of you. I know you're a spooky vampire and all, but he's still twice your size and a professional fighter. Plus, Rayonne and I have like a shit ton of weapons even if you disarm us."

Her mouth opens to retort, but Rayonne—with a smug grin—interrupts with, "Are you alone, or do you have help waiting? You sure are wasting a lot of time."

She clenches her jaw. "I'm perfectly capable of dealing with three humans alone."

Squinting at her, I say, "Past the fire . . . I don't think you thought this out very well . . ."

She shoves a fist down at her side, a low growl coming from her as her eyes flare red. Her gun snaps up, and she aims at my face.

I laugh. "Oh, I'm sorry. Am I fucking annoying you? Because you here, *right now*, impeding on my life, is pretty annoying t—" I cut myself short, pulling the trigger while she's still hung up on my words.

The crossbow launches the stake straight into her throat, the surprise making her drop the gun. Thick blood spills from her mouth as she gags and yanks the stake from where it's wedged above her collarbone.

I rush and snatch the gun, pulling the magazine out and throwing it across the room to the farthest bed.

The next thing my mind registers is being sprawled out on the floor as Agatha collides with me, then Denendrius into the two of us.

The stake goes missing from his hand, Agatha tossing it back toward the bathroom. Rayonne thrusts her stake into Agatha's chest as Denendrius tries to hold her still, but she clearly misses her heart through all the thrashing. Agatha swipes her pointed nails at Rayonne, then pulls the stake from herself when Rayonne instinctively moves her hand.

Denendrius shouts at both girls, bewilderment and confusion etched into his furious face as he tries to hold Agatha down.

"We need her phone!" I shout while trying to get back in on the action through flailing limbs.

Denendrius sits on Agatha and flinches as she knees him in the back. I scramble to her legs and get a good grip on one of her ankles since I don't have time to reload the crossbow.

I try to get her legs under control so I can sit on them and reach the open duffel bag a few feet away for a new weapon, but she pulls her leg out of my grip and kicks me full force in the chest.

A strangled noise leaves my mouth as I fall over sideways, clutching at my chest. My eyes widen, each attempted intake of breath into my spasming lungs failing. The pain radiates through me, and for a moment I'm convinced she broke my sternum.

Denendrius twists her onto her stomach and turns to look at me, but thankfully doesn't come to my rescue. He asks me a worried question I don't understand as he jams a knee between her shoulder blades, pinning her to the floor while Rayonne digs through her pockets. I pull in a sharp breath—a painful twinge resonating through me—as Rayonne gets the phone out of Agatha's pocket. She launches it across the room out of everyone's reach, and it bounces off the farthest bed and disappears behind it with a thud.

But as soon as Agatha's body levitates, Denendrius's knee

slips off her, and he's too flabbergasted to execute his next move. She's back to her feet.

"Why are you fighting so hard to keep a monster out of prison!" Agatha screeches, a few inches of air between her feet and the carpet. Her throat is healed now, only her flesh smeared with blood.

"We're not," I snap as I reload the crossbow and aim it at her. As soon as I fire off another stake, she's back on her feet and darting through the bathroom. "But we don't want your bitch ass to get any credit now that you've tried to kill us!"

I chase after her and fire another stake as she's scaling the toilet to climb out the small window. She wails as it gets her in the lower back as she's half out, but she disappears into the night, leaving a trail of blood down the wall.

I put the crossbow on the counter and stand on the toilet to close and lock the window, wincing with each breath. I'm gripping my ribs as I climb down.

"You okay?" Rayonne asks, a bottle of garlic and a cloth in hand.

"She kicked me right in the chest."

Denendrius makes a motion to my shirt like he wants me to show him, and I scowl and shake my head.

His brows rise, and he tilts his head. "Marianna."

"I'm fine, seriously," I grunt and lift my shirt while Rayonne deals with vampire-proofing the window.

Denendrius tut-tuts as we both assess the large bruise in the middle of my ribs.

"Ouch. Are you sure nothing's broken?" Rayonne descends from the toilet seat. "That looks awful."

My muscles lock, heart jumping as Denendrius probes my ribs with his fingers. The warmth of his hand instead of its usual shocking cold only makes it harder to get a new breath through my airway.

Denendrius says something that sounds comforting and smiles at me before stroking the side of my head.

Once he's confirmed I'm okay, he sighs and leans against the counter to catch his breath. His eyes flicker between Rayonne and me. The muscle in his jaw clenches, and he unleashes his frustrations by yelling Latin at us.

XI

We stare at his wide eyes until he stops himself and inhales a deep breath. He buries his face in his hands and groans loudly before motioning to the window in disbelief.

"That is what I'm worried about," I tell Rayonne once I'm done taking a hot shower. "He's clearly getting frustrated. That's twice tonight he's lost his shit."

"Yeah, we need some proper translations before he turns violent with us again."

I wince as I sit carefully on the corner of Rayonne's bed. "I'm still trying to think of ways to convince my teacher to help us, but I'm not having much luck."

She sighs and heads to the bathroom. "My turn to shower now—we'll dig through her phone when I get out. I need to clear my head."

Denendrius strips down to his boxers as Rayonne closes the bathroom door, then pulls the blanket back from our bed and crawls in. He's grumbling as he lies down, then he smiles at me when he notices me watching him and pats the bed.

"Hungry." I shake my head and stand, wandering over to the bag of snacks on the counter. "I slept while you were up."

"Ah . . ." He feels at the air with his hand, eyes narrow like he's trying to remember something. "Drink."

I frown and grab him a water, then wince as I toss it over Rayonne's bed. He catches it and chugs the entire thing, capping it and leaving it on the bedside table.

He studies me the entire time I eat my sandwich on the corner of Rayonne's bed.

"What?" My tone is like a whip.

He merely smiles.

I glower at my sandwich before I take the last few bites. When Rayonne opens the bathroom clean-faced and wearing black tights under jean shorts and a band shirt, I can feel the humidity from where I sit.

Rayonne wanders around my bed and snatches the cell phone from the floor, returning to sit beside me on hers. She flips it open and purses her lips as she scrolls through Agatha's short contact list.

"Found their number?" I ask.

She shakes her head, the smell of her apple cinnamon body spray hitting me. "No. She even cleared the old ones. Unless she memorized them or saved them under a fake name."

We look through her texts, which are almost all messages between her and each person in her contacts, trying to elicit help from them. The responses vary from "no way am I getting involved in anything to do with Denendrius" to "why do you still have my number?" and my favorite, "Why, so you can leave me stranded on the side of the road again before sunrise?"

I hold back my laughter. "At least we know she probably doesn't have anyone helping her."

She checks the call log, but there are only calls logged from hours *after* we left with Denendrius from the warehouse.

"I doubt any of these lead back to you-know-who, but I'm

going to give them all a call anyway." Rayonne dials one and takes the phone back with her into the bathroom.

"Marianna," Denendrius calls softly from the bed. He pats the blanket.

I hold my breath as I stand and snag the remote from the TV stand before I crawl on the bed to sit beside him for a better view.

He continues to study me as I search through the basic channels to pick from. Even when I decide on stand-up comedy, I can't focus on anything with his heavy gaze on me.

I peek at him over my shoulder. He dons another light smile.

What does he think of me now that he can't remember? Since he thinks we're married, does he think he got the short end of the stick by being with me? Even if he can't speak English, has he inferred from my angry tones—and apparently my resting bitch face—that I'm unsavory and not ideal to be with? How far off am I from his expectations of how a wife should be?

I wonder if he feels anything when he looks at me. He was awful at showing any of the love he claimed, but could he still feel it? Did he feel all those classic symptoms? A quicker pulse despite his heartbeat being so slow, a funny feeling in his stomach? I know I must have always been on his mind since he had an entire fantasy concocted, but did he ever *feel* anything? What was he capable of feeling anyway, aside from varying shades of fury?

Even if he doesn't have any episodic memories of us, could feeling memories remain?

"Nothing." Rayonne snaps the phone closed—and me from my thoughts—and sets it on the counter. "Great."

"At least we tried."

She grabs a sandwich and sits cross-legged on her bed. "I'm not sure what to do now," Rayonne admits before taking a bite.

"Let's go back to the apartment during the day if she didn't burn it to the ground. Agatha clearly doesn't have a good plan, so it should be safe. That, and I want to know what the hell was so important about that wall for Denendrius to rush back into a fire for."

Rayonne sits back against the wooden panel of the wall. "So, you think he has money hidden somewhere?"

My heart leaps, knowing exactly where she's going with that train of thought. "What are the chances he remembered hiding something in the wall that he didn't want to lose in the fire?"

Her brows lift. "Behind the drywall between the studs? You could fit a lot of money there."

"Maybe." I mull over that idea while settling my attention back on the TV. As Denendrius fades to sleep behind me, Rayonne works on her sandwich. Once Denendrius is fast asleep, I say, "What were you talking about when you brought up Viorel and eugenics earlier?"

She puts the plastic container from her sandwich aside and sweeps crumbs off her bed, the last piece poised between two of her dainty fingers. "Oh. People say Viorel is a connection between Children of Stars and Darklings, a survivor from some ancient eugenics mission. There is no other vampire like him that we know of. Everyone fits neatly into one of two kinds . . . except him. All I know are whisperings about him, of course. Nothing directly from him, but supposedly he's ten thousand years old."

My heart drops into my stomach. "Holy shit."

No wonder Denendrius didn't want Agatha to hand him over to Viorel.

A tickled smile shapes her lips, a breadcrumb stuck to them. "He declared himself king and built himself a new castle when the previous royal clan was brought down by crazy vampires. Nobody dared oppose him since he became the oldest vampire known after the death of the other, not that they had a reason to oppose him regardless."

Thoughts spring to the front of my head. "Wait—Alaire and Edmond mentioned a royal clan outside Sirmium that was killed. Their ruler imprisoned and tortured Denendrius before he escaped for making a mess when he was a newborn vampire."

"That's the clan, I think. I've only ever known Viorel as my king." She finishes the last bite of her sandwich before saying, "But I'm sure you can understand why he'd want to stay locked in his castle, considering what happened to the last ruler. Especially considering how Denendrius was kidnapping and killing all those Children of Stars and Darklings. Viorel must have been nervous when he started going after clan leaders without obvious reason. I imagine he didn't make it this far by leaving whatever fortress he had at the time in Romania over the millennia. He's quite special apparently, so he's a target for people like . . ." Her gaze travels to Denendrius.

My heart hammers. "Special how?"

"*Multiple* abilities. I don't know how many, but he's got a lot of precursor Darkling ones. I've heard conflicting things about his relationship with sunlight, but he's been said to hypnotize crowds and has an infallible memory and the same sort of speed and strength Darklings have."

"Are—are we going to *meet* him at the castle?" I'm not scared of much . . . but as a human, I feel like Viorel is someone I *definitely* should have a healthy fear of.

"Maybe. I really don't know," Rayonne says. "I hope we can."

Denendrius groans in his sleep, leg kicking out and narrowly missing me. I'm about to ask her another question when he launches into a sitting position, gasping for breath. His hand shakes as he lifts it to wipe the side of his face, brown eyes rimmed with white.

My eyes lock with his. "You good?"

He must understand the sentiment of my voice as the corners of his lips shakily lift. He lies back down, covering his face with the back of his hands as he tries to rein in his breath.

"We should probably stop talking about you-know-who," Rayonne whispers. "In case it's leaking into his dreams."

I nod and lie down beside him, thinking I'll try to steal a few hours of sleep to escape the pain in my chest.

A gut-twisting thought crosses my mind. What if I'm *not* allowed to go to the castle like Rayonne believes? What value could I provide to him? Do people usually need to do something for Viorel if they want to stay, or did they only give that stipulation to Agatha and Rayonne? And if I'm still marked, will he even want me around when I made Ziggy's guests so uncomfortable? Or would he require me to turn or have someone else mark me if I don't become vampire food? The what-ifs are so ample that my head spins.

What if I'm putting far too much faith in Rayonne's word?

The apartment is still standing when we pull into the full parking lot. If I didn't know any better, I'd never know there was a fire. There's no tape or signs on the door either when we grab our luggage and head to the entrance.

"I can only assume they dealt with the fire quickly," Rayonne says as we enter.

The smell of smoke lingers in the air, and I cough against the tickle in my throat. "Great."

The smell continues all the way up the stairs and into the apartment.

Denendrius slips between us as soon as I unlock the door. He drops our bags in the entryway and hastens down the hallway. With his eyebrows knitted together and his gaze tight, he swiftly tugs both closet doors open.

I watch with a furrowed brow as he drags the washing machine away from the wall and out of the closet, exposing a large drywall cutout with the piece in place.

Baffled, I rush past him and scramble around the machine, stepping over wires and tubing to get to it.

When I push on the cutout resting in place, it falls back and disappears into a pitch-black space, and I'm hit with an old smell. It's a strange mix of dust and leather.

My heart pounds and I stare back at Denendrius's concerned face. "Where does that go?" I demand, swallowing against the sudden dryness of my throat.

Considering the last thing I found hidden in Denendrius's apartment was evidence of my assault and those of dozens of other girls, I can't imagine I'm about to find anything good.

Denendrius motions for me to get out of the way, so I tentatively switch places with him, my legs numb as I stand beside the washer and Rayonne. He crawls through the hole and into the darkness. There's grumbling and stumbling, a bump on the other side of the hallway wall a few feet behind me, and then the darkness of the hole lights up with the yellow glow of a light.

"Denendrius?" I call, hoping he'll give me some insight into what I'm about to walk into.

After his astonished Latin, he calls my name.

I hold my breath as I crawl back behind the washing machine and maneuver through the hole in the wall.

"Holy shit." I stand up in the narrow room and move aside for Rayonne. Boxes are stacked in the small space, along with plastic bins and different suitcases and crates of varying ages. I immediately spot Denendrius standing in front of three massive black safes at the far end of the room. "Alaire and Edmond told me he was a pirate, so I guess I shouldn't be this surprised he has a treasure hoard in a hidden room."

"How did he get everything in here?" Rayonne's wide eyes take in the room as she steps around me.

I spot the remnants of a doorway halfway down the room, approximately where he was touching the wall on the other side when we were trying to evacuate. "I'm going to guess before he sealed this bedroom up."

"We could be here for days," she says, disappearing behind some boxes stacked taller than her. "He's had centuries to collect. I can only imagine what's in here."

Sweat starts in my hairline, and I can't help but think there's stuff he didn't want discovered. Why else did he hide an entire room from me? When he said he was done packing, he didn't let on that there were more than the boxes in the living room to move.

But now that I think of it, the stretch of wall between the living room and hallway doesn't make any architectural sense, unless there was something behind it.

When I pull in a breath, I can practically taste the dust. But an idea pops to mind. "I bet we can find something convincing enough in here for my teacher."

"Then I'm going to get digging after I open some windows." There's an impending cough audible in her voice.

I join Denendrius at the back of the room as he scrutinizes the safes. "You ran back here when the building was on fire. Was there something . . . *specific* you were trying to save?"

He only glances at me to acknowledge that I've spoken to him before crouching down in front of the safe to inspect the keypad. "Hm."

I squat down beside him. "Any ideas what the combination could be?"

Denendrius lifts his finger to the keypad, then lowers it. "*Unus?*" he mumbles to himself.

My frown's heavy on the corners of my mouth. "One? Are you guessing?"

He runs his finger over the backup keyhole, then looks at me when he says, "No."

At least he remembered that word. "You don't remember where the key is or you don't have it?"

He doesn't answer, of course, but looks over at the other two safes like he's not sure which one he should try to open.

I roll my eyes and stand. "He doesn't remember shit," I grumble to myself, standing and facing the rest of the room.

Leaving Denendrius to ponder the safes, I move toward the first thing my eyes land on, a beat-up wooden trunk—exactly what I'd expect a treasure trunk to look like with its metal banding and latches—on the wall opposite to the one we came through. I step over a smaller stack of boxes to get to it. The lid creaks when I open it.

"Wicked," I whisper, pulling a pair of brown leather boots from the top of an old tawny coat adorned with gold buttons on the cuffs. I lift it, the faint smell of sea salt spilling out of the creases when the heavy and long thing unfolds. After running my fingers over the gold-braid embellishments around the front buttons, I put it aside and pull out a heavy leather-bound book from the side of the chest. I open it. A detailed painting of a pirate ship on stiff paper with yellowed edges greets me.

"*Neptune's Curse*. 1678." I read the name of the ship inked in black along the bottom with the date. "Wow."

Denendrius, now at my side, picks up what I think is a cutlass sword from underneath where the coat was and stares at it. A flash of confusion crosses his face. "*Charles*."

"Charles?" My eyes narrow.

Denendrius rests the sword atop a nearby box and digs through the trunk with a persistent look on his face. He digs until finding another leather-bound book. From between the pages, he unwedges a detailed portrait of himself. There's stray curly strands of hair around his serious face and black eyes and what look like gold pieces weaved in a few strands of hair that I presume he tied back. *Charles Avery* is written along the top.

"You're Charles Avery?"

His shoulders lower and he sighs as his eyes shift up to mine.

"You're remembering things," I whisper, a lump in my throat. What if he remembers too much, too quickly? What if he remembers enough to fight us off and escape before we can contact Viorel?

"Um, Marianna . . . look at this." The hesitance in Rayonne's voice makes my heart beat faster.

I put the book back, my steps shaky as I step over and around stacks of bins and boxes to where I find Rayonne in the back corner. She holds an aged paper out to me.

"What?" I take it.

"Read it."

I swallow and cast my gaze down on it. With my shaky hand and the cursive on the yellowed paper, it's difficult to read, though I manage with some squinting.

September 29, 1932

    To my dearest Den,

    By the time you read this letter, I will have left already. I love you, truly, but I am choosing Richard because I don't love you like I love him. I'm sorry, but I've merely known you through spring and summer, and him since we were both so little. Can you understand that? I hope you are able.

    It was quite unlike you to threaten Richard so violently. I am now too afraid of you to give you the explanation you indeed deserve in person.

    I have been in love with him since I was ten. Though I don't regret giving myself to you, or our passionate summer, you cannot provide me with the ideal life that Richard can. I will spare you by not writing the details in this letter, but you must understand how unfair it is to me as a woman to be deprived of such a miracle. I know it is wrong of me to accept Richard's proposal after I already accepted yours, but I never thought he would ever love me.

My father and mother adore you, and you are welcome to stay at the ranch with them to continue your work with the horses, but they agree it was unfair of you not to tell me until after I agreed to marry you.

I am so thankful for all you've done for my father, and for teaching me to ride his mustangs with nearly the same grace you have.

You will find someone who loves you, I promise. You are usually so sweet and giving that you should have no issue.

I have left the ring on the counter with this letter. My best wishes to you.

"It's signed *Marianne*," I breathe.

"Yeah . . ." She hands me an old photograph. "This is what Marianne looks like."

It's a black-and-white photo of Denendrius and a girl on a porch swing. Her face is bright with a grin like she's mid-laugh. Denendrius's expression is severe, the blackness of his eyes only adding to the sternness of his face. Wearing a plain white button-up with the sleeves rolled up, he's got his arm wrapped around her shoulders, his other clutching the waist of her floral dress like he's trying to keep her at his side.

Even though the photo isn't in color, I know her hair is some shade of brown instead of how dark it looks on film, and that her eyes are brown too. She looks too much like me . . . too much like all the girls on his tapes.

An icy chill runs through me. I'm not the first girl he's tried to replace Mariana with.

"I wonder what he did to her," Rayonne whispers.

I swallow and hand the photo back so I don't have to look at it. "He killed her." Just like he took me into the woods to kill me when I broke things off with him after I found out he was stalking me. I know in my gut it's the truth and can't imagine the brutality he likely responded to her letter with. Her words must have hurt him even more than when I broke up with him.

Rayonne holds out a little wooden box. "It's full of photos from around the same time period. Do you think that would convince your teacher?"

I take it in one hand and pull the cell phone out of my pocket with the other to check the time. "School starts in thirty. Should I give it a shot?"

Her lips twist and she looks toward Denendrius, where he rummages through his pirate trunk still. "Yeah, please. Before he *really* snaps on us."

Before I leave, I take a recording of the room, then sneakily arm Rayonne with a gun when he's not looking. Next, I use the picture books to explain to him I'm leaving for a bit. He's hesitant, flat out telling me no at first, but eventually I convince him and rush out to clear my mind and lungs.

XII

Mr. Derek focuses his attention on me as he teaches, his eyes repeatedly trailing over the class before darting back to me. It feels like I'm the only one he's teaching. Even while speaking to another student, his gaze wanders back to me, and there's a faint crease between his brows that has been there since he saw me walk into class.

Even with all his staring, my mind is stuck on Marianne's letter and that photo of her and Denendrius. How many Mariannas and Mariannes have there been? How many times has he done this?

It hurts more, looking back on our first dates. He made me feel so special, like maybe I was worth something. The whole time, all he cared about was my name and face. Did he actually like anything else about me? Did he tell every girl that she was his favorite, or did he really mean it when he said it to me? As much as I don't want to be his favorite . . . *victim* . . . it would only add to the hurt if the whole time I was with him he was thinking about how he preferred past girls to me.

After too much pondering, I decide he meant it. He must have liked me as a person. Sure, there must be plenty of girls with the name and looks to fit his checklist, but if it were that simple, he'd have forced a girl into marrying him by now. I'm sure he killed Marianne when she broke up with him. He essentially killed me too in the woods, but there must have been something he actually liked about me for him to change his mind and heal me, keeping me around while I was defying him. That, and he never blood marked anyone else before.

Maybe it's wrong to think all that, but it sure makes me feel less worthless.

The more I think about it, the more I realize all the girls he's hurt fall into one of two categories. Mariana replacements, and girls who simply cater to his preferences. His tapes made it seem like he kidnapped all those girls to assault them. Did he simply use them to fill the space between the girls he wanted to try being nice to for a relationship?

When the bell rings, I sigh and wince at the pain in my chest before I stand at the side of my desk. I wait for the room to empty.

I'm already watching Mr. Derek when he looks back up at me from his desk to say, "Can you stay, please?"

I nod. "Planned on it."

We stare at one another from opposite sides of the classroom for a few long seconds until the noise of students has moved to the hallway. I close the door behind the last student before going to the front of the class and sitting atop a first-row desk facing him.

He leans back in his chair and it squeaks. "I'm worried about you, Marianna, and I'm concerned I have more to worry about than what I currently am." He mashes his lips together. The crease in his forehead is looking like it might cause long-term wrinkles. "Am I right?"

"I—" Instead of trying to find the words, I pull my backpack off and onto my lap, and take out the wooden photo box. Leaving the bag on the desktop as I stand, I approach his desk and set the box—open—in front of him. The 1930s photograph of Denendrius and Marianne is on top. "Here, the proof speaks for itself."

Mr. Derek tentatively takes the old photograph, his lips tight as he looks it over—front to back—before mumbling, "Jesus."

"That's Denendrius," I say before he tries to suggest it's his grandfather.

"That's undeniable." He inspects it. "He looks . . . stern as hell, much more familiar than the man who walked in yesterday."

"You believe me, finally?" I chew my cheek.

He places the photo on the desk next to the box. "Well, who knows the true age of the photo . . .?"

I curl my hands into fists at my sides. "Seriously? Keep looking."

He sighs and picks up the next one, a late-nineteenth-century portrait of an even meaner-looking Denendrius than *I'm* used to, though the camera quality and lack of smile are probably to blame for the deadness of his black eyes.

When too many seconds have passed without him saying anything, I cross my arms and ask, "So?"

He rests both photos back onto the untouched stack in the box and closes it. "Marianna, I don't want to call you a liar, but what you're asking me to believe—that your boyfriend is from *ancient Rome*, so we're clear, is . . . far-fetched. I'm sorry, but I'd need something significantly bigger to consider it could be true."

I curse under my breath and yank the cell phone from my pocket, navigating to the video of Denendrius's hidden room. I glance at the clock—two minutes until the bell—as I hit play and hand the phone to him. If that doesn't convince him, then I think nothing will aside from hauling in a vampire.

After tucking the wooden box back in my bag, I wring my fingers together at my stomach. I try to study his face to discern his reaction. My heart jumps when I catch a flicker of astonishment and fear.

He pauses the video and stares up at me, eyes wide with disbelief as he returns my phone. "I want to accuse you of robbing a museum, but I don't think you could swing it," he says, awe in his voice.

I smirk. "Are you starting to believe me?"

He gapes at me. "I believe . . . *something*. But you should have started with that."

The bell rings, so I snatch a pen from his desk and jot down my phone number. "Call me after school. You need to come by. You won't be able to deny any of it once you see everything."

Mr. Derek clears his throat and snatches the notepad out from under the pen when the classroom door opens. There's an awkwardness to his movements as he slips my number into his bag and leans away from me in his chair. "Right, but you know I can't because—" His words fall away as the student sits down at the back. The rest of his thoughts are clear on his face. Something like "I'm your teacher. It's inappropriate for us to socialize about something other than school outside of school."

I suppose I can't blame him for not wanting to risk being seen with a student like me, especially for something so personal, and especially if it involves an apartment. Does he worry that my "behavioral issues" alone might get him in trouble? That I'll try something or accuse him of something? I suppose I can't blame him if he thinks so, when all I've been is different sorts of trouble.

"But I need your help," I whisper, my heart sinking back to my stomach. My brain scrambles for new ideas. The backs of my eyelids burn, and he must be able to tell I'm about to cry because he sighs and looks down at his desk. "Please. You said if I needed to talk or anything—"

He nods and motions vaguely to the classroom. "*That* offer still stands," he says gently.

I clench my jaw. "Fine."

"You can come in at lunch if you'd like—"

"It's fine," I insist while turning toward the door.

I end up in the bathroom instead of class, staring at the half-covered bruising around my neck while sucking back tears. Crying better not become a habit again. Closing my eyes, I take a deep breath and consider whether to go back to the apartment to make sure Rayonne didn't swap sides again, or to make sure Denendrius didn't kill her. But I find I don't want to go back there. I barely want to leave the bathroom.

I drag myself to the library and pull a few Roman history books off the shelf, but I'm too angry and hopeless for any of the words on the page to register in my mind.

I look up from a drawing of a villa when Liz—the school counselor—walks into the library, her gaze sweeping over the tables and computers before they land on me in a chair at the back.

She waves me over and I clench my teeth, shutting the book and rising.

"Come chat," she says, turning around like she expects me to follow.

I do, and we walk quietly until we're upstairs and seated in her office.

It's weird being back in the room, sitting on the same big couch with misshapen pillows after thinking I'd never see it again. Her desk is littered with papers, and from the empty manila folder with my name on it, I can only imagine she's been desperately rooting through it.

"How are things now?" she asks from her desk chair. Somehow, the concern in her eyes is double what it was last time I came in shaking and terrified after Denendrius gave me my ring.

"I'm okay, I promise. He's acting different now." I'm not sure how else I can explain that he's not my biggest threat right now, that the vampires after him are. "Things aren't like they were before."

"How?" She tilts her head, eyes pensive.

"He apologized." He kind of did, I think. Even though he can't remember it, Denendrius would have never let a genuine apology slip past his lips when he was a vampire. And whether or not I accept his apology, it says something about him and maybe my safety.

She stacks her hands on the jean skirt covering her crossed legs. "How does his apology make you feel? Do you feel it was genuine?"

I pull one of the tacky lace pillows onto my lap and wrap my arms around it as I pull in a long, stale breath before slowly releasing it. "Confused. A little angry. I think he means it as well as he can."

Her blond brows stitch together. "Confused is completely reasonable. But can you tell me why it makes you angry?"

My fingers tighten around the lace. "It makes me . . ." I scowl at the carpet. "The confusion makes me angry. I feel like I've been thrown a curveball. I don't know how I'm supposed to react and respond to him now that he's . . . like *this*."

Liz's lips purse, the action drawing attention to the lines around her mouth. "Have you considered that his apology might be manipulation? Is he making you feel like you have to accept it and never bring it up again? Like the harm he caused you shouldn't matter anymore now that he's sorry?"

I shake my head. "That's what makes me the angriest. It seemed genuine." The strangest part is that he hasn't hit me. As angry as he's gotten with Rayonne and me, he has made no motion that might indicate he wants to.

Maybe I wouldn't need him to remember if he was human but still acted exactly the same. Maybe a shit apology and him slapping me when I have a sharp tone would make it easier to accept that he might not remember enough for it to count.

"And you believe he will never hurt you again?" From the way she says it, I can tell she doesn't believe it herself.

"I ... I've never seen him act like this. I guess he could snap but ..." My lips twist. "I don't know how to explain it, but I don't think I'm in immediate danger." If we find a way to explain everything to him, I think we can keep him happy and under control.

She nods, but she's not agreeing with me, only acknowledging my words.

"Marianna," she begins softly, "do you know about the cycle of abuse?"

Swallowing a lump, I vaguely remember Camille and Daina saying something about it. "A little."

"You're a tough girl, so I'm going to be frank with you, okay?" There's no warmth in the seriousness of her brief smile. "The other day, you came in here with a ring and asked for help to leave. Now you're in here wincing with every breath, with new bruises around your neck—some of which are unmistakably a man's *fingers*—telling me he's spontaneously changed and that he's sorry."

I stare at her, my tongue pressed into the roof of my mouth.

"I'm going to make an educated guess and say that you tried to leave, he stopped you—violently—and then a lot of begging and apologies ensued. And you changed your mind, couldn't go through with it, because maybe you believe him. Maybe he said some things that were very convincing. And I think you're right that you're not in any immediate danger—"

I feel a twinge of relief. If she believes me, maybe she won't say anything to anyone else.

"But you're back in the honeymoon stage. I'm sure you've been in it before, and I'm sure you'll be in it again. Maybe it will last six days, maybe six months. But a man who can do *that* to you, who can do something like that in the first place, can— and mostly likely will—do it again. For now, things might be okay. They might even be *great*. He might shower you with gifts and make you feel like you're on top of the world. He might act so different you won't be able to imagine that he used to get so angry. But you'll probably find yourself walking on eggshells soon, and then the abuse will come again, and then he'll reconcile with you . . . and then it'll happen all over again. The only way to break the cycle is to end the relationship."

"I can end things if he acts like that again." I could kill him if it became life and death, despite what Rayonne thinks. The blood mark can't be that deep yet.

"It's really easy to say that right now, but once you're in the moment, it's much different. There's a lot of feelings attached— codependency or love, much of the time—and it's easier to hope and believe things will be better than to go through the grief and intensity of a complete separation. The fear alone of what will happen if you try to leave can make you question whether or not it's worth it to even try."

"Things will be okay," I tell her.

The look in her eyes, the fear and hopelessness, is so vivid it makes my heart skip, and I feel awful knowing what the story will be that I leave behind.

"Marianna . . ." She exhales a deep breath. "I am extremely concerned about the extent of the abuse in your relationship. It's been a *month,* and the violence is already as severe as *strangulation*?"

I stare at her with wide eyes, my breaths short. Everyone's really going to think he killed me.

"I'm sorry," she starts, "but you cannot afford a delicate conversation. Attempted strangulations in domestic violence more often than not lead to violent death. He is going to kill you."

Technically, he already has. If he didn't have the ability to heal me, I'd be in a hole in the ground in the woods.

She sighs. "I have to ask, knowing your history. Are drugs a factor in the relationship?"

"Actually, he's the reason I'm clean right now."

The pity in her eyes makes me drop mine.

"I'm glad you're clean, at least," she says. "That's very good. I'm proud of you."

I look up and can't help my little smile. "Really?"

She nods. "Yes, of course."

"Thanks," I say, sheepishly. I can't help but feel like a fraud. I'm clean, but only because I got so addicted to Denendrius's blood that my body ignored my desire for narcotics and obeyed his loathing of them.

The bell rings, sending a jolt through me. I think about seeing Daina and Camille at lunch since I have no reason to come back to school again.

"You should stay sitting," she says gently, like she can predict my next course of action.

"I should go," I counter as the ruckus of students fills the hall. It's probably best not to leave Denendrius out of my sight for too long, as much as it's nice to have time away from him.

"I know I can't convince you to leave, but if most of your resistance is of fear of the process, and you think it's easier to stay and hope that he's really changed than risk trying to leave again, I can help. I know he picks you up after school. You don't have to go out there and meet him. I can give security a heads-up in case he tries to come in. You know what, how about I drive you down to the police station? We can call your foster mother and we'll help you through the reporting process. If that's what you'd like, of course."

I sigh and look down at my hands. "Look, Liz . . . I'm really grateful for your advice and honesty. Like, I guess, thanks for not giving up on me even though I've dodged so many meetings. I don't think your worries and whatever apply to me and my situation though. I know this is your job, but . . ."

"It's my job because I *genuinely* care. This applies to you. You're too close to it all to see it, Marianna. Nobody ever thinks it applies to their situation. But there's so many situations where it *really* does that makes it seem tricky and blurry."

I twist my fingers together, a guilty knot in my gut. It's hard to look back up at her when I'll be missing soon. Her— everyone—will think he killed me, when I'll probably be perfectly okay, maybe happy even.

"Marianna?" Liz asks.

With a gulp, I look up. "I'm okay. Thanks for all this talking to me and stuff."

Liz turns her chair to her desk and scribbles down something on a piece of paper before tearing it off her mini notepad and holding it out to me.

I take it. *School attendance line* is written above a phone number.

"That is my personal number, but you tell him it's an attendance line if he gives you grief, and that we have asked you to call in on days you're skipping. You can text me or call me. It will also work as an excuse if he doesn't let you come back to school, but you need to get a hold of someone and can't simply dial 911. It's the best I can come up with off the top of my head. But if it can help in any way . . ." Her smile is faint.

I fold it up and put it in my pocket to make her think she's helping. "Okay, thank you."

XIII

I watch the cafeteria doors from the lunch line for Camille and Daina, hoping to hell they're here today.

Sarah's steps slow when she sees me, her eyes falling to the floor until she's beside me.

"Hey," she mumbles, eyes flicking up to mine. The weariness in them is evident, like she's unsure if our friendliness extends past breakdowns in bathrooms.

I loosen my tense shoulders, returning to scrutinize the chalkboard menu. "You know, I've been here for almost three years and I haven't tried most of the shit up there." I shake my head to myself. "I don't think I've ever looked past the dailies."

"It's hit or miss," she says. "I've tried most of it."

I pull a handful of bills from my jeans and lean against the metal counter when it's my turn to order. If it's really my last day here this time, I want to make it worth it at least a little. "I want some taquitos, a tuna melt, three strawberry milks, four chocolate chunk cookies and a cheesy garlic stick." When I catch Sarah's wide eyes, I explain, "Some for later."

The middle-aged lunch lady stares at me with pen and pad in hand, her blank expression saying more than a scowl ever could.

I straighten. "Oh—um, please?"

She mumbles something to herself as she scribbles down my order, her penciled in brows lifting when she finally looks up and asks. "Is that everything?"

"No, I'm paying for hers too," I say, jerking my head toward Sarah.

Sarah shifts her weight and wraps her arms around her stomach. "Oh, it's okay. I know you're poor—"

"It's his money," I clarify. "So, literally, buy whatever the fuck you want."

She pulls in a deep breath before firing off her order. "Okay, then can I please get a chicken quesadilla, an extra-large fry, two bottles of cream soda, and five chocolate chunk cookies?" Her cheeks burn red when her eyes meet mine. "Some for later?"

My grin is wide. It feels good to provide her with even a *sliver* of revenge. I can't imagine he'd be happy about his money being spent on her.

"Good grief, girls," the lunch lady says as she lifts her pen, the paper covered in blue ink. "You're going to have to wait a minute."

Sarah and I smile at one another. They're pained smiles, but smiles nonetheless.

Though we don't decide on it aloud, Sarah and I sit at my regular table at the back together. We don't say a word to one another as we each eat our first cookie.

I can't help but think about those diary entries she wrote about me as we eat. "Did you know Den took pictures of your diary?"

Her hands move from the table and to her lap. She picks at the hem of her sweatshirt. "Yeah. He told me he was going to show you what I wrote about you. I think he was hoping it'd make you hate me more."

Flicking crumbs off my fingers, I say, "You couldn't have said anything mean enough for me not to be on your side. I know I'm a 'raging bitch' like you wrote, but girls have to have each other's backs in those situations. I wasn't sure if you knew he invaded your privacy like that."

"Okay," she whispers. "I'm still sorry."

I shrug. "Me too. But it's old news. You got your friends to beat me up, I beat you up. I'd say we're even."

She exhales a loud breath of relief. "I'm still scared for you, Marianna," she whispers. Her eyes lock with mine, a wet shine over them. "I don't believe you're going to be okay. Not one bit. Not as long as he's in your life."

"Things are different now."

She bites her bottom lip and shakes her head. "You don't really believe that, do you? I mean, have you seen yourself in the mirror?"

I grit my teeth, knowing I can't say anything to make her understand what I mean.

As a group of students pass by, Sarah leans in closer to me. "Marianna, what do you know about the things he's done? Because he's told me things that have kept me up for days now."

Dozens of graphic images flash through my mind. "It's different," is all I say. "Stop worrying about me. I'm handling it."

"If one day you don't come back to school, like go missing *for real*, I'm outing him." Her eyes challenge mine, like she's waiting for me to demand her silence. "I'll tell the police everything. I'll make sure it goes to the media. Everyone will know what he did to us. He won't be able to escape it."

I chew my cheek and let my eyes wander over the dozens of students as they smear across the cafeteria, some still in line, others seated at and on tables with mouthwatering meals. The noise of their simple existence—the jumble of laughter and squabbles—becomes too much and I feel the ache of my life, of how it's bruised my body, as I sit in my hard plastic chair.

How long will she wait when she inevitably doesn't see me after today? I blink hard and unlatch my eyes from the disorder of the wide room. "If anything happens to me, nobody would catch him anyway, Sarah."

A crease forms between her brows. "But people would still know. Wouldn't you rather them know the truth than think you overdosed or something on the street? I'm a police officer's daughter. If I say something, people have to listen."

Not wanting to burden her with the truth if she wants it off her shoulders, I say, "Okay, Sarah." Eventually, whether or not she says something, people will come to conclusions about what happened to me. And I would rather her back up what I know my friends, Mr. Derek, Carol, and Liz, will say, especially if it helps her heal. "Tell what you need to tell *if* something happens, but don't get false hope thinking it will bring any sort of justice."

The human world will never know of Denendrius's persecution. They'll never know the depth of horror he's created. My case will be as cold as my blood has run since he injected himself into my life.

She sighs as she takes a bite of her fry, her brows knitted together as she stares across the busy cafeteria while eating. But my appetite is gone, so I pick at my food, unable to help but wonder if this will really be my last day. I thought I had my last day of school before Denendrius was turned. Could I have it wrong again? Is there some chance Sarah might not have to tell everyone my boyfriend has murdered or kidnapped me? Could there be some way—some way I haven't even considered yet—that things could go back to the way they were before Denendrius stepped out of my past?

I want to believe, but the odds don't have me confident in the idea.

I stiffen when Sarah slides a piece of paper into my pocket before I can stop her. "It has my number and my dad's number on it. Don't let him find it."

"Oh—thank you—" I'm cut off by Daina and Camille throwing themselves into the seats across from us, both with teasing scowls.

"So, this is why there were no chocolate chunk cookies by the time we got to order?" Daina throws her hand toward mine and Sarah's trays. "Unbelievable."

"I'm making up for some lost time," I admit with a teasing smile that is far too happy for the actual truth of it.

Sarah lowers her head beside me, and Daina rolls her eyes. "What do you want, *Sarah*?"

Camille grumbles, but her protest is far kinder than Daina's. "Yeah, sorry, but I don't feel comfortable with you sitting with us if we're going to have to hear our benign conversations back from your friends, only weaponized."

My jaw locks and I inhale a sharp breath through my nose. I wait for Sarah to defend herself, or for an across-the-table fight, but she picks at her food. I can tell she has nothing left in her.

"Can we not? It's my last—" I catch myself. "Sarah and I are on better terms, so let's enjoy lunch."

Nobody says anything else as Camille and Daina start on their food—two hot dogs.

"My friends haven't talked to me in days anyway," Sarah mumbles. "So no real issue there."

Camille sets her food back down and studies Sarah. "Why not?"

"Doesn't matter. No real loss, anyway," she says to her tray.

Daina only provides a grunt in response.

I already have a pretty good idea why she hasn't heard from them. She's a wreck—not that it's her fault. But she doesn't have friends like Camille, Daina, and once Jenna, who will stay by your side and do what they can to help you through your shit.

Her friends are starved for drama, and if she was upset about something and wouldn't spill the beans so they could get their fix, then they'd consider her a rotten friend for not opening up. If they couldn't "help" her by doing something like jumping a girl at a school dance because Sarah's crush was more interested in her enemy, then they would look for drama elsewhere. I've gone to school with them long enough to know.

My phone buzzes in my pocket. My heart leaping, I wipe crumbs off my hands and pull it out, finding a message from Rayonne.

Rayonne: Any luck? He's getting worried about you.

At least she's not texting me with worse news.

Marianna: Shit outta luck with my teacher. C u soon.

"Is that Den texting?" Camille asks before taking a bite from her hot dog.

"He wants me to come home." I shove the phone back in my pocket.

All three of them stare at me.

"W-why?" Sarah asks.

I shrug.

"You should definitely not. What happened to you, anyway?" Daina asks.

"Long story." Do I have to rehash this a third time?

"He beat you up, clearly. Did you tell him you were going to get a restraining order like we talked about?" Camille studies me.

"No, I tried to leave."

"Shit," Camille and Daina say in unison.

I wish there was a way for us to avoid this conversation and have five minutes of normal banter before I leave and never see them again.

"It's fine. He apologized, and we're good now." My tone is final.

They all look at me, the clear worry on their faces making me clench my jaw and stare down at my tray.

I shouldn't have stuck around after talking to Mr. Derek. I should have gone back home and left our friendship at our last conversation.

My phone buzzes in my pocket again.

The only way to do this is to rip the band-aid off. "I have to go." I stand and pile my snacks into the front compartment of my backpack, ignoring their jumble of worries. Throwing my bag over my shoulder, I say, "Sorry. I love you guys, but I've got to head out."

Camille balks. "You love us? I mean, I know you do, but that's a pretty suspicious thing to say right now."

"Yeah, what's going on?" Daina presses.

I clench the straps of my backpack. "Nothing, I feel bad about the way I've handled our friendship when you guys were only trying to help."

Their eyes narrow, and Camille hides her shaky hands under the table. "Oh . . . okay," she says. "Um. It's fine. I know it wasn't personal. But thank you."

My smile only lasts a few seconds. "Okay, see you guys." I turn and head for the door.

"Wait!" Camille calls, but I don't look back to see if she follows.

I wipe my eyes as I rush out of the school.

Right away, I spot a familiar white minivan parked by the curb at the end of the sidewalk. Carol's mane of red hair is visible through the passenger window.

"No way." My steps slow. "What the hell is going on today?"

First Liz corners me, and now Carol? How many people are going to check in on me today?

Swallowing against my tight throat, I walk down the sidewalk to the minivan, my hand shaking as I grab the handle. I'm hesitant as I open the door, unsure if I should get inside. I can't help the thought of her speeding away to keep me from ever returning to Denendrius. Regardless, I climb into the passenger seat and pull the door closed behind me.

Her voice is panic-laced when she asks, "What happened? I didn't know what to do or how to find you. Your friends couldn't *remember* where he lives. He came over and took all your stuff, said I was never seeing you again—"

I hold my hands up in front of my chest, like the motion could calm her down. "Everything is okay—"

She shakes her head. "Absolutely not, look at you!"

"He—"

"What is going on? I've been trying to figure out what's going on. Mr. Henderson called me as soon as they saw you, and thank goodness they could keep you there until I got here —" Her hands shake, knuckles white on the seat belt across her chest.

That explains that, at least.

"Carol!" I interject, and she bites her bottom lip like she's trying to stop the flow of words. "Listen, please. Everything is okay . . . mostly. Denendrius can't hurt me anymore."

I tell her how Denendrius planned to take me to Italy and turn me, how I ran off, and a group of vampires grabbed me and used me for bait. That they gave Denendrius the cure, but one of their own people—Rayonne—turned on them and that she and I have Denendrius now. How he remembers nothing, and that most likely other vampires are after him. I tell her about the fire, about getting attacked by Agatha too.

"Then you can come home, right?" she says, the corner of her lip twitching in a sort-of smile. "He's no danger to you anymore. He doesn't even remember you. So you can come home? You can leave him with that girl and have her deal with everything, can't you?"

I try to think of a way to explain to her I can't, a reason that she'll accept, at least, but I come up with nothing. "It's not that simple. I can't come home."

"Why not?" she demands. "It can't be that complicated."

I try to unravel the problem in my head for her. "Even with Denendrius out of the picture, I'm stuck in his world. Who knows how many vampires have seen me with him, and so many that haven't still know my description. Never mind we've had to blab about it all now. Even if he's taken out of the picture, not everyone will get that message. There will probably still be vampires looking for him long after he's gone, or they'll come after me based on our connection. So many are looking for him in Lorimer now. I can't stick around and risk them finding me."

She looks out the windshield. "Then we'll leave Lorimer."

I cock a brow. "What about the twins?"

"I had them taken out of the home."

Heat flares in my stomach, a guilty sickness. "But . . . how could you do that? You're a far better foster parent than half the ones out there. They'd have a much better chance with you. Do you understand what half those homes are like?"

"They're so little, they have a real good chance of adoption no matter which home they're placed in until then. And it's a safety concern. You know it is."

I stare at my lap and nod. I can't confidently say that Denendrius—or other vampires—wouldn't kill her and the kids.

Her frustrated exhale makes me look up, and with far too much confidence she says, "Okay, here's what we'll do. You're going to come home with me, and you're never seeing him again. He's not your problem anymore. I'll try to get an adoption fast-tracked, we'll sell the house and start somewhere fresh."

"But what about your job?" I scowl. "Wait—what is your job, anyway?"

The corner of her lip lifts a little. "I'm a full-time foster mom since I inherited all your grandparents' money, from both sides—everything that was left to your father, and everything to your mother—and then everything from your mom and dad when they passed. I was last in the family. There's enough for us to live modestly for a long time. We can send you to an excellent school and get a tutor for some extra help too so you don't fail tenth grade again. What do you say?"

My eyes and nose burn and I blink back tears. I wish it all could come true. I wish it were possible to have that life I so desperately want, for those people to feel like my genuine family when she brings them up. "Why would you do that for me?"

"Marianna, you are my sister's daughter, adoption finalized or not. I couldn't take care of you back when you first needed me, but now that I'm allowed to and can, I'm going to. You are the only family I have left."

"I'm sorry," I whisper. "But you're not risking your life to help me live mine. You're the only family I have left too."

"Other vampires looking for you separately from him isn't a guarantee, right? It's speculation—"

I lift a brow. "It's a fair speculation, Carol. I've already been grabbed once and used for bait. I can't even risk stepping outside in the dark right now."

"Okay, but them aside, what's the worst thing that could happen if you never go back to him and go on with your life?"

My heart hammers. "The worst thing is he remembers, kills Rayonne and has his friend turn him back before looking for me. And I won't even know what's happening until he finds me and kills me, and most likely you too."

Her wide eyes are filled with a despair that tells me she's grasping for a solution when she says, "The world is a big place, so there's no guarantee he'd find you."

"You don't know what he's capable of . . ." My voice shakes. "The world is a tiny place for him, and easy to navigate when you can hypnotize anyone you want and don't have to follow any laws."

She sets her hands on the wheel and looks down the road, pulling in a deep breath. "Fine. Okay, then. I'm in," she says, stern. "Whatever you're doing, I'll help. You said she found the apartment? We'll all go back to the house and I'll list it. Once they deal with Denendrius, we'll move and take our chances with straggler vampires."

"Absolutely not! I'm not having vampires kill you like they killed—" My brain grapples over what to call them. "Mom and Dad!"

Her eyes pop wide, a surprised gasp escaping from her lips. "What?"

My hand covers my mouth. "Oh my God. I haven't had the chance to tell you."

Tears fill her eyes and she sniffles. "No, you haven't. What happened, Marianna?"

I scrunch my nose and rub the heel of my hand against my temple before twisting my hands in my lap. "I only know what Denendrius told me, and his word is . . ." I shake my head. "When he took me when I was little, vampires saw him at some point. He's had bounties on his head for centuries. They told him to either turn himself in so they could collect, or they'd kill us." I swallow, still unable to believe that he risked my life by calling their bluff. "The most important thing to Denendrius is Denendrius. So, they killed them and only left me since it's against their rules to kill children."

She wipes dampness from her face, lips trembling. "That's why they never found leads."

"Yeah."

Carol turns her face back to the window, practicing breathing like she's trying to stop a flood of emotion. With bleary eyes, she looks back at me and says, "If he's the reason my sister is dead, then I'm helping you. That makes me involved in all this already."

I pop the door open before she can have the idea to speed away. "No, Carol, I'm sorry. Like I said, I lost them, so I'm not losing you too. Even if you never see me again, at least you're alive."

"Marianna, no—" She reaches for my arm, but I hop out of the van before she can grab me, landing back on the sidewalk.

"I'm going someplace safe," I tell her. "I promise I'll say goodbye before I go. Besides, I can probably keep in touch if we're careful. Get some garlic and water, and spray it around all your doors and windows. It'll stop about half the vampire population from bugging you. If any black-eyed vampires come after you, douse them in garlic. Depending on how old they are, it'll burn like hell and might give you a chance to use a stake or something. Stay inside at night."

She unbuckles her seat belt and throws the driver's door open into honking traffic. "No!" she hollers. "No, you are not disappearing again!"

I dart down the sidewalk a safe distance and turn to see that she's still standing beside the van. "I'm sorry!" I wipe my eyes and cross the road to the Mustang when there's a gap in the flow of vehicles. "But I love you! I'll see you soon."

XIV

I feel bitter down to my core by the time I make it back to the apartment.

Denendrius grins from where he sits at the table as soon as I walk in the door, but all I can do is return a contemptuous smile.

"Happy now?" I snap at him. "I'm home like you wanted."

Rayonne stands at the counter, chopping carrots. "He's picking up English quickly. I'm wondering if he's remembering some on his own."

"Great." That's all I need now. *Him remembering.*

I throw my backpack on the floor and slump down across from Denendrius.

"Hello," he says, clearly proud of himself for knowing the word.

"Oh, fuck off," I bark.

Denendrius's expression falls, his eyes narrowing as he studies me and scratches the back of his head. "Mad?" he asks.

"Wow, you're just . . . *expanding* your vocabulary, aren't you?"

He lifts a brow.

"Yes. Mad."

Denendrius rocks back in his chair. "Hmm."

"What are you going to do about it?" I ask him. "What are you going to do about me being mad at you?"

Rayonne's low warning comes from behind me. "Marianna . . ."

"I know, relax," I hiss. "I'll stop now, sorry."

Denendrius leans sideways to reach his hand down his pocket, a soft smile on his lips as he fishes something out. Sitting properly again, he holds his hand out to me—palm up —before motioning to me.

I huff and copy him. "What?" I ask gently, forcing the hostility out of my voice.

He places something heavy in my hand, and when he pulls away with a hopeful smile, I stare at the gold bracelet in my palm, the band a circular snake devouring its own tail.

"Gold," he tells me, the word sounding funny coming off his tongue. He sounds nothing like he did speaking English when he was a vampire. He points to the snake's red eyes. "Ruby."

"This is probably really old and extremely expensive," I whisper before swallowing. It's also beautiful, and my second-favorite animal—after dogs, of course. From its slight imperfections in the shaping of the gold band, it was probably made by hand. Is it one of a kind?

Rayonne offers some clarity. "He found it in that chest from his pirate days. So, probably."

Is it a gift because he feels something for me and happened to find it? Or does he feel bad and went out of his way to find something to smooth things over with? Either way, I'm surprised he wants to give me anything when I've been rude to him, because he never would have when he was a vampire.

"Thank you," I whisper, holding it up between my fingers to

study it. There is faint writing carved into the inside of the band, too faded to make out more than the letter T. "I like it."

I have to force my hand through the thick circular band, but it fits nicely once on, and it won't accidentally fall off.

"It's an ouroboros," Rayonne says. I look over my shoulder at her as she scrapes carrots into the pan on the stove. "I looked it up when he found it. He wanted to tell you it was gold. But it's an Egyptian symbol. The Greeks and Romans used it too, as well as a bunch of other cultures."

I twist my wrist to admire it. "I think I remember it from one booklet my history teacher gave us. It represents an eternal cycle, right? Life, death, rebirth?"

She throws some chunks of chicken into the pan and it sizzles. "Exactly."

When Rayonne finishes cooking, we eat, then retire to bed so we're rested for whatever the night brings us. Hopefully Agatha doesn't try anything two nights in a row.

I wake to an empty bed and find Denendrius in the hidden room. He crouches in front of the safes, talking to himself.

"Figure it out yet?" I ask as I rub my eyes and wander to his side.

He looks up over his shoulder at me, then returns to jamming numbers into the keypad. It flashes red at him.

A word from Denendrius's grumbling catches my attention. "*Novem?*"

"Nine?"

He looks up at me, head tilted. "Nine? Yes."

"One and nine? Like nineteen? A date for something, maybe?" What are the chances of it being my birthday? The day we met in Enchanted Land? It's worth a shot.

"One-nine-nine-one." I frown when the little light flashes red. "Okay, not my birth year." I try the year we met. "One-nine-nine-six." Red again.

Denendrius motions to the other two, so I try both dates on those. I get an error each time. "Damn."

I cross my arms and lean against the middle safe, staring at him and trying to think of any other dates that could mean something to him.

Rayonne's voice comes from somewhere to my right. "You two are super loud."

"Sorry."

She paces to my side. "Why are you fixating on the safes?"

"Because he's clearly trying to remember something important—" Denendrius's abrupt excitement catches me off guard.

"*Vaha!*" He punches the year we met in backwards.

The safe flashes green. Denendrius opens it, and the first thing my eyes are drawn to is the few shelves packed with stacks of bills. Tens of thousands of dollars at a glance.

I flop down beside him. "Holy shit. I haven't seen that much money since Venganza Roja."

My heart hammers. Technically, once we deal with Denendrius, there's nothing stopping the money from being mine.

Two other shelves are full of blue and red velvet pouches. Grabbing one and pulling it open, I find a bunch of smaller matching ones. I feel nauseous with excitement as I pluck one of the smaller bags out and peek inside to see that it holds a diamond. And after searching through a few bags and a couple of their smaller interior counterparts, I assume the entire shelf is dedicated to them.

"What are they?" Rayonne asks, trying to crane her neck over Denendrius and me.

My tongue is dead in my mouth. Carefully, I turn the little bag I'm holding and a pink diamond falls into my palm. I hold it up.

Her sharp intake of breath is loud. "If this safe is full of diamonds and cash, what's in the other two?"

More money? Valuable artifacts? "I . . . I have no idea."

Rayonne's lips purse and she stares at me with a careful and wondering eye, like she's thinking the same thing I am but doesn't want to say it out loud. And I suppose after everything Denendrius has put her through, and what she went through to capture him, never mind saving my ass, she deserves at minimum a handful of diamonds.

"After," I promise her with a small nod.

"Thank you."

I knew Denendrius was wealthy, but safe-full-of-*diamonds* wealthy? Did he steal them all when he was a pirate? Robberies? A combination of different ways?

I check Denendrius's reaction to his hoard, but his eyes are locked on the bottom of the safe. Resting there is another safe, smaller, also fireproof, and only needing a key. My eyes alternate between it and Denendrius, and I'm unable to come up with a single idea of what could be inside. But considering it's in another safe, it must be more valuable than the cash and diamonds.

"Your keys," I bark at him, hand jumping to his front pocket.

"Ah. Keys," he repeats, taking them from his jeans.

He scolds me in Latin as I snatch them from his hand, but he doesn't take them back as I pick through the keys and decide on the small silver one of the bunch. Moving it toward the safe, Denendrius holds a demanding hand out. I surrender the key and he unlocks the safe and lifts the lid to expose an antique-looking black leather briefcase.

I reach out and Denendrius seizes my wrist, his grip making my heart jump.

"Denendrius—"

He looks as confused as I am. "Sorry." He frees me.

I twist my fingers in my lap, instead allowing him to take the old black leather case out of the safe. His hands are shaking when he sets it on the floor, his motions fastidious as he undoes the straps and opens it. There are dozens of glass vials aligned in rows on worn red velvet, a dark crimson liquid in each of them.

"Is that what I think it is?" My breath hitches.

"I think so," Rayonne says.

Though the vials are different, more antique looking than the one I saw full of blood mere days ago, I'm sure it must contain the same thing.

"The cure?" *Why the hell would he have these?* "He ran back in to try to save the cure?"

Her face is a mix of horror and confusion. "But they're in two fireproof safes."

I shrug. "Maybe he didn't remember that part."

She blows air between her lips. "I don't know. But I'm getting nervous about the fact that he *is* remembering."

Rayonne's not wrong about that, and it makes me queasy. "For all we know, he's only remembering bits and pieces. It doesn't even look like he knows what this is."

Trepidation flows through me as I slowly reach for the case. Thankfully, he doesn't stop me, instead leaning away so I can pick it up off the floor. I brace it against my stomach, fingers clenched around the corners as I don't dare drop it.

"That bottom row looks like a solid piece that lifts up for another compartment," Rayonne notices. She pulls at the velvet corner and it shifts.

I look around, but there's nowhere stable to rest it to investigate, so I close it back up. "Let's move to the table."

We maneuver out of the room—paying extra attention to our footing—and to the dining area, the shift in dim light to bright sunlight causing a ripple of pain through my head. The faint smell of smoke lingering doesn't help, though neither does the old smell from the hidden room.

I set the case down on the table and sneeze.

"There we go!" Rayonne lifts the bottom row of vials to reveal the hollow bottom.

Denendrius's hands open and close like he wants to swoop the case away from us when our eyes land on the handful of old journals of varying ages. Some barely have the covers intact and look like they might crumble if touched. His eyes narrow on them when Rayonne selects the one on top and flips through the delicate pages.

"I can't read this," Rayonne says as she squints at the black ink. "More Latin, I think."

She goes to put the journal back, but Denendrius takes it from her to rifle through. My mouth opens to protest as hers does, but from his tight expression and his rigid stance, I anticipate his reaction before he jerks away from me when I lift my hand out to grab it.

It's not worth fighting him, so I grab the newest-looking journal—which is probably still one or two hundred years old—but pass it off to her when I spot what looks like a bunch of letters folded together. Denendrius's name is scrawled on the front in all caps.

Taking care in unfolding them, I frown when the first one's in Latin. Since he's preoccupied with the journal, I move it to the back of the collection and find another in French. I grumble and shuffle that one behind the others too, and find a letter in Spanish, and one in English. I read the one in Spanish first, then in English. They say the same thing.

I am unsure of which year you read this, but as I write, it is 1887. You must have awoken—likely confused—with this letter, in which I will explain what I can.

In the event that you have no recollection of penning this, you should know that I am you. Perhaps you have awoken with all your memories, or without a single one. Perhaps you have awoken somewhere in between. There's no way to know, and it is unlikely that you are presently aware of the reasons that brought you to choosing to be human again. But whatever the reason, it is no longer of importance.

You are human now.

You were a vampire before waking. Depending on which time you are in, and which you remember, there may be a different interpretation of vampires. For simplicity, this means another turned you, and that you have been surviving on human blood for centuries. The contents of these vials are responsible for your current mortal state.

If you are without memory, you should know that you were born in the year AD 58 in the city of Rome. You were turned at twenty-seven years old and go by the name Denendrius. Your Roman family names no longer matter. You are better off not remembering them. You have been using the surname Sovetta for a handful of centuries now. The name belonged to a man who helped you through your darkest time before he died. He saved you when you attempted to end your life.

It is vital that you know there is a significant possibility that vampires are hunting you. They have been for a very long time. Your newfound humanity might offer you some protection, as they will continue to search for a vampire, but you must be vigilant.

There is enough money to last you multiple lifetimes by today's standards. Perhaps you should marry for love and have some children once you are accustomed to the world where you are. It is what I would do in your position.

My mind whirs. "You know what, maybe we don't need Mr. Derek at all. This is a letter to himself, in case he took the cure and woke up without his memory. Maybe it'll clear things up for him enough to calm down. Plus, he's learning English. Should we show him?" Though I'm wary of him remembering anything, I doubt the letters can provoke more than a room full of sentimental items can. Besides, if he thinks he chose to be human, maybe he'll be less inclined to turn back.

Since he likely doesn't remember anything that happened with Agatha, how does he think he became human, if we only now opened the safe? Is it possible he has more cure blood stocked away somewhere that he remembers? I can't image he'd keep all his prized possessions and money hidden in one shitty apartment. Where did he even get this? Regardless, clearly he didn't plan for someone else turning him back and intended on having the letters on him if he ever took it.

She wavers side to side. "Let me read it first—"

He grumbles something when he notices the papers in my hands, tut-tutting me before snatching them from my loose grip.

Expression deadpan, I drop my empty hands to my sides. "That decides it, then."

"It said he *wanted* to be human?" Rayonne says, flabbergasted.

Her disbelief mimics my own. "It sounded like it was a backup plan. Like he wanted the option available to him. But clearly, he hasn't wanted to use it yet since he wanted his friend to come fix him."

She massages her temple with the heel of her hand. "Curious." She sets the book back in the box. "That one's in Latin too."

Denendrius's eyes are wide as he reads, and he sits down at the table and mumbles to himself as his gaze moves back and forth across the page. When he gets to the end, he gazes right up at me with a tender smile, though there's a crease between his brows.

I stare pointedly at him. "I know what you wrote at the bottom there, but . . ." I stop myself. But what? I can't exactly reject him right now without dire consequences.

He hands the paper back to me and stares across the room in thought as I fold the letters and set them back in the case. I wish I could climb into his mind and know what he's thinking.

When he looks back at me, mouth opening and closing before he sighs, I realize all I did was create more questions in his mind.

I run my fingers over the vials. "If the cure is so rare, how did he get it?"

Her eyes brim with tears, black droplets running through her makeup and over her ghostly skin. "What if this is the reason he came after my clan?"

Horror rips through me as the pieces connect when I think over Alaire and Edmond's write-up on him. "He killed and kidnapped hundreds of Children of Stars."

"He was searching for the cure." She sniffles hard and pats at tears on her cheeks. "I could never figure out why he came after us. I thought he was bored, or that he snapped—maybe he was hunting for someone in particular and we were merely obstacles to take his frustration out on . . ."

I stare down at the notebooks, wondering what he's logged in them. If her theory is right, which would make sense since he seemed to stop hunting Children of Stars around the same time he wrote the letter to himself, it's probably full of his findings.

Rayonne glances out the window, cheeks pink as she pulls in deep breaths to combat her tears. The sky is a creamy orange and pink. She closes the case and gives her head a shake while sniffling. "We should put these back before a vampire appears outside our window. These are so valuable, especially if Denendrius killed Alessander and Thomas in his quest to find them."

With a somber sigh, I return the case to the hidden room—locking it back up—and maneuver around Denendrius, who half-blocks the hallway.

His hand brushes against mine as I walk away. "Marianna."

I turn. "What—"

Denendrius herds me backward into the wall, his hand pulling my chin up as his lips dive toward mine. I inhale sharply, the taste of wine entering my mouth as he touches his hot lips between mine like I'm fragile glass.

Slowly, I kiss him back. I hate that I do, but the fear has made it automatic.

Only this time it's not fear that allows his lips to stay on mine for longer than a second. It's sick curiosity.

Denendrius has never kissed me like this before.

My mind empties when his hand moves to my cheek to keep my head in place. His warm lips are soft on mine, at leisure like the world will halt and wait until he's finished. I'm used to his stormy kisses and hanging on as his mouth would greedily try to drown mine.

I put my hand against his chest when I think of pushing him away, but his raging heartbeat stops me. It hammers on behind my palm.

So human.

If I didn't open my eyes to look at him, I'd be convinced a different man is kissing me.

When I turn my face away—eyes burning—he doesn't fight me. He exhales a blissful breath, brown eyes glittering as he smiles.

I stare at him, my heart pounding furiously in my chest. "Why would you do that?"

When he makes a grab for my waist like he wants to pull me back in, I rush away. I wipe at my cheeks before running my fingers through my hair as I rejoin Rayonne by the table.

"I'm not sure what we should do with ourselves," Rayonne admits. "Aside from waiting for a phone call or for Viorel's men to show up. I know Agatha said they won't come until she's secured him, but I don't believe that. And if she really called them, I wouldn't be surprised if they're driving over right now."

My lips tingle, still hot from his mouth when I say, "Why don't we, like . . .?" I mash my lips together like I can squash the feel of him on them as I think. "Why don't we *go* to Romania ourselves? Waiting around for them to contact us is stupid. All three of us have passports. Let's just fly over there and go knock on the castle door."

"It's not so simple, Marianna," she insists.

I cross my arms, jamming my fists into the crooks of my elbows. "Why not? I'm seriously confused why this is so difficult. You say you don't have a contact number. That's stupid. You should have figured that out over the past year—okay, doesn't matter. But instead of waiting around for them to find *us*, let's go to the castle. I want to deal with . . ." I look over my shoulder as Denendrius comes into the room. "I want this shit to be done with. I'm *exhausted*."

She groans and ruffles her fingers through her silky hair in frustration. "That would work if we could *find the castle*, Marianna. But we can't!"

"It's a fucking castle! How hard can it be to find? Goddamn thing is probably poking through the clouds!" I wave my arms madly at my sides before crossing them tightly.

Red creeps into her porcelain skin as she argues. "*Impossible*, actually. Viorel has the entire place masked. The castle doesn't exist unless you're brought there by a vampire who is allowed to find it. Which I've heard is only his most trusted men. You can't even stumble upon it. It's somewhere in the forest—completely invisible and undetectable—and you'll be unknowingly rerouted if you go near it. It's called the Castle That Never Was because there's so many vampires who don't believe it even exists at all. The vampires who live there can't find it on their own coming and going either. That's how protected it is."

Dread trickles into me, her words deflating. "Then what do we do?"

Her smile is sympathetic. Gently, she says, "Wait. I promise, word can travel fast in the vampire community. Especially something like this. I'm sorry I've created this mess, that I didn't think every part through before acting. But I can't undo that mistake. One way or another, his men will hear Denendrius is human. They'll find us quickly, I'm sure."

I slump against the back of the counter, letting my arms fall at my sides. "I hope so."

We stand in heavy silence. Denendrius comes up beside me, completely oblivious to all the issues at hand. Does he think everything is peachy, that we merely have a few vampires to deal with on our quest for his *normal life*?

I straighten and shift my weight from side to side in thought. "We should probably stuff our go bags with money."

"Perhaps we should also find somewhere else to hide, since Agatha knows we're here?" She lifts her hands to study her nails, like she's looking for an unscathed patch of black to pick.

I wander to the fridge and grab the last energy drink on the shelf. "Absolutely not. One, there's a room full of valuable items that need protecting. And two, if you're so sure about Viorel's men tracking us down, then it would be another mistake to make it harder for them to find us."

"True. I suppose they'll track us anywhere. I forget I carry a scent with me now."

I crack the can open and take a long drink, washing the taste of Denendrius from my mouth. "Yeah, that too."

We take our bags into the room with us, and I realize as we're throwing stacks of cash in them that the confusion on his face means he probably doesn't understand it's money. Especially since he gets agitated when we touch his diamonds. We can hardly fit any of the wealth in the bag with us, but what we can fit will last us at least a couple lifetimes if we don't go crazy. We decide we can always come back for the rest when Viorel's men get Denendrius.

"We should pack some of the cure," I propose. "It could come in handy."

She agrees and reorganizes some diamonds so we each

have a velvet sack with a couple vials. We lock the rest back in the safe and return to the living room to drop our bags.

Considering my words while leaning against the end of the counter, I say, "If they don't think allowing me into the castle because you ask them to as part of your reward is okay, do you think I can buy myself in with some of this stuff? I know you said Viorel has the cure stockpiled, but if there hasn't been a vampire born with it running through their veins in centuries, don't you think he'd like to have more, as well as whatever Denendrius wrote in those journals? I bet there's some good information in there. That could be the value I provide to him for my place."

"I don't think you need to worry about that. But it's still a good idea." She peeks in the fridge and makes a disgruntled face.

I smile, feeling a little better about my odds now.

Denendrius drags his feet along the hallway carpet as he comes toward us, head down as he plays with something long between his fingers. His eyes cast up, dim with despondence.

"What's wrong?" A worrying thump of my heart ripples through me.

He settles in front of me to show the bracelet in his hands. Rubbing his thumb over some of the turquoise beads between black ones, he whispers, "Adelia."

It's his sister's? Was she wearing it when he killed her?

They're held together by a thick white cord that's stained with a rust color, but whether that's blood or age, I can't say. It's in incredible condition for being almost two thousand years old, so Denendrius must have truly cherished it.

I cover my mouth with my hand, brows drawn together in sympathy.

He pulls in a pained breath and releases a shudder. "On me," he says, holding the bracelet out.

Cringing as I grasp the fragile-looking piece of jewelry, I say, "Are you sure you want to wear it? What if it breaks?"

"*On*," he repeats with less patience.

I maneuver it around his wrist like it will crumble and hook the silver clasp. It must have been loose on her, or an anklet, as it fits snug around his wrist.

His smile is thankful as he sniffs and turns away.

XV

I order Chinese food for our late dinner before Rayonne starts cooking, and we surf through television shows while we wait. Denendrius tries to steal another kiss from me when our glances come in sync, but I pretend not to notice and retrieve a drink.

When our food arrives—fried rice, various meat dishes, and egg rolls—we eat in silence while watching a wrestling special. Rayonne is lost in thought, and it doesn't look like she enjoys the show either.

Denendrius scarfs down a heaping plate of food, excited about the new-to-him dish. But by the time Rayonne and I are done eating, there's a sheen of sweat over his forehead and he's chugging his wine down, shaky as he stands to pour himself another.

"He's going to be sick again," I grumble as I stand and follow him.

He gags halfway through his drink and only makes it as far as the sink before he's throwing up his entire dinner.

I gnaw at my cheek as Rayonne walks to my side.

"Why is he only sick when you pick what we eat?" she teases.

I mull him over, mind picking through my conversation with Alaire and Edmond, but all I can remember is how many things could go wrong upon turning back. If he only struggles to digest takeout and has missing memories, then he's lucky.

"Maybe it's the diet difference," I wonder. "He would have been on a pretty healthy menu."

"Probably. This is a smidgen of justice though." Rayonne grins.

"As long as he doesn't puke himself inside out, yeah."

He chugs three more glasses of water before shivering and turning to look at me with bleary eyes.

"Sleep," he says before stumbling to the bedroom and flopping down in bed. He groans as he crawls under the blanket and pulls it tightly around himself.

I'm relieved to have some time without him conscious.

"He's leaving us alone for a bit? Thank goodness." Rayonne releases a satisfied exhale as she falls back into the couch.

I grab a glass of wine and sit beside her on the cool leather, taking a long sip and letting the bitter taste roll over the back of my tongue. "Hopefully it's the food making him sick."

"Yes, but he deserves a bit of suffering while he waits for prolonged pain. He shouldn't be enjoying pizza and Chinese food when my Alessander and Thomas aren't even alive to eat." Her lips twist.

I can't disagree. "Can you tell me about Alessander? Is he the one who turned you?"

A ghost of a smile appears on her face, the memory nearly visible in the fond twinkle of her eye. "Yes, he was. He bought the old farm neighboring my father's; his house was down in this little valley. When I was young—fifteen, perhaps—he moved in alone. It was strange. There were rarely signs of life from his place. I periodically used to walk to the edge of our property where the valley began to check. If I looked through the trees at the perfect angle, I could see down past the thin stream to his house. I would sit on the other side of the fence near the decline and wait to see him. I didn't until one night when a storm blocked out the evening sun. He appeared as a tiny speck accompanied by a torch. I didn't watch him for long. It started to pour."

My mind spins vivid images. "Did you meet him soon after?"

She shakes her head. "No. I attempted to, but my knocks went unanswered. After a few years when the wild grass grew thick, I began hearing the echo of horses between the hills. They appeared when I was around seventeen. A couple at first. I'd sit in the grass behind the fence and observe them chasing one another, their hooves clacking against the rocks at the edge of the stream. I thought I would see him out in the day riding them, but he never did.

"Soon two horses turned into fifteen. He was yet to build a new stable or barn for them. They ate the grass and flowers and drank from the stream. His property was so large I'm not sure if he fed them himself. I never heard or saw haying. They simply existed there. They rarely neared his house, and I never saw him work with them. I kept my distance for that reason. Our own workhorse had an attitude, never mind a horse untrained. So for years I would sit there and watch their smear of coats as they ran through the rich green. There were horses of every shade, sandy Palominos and spotted Appaloosas. I remember Arabians and Clydesdales. He collected them." She grins. "I ranted to my father about it. I couldn't believe he was acquiring such expensive horses to let them go wild. The only one that was the slightest bit tame was a miniature that would come to the bottom of the hill and fail to climb it every time it saw me watching."

I can't help but smirk at the thought of the miniature horse.

Her face returns to its seriousness. "One night when I was twenty-three, I heard metallic twanging echoing outside. My first thought was that the cows had broken through the barbed wire again. I dragged myself out of bed to check and found a tall man at our fence at the top of the hill, fixing the wire for us. That tiny pony stood beside him, hoof knocking the bottom wire a few posts down from where he was working. His long brown hair made it hard to see his face, and when he noticed me, he stared up at me for a moment and left down the hill."

I watch her disappear within herself for a moment, eyes darting back and forth over her hands as she holds them clutched in her lap. She sniffs.

"Then what happened?"

Rayonne lifts her head back up, a small smile coming as an apology. "I started sneaking out at night to watch him. One night, when the full moon lit the valley up perfectly, I spotted him wandering toward the herd. What I thought were wild horses weren't so wild after all. He walked through the unbothered herd, touching their necks and sides until he decided on one. Then, without a saddle or bridle—or riding gear of any sort—he climbed onto the horse like it was nothing and trotted off."

Even now, the astonishment is clear on her face. "It amazed me how gracefully they rode together, even more so when the other horses ran with them. It was like he spoke their language." She bites her lip, a faint smile curving her lips. "Well, I didn't know it until later, but technically he did."

My eyes widen. "He could speak to horses?"

She nods. "Alessander had a wonderful mind. He was gifted with telepathy—to animals—when he was born. But I didn't know that then. A few days later, I climbed under his fence and down the hill. I was intrigued after seeing him so close. I wanted to know about his horses and why he kept to himself so much. Perhaps he was lonely and wanted someone to ride with. I wondered about the chances that he was deaf like my little sister, Harriet, and hadn't heard me knocking and calling. I was wrong though. He was trying to keep us safe by refusing contact with us."

When her lips part, a loud thump cuts her off. Denendrius grunts and grumbles from the bedroom. I roll my eyes, too enthralled in her story to care about what he's done to himself.

"Was Alessander worried about killing you?"

"Something like that. If he opened his door to me, I would have told my siblings about the man with all the wonderful horses and how nice he was. They were a rowdy bunch, and my father would have roped him into a friendship. Alessander's farm was where he went to have a breath away from humans."

"But he talked to you this time?" I wonder, my mind sifting through the possible paths her life took to vampirism. Did they fall in love and he turned her? Did he accidentally hurt her and have to fix it?

Her laugh is bright, and she shakes her head. "No, he didn't. But I wandered down again in the late afternoon to invite him for dinner. The herd was grazing at the edge of the river, tails swishing in the grass. His horses were more beautiful up close than I had imagined. I wanted to stroke one's mane on the way to the house, so I approached a glistening black giant. Its white mane and tail were poofy and well kept. It had white feathering around its hooves, and I knew that would be the horse I'd ride if I were a princess. But when I reached out to touch it, it reared. I was in the way when the rest of the herd fled. When hooves came down on me, I realized I had been correct to assume they were wild at first. I'm not sure how long I lay there with the feeling of my bones cutting through my skin and organs." She pulls her cheek taut and sighs dramatically. "Trampled to death by horses. I wouldn't recommend going out that way."

My heart hammers, my jaw slack. "And Alessander saved you?"

She bites the corner of her lip, her nod slow. "He told me later how the sound woke him, how he could smell my blood permeating the air. He saw what happened through the memories of his horses. But I was too far from the house for him to risk the sunlight, so he stood in the shadows listening to my heartbeat weakening by the hour, hoping that either my family would find me—not that they could do anything for me—or I'd live until sundown. He didn't want to risk having a horse drag me to the door, so I lay there until I passed out from the pain.

"When I woke up in a straw bed later, I felt . . . strange. I thought perhaps I'd died, as there was no pain. Surely I should be in pain after something like that." She plays with the wedding ring on her finger, tears brimming in her eyes. Her voice cracks when she says, "The first thing Alessander said when I spotted him in a wooden rocking chair across the room was 'My apologies, Beth.' Then he explained to me that technically, I was dead."

I allow for a long moment of silence to process. "Wait, Beth?"

She laughs. "That was my name when I was human. Quite boring—too common—for the person I became as a vampire, I believe."

"Then where did Rayonne come from?"

Her smile tilts. "A pet name, of sorts. My first week as a vampire was complete misery. Alessander said I lost so much of my blood that I woke up more bloodthirsty than usual. And after I saw myself in the mirror—sickly pale, red eyes, and blood-matted hair—I was an even bigger emotional mess. I looked like a demon. He said, '*Vous rayonnez*, Beth. You're a Child of Stars now. You're radiant, you'll see.' I could only laugh and scream, '*Je rayonne?*' because it felt like he was teasing me. But he was far too kind and too serious a man for teasing. But eventually I saw it. Once I was full of blood, my eyes back to normal with my sanity, I *was* radiant. And I didn't feel like Beth anymore, so my pet name became my new name."

"I like it," I say. "You've got a good story behind it."

She beams.

More questions pile on my tongue, her words having a tight clutch on my frantic heart. "What about your son? He wasn't biologically yours, then?"

She shakes her head. "He was six, a beggar boy. After Alessander brought me back to Paris with him, I saw Thomas one evening in ragged clothes outside a bakery. I walked up to him and asked where his mother was. He said he never knew her, that he ran away from an orphanage, so I took his hand and told him I was his mother from then on."

More questions are ready to spill from me when her phone rings. My heart hammers. Could it be someone with good news?

She swiftly pulls it from her pocket and flips it open, resting it against her ear. "Ziggy?" Her eyes dart up to mine, his loud—but muffled voice—leaking through. "Um—all right. Okay, I'll meet you—" She rolls her eyes at him, then to me says, "Ziggy says hello and he apologizes on behalf of his guests."

My brows hike up. "Wait—where are you going?"

"Yes, I'll hurry." She shuts her phone. "Ziggy said there's a vampire there wanting to speak to me."

A wicked grin warps my face. "About Viorel?"

Her shoulders lift to her ears. "I've no idea. I better hurry and find out."

I stand as she does. "Are you sure it's safe for you to go out there alone?"

She grabs her purse off the counter and slips the strap over her shoulder. "I'll be fine. Ziggy is going to meet me wherever I park, so I won't walk alone. I'll text you when I get to the car, and once I'm there, so you know I'm not dead. Are you sure you're comfortable here alone?"

"Well, it's not like I have the option to come with you, anyway." I lean against the side of the counter as she tucks the revolver full of wooden bullets into her purse, then takes a cigarette and poises it between her lips. "Besides, I doubt Agatha will try to burn the place down again."

Rayonne gone, I crawl into bed next to Denendrius to ensure he's still alive. He's fast asleep, thrashing and shivering like he's trapped in a horrible dream. I lie there—pondering what he could be dreaming of—until I get the first text from Rayonne, then dig into some more takeout in front of the TV.

A show is already midway through when I turn it on, a group of teenage girls walking down the locker-lined hallway of the rich high school the drama takes place in. My thumb hovers over the guide button as the scene plays out on screen: the girls plunking down at their desks, passing notes and giggling while the teacher turns to write on the board. Graduation is coming up, and the girls are complaining about how they haven't picked their dresses yet.

It's completely mundane and shouldn't be so upsetting that emotion slices through my chest. My vision turns watery.

It was one thing when having a normal future—or any future—was merely a treacherous mountain to climb. There was still a chance things could work out, that I could turn things around one day. But to know I'll never be able to have it now, even with Denendrius out of my life, even if I tried my hardest, is more painful. And knowing Carol will abandon her entire life in Lorimer to move somewhere I *might* be safe is torture. I have a parental figure on my side now, someone who wants the best for me and is willing to give me better things, and it doesn't even matter.

All I can hope is for an invitation to the castle with Rayonne, and that it will make up for everything I'll never get now. Either that, or I take Ziggy's offer.

When the mattress squeaks, I hold my breath as I wait for him to find me here crying. Instead, the bathroom door shuts, and the shower turns on.

I watch my rush of memories and imagined futures instead of the TV mere feet from my face until the water turning off breaks me out of my thoughts. I wipe tears from my cheeks as the bathroom door opens, Denendrius's quiet humming emerging at the side of the couch.

Glowering, I glance at him from the corner of my eye. He watches me as he dries his hair with a green towel, a second one wrapped around his waist. Fat droplets of water run down his defined chest and stomach. His hair is out of its tie, stopping below his collarbones.

"You're dripping water all over the carpet," I grumble. "You could've dried off in the bathroom instead of flaunting yourself."

He smiles at me, a soft and clueless smile that makes my blood boil.

"It's pretty fucked up that someone as evil as you is so attractive," I snarl. "That you're a magnetic trap for everything good, and you destroy it all. Imagine if your outside matched your inside. People would puke looking at you."

With his smile, it's almost like he's laughing at me.

"Aren't you going to react? Even if you can't understand me, don't you at least hear my tone?" I growl.

He dries his face, wicking the water from the new stubble on his jaw.

"Whatever, dude."

He sits down beside me as I turn my eyes back to the TV.

When it's clear he's more focused on the show than getting back up to find clothes, I'm too engulfed with rage to process anything on the screen. When he leans back and laughs at the TV, it feels like my bones are on fire.

"You need to get dressed!" I chastise.

I shove myself off the couch and madly dig through a box of his clothes. My hand scrapes against silk and I clench it. Discovering it's his boxers, I whip them at him and they land where I was sitting. He watches me dig, a single brow lifted, that stupidly sunny smile still smeared across his fucking face.

I find a dark green shirt and chuck it at him, followed by a pair of gray flannel pajama pants I've never seen. When he scrutinizes the pants, I step forward and yank them from his hand, replacing them with jeans.

"Is that fucking better? Or do you need a jeweled gown?" I spit.

My tone wipes his expression clear, eyes roving over me. I sit back in a heap beside him and cross my arms, leaning forward and placing them on my knees. I glare at the TV. When he dresses beside me, I huff and hang my head, my long hair shielding me from his bareness.

Denendrius brushes against my side as he sits beside me. When his fingers graze the side of my head as he draws my hair back, I release a frustrated growl and slap his hands away.

He stares at me, desperate to find an issue I know I haven't made apparent. "Marianna..."

I shoot a lethal glare at the TV.

Denendrius releases a frustrated sigh and I sneer to myself as he watches me, counting down to the moment he forces me to look at him and give him an answer. I wonder if he'll shove me to the floor or choke me. Maybe he'll settle for slamming his fist into my face. I wonder if it'll hurt less since he's no longer a vampire, or more since he would've held back his strength to avoid killing me.

Denendrius sets his jaw and leans back against the couch, eyes turning away from me and to the TV. We sit in silence through half the show. As he visibly relaxes, my heart pumps fire through me.

When something on the TV brings that airy laugh from him, I stand and face him.

"Shut up!" I scream. "You're not allowed to be happy. You're not allowed to have fun and think that everything is going to be peachy. Not when I can't even have one fucking hour with my friends without you demanding I come back home! That was the last time I'll ever see them, and you have no idea!" I reload a breath. "And you can't walk out here after a relaxing shower naked with your weapon of a body and act like it's another day! *You can't kiss me like you did!* You should be terrified that all this is happening to you, not comfortable!"

His expression drops. He nods toward the space beside him, like he wants me to sit and try to explain to him why I'm upset. Instead, I throw the back of my hand across his face.

He stands faster than I anticipate, and I nearly fall backward as his face comes within an inch of mine. His eyes burn into mine, nostrils flaring, hot air spraying against my face.

I smile. "Do it. I know you want to." I shake my head to clear my face of hair and hold my chin up, cheek waiting.

I expect him to lay hands on me. When he doesn't, something sparks in me. I shove him in the chest, and he takes a step back, growling something low at me.

"Hit me," I demand, putting more effort into slamming my open hand against the muscle in his chest.

His bottom lip twitches, and he wavers on his feet.

"Do it!" I throw my hand out again, and he gently deflects it and steps back. "*Hit me*," I snarl, taking another step forward.

His anger vanishes, and he must understand what I'm doing as he shakes his head and tries to step around me. I slap him across the face as hard as I can. The sound of skin against skin echoes through the apartment, my strength turning his head. His eyes harden as he glares back at me, sweet brown turning back to stone.

A lofty grin lifts to my lips. "Do it. Prove to me you're still the same piece of shit. Help my confusion."

"Stop." The finality of his tone does nothing to deter me.

"Stop? Why should I listen to that? You never did." I turn my head and tap my finger on my cheek. "Hit me. Make this easy! Stop being nice to me and *bruise me.*"

When his hands stay put at his sides, I shove him back before slapping him across the face again. His breath leaves him in a hard grunt, but he still doesn't retaliate.

I shout in frustration, both my hands flying at his face and chest in a flurry with no plan to stop until he hurts me. Instead, his hand captures my wrist, the room twisting around me. My back slams into his chest, his arms pinning mine down in a bear hug. My knees give under me as he forces us both onto the carpet. Sitting between his legs, I try kicking and digging my heels into them, but he throws his legs over mine.

I writhe and he shushes me, his Latin words coming out low and even.

Tears start in the corner of my eyes. "*Fuck you,*" I wail, trying to thrash free. "You ruined my life. Everything is awful and ruined. *It's not fair.*"

He holds both my arms down with one of his, moving the other one to smooth my hair down. I try to turn my face away but end up with my sore cheek against his chest. His heart thumps furiously against my ear and he rocks us, leaning his head on top of mine.

Tears blur my vision, my spit thickening in my mouth. "*Who are you?*" I sob.

For once I wish he could answer me because I have no idea.

I'm scared I don't know him anymore.

XVI

Denendrius doesn't let go of me until I'm too tired to fight, though my tears haven't found their end yet.

"You want to know one reason I'm so furious with you?" I cry as I stand and claw tears away. "Do you want to understand?"

Through my raging pain and anger, I stop caring if he remembers before we get him in a cell. I tear through the boxes in the corner of the living room, searching for his rape tapes until I—*of course*—find them packed neatly in another box of his clothes.

I throw the clothes aside and dump the box of tapes on the floor, plastic clattering.

"You're going to watch me wreck these," I say as I drop to my knees by the pile of tapes. "You're going to prove they don't matter to you. Prove you're different somehow. Prove you don't remember, and you're not playing nice and tricking me."

He surveys me as I tear through tape cases, ripping lengths of film out until there's a mass of shiny black material in a tangled mess on my lap. Denendrius makes no move to stop me from ruining his trophies. In fact, there's nothing but horrified puzzlement on his face.

He doesn't remember. If he did, surely I'd pay for this severely.

After the tenth, the mass of film ribbon knots around my fingers when I take a fistful to move it aside, only to tighten when I try to shake my hand free. My tears well as I slip my hand loose. I've barely made a dent in the pile.

Head dropped, my hair a curtain around me, my shoulders jerk as I weep. Denendrius squats down in front of me and pushes my hair aside. I stare at my lap and try to control my emotion, only to fail.

Denendrius whispers something and moves away, the sound of plastic hinges and protesting cassette gears filling the room. I peek up to see Denendrius destroying a tape. When he notices me watching, he gives me a supportive half-smile and reaches across the pile to rub my knee.

I wonder if I should tell him what they are as he rips out the film from cassette after cassette, but I worry he'll enjoy them and change his mind. Instead, I sneak a tape away from the pile to show him after the rest are unsalvageable.

After each tape he's unwound, I reach across and grab it to see if it's of me, tossing it into the pile next to me when it isn't. Eventually, he catches on that I want to see them and tosses them to me before carrying on to the next. My heart hammers the entire time, and I worry it might give out. Time lags on as he destroys them, his expression lifeless. He stops to measure my reaction every so often.

We destroy eighty-two tapes dating from 1986 to now, and I wonder why someone with such a great memory would need to record such acts.

With the last tape, I'm relieved those girls are free from having their last moments replayed. Still, I cry. The tape he took of himself assaulting me when he took me to the woods to kill me, and the two of our first meeting in Enchanted Land when I was five, are nowhere to be found. I'm not sure if that's worse or not. On the one hand, he didn't think of me like the rest of his victims—a toy to film and throw away. But on the other hand, he said I was his favorite, and that's horrible too.

When he crawls next to me and reaches to clear my face of tears, I stand and tear through the boxes in hopes of finding the missing tapes.

I'm unsure of how I feel when I find the three tapes in a green velvet sack at the bottom of a box of books. My legs are jelly, and I lean back against the entertainment center to keep upright. I pick the rape tape out of the bag and throw it against the carpet, following it to my knees as I shout and smash it with my fists until the case is in shards and the plastic windows protecting the wheels and tape shatter too.

I fall forward onto my hands to catch my breath, my legs numb beneath me.

He sits beside me, draping my hair over my shoulder and tucking it behind my ear. Denendrius rubs my back and asks me something. I merely shake, hands aching as I reach around for the Enchanted Land tapes. When I find the velvet sack, I dump the cassette tapes out, setting them on the bit of carpet I hang over. Running my fingers over the cases, I can't bring myself to wreck them.

If they don't exist, there's no evidence it happened. Denendrius can't remember—might never—and I could trick myself into believing I made it all up since I can't remember it either.

I let a hopeless exhale out and slide them back in the sack, lifting my head to the side to look at Denendrius. His anxious eyes meet mine, and I decide it wouldn't be the worst thing to have extra reminders around of how he truly was if this is how he's going to act.

He pulls me to my feet before snatching Rayonne's spare

lighter from the counter. Denendrius then sweeps the mangled mess of tiny video cassette tapes into the box.

While I watch him scramble to make me feel better, I grab the video camera and jam in the tape I set aside of a sixteen-year-old girl named Claire from 1989 in to show him afterward. I don't want to play it, but he needs to know. He needs to know why I'm so angry, how evil a person he's been, and that there's a good reason so many vampires want to kill him. And if he truly is sorry, he needs to know what all for.

Denendrius grabs my free hand and guides me toward the bathroom, stopping to throw my bottle of whiskey in the box. He throws the shower curtain back and removes the bottle. He dumps the tapes into the tub, the plastic clattering against the bottom. Then he pours whiskey over them, tears a small piece of the box and lights it before throwing it into the tub.

The flames engulf the tapes, melting the film in a hungry blaze of orange and red.

It only takes a few moments for the black smoke to billow, so I lean over and turn the shower on, the fire dying. Black ash and alcohol rush toward the drain. The evidence, the horror, washes away with it.

Either the crying or the nauseous smell of burning plastic induces a headache. I turn the fan on, thankful the smoke detector is missing from the apartment and that nobody will suspect anything with the lingering smell of the last fire.

When Denendrius tries to embrace me, I shove the camcorder against his stomach to stop him. His lips form a line and he looks down at it. I nod toward the door for him to follow to the living room, needing to escape the smoky chemical smell around us.

We pile on the couch, and I turn the camcorder on. A blue screen greets me. My nausea is instantaneous. I spin the tiny screen around so he can see, hit play, and hand it to him. The familiar sound of his sickly-sweet voice emanating from the camcorder sends a sharp pain through my chest and I succumb to tears again.

I cover my ears when Denendrius torments Claire, yet I can still hear the sounds he makes and her strangled screaming no matter how tightly I hold my palms to the sides of my head.

The minutes feel like hours . . . though maybe they really are. When there's no sound other than the noise of the camcorder being touched and moved, I clear my eyes of tears enough to study Denendrius's face.

The despairing look in his wide eyes makes my heart plummet. His juddering hand drops the camcorder in my lap, and I don't have time to shield my eyes from the image on-screen.

A brown-haired girl lies naked on the concrete of an unfinished basement lit by construction lamps, her wrists in paint-speckled silver chains twisted with wires leading to a car battery. Bite marks cover her tanned skin—more than fangs—from jaw to calf, and her throat and eyes are so red there's no way she's still alive.

He makes a gasping noise, like he hasn't breathed since I handed him the camcorder, and his eyes twitch in a way that makes me think this is all a surprise to him.

I'm not sure what reaction I was expecting from him. Not this. Not silence that makes the hair stand on my arms and makes me sweat like I'm sick. Maybe I was expecting him to act like himself. Make excuses or brush it off like it's my fault for playing it, showing him, and expecting him to care, not look revolted to his core.

I guess he did lie a lot about the things he did when he was human.

"Denendrius?" I ask carefully.

He staggers off the couch and stumbles away. I squeeze my eyes shut when I hear him dry-heaving in the bathroom.

It takes a few moments to stop myself from floating out of

my body long enough to stand. My knees ache, and I hang onto the wall as I feel my way down the hallway.

Denendrius stands facing the tub of burned tapes, taking sips of my whiskey as he stares down at them, his other arm atop his head. I can't feel the linoleum floor under my bare feet as I watch him from the doorway, completely unsure of what to do now.

"I'm sorry," I whisper. "I shouldn't have shown you that."

I've fucked everything up again now, haven't I?

I always find a way to fuck everything up.

"Denendrius?"

He twists, and I yelp as he shoves me backward into the hallway. I catch myself on the pulled-out washing machine as he slams the door in my face.

My breaths shorten. There's a tightness in my skin and brain, and it feels like bugs are crawling on me. My voice comes out too high. "Denendrius?" I try the knob, but it's locked. "Denendrius? What are you doing?"

The silence on the other side makes me grit my teeth, and I slam my palm against the door. "Please! You need to open up. Denendrius . . ." I shove the heels of my hands into my temples. "*Fuck!*"

I'm dizzy with panic as I rip through the apartment, hunting for something small and long enough to shove in the knob's pinhole. I consider breaking the door down, but I don't have the strength, and I'm not sure we can fix it again after the last time Denendrius snapped the knob to get in after me.

After too many minutes of no sound other than my sobbing and incoherent mumbling, I find a well-used lock-picking kit in the cabinet above the fridge. I wipe at my tear-drenched face as I pull out a tool with a long end while approaching the door.

"Denendrius?" I sniffle and insert the tool into the lock. The door unlocks, and I shove it open.

He sits against the wall on the floor, the bottle of alcohol safe on the counter. There are no tears in his tormented eyes when he looks up at me, which would be far more comforting than his quiet calmness. I'd feel much better if he were shaking and sobbing.

I squat down in front of him, shaky from my fear of him. "Denendrius." When his hands leap up and hold my face, I wince. "Please."

His eyes bore into mine. "You?"

My brows lower. "Me?"

One hand moves from my face, and I gasp and fall back on my rear when he reaches for the waist of my pants.

"You?" he repeats.

I push his hand away, even though it's already retreating. "Did you . . .?" *Rape me?* "Yes."

There's no change to his expression, though his eyes wander over my face and body.

Does he remember and is thinking about it? Or is he trying to fathom the truth?

Unsure what else to do other than gather up the broken pieces of tonight and sweep them away, I turn to the tub and start scooping the mess back into the box with shaky hands. Denendrius nudges me aside and cleans it up instead.

I tell myself I got my answers. He's different . . . somehow. He doesn't remember. Part of me feels a little better knowing that he might not be as big a threat right now. The other part of me feels worse.

We risk the night to throw the box into the dumpster outside in the parking lot.

Burning them, throwing the mangled pieces away . . . it doesn't give me any solace. I feel more emotionally stretched than before. And even though I know it's impossible, I still fear someone will find them and watch. There's not a place in the world I can think of where it would make me feel better to hide them. Now my name will be in a burned mess with a bunch of other girls, lost in a landfill.

Back in the apartment, I realize I've forgotten a tape when I find the camcorder left on the couch. Denendrius is shushing my low cries before I even realize they've started, pulling the tape from my clenched hand. He unwinds the tape and separates it from the plastic before throwing them both into an empty takeout container in the garbage.

When he comes back to the living room, he demands to know what's on the other two tapes.

Wanting nothing more than to lie down, I haul the Enchanted Land tapes and camcorder to the bedroom with Denendrius in tow.

I build a blanket nest around me as Denendrius crawls to my side, a nervousness surrounding him, like I might scream and kick him out of the bed.

We sit against the headboard, pillows protecting our backs from the metal bars. The only sound between us is the grinding of the camcorder as the tape plays. A blue screen appears, *play* blinking in white block letters before my little smiling face snaps into the frame.

"*Hi.*" The sound of my youthful voice is eerie, like a part of me wondered if the tape would be blank if I played it again. "That's me—Marianna." I point to my younger self.

"You?" he verifies.

I only nod.

"*Now you say hi, Den.*"

When Denendrius waves on film, he shifts in discomfort beside me.

By the end of the tape, I'm numb and don't even have the will to play the second. I shove the camera in the bedside drawer and nestle down into the sheets to stare at the ceiling.

"Now you know there's nothing heinous on that one too." My tone is listless.

Denendrius shifts down onto his side and watches me, head propped up by his hand.

I release a purposefully loud exhale. "I'm sure you have more questions than you can keep track of now."

He flops on his back, eyes locked on the ceiling.

I'm tense as I ask, "Does it seem like you? The man in the videos. Or does it feel like somebody body-snatched you?"

Denendrius doesn't look at me.

"What happened to you?" I whisper, wishing he could spontaneously speak English and answer all *my* questions. "If you didn't get killed while attacking some girl, what happened? Why did Mariana's dad kill you? If you weren't as evil as you were as a vampire, what happened? How can you go from not thinking a single thing was wrong with what you were doing to being surprised that you did it?"

There are no sudden answers like I need, only more *silence*.

I watch his face in the bit of light that spills in from the hallway. He doesn't blink for minutes at a time, his breathing so shallow I have to focus on his chest to make sure he hasn't died from shock in front of me.

I notice the stubble appearing on his jawline and reach out to touch it, the normalcy—the humanness of it—making my hand shake. It pricks the pads of my fingers when I run them over it, saying, "That shouldn't be so strange . . ."

He turns his head away from my touch. "No."

Swallowing, I clutch my hands at my chest.

"Are you okay?" I murmur after more painful minutes. What a stupid question. He isn't, but he *should* be. Vampire Denendrius would be. He would have laughed in my face for thinking that showing him those tapes would do anything.

I shed the rest of my tears until I'm light enough to float into dreamland, Denendrius stone-still beside me.

Soon, the sound of rushing water draws me closer to consciousness, seeping into my dreams and washing the sense of them away. I'm vaguely aware of the cool air against my back from the withdrawn blanket, the space beside me empty. The heavy stream of water remains at the back of my mind until it drones on for far too long and yanks me awake.

I know something is gravely wrong the moment my eyes snap open, and a surge of dread rips through me.

I'm sliding into the bathroom in only a few steps, and my heart stops. Denendrius sits in his boxers in the filling tub, holding the knife I gave Jenna vertical against his wrist.

"No!" I shriek.

At the sound of my voice, he tilts his head back a bit, and the knife jumps to his jugular.

Did he choose my knife because it's familiar to him, or was it pure coincidence?

"Stop!" I roar, anger crawling out from the deepest parts of me.

His hand freezes and he swallows against the blade, his even gaze pinned to the wall in front of him.

Rushing to him, I slip on his shirt and land on my knees at the side of the tub. "Stop," I snarl. "You're *not* killing yourself over this, you *coward*."

His hand twitches when I wrap both of mine around his wrist. He doesn't look at me, doesn't acknowledge me aside from refusing to submit to my attempts to pull the blade from his flesh. A bead of red swells under the metal when the slight movement from our fight for control nicks him.

"Stop it!" I cry. "You're going to be a man and deal with this. If everyone else has to deal with your shit, what makes you think you get to escape it? If you take your life, you're taking mine along with it. I'm not losing everything because you've suddenly realized this is all too much for you to handle!"

I'll be damned if he kills himself. It'll be over for me. How angry will Viorel be if he loses Denendrius? If Denendrius takes himself out before he gets to punish him? If he's been looking for him for so long, clearly he won't be happy if he doesn't get him. I'll pay with my life, won't I? Will Rayonne suffer too for taking Denendrius from Agatha and for creating a situation in which things could spiral out of control?

"Please," I sob. "You can't do this."

I try to pull his hand away again, but he's far too strong, even human.

Out of ideas, I resort to the only thing I can think of. I forcefully turn his face and shove my lips against his.

He exhales against my mouth, and I hear the knife clatter against the linoleum floor beside me as he turns and leans closer. I hook my arm around the back of his neck and lure him from the tub.

What does he think of my lips on his? That I love him and don't want him to die? That I'm blaming it all on his vampirism and not him? Does he think I've forgiven him?

Whatever his thoughts, he exits the tub with a flood of water. I lose my balance and fall backward, sprawled out with Denendrius barely catching himself as he slips in the water and almost crushes me beneath him.

I hold him tightly as I work my mouth against his, feeling the knife handle against my foot and kicking it further away.

He breaks away from my lips and stares down at me with his watery brown eyes, one hand lost in my hair. "I am sorry," he cries, the words twisted up in his accent.

I pull my lips into my mouth and close my eyes, tears forming in the corners. How strange those words are coming from him.

"You will be," I whisper, a fiery ache slicing through my chest and forcing a strangled breath from me. "*Oh, you will be.*"

XVII

When we're done cleaning up the water from the floor, I think of sending Rayonne a text to tell her what happened, but there's one from her popping up on my phone before I decide against it.

> **Rayonne: Staying until sunrise with Ziggy. Safer that way.**

I shoot her a text back.

> **Marianna: Cool. What did vamp want to talk to u about?**

Another text pops back up on my phone as Denendrius pours himself a glass of wine. His gaze avoids mine as soon as our eyes glimpse one another.

**Rayonne: No idea. He left before I got
there.**

"Oh, great. That can't be a good sign," I mutter to myself.

She sends me another text before I have the chance to respond.

Rayonne: See you in the morning.

I sigh and bring the phone into the room with me, dropping it onto the nightstand before jumping facefirst into the bed.

"Marianna." Denendrius clears his throat.

I roll over and sit up. "What?"

Cup in hand, he motions to himself and the bed, a line on his forehead.

"Are you asking if I'm going to object to you sleeping in here or something?" I grunt. "Whatever. Come."

Denendrius wanders over and slowly crawls onto the bed while studying my face. He rests near the edge like he doesn't want to come any closer or lie down. I'm not even sure if I should be tired anymore now, but I feel like I could sleep for weeks.

"You still want to die, don't you?" I peek at him.

He doesn't even look down at me when I talk. Is he mad I stopped him?

"Now you know what it feels like to be saved when you don't want to be." My sardonic smirk falls short, twisting into a frown. He kept me alive to wreck my life and punish me, so I suppose it's fair to return to favor.

Sighing, he scoots down on the bed to his stomach and leans his head on his folded arms atop the pillow. He stares up at me from under his lashes.

We pass through unchanging minutes until he reaches up and pushes the hair from my face and brushes his warm fingertips under my sore eyes to catch leftover tears. "Marianna," is all he says.

"I wish you had let me overdose," I admit flatly. "And that's not even because I know it would've saved me from you and all of *this*. You taking my life away from me made me realize how far I was going to waste it. I realized what I wanted the moment I knew I'd never, ever be able to have it. But at least then I had an idea of where I was headed, even if what was waiting for me wasn't great." Tears collect on my bottom lashes again.

The castle sounds like it could be a good place. Somewhere I might figure out a new life. But the more I think about it, the more I realize I don't want a new life anymore. I want to fix my old one. I want to stay with Carol and see my friends, change the way my teachers and everyone sees me.

I don't want to be known as the girl who lived a shit life before getting murdered by her boyfriend.

I wince when he hoists himself up on his elbow and kisses a stray tear away. "I am sorry," he murmurs as he nuzzles his face into the side of mine, like he thinks those words can fix everything.

Not even his begging, his bloodcurdling shrieks of pain when he's tortured, will make up for it. I know that, even now. Nothing will ever make it okay, but at least he'll pay. At least revenge will make me feel better.

My phone buzzes on the nightstand, the sound sending a jolt through me. Wondering what Rayonne wants now, I twist my arm to pick it up and open it to a text message from an unfamiliar number.

Unknown: It's Mr. Henderson. I'm calling you.

Mr. Derek, my brain corrects, and if tears didn't soak my face, I might actually snicker to myself.

His call comes through, and I'm glad he gave me a heads-up or the unfamiliar number flashing across the screen might have stopped me from answering the call. Even though I know who it is, my palms sweat and my heart skips.

I clear my throat and answer it, but he can probably still tell I was crying. "You're calling me in the middle of the night. Does that mean you believe me?"

An elevator dings in my ear before he says, "Something like that. I believe *something*, but I need more proof."

I roll my eyes. "What more proof do you need? And what else has changed your mind if it wasn't *meeting* him and seeing the crap I brought in?"

"A strange—well, threatening—phone call. I studied in Italy years ago, so I used some of my connections there to see if I could fact-check anything you were telling me. Had some friends make some more inquiring calls on my behalf too. No information connected to his name, until I got a call from a man a few minutes ago telling me that if I liked my life, I should stop poking around things that don't concern me."

My brows stitch together. "That's . . . definitely strange." Who would want Mr. Derek to stop asking questions about Denendrius? Why? "Any hints as to what he meant? Aside from likely murdering you, of course."

"No, but he asked why I was looking for information and if I knew where he was."

My eyes pop wide. "And what did you tell him?"

"I had a bad feeling, so I told him I didn't know where he was, not even really *who* he was. I lied, said I found his name in an old document and was curious."

Thank God. "Okay, good. Are you going to heed his warning?"

"Absolutely not. I'll hear you out."

I sit, relief rushing through me. After Denendrius trying to kill himself—which I feel has more to do with everything that has happened since he woke up, and not just the tapes—it would be good to have him do some translations for us so we can smooth things over. With my meddling or not, it's likely he'll stumble into more disturbing information, and maybe next time we won't be able to deal with it on our own. "Okay. I still need those papers translated."

"Should I come by after school?" he asks.

"How about before, seeing as you're awake? I don't see myself sleeping, so anytime between now and then works for me. But sooner is better than later. We're kind of in a time-sensitive situation."

"I don't think I can comfortably sleep after that phone call anyway, so now works," he says.

"Sounds good," I say before rattling off the apartment address and hanging up.

Denendrius and I lie in bed for what feels like hours, fully awake but silent, as I listen carefully for a knock at the door. I consider that I should have warned Mr. Derek about the possibility of lurking vampires. But then I'd have to explain all that to him and hope he actually believes me.

I groan and crawl out of bed for a drink, managing a full breath when there's a hesitant knock at the door. When I open it, Mr. Derek flinches like he was expecting Denendrius.

His "hello" is strained as he hauls in a milk crate full of books and papers past me, and my jaw slackens when a mane of red hair appears around the corner as I'm about to shut the door.

I do a double take. "Oh, what the hell. Carol, what are you doing here?"

She's carrying another crate, which she grips tighter—her step faltering as she enters—when Denendrius emerges from the bedroom. She swallows and looks back at me. "Derek called me again, and we filled each other in on everything we know about *this* so far. He told me you reached out to him and asked if I wanted to come along to see where you've been staying . . ." She looks around with wary scrutiny. "This place isn't very welcoming."

I shrug, not sure if it's because it's lower class than what she's used to, or if it's because of the bareness of the place. "You shouldn't have come. You should have stayed at home where it's safe."

She scoffs, nose wrinkling at the lingering smoke when she inhales sharply. "Safe is a stretch. Besides, I won't sit in that big house all alone while my sister's daughter is fighting vampires."

I lean my head back and sigh. "All right. But you realize how dangerous this is—"

"We know," they both say.

They exchange a look and then assess the apartment.

I hold my hand up, her words fully entering my system as I look at Mr. Derek. "Wait, she brought up vampires, and you didn't bat an eye. What's going on?"

"I've had a couple hours to process. I still am."

Carol lifts her chin, smiles, and begins planning with my teacher. "If we move the table between the living room and dining area, that gives us another spot for one of the blow-up mattresses . . ."

"We can fit another person on the couch . . ." Mr. Derek turns to me. "Where are you and Denendrius sleeping?"

I cross my arms. "In the bedroom."

Carol shakes her head like that's completely unacceptable. "You can move to the couch—"

"Rayonne is sleeping there," I snap.

"Well, we can figure out something temporary. Once we're at my place, there's more than enough beds and rooms for everyone to sleep comfortably *alone*," she adds.

"Hold on!" How are they going to explain to Denendrius why his "wife" can't sleep in the same bed as him in his house? That they plan on making him stay in a different house too?

This is a fight that nobody but Denendrius will win. "You guys aren't coming in here and calling the shots."

Carol crosses her arms. "I'm your foster parent, Marianna—your aunt. It's my job to make sure you—"

I wave my hands in front of me. "Nope! Absolutely not. You guys have hardly any idea what's going on. I know I'm only seventeen, but I'm kind of dealing with some stuff that's out of your realm."

"Carol is trying to look out for you," Derek interjects. "I agree with her."

My nostrils flare. "Seriously? Mr. Derek—"

He holds his hand up. "Okay, if you're going to call me that, I'd much rather you call me Derek. We've already crossed the student-teacher line here."

"Really? Okay, *Derek*." I smirk. "You guys are still trying to take over. Rayonne and I have everything under control. I only need you for translations and stuff. And, *Carol*, you can stay, fine, but this isn't the time to parent me!" They'll get us all killed. I jab a finger at Derek. "*You just learned that vampires exist. And, Carol, I left a lot of important shit out when I was talking to you.*"

When Denendrius wanders up to my side, eyeing the three of us as we bicker, they both shut up. Denendrius spits out something that sounds like a warning to them.

Carol tenses. "All right, Marianna."

"Um, I have to run back to the SUV. I brought him a couple things," Derek says. "Hopefully they'll smooth things over between me and him."

I purse my lips. "As far as I know, he doesn't actually remember being mad at you for anything."

He half-shrugs. "I-I know, but in case he does. I don't want him to"—he makes finger quotes—"fillet me like a fish."

I titter in disbelief. "Is that how he threatened you?"

"Yes. I considered calling the police, but I assumed that

would make things harder on you since they probably wouldn't do anything for me."

"Good call." I bite down on my cheek. He probably would've died for that.

As Derek steps out, Carol asks, "You said you had a safe place to go. Where is that?"

My eyes flicker to Denendrius, and I swallow. "He's remembering English," I tell her. "I don't know how much he understands compared to the bit he can speak again."

She gives me an understanding nod, a little grimace flickering through her soft features.

We stand awkwardly in silence until Denendrius asks me something, motioning to her and the door.

I rub the back of my neck, not sure what he's going on about, but I suspect he's wondering about Derek and Carol.

I introduce Carol the best I can, simply telling him she's family, and as Derek comes back in, I tell him he's my teacher. I know those words were in the books we got him, but whether or not he remembers is another thing. Regardless, he seems to understand . . . at least he relaxes.

"What did you bring him?" I ask.

He holds a large brown paper bag in hands, and I try to peer into it as he walks in. Two identical long and flat boxes are under his arms and a large canvas bag is slung over his shoulder.

"Wine, and these . . ." He sets everything on the counter before focusing his attention on the boxes. "Denendrius." He smiles up at him and motions to the boxes.

Denendrius takes a curious step closer, and we watch as he opens the first box. Inside, resting on bubble wrap, is a double-edged steel sword with a triangular tip and wooden handle with decorative carvings.

I can't read Denendrius's expression when he steps forward

and picks it up. The sight is equally terrifying and cool. He runs his finger across the blade. "Hm."

"It's a gladius." Derek unwraps a matching one from the next box. "I got them—and a few other ancient weapons—back when I was studying abroad. They're replicas, though they've been sharpened. He could probably do some serious damage with them. I was going to hang them above my fireplace, but the wife wasn't too fond of that idea."

My brow furrows. "How does your wife feel about you being here? What did you tell her?"

He blows air between his lips and hands the second sword to Denendrius. "Ex," he corrects himself.

"Oh—"

Before I can ask any more personal questions, he asks, "Do you know when he was born?"

"Um, 58 AD in the city of Rome. He told me he was close to retiring when he became a vampire."

"How old was he when he was turned?" Derek asks, doing a poor job of hiding the judgment on his face.

"Twenty-seven."

He nods like what I've said makes sense to him.

"Are we sure this is a great idea?" I watch Denendrius test the weight of the swords. His flat expression makes me wonder what the chances are he'll try to kill himself—or one of us—again. I suppose nothing is stopping him from taking us out with the rest of the weapons, though he's not highly skilled with those.

"Probably not, honestly." Derek's chuckle is strained as he pushes the sleeves of his maroon sweater to his elbows. "But if he really was a gladiator, I was hoping he could show me some things. We don't exactly have recorded fights."

"You sound like you're believing all this stuff about him now," I note.

He shrugs. "Between everything you showed me, meeting

him again, that phone call, and Carol's word, it's kind of hard to ignore."

I grin triumphantly and turn to Carol, asking, "How hard was it to convince him of vampires?"

He answers instead as her lips part. "Well, if what you were saying was true, vampirism made more sense than actual time travel."

I purse my lips. "Since you're bringing in beds and talking about us going to Carol's house, what does that mean? How much help are you anticipating giving?"

His cheek stretches as his lips twist to the side. "Were you only looking for help with a couple of translations?"

I perk up. "Why, are you offering more than that?"

"I was hoping, since I'm involved in this now, that I'll get as much as I can out of it. If you have an *actual Roman* here, I want some good information from him."

"The vampire part of this doesn't terrify you?" I squint at him.

He rubs the back of his head, fingers tangling in his chestnut hair. "I can't say it doesn't, but this is a crazy opportunity."

The chaos I've been forced into is an "opportunity" to him? My chin lifts, and I scowl. "All right. Thanks for your help then."

Derek cringes. "That came out wrong. I'm here to help you, of course. That's the most important thing, but it's not every day you learn about vampires and get to speak to an ancient person."

"I get it," I grumble.

Denendrius rests the swords back in their boxes and gives Derek a pat on his shoulder, though his face remains solemn. Derek pulls away a bit at his touch but gives Denendrius a convincing smile.

I'm entranced as my gaze shifts back to the swords in their

open boxes. Only having experience with guns and knives, my fingers itch to try them.

"Were there girl gladiators?" I ask Derek as I step forward and gingerly lift a gladius from the box. It's not nearly as heavy as I expected—perhaps a few pounds—and if Derek wasn't standing in front of me, I'd take a test jab at the air.

"It was uncommon, but yes." He takes a step to the side as I shift into a fighting stance and clench the handle.

My heart thumps and I'm giddy at how powerful I feel with it in my hand. I picture myself swinging it around. "Sick—"

As I'm about to reach for the second sword, Denendrius tut-tuts me and gently takes the gladius from my hand and places it back in the box. I push out a frustrated growl, but don't protest as I give them a longing stare.

Jerk.

"So, is he going to get all up in arms if I set up beds and move a few things?" Derek shrugs off the large canvas bag.

Denendrius is unpacking bottles of wine from the bag as I say, "Go ahead. He doesn't really know what's going on, so I think he's going with the flow for now."

Once Carol and Derek start setting up a blow-up mattress each—Derek's near the table, and Carol's between the couch and TV—Denendrius focuses on Derek with an unreadable expression as Carol and him take turns with the foot pump. Derek keeps glancing at him over his shoulder as he inflates it, like he thinks Denendrius is going to rip his spine right out of his back the minute he looks away.

"You okay?" I ask Denendrius, bumping my shoulder into his bicep as I pace to his side.

His eyelids flutter as he pulls his attention away from Derek and to me, and I realize he wasn't watching my teacher at all. What thought was he lost in?

Denendrius mumbles something to me before giving me a quick kiss and disappearing into the bedroom. I'm uncertain about him going in there alone. But when the bed squeaks from behind the closed door, I assume he's ready to crash after everything that happened tonight.

I send a quick text to Rayonne to let her know that Carol and Derek are here. Once they make their beds after another trip back to the SUV for bedding and personal items, I ask, "Are you going to bed?"

Derek straightens a green-and-yellow tartan blanket over his twin-sized blow-up mattress. "I could try, but I don't think I'll be able to. Is he?"

I wrap my arms around myself. "Yeah. Want to translate some stuff for me, then?"

Still crouched, he shuffles to a backpack he brought in, pulls a thick laptop out of it and rises to set it up on the table. "Sure."

Carol and I sit with him at the table as Derek reads Denendrius's block of words and dives headfirst into translation, mumbling to himself the entire time as he reads it over.

"I'm going with you, Marianna," Carol says after about forty minutes, voice low. There's no room for discussion in her tone. "Wherever that is. I'm not losing touch with you again."

"You have no idea what that really means," I argue.

Carol's smile is shaky. "You're probably right, but I still mean it."

"I don't even know if *I'm* allowed to go. Rayonne has her assumptions, but there's nothing concrete." I swallow.

I want so badly to believe I'll be able to go there—that it's the same place Alaire and Edmond were talking about too— but my hope for that shrinks every time I give it more thought. Despite Rayonne acting in my favor so far, I have no reason to trust her word.

"Then what are you planning if you can't?" she asks, a crease between her red brows.

My heart races and my throat dries. "I don't know. I'll figure it out when I get there. What is your plan? Because I've got my doubts that the vampire king is going to open his door for three randoms. Me alone is a long shot."

"I haven't thought that far ahead," Carol says. "I am still hoping you'll agree to move away."

I pick at my lips. "What about you, Derek? What's your plan?"

Derek pauses from the paper he's working on, pen in hand, to look up and say, "I don't know. I'm still processing all of *this*."

I huff and lean back in the metal chair. "Fair. How's the translation going, anyway?"

"Slowly." He sighs and squints at something on his laptop screen. "I'm not an expert at this, understand. It's been a handful of years. And this isn't like translating the stuff I did in college. There are some mistakes in his writing, never mind that it's frantic and in certain areas I'm not completely sure what he's trying to say. I'm spending a lot of time piecing things together."

"Can't you two talk, then?" I ask. "Wouldn't that be easier than picking through all that?"

He stares at me and slowly shakes his head. "No, Marianna. We can make educated guesses about how Latin sounds, but considering it's a dead language, we don't know exactly. Never mind the fact there would be different dialects in different areas. Take English, for example. Pronunciation is essentially the same whether you're Australian or Texan, but the way words sound—the accents—make an enormous difference if you don't speak the language. Never mind slang and the difference between Vulgar Latin and Classical Latin. I might pick a word out here and there, but it would be much easier to exchange writings back and forth than try to *hear* the words he's saying."

I purse my lips. "Rayonne and I picked out a few words he said . . . I think."

He nods and scribbles something down. "I'm sure we could pick a few out, but this is much faster. And there's less opportunity for him to get frustrated."

I grimace. "Yeah, good point."

He blows out a breath between pinched lips and sets his pencil down. "I think I've got the gist though. You tell me if this makes sense . . ."

Carol and I listen closely as he reads the translation he's constructed in English. From what Denendrius wrote, he was desperate to know the basics: where we are, what year it is, how he got here and why.

Denendrius wrote down the things he knows, and I can't breathe the entire time Derek tells me the beginning of Denendrius's story. It's a version I've never heard before.

Mariana's mother, Marciana, came to him for help one day. Her husband, Marianus, returned from a long trip as a monster and was hiding in the back of their butcher shop, refusing to come out. He was terrifying Mariana, and Marciana wanted Denendrius to help convince him to see a physician. She thought his size and gladiator status would make him think twice about using his new aggression, and that perhaps Denendrius might help her pay for better care if it meant she and Mariana wouldn't slip further into poverty without Marianus being able to help them. Denendrius agreed, worried about their safety if his sickness was causing aggression.

Marianus ripped into Denendrius's neck the moment he got too close.

The only thing he remembers after is hallucinations, and waking up hours from home in dense trees, not knowing what happened or fully understanding the reason he felt both so awful and refreshed. He drank every animal that crossed his path and somehow kept control the entire trip home for help. Until his sister, Adelia, came and surprised him with a hug and kiss as he scrambled in the front door. He sank his fangs into her neck, then lunged on his mother, who rushed to the sound of Adelia's shriek.

He slaughtered thirty-seven people in his villa by the end. All of his sisters, his mother, the slaves . . . plus everyone his father had over for a dinner party.

After fleeing Rome and hiding in a wolf den when the sun scorched him, he woke up here.

Denendrius wrote that he can still remember what each of them tasted like, and that he feels sick at the thought that he enjoyed his sister's blood, that he feels like he's had a bad spirit in him.

"He also said he feels like he's going to snap from the weight of all this," Derek reads before blowing out a breath. "Which is not great to hear."

I glance back toward the bedroom door. *He already did.*

My chest hurts, my fingers sore from twisting them in my lap. I grapple with Denendrius's story, and it's clear from Carol's dumbstruck expression that she does too. But it's the truth this time. I can feel it in my gut. He wouldn't remember his lies or why he fabricated them.

"What should I tell him?" Derek asks.

"What he wants to know." I rub the goose bumps on my arms. "He'll be fine as long as he has answers." *I hope.*

I direct Derek's translation as he painstakingly writes it, ensuring he doesn't tell Denendrius sensitive details.

My stomach burns as I retreat to the bedroom for the rest of the night, much to Carol and Derek's disapproval, and find an unfamiliar man asleep in bed.

"Dirty liar," I hiss as I crawl in beside him. "Can't believe a word out of your dirty lying mouth."

I curl my fists up so tightly that pain shoots up my forearms, wanting him to be back to his vampire self for a few seconds only so I can hammer them into his skull and ask him what gives. When I slam my head down on the pillow, his eyes pop open.

"You know, you didn't have to lie to seem like an asshole. It was already clear you were without you twisting the truth. Why would you do that?"

He doesn't answer. His tired eyes struggle to stay open, and he loses the fight. I know the answer anyway, that he lied to me about why he was turned so I wouldn't see any kindness in him, so I wouldn't have anything to exploit. Still, I can't help but wonder if he convinced himself his lies were true. Was it easier —did it alleviate some guilt—to rewrite his history than think about how he died trying to help someone else, than to think he heartlessly murdered his entire family? Is his first story— him trying to turn them—what he wishes had happened? He wanted us to have a family together, so clearly such a thing mattered to him to some degree.

His lids lift again. "Mad?" he whispers.

"No." I bite down on my bottom lip, but all my anger drips out of me. I realize I'm not mad at *him*. I'm mad at who he used to be, at what he became after this.

His smile is faint.

That thought sends a cold riptide through me. It's disorienting and I have to hang on to my own mind for a minute.

Who he used to be.

How much is left of the monster I knew? Different—yet same—body. Different memories . . . different touch . . .

I shiver. When we turn him in, what will he think if he still doesn't remember? He's going to think the worst of us, that we betrayed him. I can see the look on his face now. Will he even understand why they're torturing him?

Squeezing my eyes shut, I tell myself it doesn't matter if he remembers or not. It doesn't matter if he once beat me with cold hands when his are now warm. It doesn't matter that he's sick over his own deeds.

It can't matter.

I unload a heavy breath and close my eyes.

Denendrius brushes his lips over mine. Lids snapping open, I stare at his smooth expression. When I don't say or do anything to protest, he puts his hand on my face and tucks my bottom lip between his, his kisses like desperate strokes through the ocean, like he's trying to find land before he drowns.

I kiss him back, the taste of wine on his hot breath tugging me along. My arm circles his neck, and maybe I hang on because I'm self-destructive, or because it's easier than fighting him. It's safer. Maybe I hang on—while his wet lips shape mine with his tongue teasing my top lip—because for once it isn't terrifying.

Maybe it's because I like it. Because it reminds me a little of that first time we kissed before he ruined everything.

My admission eats me alive and sends ice water through my veins.

Denendrius shudders and holds my face tighter before slipping his hand down my side and squeezing my waist. I fear he'll take things farther than I want, but his kisses trail over my cheek and stop. He nuzzles his face into the side of mine and he lets out a tired breath.

I don't sleep. My heart thunders, and I'm glad he can't hear it anymore.

XVIII

Through all the chaos of my thoughts, I come to one conclusion: I need to get rid of Denendrius *now*. I can't afford to wait for Rayonne's game of vampire telephone to work.

That's the only way I can put an end to these strange feelings and thoughts.

As I grasp at straws for a plan of my own, a jarring thought pops to mind. I didn't see Denendrius kill Alaire with my own eyes, only Edmond. What if he got away? When Denendrius killed his brother, did he abandon me and his plan to capture him to save himself? Maybe Denendrius lied about killing Alaire. He's lied about so much else.

I suppose there's only one way to find out, if Alaire would even be willing to risk responding to me again.

I slip out of bed and tiptoe from the room. The apartment is dark as Carol and Derek sleep, the light of the moon and street-lamps leaking through the slats in the blinds and into the dining area. Reaching the table, I hold my breath as I lift Derek's laptop up, my eyes glued to his sleeping face.

Laptop secure in my hand, I back away to the hallway, then dart to the bathroom, locking the door behind me.

Sitting on the toilet lid, I open Derek's computer and turn it on, feeling lucky when there's no pass code.

After a search, I find Alaire and Edmond's decade-old forum post on a red-and-black nineties webpage of the same supernatural role-playing website that I found last time. Their coded message—how they want to find another user by the name Denendrius in exchange for a reward—is still locked.

I click the weird link at the bottom of the post again. Nothing happens this time. I wait for Derek's computer to freak out about a virus like the one at school did, but it doesn't. I keep my hopes up. Maybe he doesn't have antivirus software.

So I wait, staring at the screen with my heart beating in my throat. I think about how they tracked me down at school last time I contacted them, how Denendrius injured me so Alaire would help me and give him enough time to kill his brother, Edmond.

A pop-up appears on the web page. But it's not a chat box this time, or even Denendrius's wanted write-up.

WE ARE OFFLINE.

Click here to leave a tip.

Tears rush down my cheeks, and I cover my mouth with my sleeve to dampen a frustrated squeal.

Is it offline because he's simply away from the computer? Or because he's dead? Did I merely catch them when they were online last time?

Regardless of my questions, I decide to write him a message in case he's still around to see it. I click and a basic black-and-white text pop-up like the chat box from last time appears.

Hi Alaire. It's Marianna again. I'm sorry that contacting you last time got your brother killed, but if there's any chance you escaped that warehouse and will talk to me, I need your help again. Denendrius is human now, and he remembers nothing from when he was a vampire.

Viorel's men sent a group after him, but Agatha (the group's leader) turned Rayonne back (one of the girls helping her) with the spare vial of the cure against her will, to try to buy themselves extra time to search for Denendrius.

Agatha was going to kill me, and probably Rayonne, to cover up what she did, but we stole Denendrius from her and are trying to get him to Viorel on our own. We haven't been able to contact them. He's acting strange since they turned him back too, and I don't know what to expect from him or how safe he is to be around.

If you're willing to help me, can you get me in touch with Viorel? Rayonne said I can probably come to the castle with her. Do you think I can? You mentioned a safe place for me to go, and Rayonne said you and Edmond have been to the castle. Is that where you were planning on taking me? Or was it somewhere else?

Alaire, please get in contact with me if you made it. I don't know what to do without your help. Denendrius is remembering things, and I'm worried he's going to remember that he was about to be captured.

I write the apartment address and my phone number at the bottom before sending the message off and exiting the pages.

With no other ideas, I carefully return the laptop to the table and crawl back into bed, staring at Denendrius as he winces and grumbles in his sleep.

I wake to a loud thud beside the bed and frantic whining. As I untangle myself from the blankets in the low glow of sunlight,

Denendrius sits on the floor, half rocking and pleading with nobody as his eyes dart back and forth. He runs his hands through his hair and holds his head as he curls toward his knees.

"What's going on?" Derek demands while he, Rayonne—who I didn't even hear come home—and Carol burst into the room and flick the light on.

A tremor overtakes him, and he doesn't seem to notice us. I go to him, kneeling down at his side while I carefully reach out to touch him.

"Denendrius," I whisper. His skin is slick with sweat when I touch his shoulder. "What's wrong?"

His head snaps up, chin trembling as his teary eyes focus on mine. He blinks hard and pulls his hands from his hair to rub at his wrists like they're sore from restraints.

"Marianna—" He chokes on the rest of his sentence.

From behind me, Derek says, "Is he okay? Has he had violent nightmares like that before?"

I rub my eyes. "Yeah. I think he's having another flashback or something—"

"Out!" Denendrius roars, face contorting with fury as he notices them.

My heart skips a beat, and they stumble backward over one another into the hall.

I grab at his hands and clench them. "Hey, hey, it's fine. They're worried."

He thumps his head against the wall like he can knock the horrible images out. Tears trickle past his lashes when he squeezes his eyes closed.

"Did you remember something?" I ask.

He doesn't answer me. He says nothing for the next excruciating thirty minutes as he sits against the wall crying quietly and shaking. I stay next to him the entire time, trying to shush his cries while I continue to grapple with the extremes of his emotions.

I'm almost scared to pose the question again in case he swings back toward anger. "New memories?"

"*Ita*—yes." His eyes open and he wipes them.

"What did you remember?"

He wets his lips and pulls in a trembling breath. "Thirsty."

My heart skips. "Thirsty?" For *blood?*

Pulling his hand out from mine, he motions to the door. "Water."

"Oh—"

Derek is walking in with a glass before I can stand. He hands it to me, and Denendrius chugs it when I give it to him. He holds it back up toward Derek, who takes it before dipping out of the room again.

"Are you okay?" I murmur as I nestle tighter against his side on the floor to comfort him. Denendrius closes his eyes and leans his head on top of mine.

He shivers. "No."

"W-what did you remember?" I wince as I pose the question a third time.

"Sirmium." The name comes out with a shudder.

"Which part of it?" I ask, my tone delicate.

He lifts his head and stares down at me with his brow furrowed.

"Never mind." I sigh and point to the bed as I stand. "Sleep? You've had a . . . long night."

"Sleep," he agrees as I climb on. He struggles to stand. When he gets his legs beneath him properly, he closes the door and falls back into bed.

As soon as the door clicks open, Denendrius spins over and wrinkles his nose at Derek while lifting his brows.

Opening the door all the way to the dresser, he motions for us to keep the door open and says, "Maybe it's best if you don't close it. I think that's safer—"

Denendrius launches off the bed, his face red as he shoos

Derek out and bellows Latin at him. He motions out of the room and broadly at the rest of the apartment before himself. "Mine"—he points at Derek—"*you* sleep."

Derek nods and backs away, hands up in defense. "Okay, I understand. It's your apartment—"

Denendrius slams the door, slumps, then crawls back into bed. I run my hand over his back, feeling responsible for calming him down so he doesn't massacre everyone here.

He lays his head in my lap, one arm hooking around my back.

"Are you okay?" I whisper.

He snivels.

So, no.

As much as I want him to suck it up and go back to sleep, I know what he went through in Sirmium—being tortured for decades for making a mess when he was a newborn—must have been horrific if he's showing outward emotion over it. I probably shouldn't kick him while he's already down. Even if he's a bad person who deserved those bad things . . . which I suppose not even Alaire and Edmond were completely certain of if they thought him torching villages and leaving his victims out in the open was a cry for help. Besides, seeing him act so out of character is enough to pause my spite for the meantime.

I comb my fingers through his soft hair and smooth out the tangles, winding a rogue loose curl around my finger. There's a thousand questions burning my tongue. But they'll all go unanswered unless I can convince him to open up more to let Derek translate.

Denendrius crawls back to his pillow, and I slide my fingers down the length of his back as he moves. I lie beside him and fall asleep while waiting for his eyes to close. It feels like only five minutes have passed when I wake with the sound of midmorning chatter beyond the door.

Derek is at the table with Denendrius, who looks up at me

with bloodshot and heavy-lidded eyes as I exit the room, reaching my arms above my head for a stretch.

"Good"—a yawn interrupts me—"morning." Denendrius merely blinks at me. "You never fell asleep, did you?"

"He's been out here for a couple hours now, sitting here drinking wine, lost in thought."

I slump down in a chair, a spasm of pain from my bruised chest ricocheting through me. "Good thing he dilutes it. I'd hate to deal with him drunk."

Denendrius cocks his head at me, like he understood part of my sentence. It's also possible he's delirious after everything that's happened to him over the past few days. Hopefully, he doesn't deteriorate completely before we can get him to Viorel.

"Why does he do that, anyway? Mix his wine with water," I inquire. "It's weird."

Derek chuckles. "Aside from the social part of it, they mainly used it to purify their water and make it taste better. Their wine was much stronger than it is now—but it still must not be how he likes it since he's still diluting it—so they added water. Plus, everyone drank wine throughout the day, and it was uncouth to drink it straight."

My chin scrunches as I press my lips together. "Hm."

He gives me a tired smile and rubs his hands through his messy heap of short hair. "How're you holding up?"

There's no way to answer that question honestly. "I'm fine."

Rayonne emerges from the balcony, the smell of cigarette smoke wafting in with her and making both Derek and Denendrius wrinkle their noses.

I must have really been tired not to hear her come in this morning.

"Where's Carol?" My eyes rake over the apartment for her.

"She went to grab breakfast for us all," Rayonne says.

"Sweet." Curious, I steal a sip from Denendrius's drink. It's like drinking heavily flavored water. "Are you not going to school today, Derek?"

He rubs his hands down his face. "I called in for a sub today. I've got too much on my mind between this and my personal life."

"What's going on in your personal life?" I prod, sticking my bottom lip out while thinking about when he apologized for his shortness with me while taking my phone in class.

He rakes his fingers through his hair again, pulling in a breath between his teeth. I can tell he's trying to decide if he should tell me or not. "I'm getting a divorce."

"Bummer." I frown. "Why?"

Cringing, he says, "As much as I . . . enjoy . . . teaching you and your classmates, high school was never my intended career. I spent so much time studying overseas for a reason. I wanted to do research and be present on dig sites. But my ex-wife's family is here in Lorimer, and high school teaching was a secure job for us. I've been pushing back lately, especially since she wants to change her career and go back to school."

My face scrunches. "That's pretty unfair. It's your life."

"You're right." He shakes his head like he's trying to clear his thoughts. "I actually shouldn't be telling you this—"

I roll my eyes. "I think we've kind of crossed that line considering you're here, know about vampires and so much of *my* personal life now, and you kind of went above and beyond by joining an alliance with my aunt."

He exhales and leans back in his chair. "I suppose. I take it they won't be seeing you at school again, will they?"

I swallow a lump and clear my throat. "I can't."

I'm expecting some sort of pushback, but all I get in response is, "I can't say I agree with you dropping out, but I understand."

Dropping out. I hadn't thought of it like that before. Wrapping my arms around my stomach, I hunch over. "Did you give Denendrius that translation?"

He nods. "He didn't really say much. I tried to get him to write about what happened last night, but he won't do much more than sit there and get up to refill his cup."

"Oh." I glance up through my lashes at Denendrius, who's watching my face with his exhausted eyes. "All right."

I think Derek's only trying to make me feel better when he says, "I'll be putting in my resignation soon as well. I'm giving my ex-wife the house, but I have half our savings, so I should be secure enough to figure out what to do next."

"You don't think it's suspicious if you go missing at the same time as me?" I mumble.

He balks. "Go missing . . ." His eyes latch onto Rayonne as she wanders to the kitchen and roots around the cupboard with a scowl. "Rayonne . . . I won't have to fake my death, will I?"

She plants her palms on the counter and looks under the cupboard at him. "You might. Or you might *not*—it really depends on how all this goes. But once vampires know you're involved in our world . . . things get blurry."

It hits me what I've done. I've wrecked his life. I wanted some translations, some help, but I didn't think about what all that meant *for him*.

"I'm sorry." I avoid his eyes when they try to connect with mine. "I didn't think about what dragging you into this would do."

He ducks down to meet my eyes, smiling. "It's fine, Marianna. Since when are you so apologetic? I didn't ask for you to be sorry. It was my choice to ignore that warning call. Besides, this is the most excitement I've had in *my life*. I'm sitting across from a Roman gladiator and I have discovered a whole side of the world that I never knew about."

"Okay." I press my lips tightly together and loosen my arms around myself for a proper breath. I check on Denendrius, who looks like he's ready to fall asleep in his chair. He's got a loose grip on his cup when he takes a sip. When I pat his knee to get his attention, he flinches. "Sleep?"

Eyes half-lidded, he grunts and forces them wider while shifting in his chair. "No."

"Hungry?" Derek asks, eyes dropping to the watch on his wrist. "Carol should be back soon."

Denendrius merely stares into his near-empty glass and sighs, and I share the sentiment.

"I'm not even sure if I have an appetite."

I lean back in the chair and slouch, watching Rayonne putter around the kitchen. She finds a little pot in the stove drawer and fills it with water before setting it on the burner.

"Did you ever figure out what that vampire wanted to talk to you about?" I ask her.

She opens a cupboard next to the stove and grabs a tea bag from a fresh box. "I've no idea. He was a Darkling, so he was probably put off."

Derek's eyes flicker between us. "Someone is going to have to explain to me what Darklings are."

She explains the difference between Darklings and Children of Stars to him while she waits for her water to boil. She starts from the basics, how you can tell the difference between the two by their eyes; Darklings' only shift from red to black, while Children of Stars' go from red to their human eye color. After filling him in about everything else, she moves on to Children of Stars' abilities and how everyone thinks Darklings came from them.

I tune out half their conversation, watching Denendrius turn Adelia's bracelet around his wrist as he fidgets with the turquoise beads. A ghost of a smile flashes across his lips when he notices my attention on him.

How close were they? Did they still have a bond despite her being fifteen? From what he told me—unless he also lied about his father being a pervert to make me feel more comfortable about sleeping next to him—he at least protected her from their father in some ways.

Carol returns near the end of their conversation while Rayonne's steeping her tea. The scent of coffee, hot cheese, and eggs covers the stale smell of smoke from both Rayonne and the fire that I continue to catch a whiff of every so often.

She passes breakfast burritos to each of us, easing down in the last open chair. With Derek's laptop, papers, and books, there's no space on the small surface to eat until he clears some of it aside. Even then, Rayonne's stuck alone on the couch until Derek offers her his chair and stands next to the counter.

I scarf down two burritos, my hunger returning instantaneously. Denendrius picks at his food, lip curled as he eats stray pieces of egg, cheese, and bacon as they fall out onto the wrapper while he pokes at it.

"What's wrong with it?" I ask him with a full mouth.

He flicks a piece of tomato to the side of the wrapper.

"That's rude." I lick sour cream from the corners of my lips. "Do you not like tomatoes? You didn't mind the pizza sauce. Give me those."

He stares at me as I take his diced tomatoes and plop them in the opening of my burrito.

Derek takes a sip from his coffee after swallowing a mouthful. "They didn't actually have tomatoes in ancient Rome. Or potatoes, green beans, peppers . . ." He squints in thought for a moment. "I forget what else."

"What did they eat, then?" I take another bite.

"Gladiators supposedly ate a mostly vegetarian diet. Wheat, beans, barley." He takes another sip of coffee.

My chewing slows. "Well, he was rich. Would that make a difference?"

Derek's face widens for a flash of surprise. "Oh, really? Likely, then. Patricians ate a lot of fresh meat and fish, fruits and veggies. The plebeians rarely ate as well. Meat, veggies, and fruit still, but not nearly in the same amount. They would have relied more on bread and porridge to mix with what they had."

Denendrius continues to pick at his food, making me say, "Hmm. Well, he definitely wasn't poor with how picky he's being."

Derek smirks. "Garum was popular with most classes. It was a fish sauce. They mixed fish guts, tiny fish, and salt before leaving it to ferment in the sun."

I swallow my bite of food and fake gag. "That sounds nasty."

Denendrius scowls at me like he understood at least a portion of our exchange.

"I can't say either way. Never tried it. Want to know something grosser?"

Carol and Rayonne both say, "No."

"What?" I ask.

He grimaces while saying, "They used urine as mouthwash, amongst other things. But the ammonia disinfected and whitened teeth."

My food lodges in my throat and I cough until it goes down. *God, and I kissed him?* I haven't seen him do anything freaky like that since he woke up, at least.

Carol and Rayonne both complain about how they're trying to eat, which makes me snicker.

"Okay, okay." Derek chuckles as he takes another bite. "No more gross historical facts, I'm sorry."

Denendrius wobbles when he stands. I watch his heavy steps as he clears his throat and refills his cup in the kitchen. He chugs three full glasses before leaning against the counter. A groan rolls in the back of his throat.

"Shit." I drop my burrito and hop to my feet. "He's going to be sick again."

"Again?" Derek asks.

I help Denendrius to the bathroom, where he's reduced to

his knees in front of the toilet to retch. His arms shake as he grips the edge of the toilet seat.

Derek leans in the doorway, coffee in hand. "Is he okay?"

"I don't know," I admit. There wasn't anything about this meal that should be hard on his stomach. "He's been puking after eating sometimes."

"I'm thinking maybe it has nothing to do with the food he's eating," Rayonne chimes in as she slips past Derek to get into the bathroom.

Denendrius shivers and leans his arm across the bowl to rest his head.

I check my phone to see if I missed any messages or calls from Alaire and sigh in disappointment. "What if he's sick or something? I've heard about some horrible stuff happening to people who've been turned back."

"I sure hope not," Rayonne grumbles. "You-know-who won't be thrilled if he dies."

Denendrius groans. "*Marianna . . .*"

I step closer, not really sure how to help him. His forehead is slick with sweat when he looks up at me with bleary eyes. He stutters something before his skin pales and his eyes roll back. Body slacking, he falls sideways into me.

XIX

I plant a hand on the counter to catch myself from falling backward as Derek and Rayonne grab onto him. He slowly returns to consciousness as we prop him against the wall.

His eyelids flutter as he slurs and struggles to keep upright.

Carol appears with water, which he manages to grasp from her and swallow down.

He grunts and leans slumped against the wall, his forearms on his knees, eyes unfocused. Sweat beads down the side of his face and soaks the back of his shirt.

I wet a rag with icy water and crouch in front of him, wiping his forehead and cheeks while he focuses on breathing. When his eyes snag mine, there's a deep admiration in them despite how he struggles to hold my gaze.

"Let's get you back to bed," I tell him. "You need to sleep before you end up seriously ill."

Barely able to stand, it takes three of us to help him to the bedroom and drop him on the bed. He fumbles with pulling the blanket as he succumbs to a full-body shudder.

We leave him alone in the bedroom with a glass of water. I stand in the doorway, worried he might croak if I look away.

Denendrius rattles under the blanket, the water sloshing in the cup as he tries to drink through his cold tremors. He gulps it down, whining as he holds it out to me for more and wraps the blanket tighter.

An old conversation from a hot shower together interrupts my thoughts, and his chill becomes contagious and washes through me.

"I'm only troubled by the cold that comes with going thirsty . . ."

Cautiously, I take the glass and creep back into the hall. "Um . . . Rayonne . . . when you were a vampire, did you ever get cold when you were thirsty?"

She leans against the hallway wall. "Not really—well, a teensy chill maybe, but I've never been deprived enough to be at any level of cold that was actually bothersome. That would be *extreme* deprivation. Torture, essentially . . . why?"

Denendrius rolls sideways and into a ball, quaking so hard the blanket slides off his shoulder.

My heart hammers in my ears. "You said you still crave blood since being turned back, right?"

"Oh no." Rayonne grimaces. "Maybe the puking is psychological, like blood cravings likely are. His body can technically process the food, but maybe it freaks his brain out or something."

"Maybe." I hug myself.

"He might need blood to keep sane like I do, Marianna."

My teeth slam together, arms dropping to my sides. "Absolutely not."

I don't want to see blood touch his lips ever again.

"It might help."

"Or make him crave it more!" My fingernails bite into my palms as I ball my fists. "I am not treading there with him. He hasn't even mentioned he's having that issue."

"He might not if he is. He might not understand what he's feeling since he barely remembers being a vampire. But if it helps me, it might help him."

"I'm not fucking discussing this shit," I snarl, rotating on my heels and storming into the bedroom.

Nobody bothers me once I've closed the door.

I fall asleep once Denendrius does, though he continuously wakes me with his constant rolling and moaning. The blankets end up twisted around him, and after a few attempts trying to wrangle them back, I give up.

Eventually, I abandon napping altogether when he boots me in the calf. I lie there listening to the faint sound of everyone's chatter until I jolt out of bed at the sound of them bumping around in the hidden room.

"Hey, Marianna, I found a box of stuff I think is yours," Rayonne says from behind a wooden shipping crate as I duck into the room.

My heart skips a beat. "Odd . . ."

She points to the back corner as I squeeze between a couple stacks of boxes. A large box sits with the flaps overlapped to close it, my name written on the side in Denendrius's handwriting.

I pull in a deep breath as I kneel in front of it, holding it in my lungs as I carefully unfold the cardboard flaps to look inside. I'm blind with worry, and it takes a minute for the harmless sight of toys to register in my brain.

Allowing a breath, I wait for my heart to calm before I pull the toys from the box. They're all unpackaged and look played with. I pull a few unfamiliar dolls from the box and put them aside on the carpet, a sticker book, building blocks, and hair accessories follow.

When I spot a large book at the bottom, I shift the toys and extract a heavy black photo album I've never seen before. An orange envelope sits against the metal rings and the blank front page. I snatch it and reach inside, my fingers pinching paper.

As I withdraw them, I'm not sure whether to laugh or be appalled. "Are you kidding me? Ridiculous," I mumble flatly.

Staring at the smoothed-out sketches I crumpled and threw on my floor who knows how many months—or years—ago, I can't believe he went through the effort of picking them up and keeping them.

They're mostly drawings of horror movie monsters and rappers, a few sports cars and dogs, flawed enough for me to hate them.

Slipping them back into the envelope, I gnaw my bottom lip. Why the hell would he keep all this?

I shake my head and place the envelope on the back of the cover, flipping the white page that keeps the plastic ones safe. My breath stops behind my parted lips, my shoulders slumping.

The pages are full of photos of me. I know it was the first time he took me from how old I look. The first page makes a half-scoff, half-laugh come up from my throat. The six photos show the progression of me climbing the hood of a black '90s Mustang until I'm standing on the roof, my grin defining happiness as I have my hands lifted in the air. We're in an empty parking lot, weeds growing through the concrete. I can tell he was doing donuts from the black skid marks that lead up to the Mustang's tires. I can imagine myself giggling as he spun donuts, and my mind tricks me into smelling burning rubber.

The next pages recount the rest of our journey. There are photos of me in toy stores, one in particular where I'm sitting in the front of a full cart, holding a stuffed dolphin and grinning. Pages are filled with him and me at a sea park, a photograph of me nose to nose with a dolphin, tons of me pointing and smiling at sea animals while we sit in the crowd. My arm is in a fish tank in one of them.

Me at a park, on the swing and going down a slide. Me in a fancy hotel, wearing a swimsuit, while I stand in a Jacuzzi tub with a hilarious amount of bubbles. A photograph shows Denendrius in bed, the morning sun peeking through the open window. He's paler than usual, and even though his eyes are closed, I can guess the black of them is fading. In the following photos, he looks well fed, and I wonder where I was when he drank blood. He made a comment about me forgetting vampires, so I must have known, but did he kill in front of me, or did he leave me alone in some motel while he went out?

I know it's wrong, but I can't help but smirk when I realize I'm wearing nothing but name-brand clothing in all the photos.

The photos of me and him smiling are endless until the last few pages, where we're in an old motel. I sit under the tacky teal blanket, expression hanging as I pick at oatmeal. A picture follows where I'm giving him a forced smile. There's a handful of pictures where I'm watching morning cartoons, looking bored in my pajamas. I feel the desperation in the photographs, like he knew he was capturing our last moments together.

In the last photo, we're sitting on the hood of his car, his arm stretched out to take the photo while his other one is around me. I'm clasping the edge of his windbreaker, and I can practically see the homesickness in my young eyes, a half-smile barely breaking through my clear disappointment.

I close the photo album and blink away tears. Even if I was naive to be happy back then, I wish I could remember the feeling of freedom my younger self was ignorant enough to enjoy.

Regardless of the origin of the photos, it would be nice to have pictures of myself when I was a kid since I don't have any. I put the album aside to stuff in my bag later.

Aside from the toys that were popular when I was a kid, there are a few name-brand outfits I must have worn.

My heart stops when I move all the clothes aside and look

into the bottom of the box. There, lying diagonally across the cardboard, is the pair of black angel wings and the black lace dress I made him buy at a shop in Enchanted Land right after he lured me away. I think of the hallucinations I had of him as an angel of death when he healed me. My fingers tingle when I reach down and run the tips of them across the cheap faux feathers and over the lace. My heart jolts at the texture, and the memory of the fabric against my skin comes rushing over me. My skin pricks. A flash of indistinguishable images flood my brain, and pounding starts in my forehead.

I can't bring myself to take either article out of the box, so I reach for a baby-blue pencil case with dolphins on it. Though I can hear everyone's chatter on the other side of the room— mostly Derek excited over some Egyptian relic—I still look over my shoulder before I unzip it.

There's a tape.

My hands shake, my throat is stark dry.

Another fucking tape.

Ears ringing, I grasp it and peek at the label.

There's nothing on it.

Needing to know what's on it *immediately*, I pack the box back up and sneak out of the room, locking myself in the bathroom with the camcorder.

I'm dizzy, hot, and cold all over when I pop it in.

My own—young—screaming emanates from the camcorder, the screen black. Every muscle in my body locks, and even when it's replaced with my laughter, I still can't move.

"Was that fun?" Denendrius asks. *"Want to go again?"*

"Again! Again!" I shriek before succumbing to giggles at the sound of screeching tires appear in the background. *"Weee!"*

When the camera rolls, the view is from the car floor. Denendrius is behind the wheel of an older Mustang, in the same windbreaker and mirrored aviators as the last two tapes of him and me when I was a child. He looks behind him.

"*Okay, let's get going now. Looks like someone called to get us in trouble.*"

My little blue shoes appear in view as I kick my feet and let out a frustrated growl.

"*Need to pee before we keep driving? We'll be at my friend Sergei's in a few hours.*"

I hold the camcorder closer to my ear and lower the volume at that.

An exasperated sigh comes from the camera. "*Does that mean adventure time is over? Why do we have to see him?*"

"*That's where we're going to live. Sergei has a big house with a few extra bedrooms we can have. I'll paint yours whatever color you want. You can have a princess mural.*"

Little me squeals in excitement. "*Mermaids?*"

"*Mermaids it is.*" His grin lasts for a moment before he turns serious again. "*You know how you were telling me about having temporary parents?*"

"*Mm-hmm.*"

"*Well, Sergei is going to be a permanent parent for you now. Like a dad.*"

My ankles cross above the lens. "*I'm confused. I thought Vianna and Kenneth were going to be my permanent parents.*"

"*Not anymore, remember? Besides, they could have decided last minute they didn't want you.*" He looks toward the passenger seat where little me sits and frowns. "*It happens.*"

My sigh breathes through the tiny speaker. "*I know. It's happened before.*"

He focuses back on the road. "*You'll have lots of fun with Sergei. He's got an entire family you'll be part of.*"

"*Really? Will I have a sister there?*"

His head cocks as he looks back at me. "*No. Why? Do you want a sister?*"

"*Yes. I've always wanted a sister.*"

"Hmm. Well . . . Well, maybe. I could get you a sister if you want one so bad."

"I thought you were going to take care of me, Den," I whine.

The car slows. Another pulling up on the other side of the driver's window. They're at a stoplight, I think. *"I am going to take care of you, but like a friend. Don't worry, I'll live there with you and him, but I have no interest in bossing you around."*

"Oh, okay. That makes sense, I think."

"Is that recording?" he asks. *"I hear it whirring. We're going to run out of film."*

"Oops. Sorry, Den." I pick it up and grin widely into the lens. *"Okay. Bye-bye!"*

Denendrius's amused chuckle cuts off as the video ends.

He was planning on dumping me on Sergei, wasn't he? That must have been his big plan. Have Sergei raise me so he didn't grow up as my father figure. I wonder if Sergei would have agreed to it. Would he really do *anything* for Denendrius?

My eyes widen. I completely forgot about Sergei.

I check the phone for missed texts or calls—from him or Alaire—but there's nothing.

At least he doesn't know where we are. Maybe this kind of silence isn't odd for Denendrius, so it isn't causing him to worry too much.

A knock on the door makes me inhale sharply. Rayonne's voice comes from the other side. "Are you almost done in there? I need to shower soon."

I close the camcorder. "Uh—I was about to take one . . ." There's no way I want to walk past her with the camcorder. She'll ask me why I needed to hide it. Besides, I should probably take a shower.

"Okay, save me some hot water."

I rush through a shower and sneak out with my towel and camcorder to the bedroom to change, doing so without Denendrius waking. He's splayed out on his back, dead asleep and drenched in sweat.

Once Rayonne finishes her shower, she joins Carol—bored with the hidden room—to watch some romantic comedy on the TV.

I stick around, not wanting to dig much more, but also not wanting to leave Derek alone in case he finds something unfavorable.

"I found something . . . troubling," Derek says as I slip through the hole in the drywall.

Too late.

"What?" I walk midway down the room to where he stands next to an open wooden crate holding a glass case with a painting inside it.

He turns the image to me, and my knees wobble.

"*Pour mon amour*," Derek reads from the back. "Marianna, 1552."

I hug myself as I stare at the oil painting. It's a portrait of a wealthy girl who looks far too similar to me. Did she have it commissioned for him? Or did he have it done for her? "Put it away."

Carefully, he sets it back in the crate and wipes dust from the front of his dark orange sweater. "Marianna, what's going on here?"

I push the hair from my face. "Sociopathic insanity. He wanted to marry a girl named Mariana in Rome before he became a vampire, and he's been trying to replace her ever since. I really don't want to get into it more right now."

That's three times now . . . *how many have there been?*

"Okay." He puts the painting back in the crate.

Carol calls me from the hallway. "Are you getting hungry? Rayonne and I are discussing dinner."

I almost fall over while crawling out of the hole in the wall. "Yeah, I guess."

With Denendrius catching up on sleep and no immediate danger, we aren't sure what to do with ourselves. We order food and half-argue while we wait about our next plan of action. Carol wants us all to stay at her place, while Rayonne pushes back because she thinks moving too much will make it harder for Viorel's men to find us. It's clear Carol doesn't understand the severity of the situation when she returns to insisting that I leave with her, but Rayonne and I both set her straight.

When there's a knock at the door for our food, we all pile in front of the TV with our chicken wings and pasta. Denendrius seems back to his usual—yet quiet—self before he tried to commit suicide, even eating an entire serving of spaghetti and garlic bread without puking his brains out.

I dread the sunset when it comes, watching the oranges, pinks, and blues brushed across the sky like in an oil painting. When Derek and Carol are both done eating, Rayonne shows them our collection of vampire-hunting weapons and gives them a few pointers in the living room. The apartment fills with mock-fighting, and I feel a little better when Denendrius chuckles along. Maybe he won't snap again so soon.

Needing another drink, I abandon my empty root beer bottle on the counter and crack open the fridge. I reach into the back, grumbling about my milk being shoved behind every-thing as I grab it. When I stand, I come face-to-face with an unfamiliar onyx-eyed man as he pulls the front door closed behind him. He locks it.

Eyes boring into mine as his pupils expand in a likely attempt to hypnotize me, he whispers, "Don't make a lot of noise."

Stumbling backward, I pull in a deep breath as I slam the fridge door and holler, "Darkling! There's a fucking Darkling in the apartment!"

"I will not hurt you," he tells me as panicked scrambling starts in the living room.

"Then what do you want?" Rayonne demands as she emerges from the living room with a stake in hand, everyone in tow with their weapons. "Did you follow me from Estrella de Sangre?"

With a gladius in hand, Denendrius places himself between me and the vampire.

"Yes." His hard eyes lock on Denendrius. "And I'll only take him, now that he's human."

"What are your connections?" Rayonne takes a careful step closer, hand clenching the readied stake tighter. "What do you want with him?"

I peek around Denendrius, waiting for the Darkling's answer.

"I overheard there's a bounty on him last week. There's a man in Germany who wants him for a few million." His eyes shift between our defensive stances. "I don't want violence, just money."

Rayonne and I exchange a desperate glance. Handing Denendrius over to this man will only create more problems for us. The last thing I want is Viorel's wrath when he finds out we no longer have him.

"No," Rayonne and I say in sync.

He stands taller, shoulders tensing. "I'm not asking, only trying to approach this civilly so nobody gets hurt. I have a family to take care of and could benefit from the money. From what I've heard, his life is no loss."

"Tough shit," I snap. "You can't have him."

His eyes flare red and Rayonne hisses at me to shut up, while Derek takes a step toward me like he's going to hold me back.

As soon as Denendrius's arm twitches like he's going to attack, the Darkling takes the gladius from his hand so swiftly that I only see it appear behind the vampire on the kitchen counter.

Grabbing the back of Denendrius's shirt as he spews furious Latin, I tug him toward Rayonne and the living room, not sure what my game plan is. Before I can think of anything, Carol fires off the crossbow she's holding.

I jerk sideways. "Holy shit—"

He snarls as he catches the wooden stake in front of his face, tossing it aside. The man's foot lifts for a step, and then he's within an inch of Denendrius, whose fists come up in response.

My heart slams against my rib cage as he easily fights Denendrius off. He twists one of Denendrius's arms behind him and shoves him toward the door. Denendrius tries to writhe free, face twisting in fury when he realizes he's being overpowered.

I'm moments away from physically attempting to pry the two of them apart when I have an idea.

"Wait!" I holler. "If it's money you want, I have something worth far more than him."

He stops and turns to humor me, a black brow quirked as Denendrius spews furious Latin.

I rush into the bedroom, unzip my go bag, and find a vial of blood. Rushing back into the kitchen, I hold it up in front of me.

"It's the cure. The reason Denendrius is human again. Trust me, you'll get far more for this than him," I say.

He releases his grip on Denendrius, who merely stands where they stopped, and carefully approaches me. I hold my breath as he plucks the vial from my fingers.

"It looks like blood," he says, slit eyes flickering between us. "How do I know if this is the cure?"

Rayonne says, "Smell it."

Carefully, he pops the old cork and lifts it to his nose to inhale deeply. His brows lift and he purses his lips. "It doesn't smell like any blood I've smelled before . . ."

She nods. "I know. It will taste odd too."

"You were a vampire too?" He pulls the vial away from his face and stares at it in complete awe.

"Yes," she verifies.

I try to wrangle my breath. "So, you'll take the cure instead of him?" What are the chances he'll try to walk away with both?

His shoulders lower as he exhales, his lips curling with a peaceful smile. "Yes. You have no idea how much value this has to me."

I wipe my sweaty palms on my jeans. *That was easy.* "Seriously? Awesome."

He smiles. "Thank you. How does it work? I only have to drink it? I was ill before—will I be ill again?"

"No, it wouldn't undo all the healing," Rayonne says, "but you'll want to be somewhere safe—"

In one swift motion, he downs the blood.

Rayonne jumps forward to stop him, but she's too slow. "No!"

"What the fuck!" I shriek as he licks his lips clean. "Why would you do that *here*? You're supposed to take it and screw off!"

He looks between Rayonne and Denendrius. "Two vampires turned human in one group? I like those odds for me. I'm not leaving yet."

We gape at him as he puts the cork back in the vial and sets it down on the counter. He crosses the room to sit at the table. "What happens now?"

I stare at Rayonne. "Did you puke your brains out too when you turned back?"

"Unfortunately." She glares daggers at him.

I offer him the same look Rayonne does. "You go to the bathroom—now. You're in for a hell of a time, and I'm not cleaning furniture or carpet."

Horror passes over his face, and it's clear he put little thought into this.

He's heaving before he's even in the bathroom. Hunched over the toilet, he vomits blood and venom, red spraying across the inside of the toilet seat.

"What's your name?" Rayonne asks. "There's a chance you might not remember it."

He speaks through a pained moan. "Henry." His fingers grip the toilet seat as he looks back at us, blood running from the corners of his eyes. "Why wouldn't I remember my name?"

I cringe as he vomits more blood. "You should have asked all these questions *before* you took the blood." I hoist myself up onto the counter. "A common side effect of the cure is losing some—or all—of your memories, like Denendrius. You were in too big of a panic to get in and out of here to notice he can't even speak English."

Derek and Carol gather in the doorway, weapons still gripped in their shaky hands. They half-block Denendrius from entering. Huffing, he looks like he wants to come in and tear Henry's face off.

He's too busy whining in pain and turning himself inside out over the toilet to respond. His accuracy is poor too. Blood stains the white wall, smears on the counter and side of the toilet when he touches his bleeding eyes before grabbing around for stability.

Carol and I wipe it up together, the smell of bleach pushing Derek and Denendrius out of the bathroom and down the hall when I reassure them we're fine.

Rayonne's wide eyes shift over the blood splatter. "I need a cigarette break."

"Is this supposed to happen? Am I dying?" he asks, tears streaking through the red painting his face.

I wipe a cloth down the side of the wood counter and say, "You might be. You're going to end up passing out first, then the universe will decide or some shit."

"Oh—" He retches again. Blood seeps through his pores like sweat, and he sheds his coat when he manages a breath.

My lip curls as I stare down at him, hunched over the bowl. I'm so sick of the sound of vomiting.

"Is that what happened to Denendrius?" Carol asks as she rinses a rag in the sink.

I nod and point to the faded red stain on the edge of the carpet in the doorway.

"I think I'm dying," he cries as he slumps onto his side on the floor.

Carol's face crumples with sympathy and she holds her breath while crouching down next to him, body angled away like she thinks he might attack her. "Do you need a drink or something?"

He wipes tears from his eyes, smearing them and blood down his cheeks. "Nothing."

She bites her lip and nods while standing, turning to me for direction.

"We wait and see what happens." I scowl down at him. "Why would you do this? We've got enough shit to deal with. We don't know how to help you."

"For my wife." He hisses in pain, hand clutching his chest. "I got diagnosed with terminal cancer four years ago, and a vampire showed up at my house one day, offering to turn my wife and me for an exponential amount of money. I figured I either pay him or continue paying for the cancer treatments"— he pukes and gasps for breath—"but I had a better chance surviving the transformation than cancer. We sold our cars to pay for the blood he gave us, said it would up our chances of surviving if we drank it, and once our house sold, we paid him. He turned me first, and she was still human when I woke up. Apparently, she received a call from the doctor while I was out, telling her she was pregnant. I didn't know she went for a blood test." He gags again and coughs blood onto the floor.

"Our twins are growing quickly, and I don't want to steal anymore to support us all. It's hell explaining to our family why we've been acting so oddly. My wife refuses to turn now. If I'm not going to die, I want to go back to how things were."

I suck my teeth at him. "That's if you even remember who they are."

He squeezes his eyes closed. "Yes."

Carol and I watch as Henry does nothing more than mumble and whine on the floor, his eyes slowly losing focus on the surrounding room. He doesn't respond when I ask him if he's okay, and when he exhales a deep breath and doesn't take another, his body goes slack.

"Did he . . . die?" Carol breathes, shifting closer to me.

"Sort of," I explain. "He's going to wake up human or bloat up like a corpse."

"Jesus . . ." She backs out of the room. "I need to sit."

Tense, I crawl close to him and press two fingers against the side of his bloody neck. There's no pulse.

Rayonne returns, her eyes dull as she looks down at Henry and sighs while adjusting her black velvet skirt. "As good an idea as it was to give him the cure instead of Denendrius, now we might have *another* memory-less vampire on our hands."

I lift my chin and sneer down at him. "Nah. I'm not dealing with that. We can drop him off at the hospital. It's not our fault he busted in here."

"That works," she agrees.

I clean him up in case we have to drop him off, not wanting to attempt that when he's awake.

Denendrius pokes his head into the bathroom again, wide eyes staring down at Henry's limp body. "Me?" he asks.

"Yeah. This happened to you too," I tell him, leaning against the wall.

I'm tense and can't get a deep breath in through the next few hours as Rayonne and I take turns checking on him.

"What if he's dead?" Carol asks at some point, wrapping her cardigan tighter around herself like the thought makes her cold. She hasn't sat down since he came in.

"We'll have to dispose of him," I say as Rayonne opens her mouth. "There's no other way unless we want to get looked at for murder."

Carol's brows lower. "But his family . . ."

I shrug. "Maybe they'll think he got caught in the sunlight or something. But his wife has to know enough about the vampire world to know how dark things can get."

She rubs her hands up and down her biceps. "I guess."

"Hey," Derek whispers to her as I turn from the room,

"maybe he'll wake up with all his memories and walk out of here."

"I sure hope so," she mumbles back.

I'm not feeling very optimistic when I return to the bathroom, and I can see how stiff his neck is before I even touch my fingers to it. His muscles are tense under his skin, his jaw refusing any movement I try to force upon it. Though his eyes are blue, there's no life in them.

"Oh yeah, he's a goner," I declare coolly as I wander back to the living room. "Rigor mortis is starting."

Carol's eyes drop to the floor from where she sits next to Derek on the couch.

I blow a long breath between my lips and stretch. "All right. I guess we have to go dump him in the woods or find a barrel before he stinks."

"Let . . . let me double-check first," Derek says, giving Carol's knee a quick pat.

I let out a beat of laughter. "Suit yourself. I've seen plenty of dead bodies. He's getting stiff."

Carol's white-rimmed eyes level with mine. "When did you see bodies? Aside from . . . you know . . ." *My adoptive parents.*

"When I was in the gang. That, and Denendrius has murdered people in front of me," I divulge.

Her jaw falls open, and she scoffs at him.

Denendrius's head jerks. "What?"

She shakes her head at him as Denendrius squints at me and her to find some context.

When I follow Derek into the bathroom, he plants his hand against the wall and gasps for breath like he's going to be sick. "Okay, I believe you now."

"First body?" I ask him.

He's tense as he shifts his whole body to look at me. "Uh . . . yeah."

I wipe my prints off Henry's face and neck with a wet cloth before going back to the living room. "Nobody but Denendrius and Rayonne touch the body now," I warn Carol and Derek. "My prints and shit are in the system, and you guys don't want this traced back to you, whether or not you're here to deal with the consequences."

"What are we going to do with him?" Derek runs his hand over the side of his pale face.

I turn to Rayonne, who stands against the counter, and lift my shoulders in suggestion. "Let's dump him in the woods?"

"Yeah, that works," Rayonne agrees.

Carol gapes at me. "We can't do that."

My nose wrinkles. "Why not? Have a better plan?"

She rubs her hands up and down her arms to comfort herself. "This is horrible, Marianna. He has a family."

"Don't give me moral lecture," I groan. "He did this to himself. Either he took the blood and left, or we would have had to kill him anyway. He's a vampire. His wife will assume his disappearance is a side effect of that. Maybe she shouldn't have let him turn himself before she got her test results back. All we're doing is cleaning up his mess."

Carol gnaws at her lips and stares down at the carpet, tears in her eyes.

"You wanted in on this," I tell her gently. "This is the stuff that happens."

She merely swallows and nods. "Okay."

Rayonne doesn't pay any attention to our qualms, lost in thought as she stares back toward the bathroom. "I can't believe Agatha made me risk *this*." She exhales through her teeth. "Anyway, Denendrius can lift him. We'll throw him in the back of Derek's SUV since we're going off-road."

Derek's flesh is tinged green, and he looks moments away from collapsing on the floor. "Okay, let's get this over with."

We waste twenty minutes bickering in the bathroom over

how to get the body from the bathroom to the back of Derek's SUV.

"If we wrap him in a blanket, it's going to be pretty obvious we're carrying a body down the stairs," Rayonne says as she uncaps a glass of cold brew coffee.

I cross my arms, my heel tapping impatiently. "Would chopping him up into smaller sections and stuffing him in multiple garbage bags be less suspicious?"

"No." She rolls her eyes at me and takes a sip.

I hold my hands up. "Then what do you suggest?"

"Is there a way to do this that *doesn't* create such a colossal risk for us?" Derek interjects, rubbing his fingers into his forehead.

"Not really," Rayonne and I both say.

"Yeah, all it really takes is a hair with a follicle getting attached to him," I add.

Derek closes his eyes and sighs. "Great. And we have to take *my* SUV? It's probably got my DNA all over it."

I scratch my head. "If we're dumping him in the woods, neither Denendrius's car or Rayonne's will make it deep into them."

"I should have brought my van," Carol laments to herself from where she hides around the corner in the hallway.

Denendrius grumbles something and gives his head a shake. Leaning down over Henry, he grunts as he picks him up and throws him over his shoulder. "Go now?" he asks, full of attitude.

"We at least need to wrap him up so there's reasonable doubt if we get spotted carrying him out," I carp.

After winding a white sheet around him, Rayonne goes with Derek to bring the SUV around to the front door. Carol keeps an eye out for people behind us as I make sure the stairs are clear before Denendrius rushes Henry down.

We're out of the apartment and throwing Henry in the

trunk in under twenty seconds. As far as we know, the dark of night covered us well enough from suspicious eyes once we were out of the building. Though, there's always a risk someone saw us.

Rayonne hops into the back of the green SUV with me and Denendrius, Carol sitting next to Derek in the passenger seat.

We're quiet until we hit a speed bump and a gassy moan leaks from Henry, his body rolling into the back of the bench seat.

"Oh God," Carol squeaks from the front.

"More vampires?" Denendrius asks. He still sounds so different with the thickness of his Latin accent.

I look up at him from the middle seat. "More vampires . . . coming to kill you?"

"Yes."

Frowning, I say, "Yes? Agatha. She's probably not done with us yet."

"Ah, Agatha." He sits back straight in his seat and rubs his hands over the stubble growing on his jaw as he thinks hard.

Rayonne rests her elbow on the edge of the window. "I still have no idea what she's up to, aside from likely trying to find someone to help her. But there's five of us now, so she's going to need a few minions."

Carol looks back at us from between the front seats. "How big of a worry is she?"

Rayonne's shoulder rubs against mine when she shrugs and straightens her black bangs. "Who knows? She's capable of anything."

I chew at my nails as I study the dark and the traffic beyond the window, like Agatha might run us down in a big truck. We get out of the city without incident, an expanse of trees popping up around us on the highway.

"How far out should we go?" Derek asks.

I purse my lips. "Half an hour? Until we find a path off the highway, at least. We'll have to go in on foot at some point."

"We don't have any shovels," Carol gripes.

I adjust the seat belt around my waist and give it a frustrated yank. "That's fine. We can dump him on the ground or something. A bear or coyote will eat him and get rid of the problem."

"Have some tact, Marianna," Carol scolds.

My stomach burns and I curl my fingers into fists in my lap. "Why should I? He straight up broke into the apartment and tried to wreck our lives. We would be in so much shit if he'd taken Denendrius from us. If he hadn't killed himself, we would've had to do it. He left us all with a potential murder charge."

She doesn't respond—likely because I'm right—and nobody says anything more until Derek is mentioning a grassy path off the left side of the road.

"Take it," I grumble and brace myself as he slows and drives down the steep shoulder of the highway, jostling us in our seats. The jerking movement makes me wince in pain, and I hold my hand over the bruising on my chest.

Luckily, there are no cars to see us drive into the trees. We push through thin branches and leaves, and they close behind us like a stage curtain. Derek parks and turns the car off, and we're plunged into darkness. We unbuckle as he finds a flashlight from the glove compartment.

"Do I have to come out?" Carol asks as a yellow curve of light shines across her. "I don't want to see the body again."

I scoot off the seat and out the door after Rayonne. "Probably. Unless you want to risk fighting off any vampires that potentially stalked us here. Walk ahead with Derek and don't look back at Denendrius and me."

"All right." She unbuckles and pops the passenger door

open and steps out, twigs snapping underfoot, the hum of insects filling the air.

Does she wish she hadn't helped me now and had stayed home like I requested? Am I worth all this trouble to her? She doesn't even have an endgame, or is she still hoping to whisk me away?

What will happen to her if I get an invitation to the castle? Is it wrong of me to take it, even if that means she's alone and unprotected? Should I stay behind—if I don't have to—even if it's not my fault she threw herself into all of this? Am I a bad person for thinking of myself first? Should I feel guilty for wanting to go to Romania, even if it means I don't know when I'll see her again?

"Denendrius—" I jerk my head toward the tailgate as Carol and Derek walk. "Grab Henry."

He carries the dead vampire like it's nothing. We follow the yellow light as it sweeps through the trees, walking until we're beating at the thick green and forced to stop.

"Here," I tell Denendrius, pointing at the ground.

He drops Henry's stiff corpse in a pile of old leaves and dead branches like a sack of potatoes. Derek shines the light on his face, and he stares up at us with his cloudy eyes, blood still rimming them.

"Should we say something?" Carol whispers.

Nobody does, though inappropriate wisecracks pile on my tongue.

We all stand around Henry in an unintentional moment of silence until Denendrius ends it. "Home? I'm hungry."

XXI

My thoughts are stuck on Henry even as we hit the highway and leave him far behind us.

"Rayonne, have you ever heard of Darkling hypnotism not working on a human?" I ask.

A line appears between her brows as she scrutinizes me through the dark from where she's buckled in beside me. "Never, why?"

"I can't be hypnotized." My own confusion is clear in my voice. "I think Henry tried when he came in, but it didn't work. It didn't work for Alaire, Edmond, and Denendrius either. They didn't know why, but Alaire and Edmond gave me a bunch of fake-sounding theories to try to make me feel better."

Her expression widens. "Seriously?"

I shift in my seat. "No ideas?" Is there something seriously wrong with my brain?

A slow grin builds on Rayonne's lips. "No, but I bet a *particular* vampire would find that interesting."

I gulp. As much as I'd like answers, the thought of Viorel testing hypnotism on me makes my heart pound.

We return to the apartment for our go bags, deciding it's best to go to Carol's after all that. The chances of Viorel's men locating us in the last three hours of tonight are slim, but maybe if pesky bloodsuckers think we've declared the apartment too high-risk to stay in, they'll start looking for us elsewhere.

When we reach the apartment, we find the door cracked.

Carol half-hides behind Derek. "We locked it when we—"

"Yep, I sure did," I say, a jolt of adrenaline flooding me. I quiver with nervous jitters.

"Bloody hell," Rayonne hisses, readying her gun of wooden bullets.

I clench my teeth when I shove the door open.

A middle-aged man sits at the dining table, looking up from Denendrius's translations and smiling. I can see the black of his eyes from here.

With his blond buzz cut and generic green army coat over his white tank top, a single name pops to mind.

"Sergei?" Bile rises in my throat, and I force it back down.

Game over.

Knees buckling and legs ready to collapse beneath me, I grab onto Denendrius and he hooks his arm around my waist.

This is it now. No Romania, no revenge. I may as well have called him here myself and saved us all the hell the last few days brought.

It was all for nothing. I should have known I couldn't rely on him not knowing where Denendrius lives to keep us safe.

He stands, and the lack of hostility in the air only makes my heart pound faster. "Well, come on in. Who are your friends?"

Rayonne cocks the revolver in her grip and raises it.

My breath whooshes out of me as he appears in front of us, tearing the gun from Rayonne's hand, his eyes snagging hers.

I can't get a breath back in. Tingles cascade over my skin as my legs give out. I'd hit the floor if it weren't for Denendrius's grip. I'm completely useless as Sergei swiftly hypnotizes Rayonne, Derek, and Carol into leaving the apartment for a few hours and forgetting that he was ever there—that Denendrius and I were with them. He gets inside Denendrius's head too, telling him he should relax because they're friends, and let me go.

Sergei guides me from the doorway as I slump, letting me collapse on the carpet as soon as I'm out of the way for Denendrius to shut the door.

He pinches the fabric at the thighs of his cargo pants as he squats down in front of me, taking one of my hands in his. I can't feel the iciness of his flesh through the heat pricking my skin. "All is well," he tells me, the gruffness of his Russian-accented voice taking away from some of the clearly intended gentleness. "You are having a panic attack."

I yank my hand out of his and hold it against my chest. My head spins, my chest burning with the rapid breaths that claw their way in and out of my lungs.

The walls feel like they're burning down around me.

"I'm not here to hurt you, Marianna. But I need to know what's going on," he demands, his hard coal-black eyes flickering between Denendrius and me.

"Are you g-going to change him ba-ack?" My hands ball into fists against the carpet, the muscles seeming to contract on their own.

"No." He looks back over his shoulder pointedly at the empty cure vial on the counter. "But I would have appreciated a heads-up."

I manage my first deep breath, some tingles fading. "W-what do you mean?"

He scowls at Denendrius. "He was supposed to tell me if he went through with it, but he *insisted* he didn't want to anymore."

I'm too breathless for words as Sergei grabs my hand and helps me to my feet, though Denendrius gently takes me from him and walks me to the couch himself.

Sergei says, "I figured it would be an impulsive decision, as most things end up with him." He shakes his head at Denendrius, a playful glint in his eyes. "A heads-up would have been nice, you bastard."

Denendrius mulls him over, sitting close to my side on the cool leather, like he's not sure what he should think of Sergei.

"He understands nothing?" Sergei asks.

I lean back into the couch, my heart rate easing until hollering in the stairway about drugs, and a thud makes me flinch. "Not really."

"English?"

"Bits and pieces only, as far as I know. We've been translating Latin. Do you want me to explain to him who you are?" I pull the hair from my face, tucking long strands behind my ears.

The corner of Sergei's lip quirks up. "There's no purpose to that. If he remembers me on his own, fine. But you seem to have many friends helping you acclimate him. I'll be there if he needs me ... but he seems to be in safe hands."

He's oblivious. Perfect. "Are you sure?"

Sergei motions for us to make room on the couch for him as he fishes his wallet from the back of his pants. He sits down beside me as he opens it and takes an accordion sleeve of photos out.

"These are all of my family," he says, but from the cautious look in his eye, I can tell there's an unspoken reason for him wanting to show me his lineage. "When I died, I had two children at home with my wife: a girl and a boy"—he points to an old black-and-white photo of two blond-haired children on a metal slide with wide grins—"named Sasha and Egor. Because he saved me, I got to see them grow up. I have twelve grandchildren, twenty-three great-grandchildren, and six great-great-grandbabies now."

My mouth widens as he flips through the photos, pointing out who is who while Denendrius watches us quietly, trying to understand what we're talking about but clearly struggling. The last photo he shows me is a massive family gathering of all the family members that were still alive two years ago.

"Was it hard to watch them from afar?" I ask.

He clears his throat. "No. Denendrius helped me with hypnotism until I got the hang of it. I've spent much time with them. They remember me when I come to visit, and forget when I leave. I got to keep my wife until she passed from a heart attack at fifty-six. Through the decades, I have met every family member, and spent good time with them. It's a gift to spend Christmas with them, then leave and have them remember it all without remembering I was there with them until I want them to. I've never had to include them in this world. Denendrius has done more for me than I could ever repay."

"Wow. That must be amazing." I catch the unintentional hint of sourness in my voice. But I can't imagine having so much family, never mind having a relationship with all of them. I swallow down my envy.

He looks up from the photos, his smile pained. "It is not so bad if he cannot remember me—particularly all of them—right now. Human, or not."

I want to ask him if Denendrius threatened his family to keep him in line, but the answer to that is already clear.

I chew the corner of my lip. "Did you know he kidnapped me when I was a kid?"

He doesn't bat an eye. "Yes, I know this."

"I . . . I saw a home video where he was talking about your family and how you were going to raise me."

His brows lift, his eyes drifting to Denendrius before settling back on me. "I was *not* aware of that."

"I was curious," I mumble. "Would have you done it?"

"Ah, yes, I probably would have. I scolded him for taking you at first and recommended he give you back. I didn't know he had such big plans already."

I reflect while I pick at my nails, absorbing everything while he and Denendrius study one another for a moment that feels like it goes on forever. Maybe it's that I'm waiting for him to decide to turn Denendrius back, or for him to realize something odd is going on.

"How long was Denendrius imprisoned?" I wonder aloud.

Sergei's brow furrows. "He never discussed it with you?"

I shake my head, some of my hair falling back around my face. "No, and he's hardly told me any *truth*."

Sergei rubs his jaw. "Mm. Well, he liked to make up his own stories. I think it was easier sometimes to cope. But he told me he was there for three hundred and twelve years before he escaped."

The number makes my heart trip a beat. It's a punch in the chest. "He's acting different from when he was a vampire," I whisper. "Still angry, but considerably less. Is that what pushed him over the edge? Being tortured for so long?"

Sergei sighs and leans back into the couch, lacing his fingers together in his lap. "I think so. He's only told me a fraction of the things that happened to him there, but it sounds like the vampire who ruled the place let the guards have unrestricted access to him, allowing anything short of staking or killing him."

My head burns at the thought, and my voice shakes when I ask, "Was he only trying to get the attention of other vampires when he got captured?"

He glances at Denendrius like he's seeking permission to

continue. "That's what he told me. He said no matter how hard he searched, he couldn't find anyone like him. He freaked out, which he realized made vampires stay further away from him. But he sort of got the reaction he wanted. Someone came to stop him. He begged for help, said that he didn't know what was happening to him. I suppose they took pity on him at first. They found his maker after he fled Rome—whoever he may be—and gave the man a chance to claim Denendrius and guide him."

I swallow and notice Denendrius listening intently. "He didn't help, clearly."

Sergei lets out a scornful chuckle. "No, no, he didn't. His maker told Denendrius's captors he abandoned him for his own safety, that he intended to kill him, not turn him. How he was so dangerous, even as a human, that *they* should kill him. They took his word. He claimed Denendrius murdered his wife and child out of jealousy of their family, but Denendrius has always denied it."

I understand the inspiration for Denendrius's lie now, and I want to believe Sergei got the truth out of him.

Mariana's father sounds like he must have been an awful man. And from Denendrius's insistence that she would have grown up and married someone else, he must have abandoned them in Rome to save his own ass. How did that affect them? Did they slip even deeper into poverty? Or did Marianus end up killing his own family after tearing into Denendrius, then simply put the blame on him?

What happened to Marianus, anyway? Did Denendrius track him down and kill him?

I let Denendrius lace his fingers through mine as I ask, "Did he tell you how he escaped? I heard he drank the guards."

Sergei folds the photos and puts them back in his wallet, shifting on the couch to slide it back in his pocket. "I was not alive when this occurred, so I can only recount his story, understand." He exhales a heavy breath. "When Denendrius was being held in a fortress outside Sirmium, the man who ruled over the place was a vampire. He had a human niece. That's important to know."

My heart thumps at the memory of Alaire and Edmond's mention of a similar story.

"She used to sneak down and visit Denendrius in his cell. His story made her pity him, her curiosity growing as she did. Her presence was the only gentle thing he experienced, her voice and stories keeping him from delusion in the moments she was with him in that dark place." His lips purse and he glances back at the empty vial of blood on the counter. "She told him she knew where to find the cure for vampirism and that she could get it for him if he escaped. He often spoke of his yearning to be human and return to Rome. Since she never left that fortress, she wanted to run away with him to see the world. So they escaped together. He played weaker than he was, which threw the guards off when he attacked and drained them the next time they came into his cell, and she helped him navigate the place to get outside—"

My eyes narrow at the clashing stories. "He didn't kidnap her? That's what I heard."

"They probably would have assumed it was a kidnapping."

I hang onto his words. "And the cure? Did she have it?"

"He asked for it once they were far enough away from danger, but she never had it . . ." He shakes his head and inhales deeply. "She hoped to convince him to stay a vampire and turn her. So he drowned her in the Sava River."

I bare my teeth as I cringe. "Damn."

"Denendrius said he was a good man until that place. But after three centuries, they had tortured all the humanity out of him," he says simply.

"Is that why he tried to kill himself back then?" I ask, thinking of the man whose name he took after being saved.

"Yes. He told me he wasn't sure what else to do. He was

completely alone after he escaped and said he felt *nothing*. All he did was kill and drink. He couldn't feel anything but thirst. He was bored. Empty. He didn't want to exist if all there was for him was unquenched thirst."

"I wonder what happened to that Sovetta man who stopped him. How he died, I mean. He wrote a letter to himself to read if he turned back, explaining why he took the name."

Clearly, Denendrius felt close enough to him to use his name as his own for over a thousand years. Did he encourage the chaos that Denendrius created? Did they commit atrocities together? What *did* they do together? What was it he did—said —when he stopped Denendrius from killing himself, that convinced Denendrius to stick around and . . . *enjoy* . . . life again?

"Sovetta . . . my big *frater*—brother. Yes." Denendrius squints in thought. "Uh . . ." His mouth opens and closes as his face scrunches, like the words he requires need a little forcing out. "He died. Cannon in his chest."

His English makes my heart pound, and I swallow a thickening lump.

Sergei balks. "If he was a few centuries old, he should have survived that."

Denendrius shifts in confusion before his expression relaxes, and he shakes his head. "No. *Strella*. Ah"—he clicks his tongue—"Star Child."

"Your friend was a Child of Stars?" My chin scrunches. "Huh. That's actually surprising."

Denendrius grins and nods. "He reads minds."

I nod and laugh. "Oh, okay, well, that friendship makes sense now." A mind reader? That would have been *so useful* to Denendrius.

He merely cocks his head at me and lets out an awkward chuckle, like he thinks a good joke went over his head.

"What are your plans, you and him?" Sergei asks.

My hands sweat. "We'll probably pick a town and house once he can speak English enough to be a part of that."

He nods. "All right. I would like to be updated with all that. Whenever the wedding is, I want an invitation too, even if he doesn't remember."

His request chills me. "Okay."

"What happened to your phone?" Sergei asks as he stands. "I called it by accident and you didn't answer. Turn your ringer on."

"I don't have it anymore," I say carefully. "I smashed it."

"Ah. Because of the bug? I told him you were smart enough to figure that out."

My brows lower. *I knew it.* "Yeah, exactly."

"You call me when he remembers. He's still my maker. You understand this, Marianna?" He cocks a brow while adjusting his jacket.

I nod. "Okay, I will."

He releases me from his harsh gaze as his eyes soften, the corner of his lip lifting in a smile. "Okay, Marianna. I trust you. This is good. If he's happy, I'm happy. Call me when he remembers or you need something from me."

I'm stunned when he leaves with nothing more than a simple goodbye.

"I am still hungry," Denendrius complains as he stands and stretches his arms behind his head.

As if that's my biggest concern right now.

He grins and holds his hand out for me, and I blow out a deep breath and take it. Pulling me to my feet, he yanks me close to him and buries his lips between mine for a long kiss. When he steps back grinning, he playfully growls and half-lifts me off the floor, dragging me to the kitchen.

"You cook?" he asks as he sets me flat on my feet on the cold floor. Jerking the stove handles—like he's trying to convince me he can't figure out he has to push and turn them—he frowns. "I do not know."

"Okay, fine. What do you want me to whip up?" I drag my feet to the fridge. Probably better if I do it so he doesn't burn himself or burn the apartment down.

His smile creeps across his lips, but his brows twitch. "Hm?"

I exhale a grunt. "What food?"

Pivoting on his heels, he opens the fridge and bends over to see inside. He mumbles to himself in Latin until he decides on Italian sausages. He holds it out to me. "This meat."

"Sausages." I take the cold package.

"Okay. You cook now."

Though his tone isn't demanding, I still grit my teeth as I lean over to retrieve the pan from the oven drawer, back ramrod straight as soon as I feel his hand graze my ass. I avoid looking at him—able to feel his heavy stare—as I tear open the plastic package and toss the pale sausages on the slow-heating pan. Next, I open a can of corn and dump it in a pot on low heat, and find a spoon to stir it.

"We are alone," he whispers as he comes up behind me, his lusting breath against the side of my face as he presses himself against my back. I'm stone-still as he hooks his arm around my waist.

I can't stop my voice from shaking. "Yeah."

"Do we . . .?" His fingers trail down the front of my thigh and up again, and my skin pricks with goose bumps.

I swallow and squeeze the metal spoon handle. Denendrius pushes his body tighter against mine as he repeatedly squeezes my waist, the oven handle pressing into my hip bones. How can he possibly be in the mood for sex with all this going on around him?

"No," I breathe. "You do, I don't."

The confused noise he makes has me leaning harder into the stove, like I can pass through it for freedom.

"I was"—his hand pauses with his words, a beat of silence as he thinks—"bad husband?"

My tongue feels like it's in a knot, so I nod. It's not worth explaining all the semantics to him. I don't have the emotional energy for that.

"Hm?"

I cringe as I allow the truth past my trembling lips. "Yes. You were cruel. Mean."

"Sorry." If his apology is genuine, I can't hear it through the coveting tone in his raspy voice. His hand squeezes my side again, then moves up to wrap around my ribs below my breast. "No more mean."

My spine locks up as he kisses my shoulder. Does he not pick up on how uncomfortable I am? Or does he not care? He's known since I showed him that tape—though not all the details—of what he did. So does he not fully grasp the severity of his harm to me? Or does he not care?

"Denendrius—"

His hand wraps over mine, and he makes me stir the corn again as the water in it bubbles. Then he pulls my hand out and takes the spoon from my limp grip. He sets it on the metal stovetop and turns me around. I can feel the heat of the stove through my shirt as he presses me into it again with his firm body.

He gives me a kiss so soft I barely feel it. Pulling away, he undresses me from head to toe with his smoldering eyes. "I pick?"

"D-did you pick me?" I clasp my hands and hold them against my chest.

His brow quirks, waiting for my answer.

"Yes, you did." But not in the way he thinks.

My heart hammers as he runs the back of his hand against my cheek. "I pick good." He steps away from me and gives me a sheepish smile, like he knows he's distracting me. "Sorry. Cook."

He keeps his hands off me as I fry the sausages, though he still eye-fucks me from where he supervises beside the counter. I pretend I don't notice that he brushes his hand over the crotch of his jeans a few times, that his chest lifts and falls with heavy, lascivious breaths.

Carol, Derek, and Rayonne return as I'm finishing cooking. I'm grateful for their timing.

Denendrius's jaw sets and he clears his throat and disappears to the bedroom—shutting the door—before they've even got the front door closed behind them. Was he planning on bending me over a counter when I was done cooking or something? What would have happened if I'd protested?

Nice or not now, it's clear he's *never* been one hundred percent right in the head.

XXII

After Denendrius eats, we load the SUV with everything we need and check for a tracker before heading to Carol's. Though Carol and I worry about a surprise visit from my social worker, we accept that risk over another Darkling encounter.

Heavy rain assaults us as we cut through it while driving to where Carol's house is on the other side of the north in a newer neighborhood. The yellow blobs of light from the streetlamps look distorted through the streaks of water on the windows.

Nobody brings up Sergei, not that they could, anyway.

The brief trip from the driveway to the front door of Carol's lemonade-yellow two-story house has me soaked to my socks. A cold droplet of water runs down my spine, and I shiver while impatiently waiting for the door to be unlocked.

Denendrius grins up at the sky, water dripping down his face.

"Come on." I pull him inside, stifling my laugh.

Denendrius whistles as we enter the house, warm eyes moving past the large fireplace—wooden mantel covered in picture frames—on the immediate left, over to the staircase on the other side of it, and past the hallway to the dining area leading to the kitchen directly across from us.

"Very nice." He looks down at me. "Why not a place like this for us?"

I kick my shoes off as Carol flicks a light on that illuminates the living room on the right. "I don't know. You wanted to live close to my school. That's why you picked our home."

He leans over and undoes his sandals. "Hm. Bad idea," he says, the fact he understood all that leaving me woozy. He points around and grins. "I need this."

How would Denendrius react if he saw the mansions that some people live in? "It was supposed to be temporary, I think."

After multiple trips outside for our stuff, we go over each window and doorway with garlic since Carol isn't confident she did a thorough job. By the time we're done, I'm convinced the acrid smell is embedded in the flesh of my nose forever.

Afterward, everyone but Denendrius sits down at her nice dining room table for an exhausted meal of pizza bites.

Carol sets Derek up in a main-floor room down the hallway across from hers, and he retires to bed before the rest of us, saying he needs to go to school tomorrow. He seems relieved that it's his last day. Rayonne crashes in another room soon after, and I head upstairs to mine with Denendrius.

He grunts as we enter my white room and frowns at the twin bed in the far right corner. "We fit?" There's a floor-to-ceiling window between the bed and a tall built-in bookshelf that held my books for mere days before he came and packed up all my stuff.

"We do." I shut the door behind us and drop my bag on the gray-blue wood of the floor.

It's strange returning to this room. I didn't even have enough time to make it mine. If Denendrius had never gotten involved, would I have covered the walls in posters by now?

Would the closet at the end of my bed have even more clothes hanging behind its white accordion doors?

Part of me wants to ask him if he remembers this room, if he remembers forcing himself on me in the hot tub, but I strip down to my underwear and change into some comfortable clothes. After hauling a dead body to the woods and having a breakdown over Sergei, I don't even care that Denendrius ogles me from where he stands beside my plush white bed.

"So pretty," he whispers, tongue running over his bottom lip. He seems entranced as he unbuckles his belt and drops his pants to the floor, shirt following. "Like a goddess."

I swallow and crawl into bed, the cool sheets and the calming sound of rumbling thunder outside making exhaustion envelop me. Denendrius crawls over me, and I stiffen.

With a hand on either side of my head on the pillow, while he hovers over me in nothing but his silk boxers, he murmurs, "*I want you.*"

I pull the blanket between us. "No. Sleep, Denendrius."

He releases a dramatically disappointed sigh and bounces down beside me, elbow knocking into the wall. "My *wife*, it is your duty . . ." From his grin, I can tell he's trying to be playful and not threatening, but he *really misses the mark.*

I'm unable to blink as I stare at him, once again thankful he can't hear my heartbeat.

The humor falls from his face, the brown of his eyes losing warmth. "I upset you?"

"Yes," I breathe.

He lays his head on the pillow—turned sideways so it fits—and studies my face. "Ah."

I stare at the ceiling as he tries to get comfortable beside me.

His knees pull up against my side as he complains quietly to himself in Latin. "Marianna . . . bed is small."

"What do you want me to do about it? You should count

your blessings that they even let us go to the same room together since there's technically enough to separate us in this house."

He's silent for a long moment. "Hm?"

"Ugh. Never mind." Maybe it's a good thing he didn't understand me.

The corner of Denendrius's lips upturn, his eyes soft and glittering in the low light of the room.

I turn my face into my shoulder to break my gaze from his. "Stop looking at me like you're madly in love with me."

"Marianna."

Sighing, I turn my face back to him. "What?"

Denendrius straightens the fluffy comforter on me, the calmness of his eyes unnerving . . . so *unfamiliar*. It's strange how much humanity has changed his face.

Lifting my hand, I run my fingers along the hair growth on his jaw. "I've never seen you with facial hair before. You must have had a fresh shave the day you died."

"Hmm. You like?" he asks, lifting a brow.

My lips twist, but I nod and smile a little. He looks different, in a good way. A way that makes looking at him a little less painful.

He takes my hand from his jaw and brings it to his lips, kissing the back of it before pressing his lips to the ring on my finger.

I hold my breath when he gives me my hand back.

"Here—" I run my fingers down the back of his neck until I find the tie in his hair. It comes out easily when I pull it, and the waves and curls of his damp hair fall around my fingers. I watch his face for any signs of anger when I drop the elastic between the wall and mattress, so it'll be easier for him to forget about. "There. Better. You look even more different now."

When I run my fingers through his hair to straighten it out, he winks at me.

I bring my hands back onto my side of the bed. "Okay, sorry. We can sleep now."

His face adopts a seriousness that makes my heart pound harder.

"What?" I whisper, my throat dry.

"*Amo te*," he whispers.

My heart moves so fast that my chest hurts, and I can't get another breath in.

"I love you," he repeats, as if his Latin wasn't clear enough for me to understand.

Eyes stinging, I stare down at the blanket covering my chest. What could I possibly say back besides nothing?

"Marianna."

I swallow a lump and force my eyes to meet his. But when his hand slips out from beneath the blanket and he reaches toward my face, I can't help but flinch.

"Safe now," he murmurs to me.

The warmth of his gentle touch as he rests his fingers on my cheek is still jarring.

I inhale sharply. "I want so badly to believe you."

It would be much simpler if I could truly trust that he'll never lay hands on me again.

When a nightmare throws me into consciousness, I find Denendrius's arm across my back as he shushes my quiet cry, my face mashed in my pillow. Rolling under his arm, I stare widely at the ceiling, the heaviness and heat of his arm across my stomach helping distract me from the terror of my dream. One that started with dirty men touching me and then turned to Denendrius killing them all before pinning me down with his cold body to hurt me the same. The weight of his arm grounds me, makes me aware of my breath as my aching ribs struggle to expand under him.

He whispers something comforting, his face only inches from the side of mine. Unfortunately, whatever he says doesn't stop the tears. I hate the fact that even when he's out of my life, I'll still have the rest of my problems skulking behind me like demons with claws stuck in my back. My nightmares, fears, and distrust will continue.

Even if going to Romania works out the way everyone blindly believes it will, can I fill the emptiness that will follow me? How am I supposed to live a normal life away from normal, get a boyfriend, trust some stranger enough to spend time alone until I'm comfortable enough to give myself to them? Do that over and over again until I find the "right" one? How many times am I going to explain my past to them and hope they understand?

Can I have a love life if I want one in the castle? I suspect my human options will be limited, and I don't want to *think* about the vampire men.

Lightning cracks like a golden whip outside, illuminating my room through the thin white curtains. The rain is like tiny pebbles against the window. It drowns out some of the noise in my head.

Denendrius pulls me closer. My tank top bunches under me and I almost knock my head into the bottom of his jaw, trying to straighten it out. I turn to face him and tuck the blanket under my arm, the chill of the room a shock to my flesh as goose bumps rise. Denendrius wraps his arm around me as I shove my arm back under, the heat of his skin easily felt through my shirt. Placing my hand on his bare chest, I enjoy the reminder of his heart. I angle myself away from him, pulling my knees up against his thighs.

He nestles his face into the top of my head, his nose stuck in my hair, his thumb rubbing my cheek and catching tears.

When I eventually stop crying, I take a minute to notice. My consciousness dances close to the edge, and I sniffle violently to wake myself up, not wanting to fall back to my dreams.

He scoots down so his forehead is against mine, and I become aware of the heat of his breath pulsing against my tear-streaked face. He runs his fingers through my hair, my mind locking on the feeling. It's all I can think about. I'm so still my muscles ache, my eyes dry from not blinking, my breath heavy as it passes through my lips.

His hand slides down from my hair, my skin prickling behind his touch as his fingers trail past my throat and across the exposed part of my back before hitting the fabric of my tank top. When my breath hitches, his becomes harder against my skin. My stomach tightens.

Denendrius swallows loudly, his index finger hooking under my chin and turning my face up. My heart stops when our lips touch, my bottom lip trembling as his hand curls around the back of my stiff neck. He holds my head tighter to his, leaving me with no space to move. He tastes sweet when his tongue searches for mine, and I have to think about kissing him back, how to shape my lips around his.

It doesn't feel like I'm kissing the man who has scarred me. In the dark of the room, his lips—his heartbeat—almost convince me that man never was. With his fiery touch, the iciness of his hands in my dream melts away.

His hand moves from my neck and trails down my back. He pushes up my shirt when it reaches my waist and skates his fingers across my skin. My back arches, my chest pressing into his.

I know I'm not thinking properly when I lift my arms so he can pull the tank top over my head. But I want to feel the heat of his skin, like it might defrost that icy darkness inside me. He tosses my top somewhere behind me and buries his face in my neck.

I stifle a gasp, reminding myself he won't rip into my throat. He kisses me as I rest my hand on his head. It's hard not seeing the brown of his eyes to remind me of who he is, but his warm mouth as it trails toward my chest is convincing enough.

My fingers dance over the ridges of his muscles, his skin twitching under my touch, his kisses hardening with his breath. His unshaven face tickles my skin as I slide my fingers over his collarbone and up the nape of his neck to play with his hair. He even smells human now instead of only like pine.

Denendrius's hand glides past the waistline of my pants, running over my ass as he kisses me. I wince when he yanks me tight against him, pulling my leg over his before he returns his hand to my backside, slowly creeping between my legs.

I stiffen, my breath trapped in my throat. Without thinking, my hand reaches around and my fingers lock around his wrist before he goes too far. He pulls his head away from my chest, eyes leveling with mine, searching.

I hate myself for wanting him to touch me, for thinking that his human hands might overwrite the feeling of his harsh touches before. For thinking that if I let this happen—if he's gentle to me—maybe I can reroute my mind to this whenever I think about all the other things my body has experienced.

At least with Denendrius, I won't have those daunting questions of whether he thinks I'm pretty or not, of whether he actually likes me—even if he hasn't always shown it in the best ways—or plans on dumping me right away when he's taken what he wants. I don't have to be embarrassed, because really, he's in no position to think bad of me anyway.

Does it matter if I let this continue? It's not like it can screw me up any more than I already am.

Whatever the reason, if I hate it, I never have to do it again.

Maybe I want him to try doing something that proves he hasn't changed. I wouldn't have to worry about him remembering everything else if he did. It would almost be easier if he hurt me, then I wouldn't have to agonize over him knowing all the ways he already has. He could suffer for *this*.

Releasing his hand, I listen for footsteps in the hall or the sound of the knob turning as my hand trails up to his neck. I return my lips to his.

I lose myself in the feel of his ardent mouth as it shapes mine. I'm so used to the shock of his cold hands that I overprepare for when his hand slides under the fabric of my pants.

My lips freeze when his hand disappears from my ass, pushing my hips away from his before diving down the front of me. My breath collects at the back of my throat, and my heart beats so fast that stars trickle into my vision.

Denendrius kisses the corner of my mouth as thunder shakes the house, fingers gently exploring the space between my legs. He's gentle, no aggressive shake to his hand like I'm used to.

His lips move against mine, his breath fanning into my dry mouth. "Like?"

My ears ring. I lick my parched lips, swallowing a lump. He's already there, so I wait for the feeling that Daina always talks about, comfortable enough to allow a sliver of curiosity. Nothing happens in my body. He may as well not even be there.

Heat spreads to my face when he notices my struggle. His eyes flicker past my waist and back to my face, and I must look terrified because he gives me an encouraging smile and returns to kissing me.

He tries a different movement, but again, nothing happens. I wonder if it's because I'm broken after all my body has been through, because there's nothing about his touch that I can relate to how he used to be, and I'm sure he's well versed in the bedroom. Which means it's not something he's doing, it's *me*.

When my breath comes rapidly with that thought, the muscles in my legs stiffen with panic. A breath audibly catches in my throat, my chest lifting as it swells. He puts a hand on my cheek, his expression telling me to stop. Soft brown eyes holding mine, he acts out how I should breathe and I copy until my breath is easy again. He gives me a kind smile and pretends to loosen his shoulders and arms like he's saying "you need to relax," so I take a deep breath and imagine the stress in my muscles evaporating as I loosen.

I focus my thoughts on *him* and *now* to keep my breath even and my limbs pliable. I forbid my mind from wandering and focus on Denendrius instead of if I'm going to want to hang myself in the morning, if I'm going to be even more scared to try things with whoever I date in the future now that I know there might be something wrong with me.

So I focus on the way his practiced hands touch me, begging for my reaction as his hungry lips can't pick between showering my neck or my lips in kisses. With my knee on his hip, I lose my fingers in the soft strands of his hair, twisting them around my fingers as I think of nothing past the feeling inside me.

Maybe it's because I relax, or he does something that finally works, but it forces a gasp from me and warm tingles spread through my body.

"Ah . . ." He smiles against my mouth. "Good."

His mouth moves over my collarbones, the tip of his tongue against my skin. I shiver, my skin slick with sweat. He stops touching me for a moment, his hand wrapping around my knee as he uses it to push me onto my back. When he slips his hand back into my pants, hot lightning makes my toes curl.

With my arms around his neck, I cling to him and try to figure out a name for what I'm feeling. It makes me want him to touch me more, makes my heart thump so fast I'm dizzy.

Does this feeling mean I love him?

Would my body still react so strongly if I didn't?

My thought—that I have no idea what any of this means—startles me.

When he slowly slides my pants off under the blanket, my breath is too labored to tell him no, even if I wanted to. I run my hands down the muscles of his chest and stomach, and he bites his bottom lip and stares down at me with starving eyes.

Every bone in me wants him sweating and moaning on top of me. Maybe it's sick curiosity. Maybe I think he can fuck the bad memories out of me, for his touch to consume me so deeply I can barely remember the touch of those when I was younger.

When his fingers disappear from between my legs and he pulls down his boxers to expose himself—to show that he's ready for more—I push him away. I don't want him to stop, but I need to know he will.

When he moves away, soft eyes studying me, my throat tightens. Sweat soaks the nape of my neck, and I think I might vomit for real. Because now that I know he won't hold me down and that the "sex" won't consist of me fighting him, I have to do something so he knows I want him to keep going. I realize I have no idea how to act of my own accord in a situation like this.

I think about how I'm going to have to touch him and my stomach slams into my gut and I—

Can't breathe.

I try to move and can't. My muscles are stone. Fuzz starts in my fingertips and crawls up my arms to my face. I can't even unclench my fists. My skin feels like rubber, and I doubt I would feel it if he were to hit me.

"Marianna?"

A strangled grunt passes through my lips, and I can't even close my eyes to blink away welling tears. Because now, I'm thinking about being in my childhood bedroom and can practically feel the damp covers of the creaky double bed, the draft that would come from the broken bathroom window. I can smell the dirt, the meth smoke and weed drifting through the vents. I can almost hear the thud of a man's shoes climbing the wooden stairs to my bedroom. If my eyes were closed, I'd swear I was there.

When I quiver like I'm cold—despite feeling warm enough to sweat—Denendrius takes my hand. He whispers what I can only hope are soothing words, yanks his boxers back up, and lies down beside me. He pulls my head against his chest and runs fingers through my hair. I'm too numb to cry, so I focus on breathing and the thump of his heart against my cheek so I don't hyperventilate.

I lose control of my breath anyway, short bursts of air barely reaching my lungs before being expelled again and again between my numb lips. He covers my cheek with his hand and rubs under my eye with his thumb. I can barely feel it through the tingles tightening my skin and muscles.

Denendrius's eyes flit toward the door every once in a while, and although he says nothing, I can tell he's hoping someone doesn't come in and find me panicked and sweaty with my clothes missing. It doesn't have a lock, but I wonder if he'd get up and turn it if it did.

Slowly, I convince myself into calmness by focusing back on the raging storm outside instead of the tornado within me.

I expect him to complain, for him to try again now that I've regained my breath. But he hikes the blanket up to our chins. He helps me pull my pants up once I've snagged them with my feet and places his hand on the side of my head, sighing as he nestles into the mattress and blanket.

A hot wave of guilt pools in my stomach at the thought of his disappointment and likely frustration. He must be so mad at me now. I anticipate him rolling me over anyway, but he remains silent at my side.

"I'm sorry," I squeak.

He pulls away and gives me a what-for scowl.

I shift my eyes from his and say nothing more.

Denendrius's lips brush against mine. "I love you, Marianna." The words tickle my lips.

Goose bumps litter my skin, and I fight the urge to press my lips back to his. "I love you too," I whisper automatically.

He rolls onto his back. "Okay, sleep. Me too."

XXIII

I get the desired result from my experiment with Denendrius. When I fall back asleep—briefly, since he's waking me by climbing out of bed, mumbling about the bathroom minutes after I crash into dreamland—all I think about is him. All my horrible sexual experiences are far from my thoughts, and all I can think about is how *I felt something different.* My friends were right; just because I have trauma doesn't mean it'll be traumatic.

After Denendrius disappears for what feels like forever, I creep out of bed and slip my tank top on before tiptoeing out of my room. The light is still on in the bathroom across the hall, and when I approach the door, I can hear the shower running.

"Sex addict," I accuse under my breath.

There's bumping around below, so I head downstairs to see who else is up. I follow the slice of light across the kitchen and dining room to the pantry. Carol is stepping out of the crawl-space hatch, box in hand.

"What are you doing?" I ask as she sets a dusty box on the

table and sweeps a few cobweb strands from the top of her head.

She pulls a chair back and plops herself down in it with an overexerted huff. "I'm going through storage. Rayonne and I were talking, and she thinks I should at least see if they'll let me in the castle with you since I'm technically your parent."

I plant a hand on the tabletop and sigh. "She's being too optimistic about that."

Carol gives me a gentle smile. "She knows far more about it than the rest of us, so I'm going with it. I have to make plans for something. I'm going to put everything I want to bring into storage for now, and depending on how long we're here before they come get us, I'll probably sell the house from Romania if I can, and hire someone to sell or donate whatever's left inside."

I don't want to step on her hope, so all I say is, "What's in the box?"

She stands and flips it open. "Some of your stuff from when you were little, actually. It's on the list to bring."

"Okay." I straighten and peer into it, my eyes landing on a folded teal-and-purple sweater with the Enchanted Land logo below a silver mermaid silhouette. There are some colorful file folders along the side of the box, as well as some stuffed animals. I pick the sweater up and it unfolds. It's hard to imagine I was ever small enough to fit in it. I draw my lips into my mouth as I set it aside and unwedge a loose piece of paper.

My heart drops. On the white page, below a bright red banner with the FBI logo beside MISSING CHILD, my name is in black above a picture of my five-year-old self and my description.

The paper rattles in my hand. I unglue my eyes from it. "They kept this?"

She lifts a single shoulder in a half-shrug. "He showed up at our hotel with you twelve days later, said he found you alone, walking confused around the city. He grilled Vianna and

Kenneth about their parenting plans and ideas, like he thought you were in that situation because of neglect or something.

"I suspected him, especially since you had a meltdown when he left. Despite your easy attachment to strangers, the reaction was extreme. But they didn't buy the idea that he was a suspicious person. They assumed he was telling the truth and skipped the police to bring you straight to your parents, since you knew where they were. 'Why would a man that was smart enough to get you out of a theme park despite a quick lockdown, then evade the FBI for almost two weeks, be dumb enough to bring the kid he kidnapped back?' It made little sense to me too." She smooths the rose tablecloth covering the long wooden table.

"What did I tell you about those days I was missing?" I put the missing poster back in the box.

She blows air past her lips and shakes her head in astonishment. "*Nothing.* Not a peep about the entire ordeal. We assumed the worst, especially since you were wearing designer clothes and had your nails and toes painted when you came back. The fact that you remembered nothing wasn't a good sign either. We took you to the hospital for an exam, and there were no visible signs of trauma."

I'm relieved to know he likely didn't cross that line.

"I didn't even fight him when he took me," I mumble. "I happily left with him and let him buy me toys. Did Vianna and Kenneth know that? It took me days before I got homesick enough to demand to go home. I took his hand and walked away. Didn't that hurt them? I could have saved them so much pain if I kicked and screamed." They cared enough to adopt me, and *I left with some guy?*

Her bottom lip puckers, eyes sympathetic as she rests her hand on her chest. "Oh, honey, I don't know if you were ever told, but you have an attachment disorder. Vianna and Kenneth knew you had indiscriminate friendliness too while going through adoption. One symptom of that is going off with strangers and not checking back with your caregivers. You used to follow other families out of the grocery store and tried to get hugs and kisses from random people in the mall. It was terrifying how little fear you had of strangers. You ran off in the department store one time, and a group of teen boys brought you to security after finding you wandering around in the parking lot. It was so bad that Vianna had a leash attached from your wrist to hers at Enchanted Land, and you broke it during a fit of rage in the hotel the day you went missing."

"Oh." I bite my lip.

"You don't remember any of it?" she asks.

I sit and shake my head. "I can't remember much of anything that wasn't being locked in that bedroom. What was I like? A pain in the butt all the time?"

She chuckles softly, her smile lopsided. "No, you weren't always a pain in the butt. You were still a great kid. There was a reason they were adopting you. You were—*are*—insanely smart and talented. But you went through a lot as a little girl and it showed in your behavior." She continues when my eyes narrow. "You would have horrendous fits of rage. Hitting and biting everyone, trying to tear wallpaper off the wall. You'd rotate between hoarding food and overeating to refusing to eat. And it was very difficult to comfort you during those episodes because you refused to connect with anyone."

I wonder if I acted like that around Denendrius when he first took me. Was that one reason he wanted to pawn me off on Sergei? Or was he so used to chaos that any bad behavior didn't faze him?

When the stairs creak, I spin around. Denendrius stands on the bottom step in his boxers, rubbing his hair dry with a towel.

Carol clears her throat and stands. She closes the box after putting the sweater back in. "Can't sleep?" she asks him, jamming her hands in the pockets of her fuzzy pink housecoat.

He motions to me. "Marianna."

"Oh, you came looking for her?" Carol moves to the counter and cracks a cupboard open like she's trying to occupy herself, lips pursed as she stares at her tea options.

"Yes. Bed . . ." He jerks his head toward the stairs behind him and smiles. "You will be tired."

He's not wrong. "Fine."

It feels like it's barely noon when I wake to the bed shifting, though I can hear Derek's voice downstairs. Did he even go to the school?

Denendrius is still asleep, so I carefully swing my legs out of bed and move the curtain aside to peek at the weather outside so I can decide how to dress.

The sun struggles to break through the thick gray clouds, the rain softer now. Little streams rush down the edges of the road. My breath creates a patch of fog on the window and I can't resist writing "hi" in it.

I throw on my tracksuit since it's soft and warm, pulling my pants up as Denendrius rolls away toward the wall, mumbling something desperate in Latin in his sleep. When he kicks out, the bed springs twang.

Tiptoeing out of the room, I take the stairs two at a time and turn left to the kitchen. Derek sits at the table, papers and books strewed about.

"You didn't go to school?" I head straight to a cupboard for a glass and fill it with tap water.

He looks up from the paper he's writing on. "I went in for first and second period and handed my resignation in. I feel bad that I won't be returning to finish up, but, you know, *vampires*."

"Makes sense." Does it?

"Denendrius opened up to me about his family," Derek says with a tickled grin.

I take a sip of water and sit across from him, the kitchen behind me so I can watch for Denendrius coming down the stairs. "What? When?"

"He went back up to bed about fifteen minutes ago after downing a few glasses and eating half a loaf of Carol's bread."

My brows lift. Either he's getting sneakier, or I'm starting to sleep more heavily. "Oh. How'd you manage that one, anyway? I couldn't get him to tell me jack shit when he was a vampire."

He shrugs, dropping his pen down on the table, and gives me a soft smile. "I don't know. He was in a superb mood and answered far more questions than I thought I'd get away with asking."

My lips purse with curiosity. "Well, what did he tell you?"

Derek leans back in his chair. "Did he tell you he's adopted?"

Tiredness evades me, and I sit up from my slump. "Adopted?"

He nods. "He was a victim of exposure—" I cock a brow and he elaborates with, "It was common for Romans to leave their infants out to die if they didn't want them, or even outright kill them. Horrifying by today's standards, but it was common if the child was sick, there weren't enough resources to go around, or they simply weren't wanted."

My mouth falls open. "That's fucked up."

"Yeah, it is. He was supposedly in perfect health when his mother took him from where she found him stuffed in a clay pot on a side road. He told me she was eighteen, and her and his father had been trying—unsuccessfully—for a baby since they married when she was about fourteen. He was a rich landowner without an heir, so she brought him home one so her husband wouldn't divorce her. He took Denendrius in, but resentfully. A lot of emperors were adopted, so it wasn't looked at as a negative thing, but Denendrius told me that his father made sure to remind him that he was only alive because they saved him, and that he only did so because they had no other options and that he didn't want to destroy all the benefits his family got from his wife's family. That, and it would be especially bad if word got out that he was physically abusing her."

My eyes narrow. "Romans weren't *allowed* to beat their wives?"

"Technically, there were laws against it—during the time he was alive, at least. But I'm sure they didn't enforce it as seriously. They all saw women as property, but Denendrius isn't necessarily physical with you because he's Roman. They were a violent bunch, but the blame is on him alone. Especially given he had nearly two thousand years to change."

I recall the look on Denendrius's face when I told him at Sarah's party that it was him nobody has ever wanted. How he rammed his fists into my ribs for it. "Yeah, that all makes sense. Kind of ironic considering he hated his dad for everything he did, and he's probably worse than him."

Derek merely gives me a tight-lipped smile, a crease between his brows.

Why didn't he tell me any of this? I would've understood, not having known my biological father, and having a mother who didn't give a shit about me and made it known she would and could give me away—in any way she could. I suppose he didn't want to be emotionally vulnerable once things went . . . *sour* . . . between us.

"Does Denendrius know who abandoned him?" I wonder.

Derek shrugs. "There's no way to know for sure, but he thinks a prostitute left him, or a slave. At least that's what his adoptive mother thought. One of those is the most likely answer."

His severe abandonment issues are clear now, why he couldn't handle his creator—especially knowing now that it was Mariana's father—leaving him, why he latched on to me when I showed interest in him, and why he freaked out when I tried to leave. It wasn't his fault at first . . . but when he was a vampire? How could he expect anyone to want him when he was horrible?

"Did he tell you he was trying to convince his father to let him arrange a marriage to a plebeian girl? He was going to marry one of his father's picks, then divorce her when she was of age. Actually, the daughter of the man who ended up turning him," I say. "He wanted to be part of a loving family like hers, or something."

His brows twitch up. "That sounds a little optimistic."

"I thought it was messed up, considering she was a kid, but what do you mean?" I rub my thumb over the condensation of my glass, streaking it. "What was marriage even like?"

"Well, patricians and plebeians could marry one another, for sure. The legal age for marriage was twelve for girls—though they didn't always marry until they were a little older—and usually midtwenties for men, so her age wouldn't have been an issue if they were arranging it. But a marriage would have needed to be beneficial—either for political or financial reasons—for both families. It would have depended on what level of wealth they had as plebeians too. Marriage was more of a family decision, even if both bride and groom had to consent to it. He legally could have divorced his first wife whenever he pleased, but we don't know all the family dynamics he was stuck in. If his father ruled with an iron fist like he described to me, it could have made things that should be simple more complicated. Her family could probably never have reached Denendrius's father's expectations for a dowry, anyway."

I try to wrap my head around all that, and a headache starts in my temples. "Damn."

"Also, he was asking about his current *marriage* to you." He squints at me.

My arms are weak. "And? What did you tell him?"

He shrugs. "I wasn't sure what your story was there. He was asking about your father and dowries and all that . . . so I explained how marriage usually works in America. He seemed relieved, happy even."

"Yeah, he probably would be." I take a long drink of water and my eyes cut across the room. I notice the silence spread to each corner of the house. "Where are Carol and Rayonne?"

He puts his pen aside and folds his hands together as he adjusts in his chair, like he's waiting for a chance to say something. "They took a bunch of boxes to storage."

"Oh—"

"So, did Denendrius ever share with you what it was like to be a Darkling? Particularly the transformation? He wouldn't talk to me about it and seemed uncomfortable before going back upstairs." He clears his throat.

Good. His discomfort over the idea or memory of being a vampire makes me feel warm. "You want to be a vampire?"

The corner of his lip lifts and he picks his pen back up, fiddling with the cap. "Is that so bad? The way Rayonne talked about it was very convincing. She loathes being human again."

I wrinkle my nose. "I don't understand the appeal. The vampire world seems like nothing but a nightmare." At least, my entire experience with it has been so far.

"You would think that, Marianna," he says. "Your only experience with the world is under a deranged vampire's thumb. Rayonne told me she had a perfectly happy immortal life until Denendrius got involved."

I cross my arms and pull a grumpy face. "Still. The vampire world seems like nothing but cruelty."

He gives a what-can-you-do shrug. "You could say the same thing about our human one. You're in this world now, regardless. We both are. Nothing is going to change that. Vampirism is an idea worth entertaining."

"Rayonne says I can probably stay human," I argue.

"Yeah, maybe you can. But your opinion could change when you're not surrounded by immortality's worst. That exhaustion you're experiencing from vampires . . . I've been told you're not the only person dealing with it. Denendrius was made from unique circumstances. I doubt most vampires would be like him. The cruel things he does aren't completely a result of his vampirism, just exacerbated by it. How many vampires have been held in prison and tortured for centuries? Even when you put a human in a prison situation, it changes them. How many of your friends went to jail for drugs?"

"Quite a few."

"And how did they come out?"

I snort. "As better drug dealers or murderers . . ."

He smirks. "Right. So, you understand what I'm getting at?"

I sigh. "I guess, yeah."

"I'm not trying to pressure you. I don't want you to rule out a life opportunity because of one asshole," he says simply.

My lips twist, thoughts wandering. "Do you think he deserves to be held in some dungeon, even if he can't remember? Tortured?"

Derek tilts his head from side to side. "Prison . . . yeah. It may have unjustly screwed him up the first time, but he can't be free now. But torture? I've got mixed feelings on that one. But it's not our concern."

A pain slices through my stomach, but I'm not sure if it's from stress or hunger. "I don't know how I feel about it either," I whisper. "Seems pointless to torture a dude for things he can't remember. Doesn't really accomplish much." I twist my fingers together in my lap. "It feels like he's a different person with all his memories gone."

He nods, like he understands where I'm coming from. "Memories make a person. They influence how we see the world and our decisions. It's possible he won't make the same decisions he has in the past if he can't remember the things that brought him to make them. Sure, some things go beyond memory, but it's still a huge part of it."

I push out a hopeless breath. "I just . . . I don't know. It's so hard to be angry at him when he's acting so different. I don't have it in me anymore. I'm so tired."

Derek's eyes dart to the stairs and back to me. He leans forward a bit while saying, "You have to consider what he remembers, Marianna."

My brows pull together. "You think he remembers more than he's letting on?"

He sits back and shrugs, checking the stairs again. "I don't know. The thought *has* crossed my mind that he's playing pretend. But regardless of how bad he's acting now . . . it's *very* clear to me he's still a sociopath, even if he didn't turn into an unhinged one until later."

I wrap my arms around myself and slouch in the chair. "I don't think he remembers anything important," I argue. If he had, he probably would have jumped on the fact that Sergei showed up. "I think we'd be in big trouble."

It would still be better if he remembered nothing. He could go to jail and not be able to enjoy all the memories that got him there. That, and I'd never have to look into his knowing eyes again. His past self could drop away into the background. Already, it merely feels like a horrible nightmare. I don't want to jump back into it anymore.

"Hang on," Derek tells me, giving the table a pat. "You're spending too much emotional energy on him. It'll be over soon."

I give him a forced smile and stand to root through cupboards. None of the various snacks are appetizing.

Carol and Rayonne come home a few minutes later while I continue to ponder my options. The wind catches the door, and it slams so hard the house shakes.

There's a thud upstairs from my bedroom like Denendrius spun out of bed and onto the floor, followed by stomping while he calls my name.

I sneer at a box of fruit snacks and close the cupboard, turning around as Denendrius flies down the stairs, three at a time. His eyes sweep the room before he lets out a big breath and mumbles something.

"Are you okay?" I lean against the cupboard.

"Yes, I was dreaming and . . ." He motions to Carol and Rayonne once he realizes the source of the racket. "It is okay now."

XXIV

I skip lunch, Denendrius happily scarfing down my serving of meatloaf after he fails to convince me to eat. Instead, I lie on the couch in front of the TV and think about last night, my mind wandering over the feel of Denendrius's hands on my body. When I make myself think of him holding me down when he was a vampire and shoving his hands down my pants, the memory feels like a vivid nightmare.

Within myself, I feel an odd separation between me now, and who I was only a handful of days ago. It's a blurry line that cuts through my psyche and mind, one I don't think I can cross back over.

It feels like I've shifted into another reality.

I return to thinking about Denendrius and me the other night, and I can't help but wonder what would have happened if we'd continued.

"What's wrong?" Carol asks as she comes in and turns the volume down a smidgen.

I squint at her. "Nothing. Bored, why?"

"Your nails are bleeding."

I stare down at my hands, blood bubbling up from the torn skin of my thumb and index finger. "Oh."

I'm listless through the rest of the afternoon, feeling as heavy as the gray clouds that continue to accumulate outside. A static energy runs through me, putting me on edge. I hope I don't crack open like the clouds will.

Denendrius joins me while everyone cleans up the kitchen, wrapping his arm around my shoulders with me tucked at his side on the couch. He ponders the high school drama I watch, making confused grunts as he scratches at the thickening stubble on his jaw.

"I don't know what's happening either," I admit. "I've only watched two other episodes."

"Episodes?" he asks.

I pull in a deep breath and push it out, unable to conjure up the energy to explain.

He mumbles something in sweet Latin and squeezes me before forcefully planting a kiss atop my head. "Tired?"

"I'm eternally tired."

Denendrius gives me another kiss. "You need outside."

I roll my eyes and tighten my gaze on the TV. "Not helpful."

"Hot bath? I wash your hair? I found things for water. They smell nice." He laces his fingers through my hair and gives me a sample head massage that ends too soon.

My lips purse. I can't think of the last time I had a relaxing bath with bubbles and bath crystals—if ever. "Okay."

I twist my fingers together as we get up and walk the short distance across the area rug and to the stairs. Though I try to be sneaky going up with him, it's clear it doesn't even dawn on him we're doing anything wrong with how casually he follows me up the stairs and to the bathroom.

When he closes the door behind us, I bite at my bottom lip and fold my forearms together over my stomach.

I'm not completely sure where my nervousness stems from. From being in the same gold bathroom that Denendrius forced me to shower with him in after touching me in the hot tub? That he's going to see me naked? The latter is a little silly considering I let him touch me last night. Or is it because I'm worried about the warranted opinions of everyone downstairs if they notice us missing?

A soft smile curls his lips as he pulls his shirt over his head and sets it in a ball on the countertop. He twists the taps on and plugs the drain, testing the water before looking up at me and asking a question in Latin.

I cock a brow at him.

His grin grows, and he chuckles to himself. "Sorry. You undress now?"

Swallowing, I shift back and forth on my feet, moving out of the way when he moves to the cabinet under the sink. His motions are so relaxed that it only makes my muscles tighten.

Is he expecting to get something out of this?

Denendrius smiles up at me from the floor, a container of rose-scented pink bath crystals in hand. He points to the image of a tub on it, like that's how he figured out what they're for. "Okay?"

"Yes." I hold my breath and unzip my jacket as he sprinkles the crystals in.

"Bubbles too," I say. "Please."

Still crouched, he scoots back over to the cupboard and scans the items as he puts the crystals back. "What one is bubbles?"

I point to a purple cylindrical bottle with a few white bubbles around the brand name. "The one with the bubbles."

Denendrius chuckles as he picks it up, giving me a goofy grin while he rolls his eyes at himself. "Ah—of course."

A smile creeps onto my face and I shake my tracksuit jacket off, setting it on his shirt on the counter. He's intensely focused on making bubbles, swishing his hand back and forth, so I quickly pull the rest of my clothes off and stand with my arms crossed over my chest and my legs glued together.

"Is the water ready?" I whisper, snagging the edge of my bottom lip on the tip of my canine.

His eyes trail up me and lock on my torso, a perturbed look tightening his expression. Pointing to the faint scars from the multiple stab wounds he inflicted on me and his name that he carved into my chest, he says, "What happened?"

"You tried to kill me," I say brusquely.

He stares at me as his lips twitch together, like he's not sure how to process that. "I cannot remember. Why did I?"

"You were mad at me, but you regretted it and healed me." I should have never answered his question.

He inhales a long breath as he runs his hand through his hair to the back of his head. With a pained exhale, his hand drops to his lap. "Sorry. I do not know what else to say."

I stare at my feet and shake my head, hair falling around my head. "Can I get in?"

"Yes."

I rush to the tub and clamber inside it, leaning against the back of it and sinking down so bubbles hide my body.

"Is nice?" he asks.

The weight of his lilting Latin accent on his words makes my cheeks burn. I swallow a lump and nod.

He sits at the foot of the tub and stares fondly at me. "I am sorry, pretty girl."

I stare down at the bubbles, heart thumping so hard I'm surprised it doesn't create ripples in the water. "Thanks."

Denendrius adjusts the waist of his jeans and scowls. "I do not like. Tight."

"Miss your toga?" *Shit,* I totally could have gotten a point for that if I remembered it for my quiz. "Oh, and tunic?"

His grin is wide and toothy. "Yes."

"What did you use to wash?" I ask him, pointing to him before scrubbing my arm with bubbles.

His face is blank, gears visibly working. He looks at the shelf beside him and picks up my body wash. "At our house too. It smells like you."

I bite down on my bottom lip and smile. "In Rome?"

"*Roma* . . ." He makes a scraping motion at the skin on his arm while searching for the words. "I do not know how to say."

"That's all right."

He smiles and stands, sitting on the edge by my shoulder. "Confusing," he admits, picking up a few bottles to inspect.

I point to the bottle in his left hand. "That's shampoo. Rub it in my hair first." Then I point to the conditioner. "That goes in after a rinse. Only the bottom."

He makes a playful yet disgruntled noise. "Why so many?" He reaches across the tub and grabs the body wash. "This?"

"For your body only."

He nods and sets them all back on the shelf. "Okay, I see." Denendrius scratches at the scruff on his jaw and grumbles something.

"What's wrong? You don't like having facial hair?" I wiggle my toes above the bubbles.

"No. I am already big with long hair. I am a barbarian with this—" He vigorously rubs his hand against the side of his face like he's trying to rub the hair off. "No good."

My laugh bubbles out of me and he joins along in my amusement.

"Do you not like having long hair either?" I force a frown. Even back when I agreed to date him, it was one thing I found attractive.

He winks at me. "I do. Made my father angry. He beat me. Short is no good on me . . . and the girls like this."

I reach up and run my wet fingers over the hair on his jaw. "Well, I like it."

With a serious expression, he studies my face. "You do?"

My voice comes out small. "I do, a lot. You look good with a clean shave, but I like this a *little* better." I'd prefer never to see him with a clean shave again, but I don't want to tell him that, in case he thinks it's because it looks bad. "Maybe keep it this long"—I brush my hand over his other cheek—"but tidy it up."

He puts his hand over mine and leans into my palm. "Okay, if you like." He gives my hand a kiss and releases it, looking around until he spots a blue whale pitcher between the tub and toilet that must be left over from when Julie and James lived here. There's a tickled grin on his face as he looks at it.

I sit up properly as he scoops water, feeling too relaxed to care that my chest is now visible. "Please don't waterboard me," I tease as he lifts the pitcher to my head and pours some.

He pauses. "What?"

"A joke."

"Hmm, okay," he murmurs as he rests his hand on my forehead to soak the rest of my hair without it getting in my eyes.

He squeezes shampoo in his hand next, humming as he lathers it in my hair, fingers massaging into my scalp and running through sections.

I exhale a long breath and slouch, the warmth of the water embracing me as I enjoy the deep feel of his hands tangled in my hair.

"You feel how much I love you, yes?"

"Yes," I whisper.

"I wish to be a good modern husband now."

"That's good." I close my eyes and lean my head back when he grabs the pitcher again, wincing from the anticipation of water in my eyes—which doesn't come, thankfully—as he pours it.

He hums some more as he puts far too much conditioner in my hair and uses the waiting time to give me a shoulder massage, his thumbs digging into the tense muscles that have been tightening over time. I let myself enjoy it. My stress must have embedded itself deep as he says something in astonishment and digs his thumbs harder into my shoulders.

"Thanks," I whisper when he pulls his hands away. "This is a nice change."

I sigh when he rinses my hair with fresh water from the tap. When he grabs a pink cloth from the drawer, a hint of a smirk on his lips, my brows lift in question.

"I will wash you." He kneels beside the tub and dips the cloth in the water.

I fight my smile and lose, knowing exactly what his game is. "Uh-huh."

His grin is wide and toothy before he leans forward and presses his lips to mine. He's gentle as he washes me down with the soapy cloth, starting with my neck and shoulders and working down. As expected, he takes time to wash my chest and lingers between my legs.

"Denendrius . . ." I wrinkle my nose at him.

The cloth moves down my thigh, and he looks up at me with feigned innocence. "Hm? I am washing."

I merely chuckle. "Sure."

When he's done, I stand, and he rinses me with fresh water before taking my hand as I step out. I dry off as he brushes his teeth and rubs at his facial hair in the mirror.

"It looks good," I insist as I slip back into my clothes.

He rinses his mouth and turns around to face me. "I will make your hair?"

I squint at him. "What?"

"With pins?" He runs his fingers through my dripping strands.

"Oh." My lips twist, not feeling very confident about the outcome. "Uh . . . okay." I didn't even let Camille, Daina, or Jenna style my hair, and they actually knew what they were doing.

He leaves me impressed. After only a handful of minutes standing in front of the mirror, he's got my long hair twisted in two braids starting from either side of my head, pulled back and wound into a tight bun.

It looks far too classy for me, so much so that the sight of me makes my eyes burn.

"You hate it," he says, hands falling from my hair.

I shake my head and blink away impending tears. "No, it's pretty." So pretty I'd probably get made fun of at school for being over-the-top. I cover my gang tattoo—the main reason for always having my hair down and plain—to see if it suits me any better without the sore sight. "Too pretty for a poor girl like me."

His laugh is boisterous, and I scowl.

Resting his hands on my shoulder, he leans down so his face is next to mine. "You are a rich girl now with me. Remember the rubies."

I scratch my scalp. "How do you know how to do hair? Modern men barely know how."

He grins and straightens, taking the last bobby pin from the little plastic container we found in the drawer. "I learned from our slaves. Adelia liked me to do this."

"Did you spend a lot of time with her, then?" I wince when he jabs the pin into the back of my head.

"Yes. She was my favorite in the family. We looked so alike. Like real siblings."

I twist my fingers together on the damp counter. "I've never really had my hair done before. Actually, I haven't had a haircut since I was ten."

He stares at me in the mirror like I've said the strangest thing. "Why?"

"I was poor, remember? Someone almost adopted me though," I tell him, waiting to analyze his reaction.

He glances up at me and gives me an encouraging smile. "I was."

"My mom was a prostitute and drug addict, so they took me away from her." I can't make myself tell him the rest of the reasons.

"Who did?"

He doesn't remember calling the police to save me? Good. "The government. Prostitution is illegal."

His head snaps up like that's a crazy thing. "Is it? Hm."

"Yes. They gave me to . . . a new family." I cut myself off, wondering if I should even tell him this. Is finding some common ground worth it if he remembers?

Resting his hand on my shoulder, he smiles softly at me in the mirror. "Hm. Better like this. I take care of you."

I clear my dry throat. "Yeah."

What does he think is going to happen? Is he assuming all these vampire issues will go away and he and I will ride off into the sunset together?

He turns me around and pulls me in for a rough kiss. My heart skips.

"Happy?" he asks.

I nod and touch the braids in my hair. "Yes, thank you. I feel a little better now."

"Good." He unbuckles his pants, and I jerk away from him until he motions to the toilet.

"Right. Human." Not wanting to stick around for that, I shut the bathroom door behind me and head downstairs. Though I'm not completely alleviated from my stress, I'm calm enough now that my stomach rumbles and demands to be fed.

Carol swoops in as soon as she spots me, setting her spoon on the counter and wandering over. "Were you both in the bathroom?"

I brace myself for a lecture. "Why? I was having a bath, and he did my hair. We weren't doing anything."

"I really don't think that's appropriate," she says. Then, as if he has any say in what I do, Carol looks at Derek to back her up. "Right?"

"We're worried about you, is all," Derek adds. "We don't have to repeat ourselves."

I step onto the hardwood. "I get it. But like . . . butt out of it? I'm not sure what you expect me to do."

"Don't rock the boat," Rayonne tells them as she passes by from the kitchen to the living room, a kitten-covered cup of steaming tea in hand, "unless you want him to push us all in and leave us to drown."

They understand what she's saying, at least, as Carol and Derek exchange a glance as their shoulders slump. But from Carol's derisive grumble, she wants to tell Denendrius exactly what she thinks, especially when he comes downstairs.

Denendrius takes my hand and motions to my hair once everyone's eyes are on me. "Very pretty, yes?"

Rayonne and Derek give supportive smiles while Carol says, "It looks gorgeous, Marianna."

Warmth fills my face. "Thanks."

I gnaw through three rice cakes—despite Carol's warning that she's going to cook dinner soon—as I watch Denendrius and Derek in the backyard from the other side of the glass door. The sky still crawls with gray, and one gust of cold air was enough for me to stay inside.

Under Derek's curious eye, Denendrius thrusts and slices through the cold air with his swords like he's fighting invisible opponents. I watch in awe as he twists and turns. His skill would be clear to anyone, and there's no doubt why he mesmerized crowds, especially that little girl. If I was a kid, I'd think he was a god—incapable of dying—too. It's easy to imagine him in the amphitheater, the heat of the sun, the dust kicking up around him as he fights, dodging swords and spears as thousands scream for blood.

Did he block the sound of the audience out to concentrate better? Or did it fuel him? My mind wanders as I watch him slow down and show Derek specific techniques. I think of how many fights he could have won, how many he might have lost. What happened when another gladiator nearly gutted him? Was the crowd upset? Or did they scream for the other gladiator to finish him?

When he hands the blades to Derek, the gladii look awkward in his hands as he jabs at the air. Though I can't hear Denendrius's laugh as he leans his head back, I can tell it's loud.

Denendrius notices me and waves. I wave back and wonder what the neighbors would think if they peeked out their rain-streaked windows and saw two grown men sword fighting in the backyard during a brewing storm.

I finish my snack, and can't help but feel sour it's Derek out there learning how to fight and not me.

Screw it.

After putting my sneakers on, I slide the deck door open and brave the cold while I run across the deck, past the hot tub, and down the wooden steps to where Denendrius and Derek stand in the grass.

"My turn." I hold a demanding hand out as Denendrius accepts a gladius back from Derek. "Teach me."

From the tickled grin on Denendrius's face and his chuckle, I'm convinced he's going to deny me until Derek says, "I don't know, Marianna. They're pretty sharp."

I grit my teeth, my nostrils flaring. "If I can handle all the other weapons—"

Denendrius interrupts with, "Derek, she is *my wife.* I would not pick a weak girl."

Derek quietly agrees, mumbling something about how the other weapons aren't as big, while he stands aside with the second sword.

I shiver against a cold gust of air and a droplet of rain on my forehead as Denendrius takes my hand and folds it around the gladius's wooden handle. Automatically, I move my legs into a fighting stance, which Denendrius adjusts slightly with a tap of his foot against my right one to move it back more.

He stands against my backside, and with our bodies aligned, he uses his hand on mine to guide the gladius. I'm quivering with excitement as he slowly moves me through different techniques.

"Aim for belly." He thrusts the gladius and my hand forward as he moves my body with his. "Sometimes this—" We slash the blade through the air.

With his sword in my hand, I feel connected to him beyond our proximity, and for one moment, experience an intense ripple of envy over the fact that Mariana would have sat in the amphitheater and watched all his fights. Though I wonder what she would have thought about the sudden disappearance of her favorite gladiator. Did Marciana and Marianus keep what happened a secret? What did people think happened to Denendrius and his family?

I'm broken from my thoughts when Denendrius gives the top of my head a kiss and backs away. "Try alone."

I pull in a deep breath and summon the same concentration I use to fire my Beretta, and imagine thrusting the cold steel blade through the abdomens of vampires and slicing through their chests to their hearts. After a few minutes of Denendrius directing my mock-fighting from where he stands beside Derek, I stop to steady my breath and hold my hand out for the second sword in Derek's hand.

Denendrius tut-tuts and shakes his head. "Two? Too hard for you. A shield would have been best."

"I don't have one now," I argue.

"It does not matter. Nothing to train here, anyway." He chuckles. "You are sweet. You want to fight like me."

I swallow against my dry throat and shrug. "I've always enjoyed learning how to fight. Makes me feel safer knowing I can defend myself."

Denendrius takes the other gladius from Derek and faces me, pointing the sharp tip at me. "Okay. We fight. You learn more."

My hand shakes at the sight of him in front of me with the gladius, and I can only imagine what other gladiators must have felt in his towering presence.

"Uh . . ." Derek crosses his arms. "Are you sure, Marianna?"

"It's fine," I insist, though I flinch when Denendrius steps closer.

Denendrius and I spar painstakingly slowly as he walks me through each step and technique. He tells me we would have had to make the fight look good as well to appease the audience, and that if we were really training, we would be much more violent and physical.

Only when I'm out of breath and damp with rain and sweat, do I decide I've had enough. My face twists with delight, my cheeks warming as I notice the brightness in Denendrius's eyes.

Derek purses his lips and nods like he's impressed. "Pretty neat, considering the scattered knowledge we have of training, right?"

Denendrius laughs so hard his shoulders shake. "You see, Derek? What did I say? Marianna is much better than you. She has fire inside her. I like that."

"Think I could have been good enough one day to be accepted into a gladiator school?" I ask Denendrius with a hopeful lift of my brows.

His smile slants. "Eh, no. You are tough, but better to be a wife and mother."

"Oh . . ." I swallow my disappointment and wipe wetness from my face as the rain picks up. His words weigh on my heart as I swing the sword a little beside my leg.

I don't know why I thought I'd hear a different answer, but I suppose I shouldn't be upset when I hardly know what being a gladiator truly entailed.

My feelings must transfer to my expression as Denendrius puts his hand on my lower back and adds, "You did fantastic. A natural."

"Thanks," I mumble. "Will you teach me more another time?"

Denendrius nods, and his lips part to speak when Derek clears his throat and interrupts him.

Derek rubs the back of his neck, gaze alternating between us as he says, "Should we see if dinner is ready?"

Carol was right about me being too full for dinnertime, but to keep her from knowing that, I pick at my casserole and force bites down. The stress of the sky tucking the sun away for the day doesn't help my appetite either.

Denendrius won't keep his hands off me even as he shovels food in his mouth. Sitting beside me, he shoves his hand between my thighs a few times, finally making me spill water down the front of me. Derek stares at Denendrius with a disgusted curl of his lip upon noticing the mischievous smirk on his face.

Even as I go upstairs to change, I can't bring myself to feel more than annoyed at Denendrius. Maybe it's because I know he wasn't doing it to make me angry. Part of me also wonders if this is what would have happened if Denendrius was what I thought he was from the beginning, and I had reconnected with Carol anyway. I imagine a family meal with a real boyfriend would go similarly, from what I've seen on TV.

Carol's toe-curling shriek has me bounding from my bedroom before my pants are fully up. I clip my hip on the wooden banister as I yank my jeans up while turning the corner to the stairs. Slipping midway down the steps, I catch myself on the rail as I watch the scene unfold in the living room.

A blue-haired vampire girl stands in the middle of the room with half of a wooden broom handle through her bloody midsection, Carol holding the bristled end.

"Holy shit—go, Auntie!" I holler as my feet hit the hardwood floor. "How did she get in here?"

Denendrius appears at my side, a gladius in each hand, with cold eyes locked on the girl like he plans on embedding steel in her throat.

Derek is panting as he rushes from the kitchen, Rayonne at his side with the crossbow. "The crawlspace and up through the hatch in the pantry."

"I'm sorry," Carol breathes, "I don't know how I forgot about securing the freakin' crawlspace door."

The girl grits her bloodied teeth and fangs as she backs off the broom handle and plugs the hole in her body with her hand. She gives me a dark grin. "I'm here to collect you and Denendrius. How does it feel to be worth a million dollars, Marianna? I bet that's the most value you've ever had in your poor little mortal life."

My knees liquefy, and I have to grasp the banister to stay upright. "There's . . . there's a bounty on me?"

Denendrius glances at us, trying to figure out if he should do something. As his sword lifts, the *twang* of Rayonne's crossbow breaks his focus.

I feel the air from the stake flying past me as it embeds itself right between the vampire's collarbone and chest. She roars, yanks it out, and throws it back so hard that it clips the corner of Rayonne's jaw—leaving her in so much pain that no sound leaves her wide mouth as she buckles over, grasping at her face—and burrows itself in the drywall. Derek rushes to her side, his and Carol's voice a flurry as they try to get her to straighten so they can check beyond the blood that rushes down her neck.

Her red eyes flick up and down me as she sneers, like she thinks I'm pitiful. "Denendrius has *marked* you, after all. You're practically an extension of him. Why wouldn't there be a bounty—well, multiple, though none as good as this—on your pathetic little head?"

Is half the vampire population nothing but complete assholes? Or do I get this treatment as a side effect of being human?

My heart pounds. There's too much icy dread coursing through me for her insults to ignite anger in me. What am I to do, where am I to go, if there are bounties on my head too? If the castle doesn't pan out . . .?

Will I have no other option but to turn if I want any chance at protecting myself? But I don't want to be a vampire, so what am I to do?

The vampire reaches behind her and opens the front door. With speed none of us can react to fast enough, she takes two fistfuls of my shirt, swings me sideways, and shoves me backward through it.

The force knocks my breath and sight out of me as my back hits the front walkway. A mechanical roar fills my ears, the vibration of its source capturing me as I wade through disorientation.

When my vision adjusts, I'm cutting through the rain, the forest across the road from Carol's house swallowing me. Someone's thick arm grips me in front of them on the dirt bike we sit on. I'm too disoriented to feel the full effect of my panic.

Denendrius darts across the road after us, screaming my name with a sword in each hand.

As if lightning struck the rider, he jerks as a clap of gold illuminates the sky.

The world spins. I crash against the hard ground, the smell of wet grass filling my nose as I tumble through it. My ears ring.

Through my twisting vision, I spot the vampire who grabbed me. He lies limp on his stomach on the forest floor, the bike feet away, mud caking his blond hair. When I spot Rayonne at the edge of the trees, the revolver in hand and aimed at us, I can only assume she got a perfect shot with a wooden bullet.

Denendrius rushes past Rayonne as Derek and Carol catch up to her.

The threat of another dirt bike echoes through the trees, and I can do nothing but flinch as it rips past me and heads for Denendrius, who is halfway between me and everyone else now.

I expect Denendrius to turn the other way, to at least try to dodge the dirt bike, but he plants his feet and widens his stance. His eyes lock with the bike as it flies full throttle toward him, gladii ready to cut through blood and bone.

Just as the vampire sticks his arm out, something silver glimmering in his gloved hand as he's aimed to collide with him, Denendrius thrusts his blade through the biker's chest. The dirt bike carries on for a few yards without him as he dangles off Denendrius's sword before slipping off. There's no hesitation as Denendrius lifts a gladius up and brings it down on the vampire's head, blood spraying back across his furious face as the bike spins out and collides to a stop against the trunk of a tree.

"*Holy shit,*" I breathe, scrambling up and out of the slippery grass and almost tripping over my feet as I hasten through the chill of night to him. "The way you skewered him! That was so fucking cool!"

Denendrius's breath is brisk as he reaches me. He grins and sticks a sword into the grass, the bloodied one gripped tightly in his right hand. Pulling me against him, he dips his head down and mashes his lips against mine. I kiss him back, giddiness bubbling up inside me from the adrenaline.

The sound of more bikes approaching from the deep woods

behind us rips our lips apart. He shoves me behind him and picks up his other sword.

As soon as two bikes appear in view from opposite directions, the rider on our left flicks a gloved hand in front of himself and the bloodied gladius is torn from Denendrius's hand by an invisible force and thrown out of reach. He jerks when the second one rips away after the vampire flicks his hand to the side again.

Denendrius stares at his empty hands, completely dumbfounded.

When the rider slows and hops off the bike—with crimson eyes and bared, threatening fangs—he lets it fall onto its side in the grass. Denendrius spits a warning as he backs us up. As another bike nears on our right, I make a break for it and sprint toward the gladius as Denendrius lifts his arms to fight.

I skid through the wet grass, landing on my hands and knees beside the gladius as the bike halts a few metres away from me. My fingers latch around the gladius handle and adrenaline floods through me. Scrambling to my feet, I try to recall everything I learned mere hours ago as the blond vampire climbs off his bike and releases a mocking snicker while approaching me.

My first thought is to defend Denendrius—to at least return the gladius to him—so I twist and attempt to race back to where Denendrius and the other vampire circle one another.

Denendrius grabs the vampire's forearms when he reaches out, and he throws his body weight into him. Their arms are trapped between their chests as they push against one another, their feet slipping in the grass. He's half Denendrius's size, though I can tell with his immortal strength that he's almost ready to overpower Denendrius. But the vampire's eyes widen when Denendrius hooks his arm under his armpit. Denendrius throws the vampire forward by his arm as he turns sideways, sprawling him on his stomach and straddling his back to hook his arms underneath his chest.

It only happens in a few seconds and the vampire throws his hand out toward me as he notices me approaching. My heart rockets into my throat as an invisible force knocks my feet out from under me.

By some miracle, I don't impale myself with the sword as I fall face first and land with my arms outstretched at my sides. I struggle for breath as the blond vampire takes fistfuls of the back of my shirt.

I clutch the gladius as he fights to turn me over. As soon as he has me on my back and tries to straddle me, I focus all my might on slashing the gladius across his chest. He cries out and launches backward off me, giving me enough time to pounce onto my feet.

His black shirt is torn from hip to shoulder, and the bloody gash across his torso heals before my eyes.

He snickers harder, his face twisted in a lofty grin as he jerks toward me with a step. "You'll need to do better than that," he taunts with a husky voice.

My heart sends shock waves through me, sweat weakening my grip. Where the fuck is Rayonne with that gun?

I overlap both hands on the handle despite not knowing if it'll help or impair me and try not to let the pained outcries of Denendrius and the other vampire distract me from where they fight behind me. All I know is that the idea of having the gladius taken and used against me is terrifying.

When he bares his fangs at me, blue eyes flashing claret, I grunt and swing the gladius at his neck. He bounds back a step while fighting his laughter and shouting something the thunder covers.

With his ability to heal, I'll either have to hold him off until help arrives, or get a good enough hit that takes him enough time to recover from to sneak another strike in.

I swing for his neck again, intending to behead, and he catches the blade in his bare hands in what I can only assume is a bold attempt to intimidate me. My breath catches as our eyes lock, while strikes of lightning illuminate the forest. He must expect me to let go of the sword, but I furrow my brow and rip the gladius from his grasp. His strength does nothing to protect him from the double-edged blade.

Though he grunts in pain, he doesn't seem fazed by the blood gushing from his palms and fingers; doesn't even assess the damage as he merely smirks at me like he's having fun.

As I lift the sword above my left shoulder to slash at his throat again, his half-healed hands prepare to reach through my readying swing to capture my arm.

I change my technique at the last second, and instead of following through and letting him disarm me, I remove my right hand from the handle, swing the sword straight down to my left side, and thrust the tip of the blade toward his midsection.

"*Mother fucker!*" I roar as his flesh and muscle part for the blade while he stiffens and gasps in agony.

Cold blood sprays up through his mouth and against my face. The muscles in my arms burn, and I use my weight to lean into slicing through him. He grabs the blade with his hands to stop me. It cuts through his grip again, his wide and crimson eyes locking on mine.

"Are you having fun *now*?" I snarl at him. His presence—the fact that he thinks he's going to trade me for money—has my blood boiling and my skin hot despite the chill of night. It only fuels my strength.

The sound of another dirt bike clashes against the rolling thunder ahead of me, and from the corner of my eye, I spot Rayonne running through the trees as she lifts her gun and shouts, "Denendrius, *move!*"

Feeling the blade break through the vampire's back, I rip it out of him with a wave of crimson and shift my eyes to his unprotected neck as thick blood gushes from his mouth and runs down his chin.

I wrangle my breath and slash the blade through the front of his throat, a waterfall of red cascading down his chest and soaking his shirt. The momentum of my swing sends me twisting in the opposite direction as he chokes on his own blood and falls to his knees.

As I steady myself, my eyes land on Denendrius and the other vampire. He tries sticking Denendrius in the neck with something a few times as they brawl until Denendrius gives him a good shove and rolls away through the dirt.

The roar of the approaching dirt bike is deafening, the sound of Rayonne's shot cutting through it.

I don't see what happens to Denendrius and the other vampire, as the feel of the blond's hands circling my thigh has me spinning back around to drive the gladius into the side of his neck. The steel collides with bone and I feel the impact vibrate up the blade. I try and fail to yank the gladius back.

I'm breathless, my heart drumming against my ribs as I look up through a thickening sheet of rain in time to see the dirt bike heading straight for me. I don't have time to move—not that I could when the bleeding vampire locks his hands around my leg to keep me put—as the driver closes the space between us and sweeps me off my feet, spinning us back in the direction he came.

"*Denendrius!*" I scream.

XXV

I'm hollering as the vampire holds me across his lap and whisks me away.

I writhe and scratch uselessly at his helmet, my furious pleas for him to stop lost in the roaring thunder and muffler noises as we weave through the trees and bounce over roots.

Where am I being taken? What's going to happen to me?

When I reach for the handlebars, he jerks them from my fingers and kicks his leg under me. We come to a stop with the back tire sliding sideways through the dirt.

He shoves me off him to my feet as I kick and pummel him. I prepare myself for a violent warning.

Muffled, he angrily hollers my name as he pulls his helmet off.

"Ziggy?" I gape at his bright red eyes and bared fangs, jerking back in surprise. "What the fuck?"

He tears into his wrist with his fangs and holds it out—blood dripping into his fingerless glove—to me as he sits back on his bike and scoots forward. "Now, will you ride calmly?

Come on, I'm here to save you. But hurry, before he comes over with those swords. From the sounds of things back there, he knows how to ride that bike."

For once I'm speechless—*actually speechless.*

A muffler makes noise far behind us.

"Ah shit." He rolls his eyes at the healing wound and bites into his wrist again. "Less gaping, more drinking."

"What . . . *what the fuck?* What do you mean you're here to save me?" My heart beats so rapidly the sound of it must echo through the woods.

His hands flop into his lap as he heaves out an exasperated breath. "Well, you certainly couldn't escape when you came to visit, not with him hanging on to our every word so . . . *close* to you."

I lift my hand up, like I can command some sense out of him. "Who said I wanted to escape?"

Ziggy squints at me. "Do you not? I thought it was very clear you wanted to stay with us."

"I literally told you I was planning on going to Romania," I growl.

He scratches his head. "See, I didn't quite believe you. I thought that was more of a 'my master is going, so I must as well' thing, that you didn't really think you had a choice and planned to make the best of it. I was hoping you would seriously consider my offer to stay with my clan."

"I mean, it's an excellent offer. I haven't completely ruled it out . . . but I have to go to Romania with Denendrius."

He releases an incredulous scoff and shakes his head. "Why on earth would you *have to,* mark aside?"

I lift my chin. "So I can watch him get tortured."

"Now that's just silly." He bites into his wrist again before offering it to me. "You think you can—but in actuality, it'll probably upset you to see your master suffer."

Groaning, I say, "Would you stop biting yourself! I'm not drinking your blood."

He throws his hand down at his side. "Why not? Are you incapable of making the choice yourself?" He lifts his nose and studies me with slitted eyes. "Do I have to be a beast and force you to drink for your own good?"

I give him a death stare, unsure which words to spit.

Rolling his eyes, he says, "Oh, only once! I want you as a familiar, not a blood slave. You need his mark overwritten so you can think for yourself."

"I am thinking for myself." My words feel like hot coals spitting off my tongue. How am I supposed to know he wouldn't abuse the blood mark?

He pushes his messy hair from his face and smirks. "You are not, or you would understand what a marvelous idea this is. Come join Lance and me! We'll let you remain human for a while longer. It would be so much fun, and you would never have to worry about that bastard or the *boring* castle again."

I throw my hands out at my sides. "No! Ziggy, do you have a crush on me or something? This is all ridiculous."

His jaw drops for a little defensive gasp. "Not every boy in the world is in love with you, *Marianna*! Good grief!"

Squaring my shoulders, I say, "Then why do you want to mark me so bad?"

Ziggy forces out another annoyed breath and jerks a bit on the seat. "We want another familiar since one of ours outgrew us, and you seem like great fun. You'd get on with all the ones I already have. Lance agrees, and my friend Patricia—who can see the future, by the way—saw a whole life for us all in Las Vegas if I were to mark you by force right now."

I'm too boggled for a proper response. "That's ridiculous!"

The sound of the dirt bike nears closer, and I smirk at him.

"Damn it, Marianna! Quit being cantankerous!" he grouses, raising his voice over the sound of the muffler. "Don't make me go back home and tell Lance I did this all for nothing! You better hurry and come here, because your master is moving quickly, and he's going to catch up."

"Ziggy, I didn't ask you to save me!" I look over my shoulder as the light from Denendrius's bike—and even more surprisingly, *Carol's*—touches us and bounces off a new trickle of rain.

"Bollocks. Well, we're fucked of luck now, Marianna. He carried a sword with him. Probably to saw my head off. If you hop on quick, I might be able to zip away fast enough."

I roll my eyes and offer him a sympathetic smile, and I wonder why he's stalling. "No. But if the offer still stands, I'll keep it in mind if I end up hating the castle as much as you think I will."

He feigns hurt. "Of course it still stands. If you change your mind, work on Rayonne's too. Estrella de Sangre hasn't been the same since she left."

Denendrius leaps off the bike, sword pointed at Ziggy until I lift my hands and step between them. "*Stop*."

He shouts incomprehensible Latin but lowers his weapon.

Carol and Rayonne hop off the second bike. I glance around for Derek, but he's nowhere in sight. Did he get left behind?

Rayonne races to us, the look of betrayal clear on her face. "Ziggy?"

He holds a palm up to her. "This is not what it looks like, promise. They came into Estrella de Sangre last night and apparently heard through the grapevine that Denendrius is human again. They were offered ten million by some vampire in Munich for him and Marianna. I volunteered to go with them, but I really planned to save her. And look, now you have Denendrius back. No harm done."

She grits her teeth. "I already *had* Denendrius."

"But I didn't have Marianna," he says simply.

"You are not stealing her away with your promises of wild parties and weed. She's sticking with me," Rayonne barks.

Wait, weed's on the table? I give my head a shake and glance at Denendrius, who seems to follow at least a portion of our conversation. "Guys, shut up."

They ignore me, Ziggy arguing with, "She's going to hate it and you know it. It's a no-fun zone."

I squint suspiciously at Rayonne, who shakes her head at me and says to Ziggy, "I don't know it! And it's *safe*. You won't keep her safe from angry, vengeful vampires. You-know-where is stable."

"That's a good point," I say.

"That is not a good point at all!" Ziggy leans his head back and protests to the furious sky. "We'd protect you. We're all . . . *stable*."

Rayonne gives him an are-you-sure look and motions to the bodies behind us. "Did they not come from Estrella de Sangre?"

He crosses his arms. "That's not fair. They weren't part of the clan."

"Doesn't matter! He was nearly stabbed with a tranquilizer!" Rayonne hollers.

I cross my arms and scowl at him. "Yeah, we almost all died, dude. A heads-up would have been cool."

Ziggy pouts and grabs his helmet, shoving it back down over his head before flipping the visor up to scowl back at me. "How unfair. You're all ganging up on me now!"

I roll my eyes. "Thanks for grabbing me before that vampire could obliterate me, at least."

He grins. "You're very welcome."

"I staked that vampire, by the way," Carol interjects with a proud grin. She must catch the shock on my face as she nods once at me and says, "See, I can handle this."

With the next clap of thunder, the clouds unload fat drops of rain on us.

Rayonne shakes her head, in general disbelief, I think.

"Ziggy"—she breathes out a laugh—"go home. We're all good still."

"I am so sick of fanged fucks!" I screech as we enter the house, having stewed in slimy thoughts the whole walk back. I claw wet hair from my face, braids far too loose in my hair to look pretty now.

I'm a second away from putting my fist through Carol's nice beige wall when Denendrius wraps his arms around me and squeezes me against his chest. "You are okay," he whispers.

His hands are bloody after decapitating the vampire with the wooden bullet in his heart on the way back. Now there's no chance of it being removed and him springing back to life before sunrise. The bodies of the other vampires—decapitated—will be nothing more than ashes once the rays touch them too.

Grumbling, I shrug out of his grip and plunk down on the bottom step of the stairs. I wrap my arms around myself as I shiver in my soaked clothes. "Rayonne, how long do we have to deal with this shit?"

She glances at Denendrius before saying to me, "I'm sure it'll be over with *soon*."

"When? Because eventually, we're going to get our asses handed to us and *fucking die*."

All the eyes in the room focus on Rayonne, awaiting an answer. She squirms under our gaze and weaves through us to get to the kitchen counter, where her purse is.

"Rayonne?" Derek presses.

"I don't know what you people want me to tell you." She unzips her purse, glowering as she roots around and pulls out a cigarette and lighter. "It's been six days. Things—*travel*—take time, even for vampires, especially when they're bound to the night. You're an impatient lot." With that, she grabs an ice pack from the freezer and shoves it against her jaw. Then she jams her cigarette between her lips with a shaking hand and shivers as she walks to the deck door. She stands half inside the dining room and half out as she lights her cigarette and takes breaths with it.

Denendrius looks between us all. "Vampires . . . done?"

"Got an answer for him, Rayonne?" I ask.

Her leg bounces as she forcefully blows out a stream of smoke, wet curls tangling as she shakes her head.

Denendrius rubs the back of his neck and mumbles something to himself. "Marianna, shower?"

I grab his hand for him to help me up.

Carol frowns at me as we walk up the stairs, like she's hoping I'll protest or find an excuse not to shower with him. I mash my lips together and stare straight ahead.

My teeth rattle the entire time Denendrius and I undress and ready the shower. When we hop into the hot stream together, he releases a massive sigh and smiles.

"So cold," he complains.

"Tell me about it." I hug myself, lip quivering as I stand close to him.

It's hard to get any of the water with him in the way. He notices the issue and moves aside for me.

The night replays in my mind as I stare past him and at the gold wall through the crack of the curtain. I can't stop thinking about the bounty on my head. The fact someone wants to torture me so badly that they'll pay a million dollars makes me queasy and out of breath.

What can I do to stop them? My only hope is Romania, and who knows if we'll all survive until then if things carry on the way they have been. Between Agatha and every other random vampire, we're going to be too worn out to play this defensive game anymore.

Frustration spills out of me in the shape of tears. I shiver violently despite the rush of warm water across my flesh.

Denendrius's bottom lip protrudes as he looks down at me. "Oh, Marianna. It is okay now."

I shake my head and forcefully sniffle. "No, it's not. You have no idea how not okay things are right now."

He pulls me tight against his chest and embraces me, resting his head on top of mine. "I will keep you safe," he murmurs.

I stave off my near-hysterical breaths, though the effort steals the rest of my energy.

My tears finally find a way out when he plucks the pins from my hair. Mud, bits of grass, and bark fall at our feet before water whisks it all down the drain.

"Vampires ruin fucking everything," I cry as he rakes his fingers through my hair with shampoo. "Even my hair isn't safe. It's ruined."

"I will make it again," he whispers, planting a hot kiss on my forehead.

The water doesn't take long to run cold, and I can only assume the other two showers are being used—either for the same purpose, or to drive Denendrius and me out quicker.

I sit on the toilet wrapped in a pink towel as Denendrius runs a comb through my hair.

"Braids in the morning," he promises me.

Once the shivers subside when I'm dry and clothed, I can feel the severity of the aches in my muscles. I suppose I should be lucky I didn't break my neck tonight falling off the dirt bike or being shoved out the door.

Denendrius and I make a brief appearance downstairs to chug a few drinks before going to bed.

Thunder rattles the window in my room as I enter, a crack of lightning making me wince. "Stupid storm. We get it."

Denendrius's chuckle makes me crack a smile as we crawl into bed.

"Dislike it?" He pulls the blanket back for us. "It is relaxing."

A shiver rips up my spine. "I'm too cold to appreciate the storm."

He drags me down onto the mattress beside him. "Ah. I will warm you."

I'm far too cold to complain as he holds me tight and lifts the blanket over our heads. The dark space fills with our hot breath, the sound of my rapid heart in my ears matching well with the chaos beyond my window.

I expect his kiss before it comes. His eager mouth dominates mine. I hook my arm around him, pushing my tongue against his when I feel it search for mine.

"I love you." The words are like honey when they drip off his lips.

Warmth spreads in my chest. "I love you too," I whisper, though it doesn't feel forced this time. "How much do you love me?"

"It hurts how much." His lips crush against mine again, his hand gripping the side of my face.

I shiver—for a different reason this time—when he rolls me on my back and crawls over me. The cold of the room hits our faces as the blanket falls to our waists.

The fabric of my shirt tickles my eager skin as he shimmies it off and drops it on the floor. He presses his chest against mine. I suck in a breath when his fingers trace lines down my side, skirting under the hem of my pants and disappearing between my legs.

"So much I love you." Denendrius's voice is as soft as his touch. His lips trail down my throat, the tip of his tongue tracing a line down my flesh.

I shudder and twist my fingers in his hair. An odd sense of ease pounds through me with each of my heartbeats. There's no fear in me that he'll hold me down and break my bones or bite blood from my veins. I don't anticipate any harshness past passion.

No hesitations escape with my heavy breaths as he touches and kisses me. Not even when he pulls my pants and panties off and tosses them out of the way. Though, when he takes his boxers off and I feel *him* against my side, I can't help but tense up.

Still, I don't feel danger when he pushes my legs apart and positions his body between them.

He looks down and stiffens. His mischievous smile plummets when he sees the fading scars around my groin that I have worked hard to forget about. How many of them are from him, if any? Does *he* think they're all from him?

A wave of cold panic crashes down on me, and when I try to pull my legs away, he holds them still. His unreadable expression throws my heart into overdrive.

When tears rim my wide eyes, I inhale a shaky breath, a sob threatening.

"Oh, Marianna . . . safe now," he murmurs, chest back against mine as he consoles me with kisses.

Relief relaxes my body, and I let his hungry mouth ravage mine. My legs fall to the side as I relax. He runs his hand down my side and across my thigh, his stomach pressing against mine as he holds his weight with his forearm by my head. He loses his hand in my hair, his lips moving to my neck.

"We . . . we need a condom." Is it an excuse to stop, or has Daina made me cautious? Either way, I should know I'm not going to find one.

His head comes up, and he stares down at me. "A what?"

"C-condom. You know, so I don't get knocked up." I push the worry of diseases to the back of my mind, knowing vampirism would have cleared all that up when it healed him.

"What is . . .?"

I blow out a breath and wrap my arms around his waist. "Never mind. I don't think it matters." I haven't even had my period yet.

He merely smiles and keeps touching me as he adjusts himself over me.

"Relax," he says, hand doing something to himself—that I'm too scared to get a look of—below our waists, "or it might hurt."

I do my best to relax, but I immediately lock up, back arching when I feel him. Squeezing my arms around him, I pull in a sharp breath when I feel the sting of his slow start. He exhales a loud moan in my ear, and I take a deep breath and try not to squirm out from under him. My nerves have me shivering again.

"What I say," he scolds softly. "Sorry."

His hips rock slowly as he kisses me, and I wince at the ache. Just as I worry it will keep hurting, that I'm too scarred after all my body has been through, my body gets used to him and I let out a noise that surprises me.

He groans in pleasure as his lips trail to my ear. "Feels good?"

"Yes," I whisper.

"*Me too.*" Denendrius's moan comes louder, the sound so attractive it sends a jolt of electricity through the center of me.

I bite my bottom lip, mind clear of words to say.

He whispers Latin between kisses, hot fireflies pricking under my skin and collecting in my stomach as he moves his hips faster. His voice sends chills through me, and I imagine the nature of his words to be as nice as they sound. I hold my hand to his hip and lose the other in his hair as I hold him tight to me. With my head against his sweaty chest, the sound of his racing heart is glorious.

I'm surprised that my mind doesn't wander back to those

dark and terrifying nights. The feeling is so far from being the same.

"You like?" he asks for what must be the tenth time.

"Yes," I admit, more to myself than him.

I let myself enjoy the way my body responds to his, shoving the stray negative thoughts away before they have a chance to form fully in my mind.

He lets out a moan so loud that my eyes widen.

"*You're being too loud,*" I hiss.

"Why?" he grunts before adding, "You not want to hear how much I enjoy you?"

"*Everyone is going to hear.*"

He pulls his sweaty chest away from me and tongues his bottom lip. "Problem?" Denendrius grins, his eyes lustrous as they bore into mine.

I bite down on my bottom lip to stop sounds from escaping from me and nod.

Crushing his body back against mine, he lets out a moan that sends another electric ripple through me and makes my heartbeat spike.

"Stop it—" I slap my hand over my mouth when he reaches between us to touch me and a high-pitched noise is forced from the back of my throat with a gasp.

He pulls my hand away from my mouth and grins. "I want to hear."

I bite back my laugh. "No!"

Maybe it's the endorphins, or the fact that we might get caught, but I'm flabbergasted when I realize I'm enjoying myself. I thought for sure my first *real* time would have me breaking down at the mere feel.

This will be a much better memory for my body to cling to. Though it's still Denendrius, it wouldn't be so bad to think of this whenever the topic or thought of sex comes up instead of my only other references.

"*Oh, Marianna,*" he whines as he mashes his lips against mine, his kisses barely lasting a moment each before he's interrupted by noisy bursts of pleasure.

I playfully press my hand over his mouth. "Stop it—" My back arcs and he hooks one of his arms under me to hold me tight to him.

Other arm by my head to stabilize himself, he gasps as he shakes his head away from my grip. "*You* are the loud one now."

My volume—paired with the words I've been uttering—doesn't fully dawn on me until Derek is bursting into the room.

XXVI

Denendrius scrambles off me and the bed as soon as Derek's hands land on him.

"Derek, what the fuck!" I holler, my voice drowned out by Denendrius's snarled Latin as he slams his hand into Derek's shoulder and sends him stumbling backward.

It's pure chaos. I can't decipher anything through the flurry of voices or move fast enough to insert myself between them.

"*Stop!*" I shriek, pulling the sheet tight around myself as I leap out of bed. "Both of you! Stop!"

They're both too furious with one another—Derek shoving at Denendrius while calling him names and uttering threats, Denendrius pushing back in warning—to pay me any attention. They get to the threshold of the room, the mix of Latin and English so loud I want to slam my hands over my ears.

Instead, I add to the noise by shouting, "Derek, stop before he—"

In his unbridled rage, Denendrius bounces Derek's head against the wood banister. The crack of his skull against wood ricochets through the house and brings total silence. He's out cold upon contact, crumpling to the floor.

I can't pull enough air into my lungs to let sound out. Carol and Rayonne rush up the stairs to Derek and huddle around him, calling his name as they shake and fail to rouse him.

Even with Derek down, Denendrius returns to spewing enraged Latin.

"Stop it!" I bellow and scramble to Denendrius, fingernails digging into his arm while I try to pull him away so Carol and Rayonne can properly tend to Derek. His foot comes up a bit, and I'm not sure if it's to counteract my force or if he plans to stomp on Derek's head, since he locks his eyes on him still. "Did you fucking kill him? Fucking hell! Denendrius!"

Denendrius tears out of my grip. His hand shoots out, grabbing the bottom of my jaw so hard that my teeth click together and his thumb and fingers dig into my cheeks, the heel of his hand pressing into my throat. My heart spasms in my chest, and I yelp as Carol and Rayonne scramble off the floor.

Every shred of fear I've ever had in his presence torrents through me at once when his eyes lock on mine. I don't see brown, just the black pits of hell that used to run so deep within him.

Tears burn my eyes. "*Denendrius,*" I squeak.

Anger leaves him like a cast-out demon. He blinks at me, then looks back to where Derek lies and where Carol and Rayonne have stopped short—stunned—now that he's unlatched his hand from my face.

"Oh no, Marianna . . ." He reaches out to me as I back away, his brown eyes soft again.

My fear leaves with his fury, seemingly in sync, but the adrenaline remains like poison in my veins and I feel like I'm shutting down. I sit on the edge of the bed, wrapped in the sheet and a numb nothing.

Denendrius's face twists with pain, eyes desperate as they

hold mine. "I didn't . . ." His mouth opens and closes, searching for words. "I don't know why I did this." He struggles for breath and rests his forearms on his head. "Marianna, I am so sorry."

I lower my gaze to the white sheet that I grip to my naked body.

"Carol, am I in trouble if he is dead? It is *his* fault." The panic in Denendrius's sweet voice is clear.

"Are you serious, Denendrius?" Carol snarls.

Rayonne murmurs, "You're okay, Derek. Can you look at me?"

When I lift my head, I hold my breath until they finally get him sitting up against the railing. He groans, unfocused eyes rolling in their sockets.

Denendrius breathes in relief, then turns to me. He kneels on the floor in front of me, hands scooping up mine. "Marianna . . . I am so sorry. I never . . . Marianna, he made me so mad—"

"Please don't," I whisper. My hands are limp in his. "Get some pants on."

He grabs his boxers and shoves his legs into them, desperate eyes searching my face. "Marianna, please don't be mad—"

"I'm not mad," I whisper.

"I hurt you."

"*Yeah.*" I swallow a lump and it catches in my sore throat, the front of it still feeling compressed from the pressure of his hand.

Carol storms back into the room. "Get away from her—"

"Go help Rayonne with Derek," I demand flatly. "I'm fine. We were messing around."

She wavers where she stands. "He wasn't . . .?"

"No, he wasn't. Jesus. Go, *please.*"

She exhales a long breath and nods before leaving the room.

I stay sitting on the bed and stare at my hands as they

clench the sheet while I listen to Rayonne and Carol help Derek down the stairs. Tears rush from my eyes. I sniffle and cry quietly, unmoving as Denendrius rushes out of the room and returns with a brush.

He fixes my hair and braids it again, mumbling apologies and explanations the entire time in his broken English.

"I am so sorry," he whispers frantically, placing pins to keep the hairdo in place. "I never hurt you again. I promise. I don't know why I did that."

I wipe my eyes with the backs of my hands, my voice squeaking as I say, "Okay."

"Do you forgive me?" His desperate eyes bore into mine like a puppy who got in trouble for nipping at someone.

But I do.

Maybe it's because I really believe him this time, that I think this wouldn't have happened if Derek hadn't interrupted him in an intimate moment, if I hadn't been so aggressive when he was already amped up.

"I love you." He reaches up and strokes my cheek with the back of his hand.

Maybe a little of part of me fears finding out what happens if I don't accept his apology.

I lean into Denendrius, and he wraps his arms around me.

"It is not like me," he whispers, a crack in his voice. "I hate me for hurting you."

My lips press against his collarbone, the sound of his raging heart against my ear helping me feel better.

"Why did he . . .?" He lets out a dumbfounded huff. "You are my wife."

Can he *really* not think of the reason?

"He probably thought you were . . . *raping* . . . me." The word catches in my throat.

Denendrius's heart stumbles at my words, and his silence speaks for itself.

Rayonne watches me as I come down the steps, leaving Denendrius to work through his guilt alone. I told him he better get over it before I return from checking on Derek, because I don't want to hear another apology tonight.

"You're sleeping with him?" she asks, the concern on her face clear.

I cross my arms and shrug, waiting for a lecture.

She picks up her cup, steam drifting up off the tea-yellow surface. "All right." She turns her eyes back to the TV and mumbles, "Shit."

My deep scowl hurts my face. That's all she has to say?

I follow the deck light into the dim dining area as it shines through the glass.

"Marianna, can you bring me a new ice pack?" Derek's strained voice carries in through the half-open deck door.

I find one waiting in the freezer and snatch it, wrapping it in a tea towel before meeting him outside. Rain still pours from the inky sky beyond the deck's overhang.

"How are you feeling?" I hand him the ice pack and sit in a wooden deck chair that's left of his and angled toward him. Carol must have sat in it last to monitor him.

"Fairly concussed." He sets the defrosted pack on the deck beside him before taking the one from my hand and wincing as he holds it against the side of his head. "I'd haul myself into the ER if I was in any other situation."

"After having your head bounced off a wooden rail, yeah, I can imagine."

He shifts the ice and groans before saying, "It's clear he hasn't changed."

I inhale a deep, humid breath and release a strangled chuckle. "To be fair, I don't think anyone would react well to someone barging into the room and prying them off the person they're having sex with."

His frown deepens, and a crease appears between his brows. "I thought he was raping you, Marianna."

I swallow a lump before it can block the breath in my throat, and my eyes drop to my lap.

There's an angry undertone to his worry as he speaks. "Was he? Because I know enough about your history and his that my brain leaped to that conclusion the moment I opened the door and saw him naked."

"He wasn't hurting me," I insist, looking back up at him. "He's twice your size and ten times your strength, so I don't understand why you thought you could win a fight with him."

"I was trying to protect you," he says gently. "That's all. I knew I wouldn't win, but I got him off you at least."

"Oh." He risked the real possibility of Denendrius killing him for me? I have the thought that Derek did something a father would do. Except I know that I'm not worth someone else risking their life. Even Denendrius—the person who thinks they love me the most—has picked his life over mine in the past. He may love me, but he's not stupid. But knowing that makes what Derek did mean more.

"Thank you, sort of." My smile is more of a grimace.

Derek might have saved me if I had been in real danger.

He leans forward and gives my knee a squeeze. "Of course, Marianna." With a heavy breath, he shakes his head. "I just—" He grits his teeth. "You know I'm thirty-one, right? Barely older than him. I can't even imagine looking at any of my students like that—never mind..."

I feel the deep line in my forehead as I analyze his words. I never thought about the fact that they're practically the same age.

"Do you wish you could go to the ER? Like, leave, I mean?" I bite my cheek and try to swallow down the discomfort of his words.

"I can't leave." He winces as he adjusts his hand on the ice pack and props his elbow on the arm of the chair.

"Well, not because of vampires, I know. But do you want to leave?"

He gives me a small smile, then flinches when the movement must make pain radiate up to his head. "No. Despite the . . . stress, I'm enjoying spending time with you—and Rayonne and Carol, of course. My life has more meaning right now digging through history and helping you all out than it did as a high school teacher."

I bite my bottom lip before saying, "But we've basically ruined your life."

He chuckles. "No, I don't think so. I've been doing a lot of thinking . . . and talking to Rayonne. The idea of vampirism . . . getting to experience history firsthand . . . sounds amazing. I think I want to go that route after all this. I like the idea of being a Darkling, though I know it's astronomically riskier."

I wring my fingers in my lap. "Even if you can't go to Romania?"

He nods. "Yes. Rayonne's excitement is wearing off on me. She told me she would have turned back already if it wasn't such a tremendous risk to take. She doesn't want to die before she sees this through."

"Glad you figured something out," I mumble, trying not to feel sour.

He gives me a pained but confident smile. "You'll be okay, Marianna."

How can he believe that? "You don't know that. My life's ruined. I'll have nothing remotely normal now."

Derek grunts. "Okay, so you've had it hard. I won't try to convince you of how you should feel about everything up to this point, but your future isn't ruined. And who said you need a normal life? I feel you're using normal and happy interchangeably. You can have a good, happy life without it being normal."

I bite my bottom lip and don't know why I never had the thought myself. "I guess."

"What does normal mean to you, anyway?" he asks.

I shrug and stare across the empty green of the backyard, the back fence shaded with shadows. "I want a good job. Not office job kind of normal, but an artist maybe—I don't know what kind. Doing tattoos would be cool, but so would having a painting in a gallery or something. I'd like to live in a nice house and grow old with a husband . . . maybe some kids . . . but I'm not sure if I'd make a good mom even though I could take care of my foster siblings. Not the PTA kind of mom though. I guess I don't need to think about that anymore, but I'd like the option."

"Is there a reason you want that, or do you think that's how your life should be because it's what you've been told?" He pulls the ice pack away from his head.

"I *wanted* that." A cold gust of air blows against me, and I pull my sleeves over my hands and shiver.

Wanted. Because it's impossible now.

He straightens his ruffled brown hair, the section that was under the ice pack wet. "Well, I know as much about the castle as you do, but who says you can't have some of those things in a different way than what's normal? I wouldn't rule it all out. You don't know the future you could have waiting for you. Don't shoot for normal, even if vampires don't end up a part of your life. You should aim for happy."

It's good advice, yet it's difficult to unclasp my fingers from the idealistic life I've fantasized about. It's much easier to hang on than let go and fall into whatever is clawing at me and waiting below. Even if I can't pull myself back up to that dream, it's a lot less scary to hang on to it.

Besides, it's hard to aim for happy when I'm focused on staying alive *and* untortured.

"I don't think I'm going to have that, in any which way," I admit, twisting my fingers together painfully in my lap. "I want it badly, but that doesn't mean I can have it."

He frowns. "Why not? Vampire or human, you should be able to find something and someone that makes you happy."

"As much as I like the idea of wearing a dress and getting married, I'm not the type of girl that gets that." There's no humor in my chuckle. "I have nothing going for me. I guess I'm lucky I won't need to get a job now, because there's no way anyone would hire me with my criminal record and lack of school." My eyes burn, but I hold my tears back.

He stares at me. "Is that why you're doing this with Denendrius? Because you think you deserve him and can't do better? That you're not worth anything? It seems like you're self-harming by having sex with him, Marianna."

I stare down at my knotted fingers. "I don't know why I am. But it's not like I should think I can do much better, regardless."

Denendrius doesn't deserve me with how he was as a vampire, but if this is as bad as he gets as a human? I could cope with that. Of course, I don't dare tell Derek he's right. Denendrius is the kind of guy who would date someone like me. I thought maybe I had value to someone more than that at first, but after everything went awry after our first few dates, I woke up. If he wasn't crazy, why would he have wanted to date me in the first place? Even CJ probably would have dumped me once he realized he was delusional about my worth.

There's an edge to Derek's voice, and the chair creaks as he shifts closer. "I think that's a very dangerous mindset to have about yourself, Marianna. And it's very untrue." His worried eyes lock with mine. "I think you can find someone who understands you and likes you, without having to settle. If you don't see any value in yourself, you're going to put up with a lot more crap. You're better off alone than lowering your standards. You need to keep them up, even if you don't think you're good enough for the guys that fit them."

Easier said than done. What are my standards supposed to be, anyway?

"Work on yourself," he tells me. "You don't need to worry about dating at all. Get yourself to a point where you can open up, where you feel better about yourself, and dating will probably be a lot easier."

"So, years."

He sighs. "I think you should wait until this blood mark is taken care of before you think too hard about things. I bet you'll feel much better once you're not connected to that psycho pervert up there. Wait until you can see the forest for the trees."

I clench my hands into fists, tendons popping up under my skin. "I take it Rayonne told you about my blood mark?"

"Yes, she did."

I jerk to my feet, arms crossed firmly over my chest. "Not all my thoughts and decisions are because of him. I do have some free will here."

He rises to his feet but rests his weight on the back of the chair. "How do you know what's what until he's out of your head? Wait until you're away from all this before you decide you're doomed."

Sure, and then I have to pick apart my own thoughts from whatever vampire marks me next since they're going to keep Denendrius alive to torture for who knows how long. That, or I cave and become a vampire so I can think without being attached to anyone. Though with being a vampire, I suppose that'll change the way I see the world a bit too.

"I guess," I grumble.

I might as well cut my brain out at this point.

He wishes me goodnight, and we step back inside together.

The living room is dark, the TV off. Rayonne must have gone to bed.

Stomach complaining, I search for food in the dim kitchen. Nothing is appetizing, and I'd rather starve than pick something that takes more effort than opening a package.

I sigh as I shut the fridge for the third time. I'm about to check on Denendrius and sleep when Carol comes out of her bedroom in a floral bathrobe with her wet hair up in a matching towel.

"Are you okay?" she asks me, tying the belt on her robe tighter as she walks barefoot into the kitchen.

"I'm fine," I tell her, "promise."

Carol flicks a switch and a row of lights under the cupboards illuminates. "Can't sleep?" She looks like she wants to ask so much more, but she presses her lips into a firm line and leans against the counter.

"I was going to find something to eat, but I don't have the energy."

"What do you want? I'll make you something." She straightens and heads past me toward the fridge.

"Um." Her offer makes me uncomfortable. "It's fine. I can do it; I'm just being lazy."

Her chuckle is quiet, tired. "Marianna, I'm your guardian. It's my responsibility to take care of you. You're not expected to cook for yourself all the time. I haven't had a chance to do much for you anyway, so it'll make me feel better."

I pick at my nails. It's been a handful of years since a guardian aside from her has offered to cook me a meal outside of regular hours and didn't act like it was a burden, or like I *should* be completely independent because I was capable. Maybe if I had been a better kid, they would have paired me with parents equipped to give a shit.

I swallow my lump of guilt. "Sure. Thanks."

She cracks the fridge open, glass bottles rattling in the door as the yellow light spills out. "What are you feeling like? Sandwich? Macaroni?" She closes it and leans over to pull open the freezer. "Pizza bites? Pierogies?"

"Sandwich is fine."

"Okay." She opens the fridge again and collects sandwich ingredients. "Is Denendrius sleeping?" she asks, eyes cutting to the stairs as she splays ham, cheese, and a few condiments out on the counter.

I shrug as slump down in a table chair. "I have no idea."

She sighs as she opens the wooden breadbox on the back of the counter to grab a loaf. "How many do you want?"

"One." My leg bounces. What is he doing up there? "How different is Denendrius acting now compared to all the times you met him?"

Lines appear on her forehead as her brows jerk together. She pulls two slices of bread from the bag and sets them on a lilac-colored plate. "I'm not sure what you mean."

My leg bounces faster, and I lower my voice so only she can hear me from where she stands a few feet away. "I know you don't like him at all, but does he *seem* better?"

She unscrews the mayo and slathers some on a slice of bread before matching my volume and saying, "Well, I still feel like I'm walking on eggshells around him . . . but you want me to tell you he seems different, right?"

"Doesn't he?"

She shrugs and licks mayo off the side of her finger. "Yes? No? Memories or not, I still see so many similarities between him now and him before."

"Similarities? Like what?" The occasional fit of anger, maybe, but he's still much calmer these days.

"Aside from how he got physical with you up there? He still looks at you the same way, for starters."

I scowl. Does he? "I don't see it."

"You probably don't." She applies mayo to the other slice of bread. "But he looks at you like you're an object. Even the way he moves around you, the glares he gives us . . . he thinks he owns you. Like you're his pet or something."

"I never noticed that." Not *now*, at least. "Aside from that?"

She sighs. "Sure, Marianna. He's a lot different. But that can change in an instant."

I bite at my nail. "Do you think if he never remembers that he would stay like this . . . or turn into a good person?"

Her expression sours, the force she uses to squeeze mustard onto my bread severe. "No. Some people can't be rehabilitated, Marianna. Not past a certain point. He's far, far past the point of rehabilitation. Maybe if someone had helped him in the beginning instead of locking him up, but it's too late now. All anyone can do now is keep him away from other people . . . or, you know . . ."

Kill him.

I bite at my bottom lip as I ponder her words. "Did you know he feels sorry about killing his family? He feels horrible about how he treated me. He was literally sick over some things he did."

Her jaw sets. She slaps a few pieces of ham on one slice and says, "There's no way we can know how well he feels empathy. He's a master manipulator. I wouldn't put it past him to fake his tears for your sympathy."

"What if he can feel empathy?" I whisper, looking over my shoulder to make sure he's not standing at the top of the stairs, listening.

"It's not even worth considering. You're not a rehabilitation center for sick men, Marianna," she says, her tone cutting. "You should focus on nothing more than your own sanity while we deal with this."

"But *what if he can* be fixed now?" I ask again. "Derek said memories make people. What if he never remembers and stays how he was before he turned?"

The way Carol stares at me—like she doesn't know me . . . like she fears me—makes me lower my head.

"I'm not going to explain to you what's wrong with that question . . . you already know. You're not thinking clearly."

"I *am* thinking clearly," I grumble.

But the idea infects my brain like an unshakable, intrusive thought.

My mind bombards me with images of Denendrius—the same Denendrius that had me giggling while we were having sex—in a dark room, bloodied and chained and not fully understanding why he's there. In the image, he stares at me with tears in his lost eyes.

Carol carries my sandwich over and sits in a chair next to me, pitying eyes holding mine. "I won't give you grief for feeling bad for him, honey. Though I can't say I would in your position. Being abandoned as a baby, neglected, and raised in a misogynistic society with a father who modeled abuse . . . then trying to help someone and paying for it . . . it's tragic. It's very easy to see why he ended up this way."

She rests her hand on my arm. "But none of that matters. Even if he could be fixed—which I completely disagree that he can—no amount of philosophical reasoning matters. At the end of the day, he's going where he's going, and there's nothing that can change that. You can acknowledge it all, but don't let the thought go beyond that."

I pick at my crust and release a painful breath. "What does that say about me? I didn't really have a chance, either. I was in a gang. How many deaths have I contributed to? How many bullets hit people when I was firing out car windows? I peddled drugs. How many people overdosed that I sold to?"

Her bottom lip puckers. "That's different, Marianna. You were a child, and they indoctrinated you. He's a grown man who has spent almost two thousand years tormenting people for fun. Had you grown up in a healthy environment, you would have been like every other kid."

My sandwich stops looking like food. "I was twelve when I first killed someone. It was my gang initiation. I fired a shot into a man's chest without a second thought, and he didn't even see me coming. He was from a rival gang, and I got him behind his auntie's house. The police didn't even glance in our direction when they looked for someone to blame. He had crack in his system, so they assumed it was a drug deal gone wrong."

She presses her lips in a tight line, the corners down-turned. "Marianna—"

My stomach burns and I feel queasy, the memory rolling through me like acid. "And do you want to know what I felt? *Happy.* I was happy I finally did something to warrant love. I went back to the gang house with his bloodied bandana and they patted me on the back. They told the other members to look up to me, that I did good for our family. I was told not to feel bad, that he would have killed one of us, eventually. To this day I've had no one as proud of me for anything like when I killed him. Maybe Denendrius and I are perfect for one another. We're both murderers, right? Maybe he's what I deserve."

"Honey . . ." It's obvious she wants to tell me it's okay, but we both know it's not.

"I should have a life sentence for some of the things I've done." Picking up my sandwich, I force myself to eat it so she didn't waste her time.

Carols chews at her lip as she studies me, the conflict clear in her teary eyes. She's speechless, of course. What could someone possibly say to that?

She pulls in a stabilizing breath and slowly pushes it out. "Well, I think the world has punished you enough now."

Maybe, maybe not. It sure doesn't feel like I'm done being punished.

XXVII

Denendrius sits up in bed and rubs his eyes when I come in. I sigh and force my heavy legs to move me across the room and to him.

He tests a smile as I crawl into the bed beside him, checking my resistance when he grabs my waist and gently pulls me toward him. I let him know everything is fine by falling into him and curling up at his side.

"Do you remember me from when you were a vampire?" As soon as I ask, I wish I could take the question back. Do I want to know?

"No." He smooths the back of my hair.

I rest my palm over his heart. "Then how do you know you love me?"

There's a smile in his voice as he says, "My heart remembers."

I pull away and look up at him, overwhelmed by thoughts as I stare at his sweet smile.

My mouth burns. How can I sleep with him, laugh with

him, then let him be tortured? Should that make me an awful person? A little slip of anger in a justified place means nothing. He's not who he was. It's like he's been ... reset.

I run my fingers over the fading marks on his cheek from my nails. In a few days, those, as well as the ones on his hands, will be nothing more than a distant memory, not even deep enough to leave a scar like the ones he left on me.

My thoughts ebb through me, and I don't hold them back. Whether the thoughts are right or wrong to have, I accept that they're mine, that I feel how I feel. I can't change them any more than I can change the situation I'm in. Maybe I should still hate him at this moment, want to claw his eyes out and break both his kneecaps, keep him in a room alone until it's time to move him to a cell ...

But I don't feel like that anymore.

I allow myself to accept what I want, no matter what kind of person it makes me—desperate, weak, stupid or insane. Maybe as someone who isn't and has never been normal, I shouldn't expect myself to have normal thoughts. Everyone can blame the blood mark as much as they want. But these thoughts come as all the others. They aren't loud and don't feel forced into my brain.

I want to believe that this Denendrius is completely uncoupled from who he was as a vampire. That there's two different people who shared the same body, that one came and went with immortality. That one built itself on the foundation of the other. I want to kiss him, feel him, hear how he loves me, and plans to keep true to his promise never to hurt me again.

I don't want him to suffer. I don't want to be an angry, vengeful person who punishes whether or not it's logical to punish. Do I have to be one more person who hurts him when he only needs help?

Maybe I'm so fucking sick of everyone in the entire goddamn world telling me what I should and shouldn't want or do. Derek can talk me up all he wants, but I am who I am. A victim of my upbringing and circumstance like Denendrius.

I can fix myself if I try, do my best to be a good person and friend, instead of trying to convince myself that I am by drunkenly telling people like CJ. But I've still killed and beaten people, sold drugs and stolen cars. Am I deluded—arrogant, even—to expect someone better to date me? If I don't want to date anyone worse than me, then why should I expect someone else to?

Fighting is so tiring. I should stop demanding more from the universe, like it should care what I want or what I think should be fair, and work with what I've got.

I surface from my thoughts and find Denendrius lost in his own.

"What are you thinking about?" I whisper, skating the tips of my fingers down his bare arm, leaving goose bumps behind. Even the wound on his shoulder is healing nicely.

Denendrius blinks hard before his eyes lift to mine. He rests his palm against the side of my face and brushes his thumb beneath my eye.

"Your eyes remind me of Marciana's. Like cinnamon." His smile is soft, and he runs his fingers through my hair. "Hers was darker." He runs his index finger across my bottom lip. "Same lips."

I swallow a jealous bout of words, my eyes dropping from his. I watch his mouth instead, the hot breath from it gentle against my face. If only he knew I look like so many of his victims. A cold shiver runs through me. When he was a vampire, did he ever look at me and compare certain parts of me to girls he raped and killed?

"What was Mariana's mother like?" I ask. Surely, she wouldn't be anything like me in personality.

An odd smile passes over his lips—pained, perhaps—as he

says, "I don't have all the words to say . . ." His lips purse. "She was a good person. Very kind."

I cringe when I say, "Denendrius . . . are you sure you weren't in love with Mariana's *mom* and not her?"

He scowls at me, the offense clear on his face. "No. She was in love with Marianus, so I never had the thought. They were lucky to have love within their arrangement. I was to marry her daughter one day. We would have loved each other like they did."

I cringe as I say, "But you never met her, and she was a kid . . . how would you know?"

His jaw sets, and he inhales a long breath through his nose. I can't help but think I've angered him.

"She would have grown up to be like Marciana. She was an excellent mother, a good person. Mariana would have turned out like her. I would have loved her."

"But how can you know?"

His voice is hard. "She would have."

"All right," I whisper, knowing better than to fight his denial, vampire or not.

He sets his palm back on my cheek. "You should not be jealous. We are married. I was not in love with her. I have never been in love before, except with you. Nothing matters now but you."

"I believe you." I bite my bottom lip.

When he leans close and his lips graze mine, it's like he's asking for permission. I rest my hand on his jaw and close my eyes while I roughly shove my lips against his. I nip at his bottom lip and he bares his teeth playfully, brows lowering as a low groan rolls up his throat.

I pull away and wet my lips, my roaring heart spreading warmth through me.

"I was not done with you . . ." He trails off, the suggestion in his words clear. He takes a fistful of my shirt and yanks me closer.

We continue where we left off before being interrupted, with him on top of me while I grip tightly to him. There's no humor between us now, only a heavy seriousness, something desperate entwined with our bodies.

He glances back over his shoulder at the door a few times—rougher with me in those brief moments—like he's daring Derek to come back and interfere again.

I'm confused—a little disappointed—when he climbs off me and lies down by my side.

"Oh . . . okay. Did you . . . are you *done*?" I whisper, heat in my face as I squirm, feeling awkward.

"No. Come here."

My lip trembles. I sit and scoot closer, eyes scaling up and down his body while I pat my hair to make sure it hasn't come fully undone again. "Did I do something wrong?"

"I want you a different way." His smile is mischievous.

"Oh . . . how?" I fold my hands in my lap and wait for more direction.

His eyes narrow slightly. "Do you know some things I like?" he asks, like he's hoping he's already told me and that I'm okay with it.

"Uh . . ." Where the fuck is he going with this?

He wraps his hand around the back of my head, giving me a gentle pull down as he studies my face with nervous eyes like he thinks I'm going freak out at him.

I just shrug. "Okay."

He's oddly thrilled when we continue that way for a few minutes.

"What do you like?" His head tilts against the pillow as I straighten.

"I . . ." I shake my head. "I . . ." Have no idea how to answer that. I've avoided figuring that out.

"Okay." He runs his hand down the side of my face and clearly comes to some conclusion on his own. He lays me back down on my back. "You never feel good before? Not *alone*?"

Aside from tonight? I swallow and shake my head, jitters taking over me.

I may, unfortunately, know more than I should about the male body and what makes it work, but *mine* has always been left a mystery to me. I didn't want to give myself any attention after how much my body was already forced to have.

He's got a tickled smirk on his face as he runs his hand along my thigh. "You don't have to be so dutiful with me. I love you. I want us like modern husband and wife."

"Oh. I'm not trying to be *proper* or whatever. I . . ." I bite at my bottom lip, not sure what to tell him. "I'm nervous."

"I will teach you," he says with a devilish smile. "I want fun, not only to make babies."

A nervous shiver runs through me, and I hold my hands in tight fists against my chest as he puts one hand on each of my knees and pushes my legs apart. I'm stiff as he kisses down my thigh while carefully watching my reaction. I hold my breath when his fans against me.

By the end, I'm drenched in sweat, my muscles sore and body hot from toe-curling spasms.

But it felt good.

I'm too tired to move as he crawls back on me, and I'm surprised that there's still more pleasure left for my body to go through.

My moans make my eyes sting, the fact that I'm doing something—taking power back—that tormented me for years makes me oddly proud, even if I'm finding that control with Denendrius.

My body is starting to feel like it's mine again.

His body tenses on mine and he releases a long groan, lips vicious as he kisses me.

"Are you done now?" I ask when he pulls his lips from mine and sighs in satisfaction.

"Yes."

Denendrius rolls off me, and when I turn on my side, he slaps my ass so hard that I yelp.

"Oh—sorry." He cringes, like he didn't mean to do it so hard.

I let it slide and lay my head on his chest. "You know a lot of stuff," I note while trying to catch my breath, his lungs heaving under my head.

"I had lots of sex." It doesn't sound like he's bragging, just explaining with a simple fact.

My stomach burns, and it must be jealousy as I ask, "With who?"

He shrugs. "Eh . . . brothel, sometimes. The nice ones, with the expensive girls. Some free girls that like me, but it is not so easy."

I stare at him, trying to process his words. They're too much to swallow at once, and far too *casual*. "Why?" I realize he would have never had real dating experience, that it would have been straight to whatever marriage they arranged.

His eyes narrow, like he's confused by my question. "Unmarried virgin girls have to stay that way for their first husband. Terrible to take that."

The corner of my lip pulls back, and I can feel the bitchiness on my face. "But the men?"

"What?" He scratches his jaw.

"They had sex whenever they wanted?"

He fights a smile, and it looks like he wants to laugh at me. "Yes, Marianna."

I swallow.

"Derek explained much to me." He pats my thigh and chuckles. "Very different. It's okay. Better feeling with love, anyway."

Thankfully, I remember one of Daina's tips and get up to pee. My legs are as useful as cooked spaghetti, and I land on the floor while gripping the edge of the mattress.

Denendrius laughs from the bed, the springs creaking under him as he rolls over to look down at me. "So good?" He kisses the air at me and grins.

I grumble and stand.

"Bath?" he suggests.

When I agree to a shower instead, he carries me to the bathroom and sets me on the toilet while he readies the water.

Once we're in the hot stream, washing sweat and sex off us, he says, "I am so lucky. Best wife. You do things for me that I had to pay girls for."

My jaw falls open, and I'm so confused that I only use half my force to slap him in the chest.

Thankfully, he laughs. "Sorry. It is true."

My face scrunches, my hand searching the air at my side for logic. "Why would you have to pay a fucking prostitute for that?"

"It is deviant for me to do such acts with you."

My cackle hurts my throat. "What? Everything we did was totally *normal*."

"Is it?" His perplexed expression only makes me laugh harder.

"Yes, it's perfectly normal. You've always gone against the grain, then, no matter the norms, huh?"

"I don't know what you mean." He rubs bubbles across his chest. "Grain?"

I shake my head, too tired to explain. "Never mind."

The sound of the bedroom door closing carefully draws me out of a dream. I sit and rub my eyes. Denendrius is dead asleep, his arm draped over my lap. From the weak light, it's too early to justify being awake after my long night.

Wanting to know who peeked in and why, I slip out from under him and the covers and tiptoe out of the room. I pause at the top of the stairs when I hear low voices and catch a whiff of coffee.

A kitchen chair slides against the floor as Derek whispers, "They're both sleeping still."

Muscles rigid, I perch out of sight behind the banister to listen to their quiet conversation.

"What are we going to do?" Carol murmurs.

I strain to hear Rayonne's response. "I think it's time for me to check out some clans in New York City. Ziggy said he'll come with me if we hear nothing from Viorel's people by tonight."

There's hesitation in Derek's voice. "I don't know if that's a safe idea considering you're human now."

"What are our other options, then? Because we're going to be ripped apart from the *inside* soon. Either he's going to remember what's going on here, or she's going to tell him. We'll have to . . . I don't know . . . keep him drugged to stop him from leaving."

She? *Me?* My stomach turns. I'm not a snitch.

Derek sighs. "They know he's in Lorimer, right? It's a week since he's been human. Like you said before, they're bound to figure out where we are sooner rather than later, right? We can't be *that* elusive."

"Sure, they'll find us, but are you certain they will before he kills us in our sleep?" Rayonne counters. "I'm genuinely worried for our safety. Marianna's under his complete control, and I've seen how bad blood marks can get. She's been latching on to ways to keep him alive since Agatha turned him back. She was dead set on killing him but wouldn't go through with it, and then she focused in on needing him to remember before he deserved death. Now that he's remembering things, she's somehow convinced herself that he's two different people. I mean, she's had a complete shift in attitude. It's eerie."

My face burns. How many times have I explained my reasoning? They can't blame the blood mark just because they don't agree with me.

"We don't know what he's been telling her when they're alone," Derek adds.

How could that possibly be any of their business?

Carol says, "Then we need to separate them. Before we end up dealing with a teen pregnancy on top of it all."

There's no humor in Derek's low chuckle. "Yeah, with the pain in my head, I'm going to have to disagree. I'm not trying that again unless she really needs immediate help."

"So, New York City," Rayonne says.

"Okay, but I still think they need to be split up," Carol pushes. "If I can get Marianna in a car with me, *I'll drive*. You guys can incapacitate Denendrius somehow."

Frustration leeches from Rayonne's voice. "You don't understand how blood marks work, Carol. We're essentially dealing with a deadly version of Stockholm Syndrome. She's *literally* connected to him, far beyond a mental and emotional level. Messing with that will have consequences. Their souls, energy, whatever you want to call it, are tied, getting stronger the more time they spend together. He probably had her drinking from him all the time too. I've seen blood slaves commit murder, self-harm . . . many things and rationalize it and think it was their choice, because of the mark. It's insanely easy to abuse if the vampire wants to. She'll care more about preserving his life than her own if it comes down to it, and I don't want to create a situation like that. I'm honestly impressed it took so long to get this bad.

"Besides, even if you took her across the world, I promise she'd find her way back to him if she ever tried . . . which she would. She'd make seemingly random decisions that lead her to him—*us*—and she'd have an entire trip to stew about the separation while feeding off whatever his feelings were about it while he was with us. Yeah, if we keep them together, she'll get worse, but we don't really have the option. I thought the mark would go away when he turned back, but I was wrong."

What absolute fucking assholes. My body vibrates with anger, and I grip the wooden banister balusters so hard I might rip one from its place. If they tried to force me away against my will, could they really blame me for any retaliation when it's *against my will*?

Carol grumbles, then says, "Got it."

Rayonne sighs and adds, "Once we're with Viorel's men, I'm assuming they'll have someone else mark her to break her connection to Denendrius. I can't imagine they'd let that continue, especially if it's Viorel and his clan's safety at risk."

My heart stops. They'll have *some other vampire mark me*?

They can't do that. They can't!

I grind my teeth, flashes of fiery anger cascading over me.

Fucking.

ASSHOLES.

I didn't want to be marked by Denendrius, but there's no harm right now. Who knows what some other vampire would have me do if he controlled me? Despite what they believe, I know my mark to Denendrius isn't so deep that it's taken over my thoughts and will.

That's not happening. It can't. I will not fucking allow it.

But at least I know Denendrius will never allow that. He'll protect me from some other vampire trying to take me as his own.

I scurry back to the bedroom, holding my breath as I close the door behind me and slip back into bed. My head pounds, eyes burning. I curl up close to Denendrius and wrap my arms around my midsection. My gut burns with guilt and panic.

Tell him.

The thought makes my head spin.

Tell him.

I have to bite down on my tongue to stop the building words from tumbling out.

I know I should tell him. How can I keep it from him that there's more going on than vampires coming to kill him, that they're planning on turning him in to Viorel? But then, what if I tell him? He'll kill them. But I can't let them take him either. I can't let them pour someone else's blood down my throat.

But I don't snitch no matter how badly the words want out.

I feel like such a bitch. How can I sleep with him, tell him I love him, and not tell him he's in horrible danger?

Maybe there's really no point in scaring him. What are the chances they'll actually come for us? There's nothing but Rayonne's hope to go on. They probably won't even come.

Whether that's actually true, it makes me feel good enough to fall back asleep.

XXVIII

The thick smell of frying bacon lures me into consciousness. I give Denendrius a shake before heading downstairs, pretending like I didn't overhear them conspiring against me.

They're not as casual, all eyes turning to me from different parts of the kitchen as I enter.

"Morning," I gripe, hoping they interpret the disdain for them in my voice as a lack of desire to be awake. I flop down at the table in front of a plate of bacon and eggs that Carol points out to me.

I say nothing as I pick up my glass of orange juice, wondering what the chances are that they'd drug me and haul me away.

Denendrius's heavy steps down the stairs take my attention. He adjusts the hem of his green T-shirt over his blue jeans as he steps onto the floor and stares straight—emotionless—at Derek. Derek grips his plate, a vein popping up in his tense neck as he stops and stares back.

Rayonne's chewing slows beside me.

"I'm sorry, Denendrius." Derek cringes as he says the words, like even bringing up last night might get his head bashed in.

Denendrius's smile brings the stress level down in the room. "Ah. Me too."

Derek's shoulders lower with an exhale and he nods while pulling a chair back and sitting. "Okay. We'll forget it ever happened." He sets his plate down and points to another on the counter. "There's one made for you."

Denendrius scrutinizes Carol's plate as she passes him to get to her own chair.

"How are you feeling today, honey?" Carol asks me as she sits across the table from me, beside Derek.

Does she *really* want to know? "I'm fine." I push a hill of scrambled eggs onto my fork.

Denendrius grunts something as he throws himself down in a chair next to me, plate half-colliding with the tabletop. He flinches and rubs his back.

"Are you okay?" I ask him with a mouthful of eggs.

He gives me a pained smile and nods. As usual, he eats with his hands and completely ignores the utensils that Carol sets beside his plate like he's trying to make a point.

Once we're finished eating, Denendrius stands and stretches before saying, "I want to go home now."

Derek and Carol exchange a glance, a quick conversation happening between the odd looks that cross their faces.

"I think it's better if we all stay here," Derek says carefully, Carol backing him up with a firm nod.

Denendrius scoffs before a sharp beat of laughter leaves him. "I was not asking." He holds his hand out. "If no one will take me, give me keys and I will go."

Derek sets his plate at the end of the counter and crosses his arms. "Do you remember how to drive?"

Denendrius lifts his chin and rests a hand on my back. "No. Marianna drives."

Derek's lips part to protest more until Rayonne stands with her empty plate and interjects with, "I think going back to the apartment is a good idea, actually."

Derek and Carol have no choice but to cave, and after we clean the kitchen and pack up the SUV, we're off again.

The apartment is exactly as we left it when we return. Rayonne, Carol, and I waste our afternoon watching a romantic comedy while Derek and Denendrius sit back at the table together, poring over whatever complicated translation they huddle around. On the surface, they seem to get along again.

"Oh," Rayonne says near the end of the movie. "I can show you that picture I mentioned earlier, Carol."

I lean against the arm of the couch as I turn to see them. "Picture?"

Rayonne wipes at the bottom of her eyes, a particle of fallen black eyeshadow smearing across her pale skin. "Of Alessander. I was telling Carol about him the other day."

Once the movie is over, she rises and disappears somewhere near the front door, loudly digging through her suitcase. Returning, she sits back between us and crosses her fishnet-covered legs.

Rayonne opens a fancy silver cigarette case, a single small sepia photograph in it that's bent and crumpled at the corners. Rayonne sits beside a man I presume to be Alessander on an old sofa, a blond-haired Thomas between them. Alessander's long dark hair hangs over his suit, his eyes ancient and wise. Though none of the three are smiling, the joy in Rayonne's eyes leaps from the nineteenth-century photo.

"You three were an attractive family." I can't stop my eyes from traveling over to Denendrius. He's so deep in reading something that he doesn't notice me watching him. I give my attention back to Rayonne.

"Agreed," Carol adds. "I'm sorry."

Rayonne stares fondly at the photo, rubbing her thumb over both Alessander's and Thomas's face.

"Do you think you'll ever date again?" Carol asks gently. "Not that you have to, of course."

She snaps the case closed. There's heavy pain in her eyes when she whispers, "No. I don't think I can ever love another. I already had my epic love story. Anything else would pale in comparison."

We watch the beginning of the next film, and I wonder about Carol's dating life, realizing I know little about it.

"Do you have a boyfriend, Auntie?" I purse my lips.

Her eyes automatically flicker to Derek before settling back on the TV. Pink appears under her fair skin, a hint of a smile on her lips. "I don't. I haven't had a boyfriend in a couple years."

Interesting. Is she seeing him in secret, or does she have a crush on him?

From the corner of my eye, I catch Derek look up and toward Carol as he passes a paper to Denendrius.

Very interesting.

My attention moves to Denendrius when he gets up and walks around the table to the balcony door. He slides it open and steps outside. My feet hurry after him, and when I push the blinds aside, he's leaning against the wooden rail, staring at the parking lot below.

"Don't jump," I tease. The door is sticky in its frame, and my fingers are throbbing by the time I get it slid shut behind us. Standing close to him, our arms touch.

He doesn't look down at me.

I give him a nudge. "Seriously, though, you better not be thinking about it. You'll break both your legs."

"All I want is fresh air."

"Okay, sorry." I snag my bottom lip between my teeth and bite down. "What were you and Derek talking about?"

"Rome." Denendrius's eyes flicker sideways before he rubs

them and exhales. His gaze lands on the abandoned lot—a pile of stone and rubble—across the street as he leans over and rests his chin in his palm, his elbow on the rail.

I curl my fingers around the splintering wood and lean my tender ribs against it. "An apartment building used to stand there before a meth lab exploded and burned it down when I was seven. I used to spray paint there when I got older." I rap my nails on the railing. "You were in Lorimer sometime around then. Do you remember? My mother's house was a few neighborhoods away, but I still remember hearing the sirens and how black smoke filled the sky. Did you have this apartment then? Maybe you saw it happen. You might have seen me tagging a couple years ago, actually . . ."

"I don't remember, Marianna."

"Okay." I bite my lip harder this time.

I think of him standing where he is now, staring across the street at thirteen-year-old me as I climbed the beaten metal fence and spray-painted gang signs so everyone would know this neighborhood belonged to us. I shake a chill that tries to run down my spine, trying not to think of all the ways he has puppeteered my life.

"Are you mad at me?" I blurt, unable to help the question.

He unlatches his gaze from the abandoned lot and stares down at me. "No."

I pick at my lips. "Are . . . are you sure? You're not saying much today."

Denendrius gazes back across the lot as he straightens. "I'm not mad at you, Marianna. I'm thinking a lot."

I run my hand across his back and his muscles tense under my touch. Swallowing, I pull my hand away. "Oh . . . what about?"

He points at the abandoned lot. "Should I remember something about it?"

I take a relieved breath. "Yeah, probably. You've had this

place for a while. You probably saw me over there getting into trouble."

"Perhaps." He rubs the back of his neck and winces. "But I don't remember that."

Twisting my ouroboros bracelet around my wrist, I say, "That's okay. It's not important. You were probably mad I was hanging out with those types of people."

"Hmm."

I scrape my thumbnail against the wet wood, brown paint peeling off. The humid wind ruffles my hair around me, the smell of rain imminent. The rolling gray above promises it soon and the obscured sun makes it feel like it's closer to sunset than it actually is.

"It's going to rain—"

"I want a new house." Denendrius folds his arms across the rail and leans on them.

I swallow. "I know. That kind of stuff takes time though."

He grumbles something in Latin and shifts his weight to his other foot.

"Is there a reason to hurry?"

He stares down at the rear parking lot below, eyes tightening on a green car as it backs out of its spot. "You know of *lemures*? Restless ghosts?"

I stare at him, goose bumps lifting on my bare arms. "Why?"

"I am sick here from them."

Wrapping my arms around myself, I ask, "Then why did you want to leave Carol's?"

"I did not think it was this place until we returned. I have strange things in my mind here." The bottom of his eyes twitch and he blinks hard.

Memories? "W—what do you mean?"

He rubs the back of his neck as he straightens again. "I saw a girl on the bathroom floor. For one moment. She looked at me and disappeared."

I lean away from him. "What girl?"

"Bloody girl. A ghost." He stares at me with haunted eyes.

"A ghost." I blow out a breath. I can't say whether or not I believe they exist, but I want to be someone who does. Yet if anywhere is going to have them, the apartment probably would. Half the shit in that secret room is probably haunted. He likely killed people here too.

He grunts before saying, "Yes. Derek said I cannot worship my gods here. I think they are angry with me. He said I cannot do blood sacrifice."

"Ah."

He sucks at his teeth and huffs dramatically. "He called it animal cruelty, and it is not simple to go buy livestock in the city."

I snort, bracing myself as I say, "I hate to break it to you, but nobody worships Roman gods anymore. It's considered mythology."

"All stupid, then. Who do they worship?" He blinks rapidly at me while giving his head a quick shake, like I've told him something utterly preposterous.

"In America? Mostly Jesus."

His eyes narrow. "Who?"

My raspy laugh fights its way out, and it sounds like I'm sucking at air. "Christianity? Wasn't he alive around the same time as you?"

He thinks for a minute, then a grin spreads across his face. "Ah." He holds his arms out at his sides like a cross. "Yes?"

"Yeah, that's the guy you're thinking of."

He sniffs. "Troublemaker, him."

"Did he really exist?" I ask Denendrius, thinking I might get some sort of insider knowledge.

Denendrius shrugs. "How am I to know? I never met him. Nobody I know met him." He vaguely motions to the buildings. "They all worship Jesus?"

I brush my hair out of my face and wrinkle my nose when a tiny drop of water lands on the bridge of it. "Some of them. There's a lot of different religions people can pick from."

His face is full of hesitant hope. "Do you believe in my gods?"

I touch his bare arm when I let him down easy. "I don't really believe in anything."

He half-sneers at me. "Is this why we have no altar?"

I playfully roll my eyes. "I don't know how much you actually believed in your own gods, Denendrius. You kind of started comparing yourself to Mars." I lean against the railing and place my hand on his, the warmth of it nice compared to the chill of the air that hugs us.

He turns his hand, laces his fingers through mine, and grimaces. "Oh . . . I will be in trouble for that, I think."

Dinner ends with Denendrius drinking four glasses of diluted wine before puking it up with his shawarma.

I rub my hand in a circle between his shoulder blades, his shirt sweaty and clinging to him as he kneels in front of the toilet.

"This house," he whines before retching again and whispering something in hoarse Latin.

"You're not sick because of ghosts, Denendrius. It's the cure." The cure makes more sense, anyway.

He slurs something as he wavers under my hand, then feebly scratches at his shirt and chest.

"Are you okay—"

Denendrius falls sideways onto the floor with a thud, his eyes rolled back and skin a sickly gray.

"Derek!" I holler, dropping to Denendrius's side.

Derek, along with Carol and Rayonne, rushes to the bathroom and helps me sit Denendrius upright.

He comes to, slurring Latin as he leans slumped against the wall, his forearms on his knees as his delirious eyes struggle to focus on me. Sweat beads down the side of his face.

I wet a rag with cold water and crouch in front of him—while Carol fetches water for him—wiping his forehead and cheeks while he focuses on breathing. I send Rayonne and Derek away, feeling like I'm suffocating in the small space. They can't be much help, anyway.

When his eyes snag mine, there's a deep admiration in them before his head slumps. My heart leaps. Putting the rag aside, I grab the drink from Carol before she leaves us and bring it to his lips.

"Denendrius," I murmur, trying to pour the drink without spilling it or choking him. "Drink."

There's a dullness to his eyes as his large hand overlaps mine and part of my bracelet on my wrist to keep the cup still so he can drink it down.

Finished, he inches his hand away as a shiver rips through him. When he lifts his head to look at me, the darkness in his eye is eerily familiar. *Tormented and cold.* "Tatiana?"

I shift away from him, shaking my head. My blood runs cold, my breath frozen in my lungs. *Tatiana?*

His gaze swings around the room, but from the confusion on his face, I can tell he and I aren't seeing the same things.

Painfully slow, I rise to my feet and take a step back toward the door. "Derek!" I call loud enough to get his attention from the kitchen. "Maybe you should come back—"

Denendrius is on his feet at once, screaming Latin as he grabs me by the throat and twists me to hold me like a shield in front of himself as he faces the door. When Derek rushes to the doorway, Denendrius only screams demands louder while he presses his forearm into my throat. My ears ring, the chokehold so tight my lungs burn. Tatiana's name is mixed in with his shouts, and through Derek's—and now Carol's—panicked attempts to deescalate him, he whispers something sweet-sounding in my ear, the name attached to the end of his words.

My vision swims as I claw at his arm with my dull nails, too full of terror to make my legs do anything useful. My hearing fades with my vision, and I realize Denendrius was definitely holding back his strength when he was a vampire as I lose consciousness.

It feels like only a few seconds have passed when my eyes flutter open. The bedroom light fixture hangs above my head, and I rouse with movement beneath me.

My voice comes out hoarse. "Denendrius?"

When his head appears in my vision, bloodshot eyes holding mine, I realize I'm lying on his lap in bed.

His words sound garbled when he talks, and he brushes his fingers against my cheek.

"He snapped out of it as soon as you went limp," Rayonne explains from the doorway.

I groan and roll off his lap onto the cold blanket, rubbing my sore throat while I sit with my folded legs under me. "Fuck."

Denendrius reaches out and tucks part of my hair behind my ear, so he can see my face better from where he sits against the headboard.

"And he suddenly doesn't remember English again," she adds.

My head snaps up, hair falling back around my face. "What?" I gape, airless again. Twisting back to him, I ask, "Can you understand me at least?"

Pain warps his sickly expression, and he rakes his hands through the center of his hair, fisting a bunch at the back of his head as his hand shakes. From the sheen over his eyes and the way his lips stumble together, I can tell that he remembers everything but the words he needs.

I crawl back over to him and rest my hand on his knee. "It's okay. It'll come back." *Hopefully.*

His chin scrunches, the corners of his lips pulled down. His body jerks with a deep shiver as he chokes on a gasp.

"Lay down," I tell him, pulling at the blanket under him. "Maybe you'll wake up and remember."

He reaches out and grips the stomach of my shirt as he maneuvers between the sheets. Is he scared of me leaving his side? Does he think I might try to since he's hurt me twice? The desperate look in his eyes, the way his lips fall open without the words he needs, makes me think I'm right.

"You had a flashback. You didn't do it on purpose." I stroke his cheek, and he shudders at my touch and closes his eyes. Clearing my throat, I add. "I'm *okay.*"

Rayonne lets out a weird breath that has me looking back at her. "What?"

"This is making me incredibly nervous, Marianna."

Carol walks up behind Rayonne and exhales a loud breath of relief when she sees me awake. "Oh good. I thought he was going to break your neck."

"It's a little sore." I clear my throat again. "Can you get me a drink, please? I should stay here with him."

Denendrius grits his teeth and breathes through them, face twisted in equal parts fear and frustration as he mashes his head into the pillow.

I huddle down next to him after my drink while everyone else sets up their beds for later. Wide awake despite my brain's exhaustion, I lie on my stomach and watch a mix of fail videos and anything else that holds my attention for over five seconds on the phone, trying to distract myself from reality. Denendrius succumbs to quiet sorrow beside me, the time between his slow blinks extending. Soon his eyes lose focus on the screen and he closes them, a deep sigh blowing against my bare shoulder.

I run my index finger down the bridge of his nose and

across the shortened hair of his upper lip as he peeks at me. Derek got him a beard trimmer on the way back to the apartment as a peace offering.

"I love you," I whisper, leaning close to touch the tip of my nose against his.

There's no sign on his face that he has any idea what I'm saying.

"Shit," I grumble as I flop onto my back.

XXIX

A crack of lightning jolts me awake to an empty bed, the apartment too quiet and my nerves too frayed for Denendrius to be near.

When I check the phone, it's only ten p.m. despite feeling so much later.

Rumbling thunder forces more adrenaline into my veins as I bolt from the room.

The front door is wide open.

"Oh, no—Denendrius!" I bellow. What if he forgot more than English in his disorientation? Or what if it flooded him all at once and he's trying to escape?

There's movement in the living room, and I flee a clash of questions to find him.

I race right past my shoes and out the front door, my feet pounding down the wet carpet of the steps as my panicked breath fills the stairwell. When I approach the glass door of the building, I throw myself against the metal bar to open it. A cold gust of wind catches me as I step into the parking lot, whipping my hair around me like a tornado and assaulting me with icy drops of rain.

"Denendrius!" I call, voice lost to the storm.

I rule out Denendrius remembering and leaving when I find his car parked in its usual spot.

Which means Denendrius could be anywhere, and there could be vampires around.

Did a Darkling subdue him and sneak past us?

I wrap my arms around my stomach, thoughts in an incoherent flurry. Where do I look? What do I do?

My only thought is to search and call Sergei if I have no luck.

Unsure of which direction to take, I move straight down the road toward the convenience store. It only takes a few blocks before the cold has numbed my feet too much to feel the damp concrete against my soles, and it feels like my breath is made up of wind. When I reach the door of the store and duck inside, it's like I've stepped out of a giant fan.

"Ma'am?" the cashier asks carefully from behind the glass divider at the register.

I wrangle enough breath to sputter, "Have you seen a tall white guy, brown hair and eyes, possibly crazy looking?"

He shakes his head. "No. You're the only one I've seen in an hour."

"Fuck." I groan and throw myself back into the storm.

I decide to go around the block and head back to the apartment to call Sergei. I'd much rather risk him than whatever else might wait for Denendrius—and us, if we lose him. At least Sergei thinks this is all Den's choice.

I'll use the other door in case Denendrius was simply exploring the building, I decide, scolding myself for not checking the numerous halls for him first. My skin is sore and numb from the harshness of the rain by the time I walk around the L-shaped building and to the other entryway.

When I round the side of the brown building, movement catches my eye from the abandoned property across the street. Through a sheet of heavy rain, I spot a man big enough to be Denendrius and take off through the parking lot and across the desolate road. I scale the bent chicken wire fence and plummet into the tall grass, my soaked clothes weighing me down. I navigate through tall grass twisted with weeds, rebar and crumbling chunks of concrete from where a building once stood.

Denendrius kneels shirtless in a patch of torn-up grass and dirt, his hands muddy as he stares at the disturbed ground that's four feet deep in some places. His jeans are soaked red, streaks of crimson running down his face, neck, and chest where the rain has cut down it.

"Holy shit . . . Denendrius," I breathe as I come upon him. "Please tell me you're not burying someone."

I plant my hands on the knees of my soaked jeans, trying to catch my breath. My wet hair dangles around me and my feet sink, mud between my toes.

He falls forward onto his hands and scrapes his fingers through the dirt. I squat down next to him. When I touch my fingers to the frigid skin of his back, he jerks from beneath my touch, his breath loud enough to break through the storm's volume as he claws faster at the ground.

Moving back, I straighten. "Denendrius . . . what are you doing?"

He glances up at me, brown eyes so tortured I feel a chill colder than what the storm brings. I catch sight of his teeth, dark red with blood.

I try to keep my breath in check. "What did you do?"

Noticing the long cut across his forearm, all I can do is hope that all the blood is from it and that maybe he drank from himself.

Denendrius huffs as he continues to dig, mud caking his hands as he scrapes it aside. After a few minutes of lightning cracks and rolling thunder, his hand tangles in something that a shot of lightning reveals as torn fabric, caked in dirt and vaguely pink.

"Stop digging," I hiss.

His fingers claw up more mud, enough for the fabric to move and reveal the dirty, bony fingers of a corpse.

My breath expands in my throat and I step away, eyes scouring the roads like the police are already on their way.

He stares at the bit of exposed remains with a flat face and distant eyes before rising to his feet and turning to me. He points to her, then to himself, his Adam's apple bobbing like he's choking on the words.

"You killed her," I interpret.

He looks back down, red-rimmed eyes filled with knowing.

"You remembered something, right? That's how you knew she was there." I feel horror roll through me with the thunder, water running down my back. "How long ago did you kill her?"

The sound of my voice doesn't reach him, and I'm not sure he'd respond even if he understood my words.

How long has she been there? When he started coming to Lorimer years ago? When he got the apartment a few years back? Either way, that means he remembered something recent.

A thunderclap overpowers the sound of his voice, but there's enough light from the streetlights and electric sky that I can read his lips.

"Two years ago."

He's remembering English again, and *recent events now*? He could remember me and how angry I made him.

My stomach clenches, the thought more terrifying than the body at our feet.

"Allison . . ." Denendrius crouches down, staring help-lessly at the grave as he removes more dirt from her. He uncovers a cracked and muddy skull with a shattered jaw and eye socket, the neck twisted. It's easy to imagine how she died.

He releases his breath, wiping his nose with the back of his hand enough times to make me realize some of the wetness on his face is from tears. He refrains from meeting my eyes as he stands again and turns around, head low as he takes a step toward home.

I grab his arm, desperately trying to pull him back. "What are you going to do about this?"

"Leave her. She's restless."

Dropping his arm, I say, "You want her to be found?"

He swallows, his feet shuffling in the dirt as he angles his body toward the apartment. "Yes. I want the ghosts to go."

We rush back to the apartment, the muscles in my hands so stiff from the cold that I struggle to open the door. Walking up four flights of stairs proves no easier. My joints resist with each step, and Denendrius and I shiver so hard I'm surprised we don't both shake right out of our skin.

As soon as we're into the apartment, Denendrius pushes past Rayonne and into the kitchen to retch in the sink. Blood sprays against the stainless steel and up onto the off-white square backslash.

"I think he's sick. Where are Carol and Derek?" When I step closer to him, he groans at me and holds his hand up a bit to ward me off.

"They started looking around the surrounding blocks for him." She pulls her flip phone from a hidden pocket in her billowy black skirt. "I'll tell them you're back."

The muscles in Denendrius's back and shoulders contract as he pukes again. I grab him a glass of water and he begins to chug it. Halfway through the glass, he pukes crimson into it before he has a chance to turn his head to the sink, dumping it as his stomach continues to empty.

My hands vibrate violently at my sides, more from

worry now.

Rayonne looks back at the bag of weapons beside the table. "That's a lot of blood to be puking up. Who did you kill, Denendrius?"

Denendrius groans before coughing, his voice strained. "Nobody. I am sick. The blood is from my stomach."

"Yeah? Why is your arm injured?" Her eyes narrow in distrust.

"I went across the street. The metal fence cut me. *I am sick*," he growls.

I chew my cheek. The cut definitely looks like it's from a knife. It's too perfect of a wound.

Rayonne puts her phone on the counter and takes a step closer. Though her tone is caring, there's a hint of a challenge, like she's daring him to come up with a lie. "If you're that sick to be puking up so much blood, you could need emergency stomach surgery."

He turns the tap on and wets his hands with warm water before splashing it on himself—and half on the floor and counter.

"I am fine," he snarls at her, throwing a lethal glare over his shoulder.

Her lips press into a tight line. "What are your thoughts, Marianna?"

Dread drips into me. I shake my shoulders to try to rid myself of the feeling. "Denendrius . . . come on."

His jaw sets and he reaches across the kitchen to the knife drawer. The blades scrape against one another as he forces the drawer open. Without too much thought, he grabs a paring knife from the top and slaps it on the counter near the stove before twisting to vomit in the sink again.

After spitting a mouthful of dark red saliva into the sink, he says, "I cut myself, okay?"

"Are you craving blood?" My voice shakes, and I lift my

hands to my sore cheeks.

His lip curls back like he can't believe I'd ask him that. "*No.*"

Rayonne's leg shakes. "If you are, it's okay, Denendrius. I crave blood since I turned back human."

He slams his palms on the counter and heaves over the sink before snarling, "*I am not!*"

Rayonne and I both take a step back.

"Then why on earth did you cut yourself, if not to drink from the wound?" Rayonne prods.

"Because it made me feel better," he explains with a wry smile.

Her eyes flicker to me. "What . . .?"

"You wanted to know," he spits.

"That still doesn't explain why you're puking blood—" She bites back the rest of her words.

The look in his eye is dangerous, like one more question will have violent rage spilling from him like a volcano. He turns on his heels and heads down the hall.

My muscles protest with my swift movements as I chase after him to the bathroom, shutting the door behind us. "Can you tell *me* the truth?"

He ignores me as he pulls the shower curtain closed before reaching behind it to turn the water on.

"Den?" My fingers twitch as I strip naked, giving him no choice but to share the hot water with me.

Total silence.

He unbuckles his belt and drops everything, and I can't help but think he's going out of his way to avoid looking at me.

"Den? Are you mad at me?"

"Why you call me that? Den?" His voice is sour with irritation, his eyes sharp as they cut over me.

"Sorry, Denendrius." He doesn't have many recent memories still, then. That's good.

His lips purse as he looks me up and down. "It's okay." He

holds the shower curtain back for me. "Go on, be warm."

My shivers slow under the hot water, but I still ache down to my bones from the storm's abuse.

Denendrius puts his chilly hands on my waist, and I yelp and sputter curses.

The seriousness hardening his face softens at my reaction, and he lowers his hands. "I'm not craving blood," he promises. "I . . ." He sighs. "I dreamed about feeling sick from being thirsty as a vampire. I am feeling so sick lately, I thought maybe it would help me feel better like it does Rayonne. It made me feel sicker."

I unload a weighted breath, shoulders lowering. "Oh."

His small smile twitches, so far from reaching his eyes. "It makes me sound strange."

"I'm used to strange."

Exhaustion clutches me again, and I yearn for a day where I can truly rest. The fact one seems so far away—if any are waiting at all—only makes my head yearn for a pillow. I could probably sleep for a week straight. "I think I'm going to get a cold from running around so much in the rain the past few days."

He curls his fingers around my waist again. "I would take care of you."

"Sweet." I lean my head back so hot water can rush through my hair, and a smile passes over my lips. It only lasts a moment as I think about the girl outside and his flashback earlier.

"Were you remembering Sirmium?" I whisper.

Was Tatiana the girl from the story Sergei told me? Was he remembering her helping him escape? Did he choke her out too, then? Or did he not know his strength while he was trapped in the memory?

"I'm too tired to talk about so many things."

"Okay." My feet ache so terribly from the sidewalk and pebbles that the hard bottom of the tub becomes too much to stand on. I hold the plastic side of the shower as I sink down and sit at the bottom of the tub, a cold draft from the crack in the curtain wafting across my back. I rattle so hard I feel a twinge in my neck.

The pain only forces my waiting tears forward, and I lean my forehead on my knees as I sniffle and try to hide them.

My thoughts are too messy, and I can feel myself breaking off into little pieces inside. It's like I'm standing on a thin chunk of ice in the ocean, the heat of this situation weakening the platform of my life. Soon it will melt away and I'll be left to the dangerous deep with sharks waiting to snap me up. I'm so far from land that all there is to do is wait.

But what am I even waiting for? There's no safety close enough to float to.

I'm hardly worried about another vampire marking me, or what my life would be like in Romania. My hope for such a thing even happening has dissolved. But now there's another section crackling, ready to break off.

Denendrius's sanity.

I worried something like this would happen . . . but he seemed stable enough. There's nothing I'll be able to do to stop them from subduing him if it came to it. Is he going to get worse?

I lift my head when Denendrius's feet squeak against the bottom of the tub and he grunts. He maneuvers down in front of me, a long leg on either side of me. Leaning his forehead against mine, he releases a blissful exhale and says, "What would happen if we abandoned this place?"

He probably has this place under a fake ID, and I wouldn't be surprised if he either gave the landlord a good chunk of money or hypnotized him. But since I know we can't leave regardless, I say, "I don't know. It's usually a lot of paperwork to get a new place, especially if you want to buy one. It would take weeks."

He grumbles in frustrated Latin. "Okay. We will start soon. I will feel better in a new home. Then everybody can leave."

What if being in this apartment really is triggering him? What if being *here* is what makes him worse? That, and the vampires constantly trying to kill us can't be helping.

We get out of the shower once we're both thawed, and I convince Carol everything is fine.

Much to her protests, I pour myself a glass of whiskey in an attempt to warm my insides and bring it with me to the bedroom. I can't stop my thoughts from circling around Allison's body outside as I take small sips. How long will it take someone to stumble upon her grave? What will happen when they do?

When I'm convinced that Denendrius is asleep, I scoot away from him and snag the cell phone. I wince against the brightness of the screen as I type "Lorimer missing teen Allison."

The list of results is depressingly short, but from a website made last year by a family member, I'm faced with a copy of a newspaper article from two years ago.

Desperate Search for Missing Teen Begins

LORIMER POLICE are hunting for sixteen-year-old Allison Johnston and are requesting any knowledge the public may have of Johnston's violent kidnapping. Last seen arriving at the home where she babysits, Allison was wearing a hot-pink sweater and a blue jean skirt. Pictured above, Allison is slim at 5 feet 2 inches tall and 110 pounds, with long brown hair and hazel eyes. The family who hired Allison called the police when they returned home to find their two sons locked in a closet and signs of a violent struggle in the bedroom where Johnston was sleeping. Allison's family is praying for the return of their daughter. Police are asking the public to remain vigilant and report any suspicious activity.

I stare at the haunting black-and-white photo of Allison, and I can't help but wonder if she was on any of those tapes. If I saw her name, I don't remember.

"What did I do with her?" Denendrius's voice almost makes me jump out of my skin.

My throat tightens and I swallow against it. "I—I don't know." Not exactly, at least.

He reaches out and runs his fingers against the side of my face. "Do you hate me for it?"

I stare down at him. "I hate who you were, and that you did it, yes."

A crease forms between his brows. "Me too. It is hard to understand how I did all those things. None of the memories feel like mine."

My chest is tight as I put the phone on the bedside table, swallow down the rest of my whiskey, and face him with my head on the pillow. "You don't remember why you did any of it?"

The world may never forget what he did, but I still don't want him to remember. Maybe that's selfish, but I don't think I could handle him having the memories of what he did to me again. It's better off if they exist nowhere else but behind a door in my mind, locked away for good.

His Adam's apple bobs as he swallows, his voice coming out hoarse. "I'm scared to remember, Marianna."

I cup his jaw with my sore fingers and scoot closer to press my lips against his—

The sound of the apartment door being kicked open deafens me. I instinctively leap out of bed. Denendrius kicks the blanket off, the sound of Rayonne's shrill scream curdling the contents of my stomach before there's a heavy thud in sync with her silence.

XXX

"I swear, it's just us in here!" Derek hollers, his voice a desperate pitch that shocks my nerves.

I'm dizzy with panic as I scramble for my revolver in the nightstand and yank it from the drawer.

A man knocks on the door and laughs. I'd lock it if I didn't risk getting the door booted into my face. Denendrius shoves his legs into his pants as I point the gun, not sure how high I should aim for whoever is coming in. I hold my breath and hope whoever is on the other side isn't too strong for a wooden bullet. If I'm not dealing with humans—doubtful from Rayonne's reaction—then since they were impervious to the garlic, Darklings must be after us.

My heart's ready to give out as the knob slowly rotates, like whoever is on the other side is trying to make us squirm in nauseous anticipation. My teeth clench, my hand sweaty on the gun.

The bedroom door flies inward, a shotgun aimed at my chest.

"*Hola, puta,*" a tattooed man says with a sardonic twist of a smile. His eyes are dark with disdain as they wander to Denendrius. "*Diablo.*"

He steps out of the way for another member of Red Revenge, who comes in with a handful of neon-orange zip ties.

I recognize him—Paco—as one man Carlos had beat me when I was in the gang house's basement. He has double the tattoos now. From the black I glimpsed on the inside of his bottom lip when he spoke, I'm sure it says *padre*, which only means he's in charge now. Carlos and Julio had the same lip tattoo when they were leading us. Paco must be near thirty by now, and from the look in his blown-out pupils, he's coked out of his mind.

"How the fuck," I breathe. "Paco?"

Paco's deep brown eyes twinkle, and he rubs his inked hand over his buzz cut and adjusts his grip on the shotgun. "Put the goddamn gun down, Marianna."

"No," I growl, my heart spasming in my chest. "Why the fuck would I do that?"

Denendrius steps around the end of the bed, shoulders squared. He snarls something, and I can tell he's going to try to pry the shotgun from Paco's grip.

"Denendrius, don't—"

Paco slams the butt of the shotgun into Denendrius's sternum, the air forced from his lungs as he wheezes and clutches at his chest. He topples over on his knees, and I fight the urge to rush to him. In Spanish, Paco tells his partner in crime—calling him Danny—to double-zip-tie his wrists.

He aims the gun back up at me, lifting it to stare crudely down the barrel. "Put it down or I send your man back to hell. I got slugs in this shit."

I grimace and lower the revolver. He reaches forward and tears it from my grip, lifting the bottom of his white tank top, exposing more ink, to jam it in the waist of his jeans.

Denendrius catches his breath as the first zip tie tightens around his wrist, and he kicks out at Danny before Paco hammers him in the side of the head with the shotgun. He grunts, too confused to stop the next zip tie that binds his wrists together.

"What do you want with us?" Derek asks with a hoarse voice from the living room, all his bravery clearly spent on speaking up.

An unfamiliar girl laughs from the living room, and Paco shouts his response. "This guy fucking *ate* one of my brothers, and this bitch shot one." He shakes his head in disgust at me before stepping closer to snarl, "How are you still alive? You should be dead."

He jams the cold barrel between my brows, and my eyes cross, breath trapped in my throat.

Paco bites his bottom lip, eyes searching mine for secrets as he cocks the gun. "Do you die if I pull the trigger?"

"What do you think, *loco*?" I spit.

A sick laugh bubbles up past his lips and he lowers the gun. "I think whatever you fuckers are on will not bring you back this time." He motions with his head for Danny to zip-tie my hands.

"Fuck you," I snarl.

Paco turns the butt of the shotgun around and I feel the carpet against my cheek, hot pain enveloping my head as plastic locks around my wrists. I groan and hear Denendrius protest and mumble my name before another thud.

Rayonne's shrieks and sobs and Carol's teary pleading seep through my semiconsciousness until their terror brings me to the twisting sight of the apartment parking lot. I'm laid out on a brown leather bench seat, a blur of black hair and limbs beyond the vehicle's door. The gangster holding Rayonne tries to shove her into the seat, but she kicks her feet against the frame of the vehicle. He slams her on the ground, her arms and legs flailing until he holds the tip of a knife against her throat. She's quiet until he pulls a red bandana from his back pocket, her squeals muffled as he shoves it into mouth while she writhes. His fist slams against her face until she's unconscious, her body limp as he tosses her on the leather seat in front of me as I fade.

The feeling of my head rattling against glass brings me back to consciousness and I find myself staring through a tinted window at gray asphalt and dotted yellow lines. My head pounds when I try to lift it, and my ears ring. Turning my eyes up, I see the buildings are sparse around us, the streetlights nonexistent.

"Why are you taking us out of the city?" Derek asks from the seat in front of me, Carol hugging herself beside him with Rayonne on the right of her.

Paco's laugh comes from my right side.

I answer for him, half my words slurred. "They're going to kill us and dump our bodies in the forest." I clear my throat. "It's what we used to do."

There's a grin in Paco's voice. "You have a good memory, *puta*."

I sniff, blood running down my nose as I lift my head. Denendrius sits tall beside me, sharp eyes straight ahead as he ignores the shotgun barrel Paco has placed at an angle under his ear.

Rayonne whines and fights to lift her head. The left side of her face is bloody and swelling, the bandana tied and parting her split lips. Black makeup runs down her cheeks. She shakes and her emotion brings a smile to Paco's lips, and he reaches forward and runs his hand over the back of her tangled hair, making her grimace and sob.

"Marianna, what's going on?" Derek pleads limply, turning around in the seat in front of me to look back. He puts an arm around Carol, who's covering her face with her quivering hands.

I clear my dry throat. "I don't—"

Paco interrupts. "Reckoning day, Marianna. You killed Carlos. You and that fucker Julio were stealing blow and fudging the numbers to sell it on your own, and you already planned to kill Carlos before you did it so Julio could run things. We were up for hours weighing shit and crunching numbers, and it was still wrong after Julio gave us his word. Why do you think nobody let you out of that basement but him?"

I close my eyes. "Honest to God, we weren't."

"No? Then why did I catch that motherfucker with bricks in his trunk? Why did I find stacks in his mama's house?" he demands.

I grit my teeth, the taste of blood on my tongue churning my stomach. "I don't know. Maybe he was, but *not me*. I rounded up to the closest figure that made sense, thought I missed a couple digits because I kept thinking about getting raided and I was used to having Julio's help."

"Boo-fucking-hoo," he mocks.

I sit upright, hot coals heavy in my stomach. Adrenaline pounds through me so hard that it pushes some of the agony away. "Fuck you. I usually knew my fucking shit. Don't forget, Carlos had me counting for a reason. Julio told me before I even did the math what the tally should be, and when I counted, it was only a few pounds off from what he said was ready for the dealers. I thought I might have misheard him and wrote what I thought I counted. If Julio really was stealing shit, then he was hoping I'd take his word. You wouldn't have known product was missing if I hadn't fucked up."

He laughs. "If you ain't lying, he fucked you real good too." He adjusts in his seat and tries to wipe his grin away when he runs his hand over his nose and mouth. It grows, his laughter coming harder. "Aye . . . he fucked you real good, then. Tell *him* how pissed you are when you join him in hell."

My jaw locks and I lean my head back, inhaling loudly.

I wince when Derek speaks. "Why would you kill her for being a scapegoat?"

Paco's finger twitches over the trigger, the barrel of the gun shifting a few inches away from Denendrius's throat and toward the seat ahead where Derek sits.

"Don't talk—"

Paco cuts me off. "It doesn't matter! She killed Carlos in cold blood." He points to his eye. "I saw this bitch come upstairs behind Julio. He set his gun down the counter for her." His eyes turn to me. "You grabbed it as soon as Carlos saw Julio let you out, and you were already aiming through their punches. You didn't even give a damn! You popped him one and let Julio deal with the uproar. Carlos did so much for you and you fucking do him like that?"

My lip curls. "Because he tied me to a chair and locked me in the basement to have me beaten. He was going to traffic me. Don't pretend you wouldn't do the same."

He shakes his head, teeth bared. "You make mistakes, *puta*, you pay the price. He would have done it to any of us. You forget how he bailed you out of jail? How he got you off needles and put fucking food in your mouth and clothes on you? You would have been sleeping on the sidewalk or stuck with those creepy foster parents that one time if it weren't for him. He *always* vouched for you." Paco leans toward me and into Denendrius's space. "You tell Carlos what an ungrateful little bitch you are once the bears are done with you."

I think about the placement I got when Carlos was still in charge, how he let me sleep at his place because I was waking up to my foster father standing in my doorway in the middle of the night. It took my social worker far too long to move me, and if it weren't for Carlos, I would have been on the street or there for him to get the nerve to come in one night.

"Carlos was still a bastard," I snarl.

Derek opens his mouth again, and I wish he'd stop so I'd have time to think and come to terms with dying. "She's seventeen . . . are you really going to kill a kid?"

Paco spits onto the floor of the SUV. "I've killed younger for less. I don't give a shit! If Marianna was old enough to live this life, to sell drugs and steal cars, to *murder* for us, she's old enough to die. Only God can free you from this life."

Derek is finally out of words. His lips form a tight line and he looks from me to Rayonne, his arm tightening on Carol.

Rayonne mumbles something that I miss.

Danny—who sits crouched on the floor between the driver's and passenger seat facing the three of them with a semiautomatic pistol—pulls the bandana from her mouth.

"Are you going to kill us too? What did we do?" she cries.

Paco laughs, Danny and the two up front echoing. "It's nothing personal. But maybe you should have picked who you associate with better. Hm?"

Her tears come again, and it's strange to see her so afraid of a street gang when she's barely flinched in the face of vampires.

Denendrius leans in close to Paco—maybe to intimidate him, maybe because he's dizzy from being beaten—and scrutinizes his tattoos. His head turns to me, eyes pinning the tattoo on my neck. Denendrius's eyes narrow before his sharp gaze points forward.

Is he coming up with a plan and waiting to act? Why is he so quiet?

I hold my breath when we turn down a wide dirt road with a mass of trees on either side of it, questions spinning in my mind when a pair of yellow headlights slice through the dark. I squint against them, feeling like pins have been shots into my eyes. The outline of a woman slinks toward the SUV, and as she nears, my mind empties of words.

Rayonne gasps as the sliding door rolls open. "Agatha?"

Her eyes lock straight onto Paco. "You can hand him over now since I led you to Marianna," she demands, the heel of her black leather boot bouncing in the dirt with impatience.

He snickers and cocks his shotgun. "Settle down, *chica*. I want more than that now. Why do you want this man so bad, huh? 'Cause I was thinking . . . he must be pretty special. I wouldn't mind killing him myself after he tore up my brother. Since Marianna has been around him, she doesn't seem to die either, and I know no heroin is responsible for that. Why don't you fucking persuade me some more?"

Agatha stares at the gun, lips twitching before she spits out, "We had a deal. I tell you where Marianna is and you bring him and that goth bitch to me. You can keep the other two, I don't give a shit."

The girl in the driver's seat laughs in disbelief, her support fueling Paco's haughty grin. "You expect me to take on the burden of two more bodies? Fuck your deal," he spits. "Who do you think your ass is dealing with?" He points behind him with his thumb, smile fading. "That's my fucking city, you understand? You come onto my turf, knock on our door like a goddamn pig and start asking questions, and now you're calling shots?"

Agatha stands tall, nostrils flaring, eyes calculative. "*Fine.* I'll gladly take them. And you want the drugs they're on? They're in the van—crated—so you'll have to come look for yourself."

Paco's head sways as he rubs his jaw, thinking. "Why don't you *tell me* what it is?"

A blank look flashes through her eyes, and her mouth opens and closes.

"It's research chemicals," I interject, thinking about how Carlos was always interested in chasing the newest and craziest high he could get his hands on. "They don't have a name that's not a scientific mouthful, but it's fucking *sweeeet*."

It's not that I want to help Agatha, but I've had far more luck taking her down over Red Revenge. Clearly, she's got something planned for him, so if I can get Paco and his crew out of the way . . .

"Don't take them," Denendrius warns Paco, eyes remaining locked on Danny. "You need to be strong. Marianna almost was not. Very risky. But perhaps . . ." He glances at Paco from the corner of his eye. "Hm. Perhaps you shouldn't. You are probably only a little stronger than her . . ."

Paco grits his teeth, shoving his face closer to the side of Denendrius's. "You don't tell me what I can't fucking handle." He hops out of the car, shotgun in hand, and sniffles loudly. To Agatha, he spits, "Show me."

The corner of Denendrius's lip lifts in a half-smirk. I don't appreciate the weak girl stereotype, but I guess the attempt to emasculate Paco worked.

My muscles lock as I watch Agatha stare up at him. The blue of her eyes shifts in the low light. Paco's lips part to speak and Agatha lunges, dark blood spraying across windows and the seat as her fangs tear into his throat. Paco screams, Danny firing off a shot that misses Agatha and echoes into the thick woods behind her.

Agatha drops Paco in a screeching and writhing heap in the dirt. "Good luck," she snarls. "You'll need it." Her eyes lift to mine and she gives me a devilish grin while running her bloody tongue over her fangs.

The girl leaps from the driver's seat, headlights illuminating her black-and-red flannel button-up as she races around the front of the SUV to Paco. She leans down and tries to help him to his feet, but he shoves her aside while writhing and holding his neck as he screams in Spanish.

Agatha picks up Paco's shotgun and points it at Denendrius.

When a man steps out from the utility van she came in, my heart plummets through me.

"You're not taking Denendrius," I snarl, hooking my fingers in the sweaty fabric of his T-shirt.

Her finger twitches over the trigger, aim sweeping from Denendrius to Derek, Carol, and Rayonne. "Out."

"No," I object as everyone but Denendrius obeys her orders. "You're not taking them. Carol—"

Agatha flashes her fangs at me. "Oh, don't you worry about your aunt and teacher. I'm thirsty, so I'll give them quick deaths. I'm saving all my energy for Rayonne."

Refusing to sit idle, I lean back into the seat and boot Danny square in the face as he tries to climb over to me. There's a crunch, and I feel something give under my bare heel. The momentum sends him back against the dashboard between the driver and passenger seat, and I scramble over the back of the bench for his gun that fell on the leather. My fingers touch the cold metal, but he breaks it from my grasp, whipping me across the side of the head with it. My ears ring, the taste of blood strong on my tongue. An arm curls around my throat as I struggle and try to blink away stars. I freeze when metal presses into my temple.

When my vision straightens, it's Danny with his arm wrapped around my throat, my back pressed into his chest as we lie twisted on the seat where Carol sat. I freeze, knowing the gun against my head isn't a bluff.

"*No te muevas*," he commands in my ear as he lets out a wet cough.

As directed, I don't move. I gnash my teeth, barely able to swallow under the pressure of his forearm.

Agatha steps forward and shoves the barrel of the shotgun against Denendrius's chest. The man she beckoned from the utility van snatches Rayonne with inhuman speed, his black eyes strong against the sick paleness of his flesh. He looks bigger than Denendrius, and she screeches and claws at him.

Carol's desperate eyes and terror-crumpled face turn to me from where she stands in the dirt. Her chest lifts and falls in short breaths.

Agatha forces their steps forward. At least they'll have better odds all together. There's no mercy where I'm headed, but at least I've had a year to come to terms with the likelihood of the gang killing me.

When the SUV jerks, I look up and find Paco crawling into the driver's seat. The girl races around the vehicle as he cranks it into reverse.

"Denendrius!" I cry as the SUV flies backward.

The Darkling—swiftly disappearing with Rayonne and returning without her—yanks Denendrius out of his seat and into the dirt, Paco's girl left behind screaming his name.

Denendrius's raspy voice calls for me as he disappears from my sight. My heart hammers, throat dry as I try to writhe in Danny's chokehold to get to the open door.

We race backward until Paco breaks hard and whips the vehicle ninety degrees onto the highway. I'm wrenched out of Danny's arms, the movement slamming the vehicle door shut before I can scramble to it to risk the speed and highway for freedom.

Paco steers frantically, the SUV fishtailing as he races down the highway. I struggle to catch my bearings as we jerk side to side. He clutches his bandana against his gushing neck, screaming at Danny and the man in the passenger seat—who has been so quiet I hardly noticed he was there—in Spanish to keep an eye out for the demons, to shoot if the van tries to stop us.

"Where are we going?" I demand.

His head whips back to face me. "Wouldn't you like to

fucking know," he seethes. "You knew what they were, didn't you?"

I clamber into the back seat, kicking Danny in the chest when he tries to get up. Blood gushes from his broken nose.

My heart races faster the farther we travel from Denendrius. Tears well in my eyes, and all I can think about is how I'll never see him again.

At least he won't think it's me who let him get tortured.

"Didn't you!" Paco screams.

My brows drop, eyes tightening while I will my tears not to fall. "No," I lie, teeth bared.

Paco swerves when the van's headlights shine through the SUV from behind. "Fuck!"

I pull against the zip ties. "They're not coming after us," I promise.

"How do you know?" he snarls, his bloody hand slipping on the steering wheel.

The van passes us before I can answer, tripling its speed and stopping dead in the road ahead with screeching tires. The sliding door opens. In our headlights, Agatha's back slams into the pavement with Denendrius on top of her. The zip ties are missing from his bloody wrists. He jams his thumbs into her eyes as she claws and kicks at him, her body trying to lift from the ground as he repeatedly cracks her head against the highway.

My hope soars until Agatha's partner leaps out of the driver's side. He throws Denendrius off Agatha—who is screaming and clutching at her face—and wrangles him back into the van. In a blink, they're driving off again.

Paco slams on the gas, swinging the SUV around the van. I press my palm against the chilled window, watching wide-eyed until their headlights outshine the image of the van.

Denendrius ...

Paco and the gangster beside him ramble in Spanish about

how she bit him as Danny slides into the seat beside me, gun on his lap.

Paco eyes me in the rearview mirror. "What'd she do to me?"

I swallow and wet my lips. "She bit you . . . but you'll be fine."

His hand tightens on the wheel, and he clears his throat. "Bitch, I don't feel fine! Am I going to turn into a monster or some shit?"

"No," I assure him, slowly sliding my seat belt on when all eyes shift to Paco. "You would have had to drink her blood to turn."

He shifts and rolls down the window. "I don't know." He wipes sweat from his forehead. "I don't feel good."

I swallow a nervous lump. "Well, to be fair, you got your throat ripped the fuck out. You're gushing blood."

Danny speaks beside me. "Yo, Paco. Maybe we should forget about this bitch and snatch a doctor."

Paco's eyes flicker to my reflection again, and I hide the shake in my zip-tied hands by stuffing them between my thighs.

The passenger's voice comes deep, his Spanish thick as he tells Paco to go back into Lorimer, that he has addresses belonging to doctors they can check out. He doesn't think they should kill me until they have fixed Paco up in case they need information.

Paco grows visibly uncomfortable over the next few minutes but refuses to allow either man to take over driving. He shifts between sweating and shivering, the vents and dials on the dashboard struggling to keep up with the constant temperature changes. His breath is loud as he works through the pain shaping his face.

When we swerve—not enough to scream danger to anyone else but me—I brace myself against the cold seat and hold my breath.

Paco's eyes flutter, his body wavering as his bloody hands slip off the wheel to fall by his side. His chest crashes into the wheel. The car speeds up, his dead weight heavy on the gas. Blood pounds in my ears and my breath strangles me while I watch the passenger reach for the wheel. He tries to turn it to straighten us, only for Paco's body to slide sideways and yank the wheel to the right and out of his hand. I cover my head and close my eyes as the grassy ditch appears outside the windshield.

The night's silence fills with the echo of groaning and crunching metal. Glass shatters while a gun fires. My mind spins as we roll, unable to tell if I'm up or down. The smell of dirt and grass mixes with sharp grain-sized shards of glass in my nose.

When we finally stop, it takes a minute for my balance to catch on. The sound of Danny groaning behind me in the trunk makes me pull my arms away from my head. My sight escapes me as I look around. When my brain recalibrates, it's to an upside-down image of shattered windows and twisted metal in the dim light provided by the dashboard glow and headlights.

Paco is missing from the front seat, and a quick visual sweep of the SUV suggests he was thrown through the windshield. The gangster that was sitting in the passenger seat moments before lies on the ceiling of the car, a bent and broken arm a few feet from me. Gurgling accompanies his breathing, the side of his bald head caved in and bloody.

Danny stirs behind me, another groan finding its way past the ringing in my ears. My heart is frantic as I lean forward, zip-tied hands moving to unbuckle my seat belt. I grunt when I land on my shoulders in a pile of glass. Twisting onto my side, I wiggle toward the broken window, the frame so bent there's only a small space for me to shimmy through.

My hands are useless, so I pull myself forward with my elbows. I suck in air as glass pokes through my jeans and sweater, a raw edge of metal digging into my stomach, another tearing the neck of my shirt. A hand circles my ankle when my upper body finds grass. I clench my teeth and turn onto my back, the feel of metal against my spine as I kick away Danny's hands.

He hollers in Spanish while he scrambles for his gun, his hands rooting through the glass. I waver as I roll onto my feet, the sound of his pistol cocking forcing my feet forward.

Paco lies in the grass to my left, unconscious and somewhere between life and death. My dizziness feels like resistance around me when I bolt toward the trees, hoping I can get far enough away before he wakes up or before Danny can catch me. My head aches and my feet slide in the grass. I feel like I'm racing across a rocking boat.

I gasp when Danny fires a shot off, the bullet disappearing into the grass a few feet to my right. Glancing over my shoulder, I see he's hunched over Paco, gun aimed in my direction as he tries to rouse him.

"Marianna!" he bellows while leaping up, another shot firing.

My legs move faster and refuse to slow even as I break through the trees. Leaves and branches whip me as I run with my hands in front of my chest. The forest's canopy wards off moonlight, offering me both protection and danger the deeper I get.

Danny calls my name as I hear branches snap in his wake. Thankfully, the forest is too dark for him to see me. I stumble over roots and fallen branches, stifling my breath like crashing through greenery isn't loud enough to give me away. I veer off on a right angle, trying not to think about how hard it will be to find my way back in the morning if I survive the night.

How long will I have to run before Danny gives up? How long until Paco wakes up and sniffs me out?

I push forward despite my worries, my throat dry and

aching, my legs threatening to give out. I don't know where I plan on going, and I know I'll get lost in the forest the deeper into it I run. Though, I'd rather get lost than shot. Eventually, the sound of Danny chasing me fades, and I wonder if he gave up, or if we are merely both lost now.

I hunch over against a tree at the edge of a small clearing lit by moonlight. Pine and earth fill my nose as I try to catch my breath. My hand sticks to the bark and I grimace and shake away something that crawls over my skin. My adrenaline drains and I exhale a dry breath through my raw throat. Should I keep walking, or should I hunker down here and wait for sunrise?

My body doesn't give me a choice. Dizziness overcomes me now that I'm still, and it feels like up is down as I grip the tree. That familiar nausea that comes with passing out greets me, and I have the thought that maybe my adrenaline is covering up a grievous injury I'm about to succumb to.

XXXI

A hundred thoughts pass through a painful moment. I might not have to worry about Denendrius remembering, about whether I'll be able to go back to a normal life once he's out of mine, or if I should accept my new place in the world of vampires. I won't have to worry about anything if I'm dying.

The world twirls faster, and me sideways, until it feels like I'm spinning off my feet into dirt and twigs. I lie gasping for breath while my head pounds. The stars that enter my vision a fabrication of my mind as it fights for me. They twirl and smear into the blackness of the sky.

There's a yellow flicker in the twisting darkness, then another, and a dozen more until the night retreats.

The trees have vanished, though the cold clings tighter.

A cold and damp stone room snaps into place around me, my eyes focusing on a four-poster bed made from human bone, black chiffon and velvet draped down around it.

My heart pounds when lanky fingers and pointed nails part

the drapery, and a black-clothed mass slips through it and stands to face me.

I feel compelled to step back at the sight of him, his long black gown disguising him with the shadows that the candlelight doesn't reach. His pale skin is practically translucent, the candlelight highlighting his blue veins and the wine red of his lids and under eyes. I can't tell how old he would have been when he died, even though I suspect it was somewhere between twenty-five and forty. With his strong features, he's attractive despite how monstrous vampirism makes him look. His long and thick brown hair hangs and makes his cheekbones and nose appear sharper than they already are.

"How *curious* that you should appear in my dreams." I can feel the power of his voice in my core as it bounces off the stone walls. His accent is strange, like he's doing his best to match the language he speaks. "Who are you?"

My heart pounds so hard I'm surprised I haven't passed back out. "M-Marianna—" The dark twinkle sparkling in his crimson eyes takes the rest of my breath from me.

"So, you're Denendrius's newest fix . . ." He tilts his head to study me, a fanged grin stretching his lips as his eyes travel up from my chest, my shirt torn right above my bra to expose the crude scar of his name. "*Of course* your name is Marianna."

I gulp and glance around the room I can only suspect is in a castle. "Are—are you *Viorel*?"

There's a flicker of a smile on his ghostly-red lips. "Yes."

"Where am I?" I demand, but the shake in my voice makes my words sound like a plea. "How did I get here?"

How long was I out? Did Viorel's men find me in the forest?

His garnet eyes narrow, his brown brows twitching closer. "You're in my chamber . . . Though you're not *really* here. Very curious."

Still unconscious.

I look behind me for the winding highway or the stretch of

forest I collapsed in, but there's nothing dreamlike to this dream—to the gray stone wall a mere foot from my back.

Dream or not, where do I run? Every fiber in my body screams at me not to trust Viorel, though my rational mind can't come up with reasons that don't lead back to whatever fears Denendrius had when he was a vampire.

I feel an inch tall before Viorel, internally shaken and more terrified staring into his eyes than I ever have standing before Denendrius. Could he squash me with a scowl? I rest my sweaty palm on my chest, like I might have to stop my heart from leaping out.

I think it might when he gnashes his teeth and bares them —fangs and all—at me as he drops his burning gaze to where my hand rests.

Arm too heavy with dread to keep up, my heart is left unprotected as my hand drops back to my side. When his eyes follow my hand, I realize his fixation is on my gold ouroboros bracelet.

The candle flames stretch taller, the room brighter as Viorel erupts. "*Where is he?*" he roars. The air feels like it's on fire as it passes in and out of my lungs. "*Where is Denendrius?*"

My tongue sticks to the roof of my mouth, my eyes wide and unblinking. Sweat and blood makes my clothes stick to me.

The space between us feels halved, though neither of us has moved.

"*Tell me!*" he bellows, his voice so powerful I can't help but imagine the stone of the walls loosening and coming down on me.

I stumble back into the wall, the icy bite of the stone vivid against my skin. I shake my head as I picture Denendrius being hauled away down the highway.

He inhales a sharp breath of surprise and his eyes snap shut, the candle flames falling to the tops of their wicks. When he opens his eyes, the fury in his gaze is snuffed to a smolder.

"I apologize, Marianna. My anger is not meant for you." He exhales heavily. "Please forgive me. I truly mean you no harm."

I can barely make my tongue move. "I-I forgive you."

His eyes turn pleading, though they're filled with caution. "Tell me where you are, if you are able. Where has Denendrius hidden you away from the world?"

"You're . . . you're not already looking?" I choke out. Was I right to think Rayonne was being overly optimistic? Should he not know that we are in Lorimer at least?

"I have yet to cease searching for him," is all he says, pain in his eyes. "I never will. Pray tell, Marianna. Where in this wretched world is he? Save us both grief."

"I—" The thought of Denendrius on his knees before Viorel enters my mind, human and shaking and not understanding why and what's happening to him. "I'm—" My breath strangles me.

When he takes a step closer to me, hand reaching out, I shiver like I'm trapped in the rain and squeeze myself tighter to the stone wall, like I can fall through it and back into the woods.

"You cannot physically tell me, can you?" he shakes his head in pity. "Once I possess you, I'll *free you*." He winks at me, his fanged grin returning with a silent burst of laughter.

He'll mark me?

My mouth opens to retort, but I don't have the breath required for words.

"*Marianna!*" a familiar voice echoes through the room, though there's nobody else here when I look around.

Ziggy?

"You can trust me, Marianna," he says with a wintry smile. Everything from his fangs to the way he seems to float over the cold floor screams otherwise. "I know I may appear quite terrifying. But you *must* remember, *I am not your villain.*"

"I—" I sink to the hard floor and wrap my arms around myself as my vision blots.

"*Marianna! Wake up! Oh, fuck! Wake up!*" Ziggy's voice sounds as real as Viorel's. "*You better not die on me too!*"

Viorel's eyes trail down my arm again before locking back with my wide eyes. "Wake up, my dear Marianna."

My eyes snap open, a heavy calm enveloping me from where I rest in Ziggy's arms, my cheek pressed against his quiet chest. His band T-shirt is soaked and reeks of blood.

Past his head, the moon stares down at me with its round face, the clouds like cotton over the stars.

Pain ricochets through me when I turn my head to see his face.

"I've got you," he murmurs. "You're all right."

His face is blood-splattered, a disturbed look in his red eyes as he carries me to a lime-green sports car that idles on the side of the empty highway.

When Carol's pained cry emanates from an open window, the questions spinning through my mind leave me disoriented.

"She's okay, I promise," Ziggy says, though he begins to hasten.

The passenger door opens, the interior light illuminating Denendrius in the passenger seat and Rayonne on the other side of him behind the wheel.

Denendrius pulls in a deep breath as he holds his arms out to me.

Ziggy hesitates in front of Denendrius when we reach the car, his fingers tightening on me, his chest stiff with a held breath. His huff is faint before he sets me on Denendrius's lap.

"I love you," Denendrius breathes while embracing me, his blood-smeared arms so tight around me I can't pull in a breath of my own.

I think of Viorel's fury when I say, "I love you too."

When the passenger door slams, I jerk out of Denendrius's

grip, my eyes landing on Carol and Derek in the back seat. It's too much of a sight to take in at once. There's so much blood I almost avert my eyes, not sure I can handle deciphering it all.

Carol sits upright in the seat behind Rayonne, her bloody and bruised face against the window. Her leg is at a strange angle in her red-soaked green leggings.

Though I can see the relief in her eyes at the sight of me, the tears that run from them and past her slack jaw tell me I won't be hearing her voice express that sentiment for a while.

Derek lies on his side, limp legs draped over Carol's lap, his head against what little beige leather is visible beneath him and the gore. There's hardly any life left in his half-lidded eyes. I'm not even sure he can see me right in front of him. Blood trails from his ears and mouth, his cheekbone collapsed, jaw closed at an unnatural angle. There are four long slashes through his brown sweater, like Agatha took a swipe at his chest. From the blood that bubbles up in the fabric with each of his breaths, it looks like she would have been quite close when she did it.

"What happened?" My voice is an octave too high.

Nobody answers.

"Go on, Rayonne," Ziggy says as he climbs into the back seat, maneuvering his lap under Derek's limp head.

She cranks the car into drive and winces as she steps on the gas.

"You're going to die, my friend," Ziggy tells Derek as he looks him over, placing a bare hand on the side of his face as the tires turn beneath us. "Do you want to stop it?"

Blood drips from the corner of Derek's mouth, and a tear runs into the bridge of his nose.

"Do you want to be a vampire?" Ziggy asks softly. "I can turn you right now."

The only sound Derek makes is a low gurgle, his breath coming out of him like a sick wheeze.

Ziggy scoops one of Derek's hands up and laces their fingers together. "Squeeze my hand, and I'll make the pain stop."

I hold my breath, unblinking as I stare at their hands.

There's a twitch in Derek's fingers . . . then, like he's using the very last of his strength, he exhales and squeezes Ziggy's hand.

"Okay," Ziggy whispers. He unlinks their hands and runs his fingers tenderly down the side of Derek's face. "Everything will be okay now."

Ziggy closes his eyes and takes a few purposeful breaths. Without opening them, he leans his head back and inhales sharply. His crimson-coated fangs extend, and I can't help but hold my breath when he throws his head down and buries them into Derek's throat.

This is my fault. It's the only thought that darts through my head. *I couldn't leave Derek alone.*

The pain forces Derek's eyes wide, a low whimper slipping past his lips. Ziggy rips his fangs out of his throat, gasping for breath as he leans his head back against the headrest and whines about there being so much blood. He pats Derek's shoulder and licks his lips clean.

When Derek's eyes close, I cross my legs over Denendrius's lap and face him. He wraps his arms around me. After rubbing my raw wrists—Ziggy must have relieved me of the zip ties—I rest my hand on Denendrius's chest, the feel of his heart calming me.

"What happened?" Denendrius asks.

Rayonne glances at me, wet curls cascading over her shoulder as she too waits for my answer.

I straighten. "Paco turned behind the wheel and we crashed. Danny chased me into the woods and I . . ." I bite my tongue at the thought of Viorel, a flicker of anger in my chest at Rayonne for being so convinced that they'd find us "any day now" when in reality, Viorel didn't seem to know where we are at all. Understanding—maybe a little pity—comes like a hard blow, and my anger is no more. Was she telling all of us what she hoped was true? Has she been desperately hopeful to the point of delusion?

"I killed him," Ziggy says from the back seat, eyes closed again as he runs his hand through the long part of his hair. "He was searching the woods for you. Ripped out the heart of his turning friend."

I relax into Denendrius's arms. "Thanks."

"Are you hurt?" Denendrius asks, lifting a hand and gingerly touching my forehead. There's blood on the pads of his fingers when he pulls them away.

"I think I'm okay," I assure him.

He wraps his hand around the side of my head and pulls my lips against his for a long kiss. Viorel's red eyes burn in my mind, and the taste of blood on his breath has me thinking of Viorel forcing his down my throat.

I try to convince myself it was a vivid dream from hitting my head. Yet it feels like a memory.

The taste of blood on Denendrius's tongue makes my stomach pinch, and I pull away from him and wipe my mouth.

"Sorry." He pulls the corner of his mouth with his finger to show me the gash inside his cheek.

"Ouch." My attention turns back to Ziggy with his depressed sigh.

Ziggy's hand twitches as he pulls a smartphone from the interior pocket of his patch-covered black jean vest. He gulps as he dials and holds it to his ear. "Hi, love . . ." The tears in his black-rimmed eyes are instant. "No, love, just me. I suppose you fighting and dying was what kept everyone else alive in that vision. Rayonne and all her friends are . . . mostly okay." He blinks hard, tears released through his makeup as he nods. "Yes, Lance, but I'm still glad you stayed behind. I'll be home soon. I've got some things to finish up . . . I love you too."

I swallow a lump and look between him and Rayonne as he hangs up. "Can someone tell me what happened now?"

Ziggy is too busy trying to hold back tears to respond.

Rayonne's voice is limp when she explains. "I'm marked by Ziggy, so he knew something was wrong and started calling me. I answered without Agatha noticing, and with what he overheard and the mark, Ziggy figured out where we were . . ." Her grip tightens on the wheel. "Ziggy brought six people from Estrella de Sangre to help. Agatha and that Darkling killed all of them. It was *brutal.*" She shudders and glances over her shoulder at Derek. "It was so fast I'm still trying to figure out exactly what happened. But that Darkling is dead. Agatha . . . I have no idea. Derek and Carol were too injured, I had to help them."

"Fuck." I have no other words.

"I need to go to the hospital," Carol cries from the back seat. Tears soak her bruised cheeks. "I'm hurt bad. I don't know how much longer I can stay awake. I'm probably going to go into shock."

"I've got nothing left in me to calm you, but do you want me to turn you too?" Ziggy's smirk is lopsided and weak. It looks like he already knows her answer.

Her lips tremble together, her breath uneven as she lifts a weak arm and brushes the wetness on her face away. "No, thank you."

Ziggy pats her forearm as if to say "there, there."

"Please take me to the hospital," Carol pleads.

Rayonne and I exchange an unsure glance. I can tell she wants to say yes as much as I do, but can we? Do we even know the risk if she's not sure what happened to Agatha? What kind of danger still lurks?

"I don't know how . . ." She would have no issue with the staff . . . but *us*? I wouldn't be surprised if Liz and my friends are already getting the police involved. Although, what will people think of Carol's absence from the human world? Have they been calling her, asking about me? Has she ignored them if they have, or is she pretending she hasn't heard from me yet?

A deep sob escapes her, the sound a hot knife in my heart. "Just leave me on some road, pretend it's a hit-and-run." She grits her teeth in pain. "I only need them to fix my leg and arm and pump me full of painkillers. I'll get out as soon as I can."

"It's not a bad idea," Ziggy says. "Unless she turns, there's not much we can do. I can't heal like Darklings can. The change happens too quickly."

"Okay," I agree with a deep swallow.

I wish Carol had listened to me and stayed out of this. The fact she cared enough about me to put herself in this sort of danger is hard to wrap my head around.

"How much longer until Lorimer?" Carol moans through gnashed teeth. Is she holding back her screams? Fighting to stay awake?

Rayonne says, "About an hour."

Carol covers her eyes with her forearm, her hand in a tight fist.

"I don't carry painkillers these days," Ziggy murmurs, hand resting back on her arm. "But I can give you blood. Though it won't heal you enough to make a real difference, it will help with the pain."

She sniffles while lowering her arm. "Won't that mark me, like Marianna?"

"Yes, but the one time won't do so much." He's fighting a little smile as he says, "Perhaps it'll make you want to be my friend, but I don't carry bad intentions, Carol."

She bites down on her bottom lip, blood bubbling out of the cut on the edge as she contemplates.

Ziggy holds his hand over his heart, covering a black-and-white patch of a skull with a dagger through the center of its forehead. "I'd never use it for bad. Rayonne and my familiars all have as free a mind as it allows—that's how I prefer them. Besides, it might not be the worst idea to be connected to a vampire if you're to go off to the hospital on your own. I'd feel it straight away if something horrible happened to you."

Is that why Ziggy marked Rayonne? So he could keep track of his newly human best friend?

Carol's teeth chatter as her eyes shift to mine. "What does it feel like?"

I shrug. "I never knew he marked me until I was told."

Carol blots her eyes with the sleeve of her peach sweater. "Okay," she squeaks. "If it'll help."

His eyes burn red again as he bites through the tanned flesh of his wrist. Reaching across himself, he holds the incisions to her mouth, and she covers them with her lips. She squeezes her green eyes closed as she drinks.

He leans his head back and closes his eyes as she drinks from him, two long minutes passing before he squints one at her.

It must be quite calming to be connected to Ziggy. The muscles in her eyes and face relax, and I can tell she's fast asleep before he pulls his wrist away to pat a tangled bit of orange curls by her temple as the wound vanishes. There's no sign of pain on her face. Her bloodied lips part slightly for even breaths.

"She'll be okay." He looks down at Derek, and my eyes follow.

I can't tell through the dim light and all his injuries if he's still awake or not, though he's unnaturally still. Has he merely been in so much pain that a new infusion of it hardly made much of a difference?

"I'm sure Derek will make it, but he shouldn't be around you all when he wakes," Ziggy says. "I'll take him to Estrella de Sangre, for the day at least, see what kind of state he's in. He's lost so much blood he might be more bloodthirsty, though knowing what's happening to him will have his mind in a better place."

"He was already asking a lot of questions about vampirism," I tell him. "But I don't know how serious he really was about turning."

"He was very serious," Denendrius chimes in.

Ziggy nods. "That's good. Perhaps this won't be so difficult on him like it is most."

"Hopefully," I whisper.

Maybe I won't feel so bad if he's content with this outcome.

XXXII

Ziggy stops in the middle of a dark street within walking distance from Carol's house. She grimaces as she shifts out from under Derek's limp body to open the door.

"Love you," I tell her.

Her smile is more of a pained flinch. "Love you too, honey. I'll be okay."

I can only hope.

I chew my cheek as she hisses in agony and maneuvers out of the back seat. She sits herself on the asphalt, dirt marking her pale skin as she lays herself down.

Ziggy gives her a little wave, his lips slanted in pity, before he shuts the door and tells Rayonne to drive.

We park down an alley another block away and turn the car off. Ziggy calls 911 and reports a hit-and-run. We hear the ambulance come and go ten minutes later.

All I can think as we head home is that maybe I should have thought of a better way to convince her to stay out of things. Maybe I shouldn't have gotten in the van to talk to her. Though

I've enjoyed spending what little time I have left with her, the demons of my life have now successfully bled into hers.

"Hopefully no vampires get to her at the hospital," I whisper as we pass a green light halfway home.

"She's marked now," Ziggy says. "Many won't be so inclined to touch her. Messing with another vampire's familiar or blood slave is a line most won't cross. Though I'm sure that wouldn't deter Agatha and her ilk." He rolls his eyes. "Besides, if I have to feel her die, I will rain hell upon her killer."

My lips purse, and I think back to what I overheard Rayonne tell Carol and Derek about the mark. "You can feel when they die? How?"

He nods. "It's difficult to explain. One of those things you must experience to understand fully, but the best way I can describe it is a soul string. Much of it is *simply knowing* intuitively as a vampire. It's a harrowing feeling to have that line severed by death, even worse with a strong bond. One of my familiars was killed in a head-on collision a few years ago. It's a helpless feeling, especially when there's nothing you can do. It was daylight, so I sat there in my bed, feeling her die."

I swallow, eyes shifting to Denendrius's. "Can you still feel that you marked me, even though it's not very strong?"

"No, it's *strong*," Ziggy interrupts. "Stronger than when we first met."

I scowl at him before connecting my eyes with Denendrius's as I wait for his answer.

Denendrius runs his hands down my arms and smiles. "Yes. I did not know what I felt at first. But I knew the whole time we were apart you were alive."

No wonder Denendrius could find me so many times so easily when he was a vampire. Now, it doesn't feel like such a bad thing. If I ever got kidnapped again, I know he'd locate me.

"You must not have had any marked humans attached to

you when you turned back, then?" I ask Rayonne, thinking she would have known the mark carries on if she had.

She shakes her head as she turns a sharp corner. "No. Aside from my son, I have never cared for the feeling. Unless you learn how to push it to the back of your consciousness, it's a very busy feeling."

Ziggy smiles. "See, that's what I love. I never feel alone even when I am. I love being tangled in all those strings."

I assume that's why Denendrius marked no one, then, never mind the risk it would have created with making a human a direct ticket back to him. If he hadn't marked me, would he have avoided being caught?

Fear burrows back into me once we arrive at the apartment, Ziggy dropping us off and whisking Derek away. I'm tense with each step up to our apartment, and Denendrius must be as well as he makes a point to stand in front of Rayonne and me.

They must have kicked the apartment door open earlier for no other reason than dramatics, as the door frame is unharmed while the brass deadbolt keyhole is horribly scratched. It's slightly ajar, and we must have insane luck that nobody robbed us over the handful of hours we were gone.

After a quick check through the apartment, there's no sign anyone else stepped inside.

Rayonne heads to the freezer and grabs a frozen bag of peas. After breaking it up, she molds it around her bruised and bloody face. Her pained but equally relieved sigh is muffled. She must have no energy to walk anymore, as she sprawls out on the kitchen floor on her back and moans.

Denendrius steps over her to get to his wine as I wipe dirt from my feet on the carpet in front of the door while locking it behind me. He drinks straight from the bottle, the dark liquid sloshing as he gulps half of it back. But wine and frozen peas will not be enough to rid the ache that surrounds me like a second skin. I step over Rayonne—almost slipping on her black curls—to pour myself a glass of whiskey.

After wiping his mouth with the back of his hand, he jerks his head toward the hall. "Bath?"

"Shower." I throw back my glass of whiskey and clear my throat, following him down the hall.

Rayonne is still lying on the floor once Denendrius and I have cleansed all the blood and dirt from ourselves.

"I miss vampire healing," she gripes, her voice cracking. She sniffles. "This is horrible."

"Well, you had your face bashed in." I step over her again to reach the alcohol, wishing I had some painkillers.

"Sleep?" Denendrius asks from the bedroom doorway as I pour myself another glass of whiskey.

"Go ahead. I won't be able to until I know Carol and Derek are okay." I take a sip, the first glass having already numbed some of my aches.

"Okay." He walks over to give me a kiss before retreating to the bedroom, shutting the door behind him.

I sit down against the cupboard next to Rayonne. "Going to lie there all night?"

"Probably."

"Want a pillow?" I almost stop myself from offering her one when I think about how Viorel has no idea where we are.

She merely grunts.

"I know I already asked, but what the hell happened? To Carol and Derek, at least . . ."

Pulling the peas away from her face, she touches a few bruised spots on her face. "Ziggy and his friends stopped the van. Well, Ziggy *leaped* onto the hood and smashed the windshield. That Darkling wanted *none of it*. Stopped the vehicle and got out, and they swooped in with the car. Everything descended into chaos after that. They brought weapons, thankfully. Most of it was a blur. Derek tried to take Agatha and lost.

A vampire fell on Carol, but she doesn't know who. Honestly, with that Darkling, most of it happened too quickly to see. They got his heart out of his chest though."

I take a long drink of my whiskey. "Jesus." My eyes flicker to the bedroom, and I lower my voice. "What does he know?" Did Agatha let the cat out of the bag?

She grunts and puts the peas back on her face. "Nothing. She was only taunting me and Denendrius until he broke out of his zip ties. After Denendrius gouged her eyes out, she was pretty quiet, occasionally talking German with that Darkling. But she mostly texted until Ziggy showed up."

"Good." I'm impressed he hasn't figured *something* out yet, though he likely will sooner or later if I keep pushing back on him and his wish for a new home.

I sip my whiskey, back aching from leaning against the wooden cabinet. By the time I'm done drinking the golden drink, my belly is warm, and my loose limbs and muscles are too numb to feel the full depth of the pain now.

Rayonne's limbs jerk on the floor, a surprised gasp coming from her as she sits and rubs her eyes after the makeshift ice pack falls away and onto the floor. I didn't realize she fell asleep.

"What's up?" My eyes narrow.

She groans. "A tremendous wave of pain ripped through me."

I point to the bottle of whiskey above my head. "It helps."

She brushes her fingers over her bloodied lip, her face scrunched as she inhales sharply while standing. "I need a cigarette first."

Still having no desire to smoke one, I call Carol while I wait for her to get back.

She doesn't answer, which has me worried until she calls right after I disconnect. There's a nervous shake in her voice. "Hello?"

"Oh, shit, I didn't give you this number. It's Marianna. Are you okay?"

Her exhale makes the line sound fuzzy. "*Oh.*" She chuckles. "Yes, I am. They've got me on some painkillers. I've got obnoxious casts for a handful of weeks too. But better than dead."

I pull myself up with help from the counter's edge. "That's good. Are they keeping you?"

"No, I'll be back when the sun comes up. How are you? Any update on . . . ?" She stops herself from saying his name, which is a smart move.

"Not yet. I'll ask Rayonne."

Her sniffle is loud. "Okay."

My lips twist and I lean against the counter, glancing at Rayonne, who stands—restlessly—near the cracked balcony door with a skinny smoke poised between her fingers. "How do you feel about his new . . . change?"

There's a long pause on the line, nothing but the noisy hospital in my ear. "If he's happy, I'm happy for him."

"You like him," I state.

It's like she's trying to hold back her words when she says, "He and I have sort of been talking since Denendrius threatened him. We were talking about you first, but . . . you know."

My eyes widen. "*Wow.*"

Her words leap through the phone. "Are you upset?"

"No, surprised. I like Derek. He'd be a good fathe—uncle." I grab the bottle of whiskey and pour enough to cover the bottom of the glass.

There's a smile in her voice. "I'm glad you approve. I'm going to get some rest, and I'll take a taxi back in the morning. Get some sleep too."

A hazy nightmare of Viorel tying me to a post of his bone-carved bed to force blood down my throat lurches me awake. A scream claws up my throat, but I snap my teeth together to stop it from escaping.

Denendrius sits up and wraps his arms around me. "Nightmare?"

"Yes," I squeak, too shaken even for tears.

"Me too," he whispers. "What did you dream of?"

I fist the blankets and stare into the dark, acutely aware of the sweat on my neck and down my back. "About being kidnapped by vampires," I say, skirting around the truth. "It really bugs me that someone wants to pay to torture me."

I'm so sick of people being paid to *have me*. A hundred nasty feelings charge through me at the mere thought.

He leans his forehead against the side of my head, burying his nose in my hair. "I will keep you safe."

It's sweet how he thinks he can.

"What did you dream of?" I whisper, unlatching my hand from the blanket to touch the side of his face.

"Sirmium," Denendrius whispers. "Always Sirmium. The torture."

I might actually barf.

Guilt erodes my gut.

Tell him.

Just tell him.

They almost took him tonight to be tortured endlessly, and I can't even let him know?

His nightmares could be real again, and I won't even warn him . . .

What a bitch.

I drop my hand from his face and lie down. He nestles down beside me and presses his hot mouth against my cheek in a soft kiss while I stare at the ceiling.

"I love you, Marianna," he whispers.

"I love you too."

How dare I say it back.

How can I complain about all the ways he treated me when he claimed to love me, when I am betraying him now? If there's one thing Denendrius didn't do when he was a vampire, it was allow other people to hurt me. Yet, here I am, crossing that line, *betraying him.*

I know everyone would say it's because he deserves it, but it's so hard to agree with them these days when his hands are so gentle with me.

How can someone who makes me feel this way deserve harm? Really, he's all I've got now.

I think about everything Derek and Carol said and I feel like I'm spiraling through reality, a different-colored lens over each of my eyes, the colors slowly smearing together to form something new. I know how I should feel, know what I should say and how I should act . . . but none of it makes sense to my heart. It's all a little confusing, but I guess that's how all parts of life are.

Things don't have to be perfect between Denendrius and me. That's a little impossible with people who are so imperfect anyway. How can two abnormal people be normal together?

But everything is rosy and warm with Denendrius. The darkness, the void of my life, is a little less scary with a red tinge to it.

And maybe this mark of ours isn't so bad. Denendrius can keep me safe better. It's not like he's using it for evil now. That, and it has miraculously cured me of my nicotine and drug addiction. It's hard not to be grateful for that when it's possessed me my whole life. I haven't even thought about having a cigarette or shooting up in days. Even thinking about it now, *I feel nothing toward it.*

Why are blood marks only bad when they're in regard to me?

I doubt anyone will question every idea Carol and Rayonne have now with Ziggy's mark on them. If Carol decides she wants to spend more time with him, I bet nobody will think anything of it. And what if Derek overwrites Ziggy's mark with his own? What if Carol and Derek fall in love, get married and spend forever together? Will everyone think it's all because of the mark?

Everyone has always expected me to act like an adult growing up. Maybe they shouldn't complain now that I am. So what if I want to stay with him where it's comfortable and familiar?

Perhaps Rayonne is right. If the time comes, I won't allow them to tear Denendrius brutally away from me. It's time to stop letting grown-ups, *vampires*, and everyone else decide my life.

If I don't want Denendrius to go, he doesn't fucking go. He's mine, not some ticket for them to cash in. If I don't want another vampire to mark me, do they really think they can force me?

And it's not because of the mark, it's because it's what's right. For once, I want to do the right thing. And the right thing isn't letting Denendrius suffer. Besides, the man everyone is after is already dead.

I snuggle close to Denendrius, his sleepy breathing tickling the side of my face.

Maybe we do need a new place without so many ghosts. I bet he would really thrive out of this chaos.

XXXIII

With Denendrius and Rayonne still sleeping, I creep into the dining area after another nightmare of Viorel. Quietly, I sit down at the table and flip to a fresh page in one of Derek's notebooks, plucking one of the many pencils from his messy pile of writing instruments.

Setting pencil to paper, I use the fresh glow of sunlight to draw the image of Viorel out of my head. He's still vivid in my mind, his death-white skin and crimson eyes that could probably suck the life from someone. I can still feel the bite of his fangs from my dream, how they tore through my skin like butter, how the venom on them burned.

A shiver rolls through me when I'm done drawing, Viorel staring up at me from the page. It's difficult to question the validity of my experience meeting him when his face is so far from something I could manifest on my own.

A light knock on the door has Rayonne stirring a handful of feet away, and me fumbling with the notebook as I hide it beneath one of Derek's Latin books a moment before Rayonne pops her head off her pillow.

I already suspect it's Carol before she identifies herself from the other side. After rushing to the door, I yank it open and find her standing with a crutch.

"Morning." She smiles, a medicated glaze over her eyes.

"Feeling better?" I smirk as I step out of her way.

She hobbles in, her leg in a white cast from her foot to thigh, a matching one on the opposite arm. "Better. Not keen on the fact that I'm trapped in this for weeks. How are you feeling?"

I shrug, a hot ache radiating through my neck and pounding in my head. "Feeling better than Rayonne looks, at least."

Rayonne sits and rubs her bloodshot eyes, flinching with each loud breath. "You're full of Denendrius's blood still, Marianna," Rayonne grumbles. "Of course you feel better than me."

I roll my eyes, focusing on the fact she's hurting more than me to keep an ember of anger from igniting inside me.

Rayonne throws her blanket aside and climbs off the blow-up mattress. "Hey, Carol."

I close the door behind Carol as she asks, "Have you heard anything about Derek yet?"

"Yeah. I got a text right before sunrise." She roots through the folds of the blanket for her cell phone and flips it open when she finds it, rubbing her black eye before reading, "Derek woke up. Aside from newborn woes, he's ecstatic. He's going to have to stay with Ziggy's clan for a bit." Rayonne looks up at Carol. "We could probably go visit him in a few days, if you'd like. We'll have to keep our distance though."

Carol pulls in a shaky breath and tucks her hair—clean now—behind her ear. "Yeah. That'd be nice."

I'm glad Derek is happy.

I leave them to talk and go to the bathroom. When I return with brushed hair and teeth, Rayonne is cooking breakfast and Carol is sprawled out on Derek's bed, half asleep and nose occasionally sniffling at the smell of bacon that fills the apartment.

Rayonne knocks an empty bottle of wine off the counter when she tries to move another aside, the green glass breaking and spreading in chunks across the floor. Denendrius scrambles out of the bedroom, complaining at us in Latin when his eyes land on the mess.

I clean up the glass for Rayonne so she doesn't have to stop cooking, while Denendrius loiters for a few minutes in a huff before he disappears into the bathroom.

Once breakfast is ready, Denendrius and I plate up and sit shoulder to shoulder on the couch like we're magnetized.

"I don't think Rayonne has your best interest in mind," Denendrius whispers, nudging me. When I look away from the boxing ring on TV, he juts his jaw toward where Rayonne and Carol sit on Derek's mattress. Carol picks at her food as she leans against the wall, Rayonne's back to us.

It is a little odd that they're way over there talking together, especially since I know they all talk behind my back.

I hadn't given our quick friendship—or alliance—much thought before. We got along, but was she pretending to like me?

My eyes flicker back down to my plate when Rayonne gets up and helps Carol stand before going back to the kitchen. "Why do you think that?"

"I think she has a plan," Denendrius whispers, turning up the TV. "It seems we are waiting for something. How did you become friends with her? You don't seem close for girls . . ."

"Agatha turned you back, Denendrius. She turned her back too, so she helped us because Agatha betrayed her."

His face scrunches, clearly not understanding. "She's using you. I think she wants to trade me in. It would be smart to go to a new house if we are being hunted."

"You're not wrong about a new house," I say under my breath.

"I think she is using you to control me until somebody comes."

I swallow. I suppose it was only a matter of time.

"I don't know," I argue, not having the faculties to deal with a blowout right now. "I think she's staying around here because of Ziggy. If we go somewhere else, we have nobody to help us. Vampires are going to find us no matter where we go."

"Maybe, but she was a vampire," he counters. "She still drinks human blood. Do you believe she has any regard for human life, or your life? She's had decades to become a talented actress. She's planning something. I think she's going to hurt you."

My mind wanders to Viorel, how he wants to mark me, and how insistent Rayonne is that I can have a place in the castle. What if she knows more than she's told me? What if Denendrius is right? Is it possible she's had contact with Viorel's men the whole time but has been stringing me along for some unknown reason, or waiting for them to get here?

Rayonne spent years playing for Agatha's team, accepting abuse from her for the sake of revenge. She admitted her entire purpose for living has been to kill Denendrius . . .

It's too much to swallow at once. My head aches enough. "There might be a tiny truth in that. But even if she was only using me at first, I think things are genuine—"

"No." His hot breath beats against the back of my ear when he whispers, "She is pretending to be your friend."

I pick at the edge of my plate while I try to think of ways to argue with him. I come up empty. My lip trembles as Rayonne answers a call in the kitchen. Could she be talking to someone right now?

He wraps his arm around my shoulders. "It hurts me to say, but I don't think she would even speak to someone like you if there wasn't so much in this for her. There's probably another reason why she didn't want to bring you back to Estrella de Sangre. Ziggy likes you . . . but I think that was the problem. He invited you to his clan. She must not have liked that."

Tears well in my eyes.

"Oh, no . . ." Denendrius holds me tighter. "I did not mean to make you cry. I believe you deserve the truth. Nobody else is offering it to you. They're all in this for selfish reasons. Apart from Carol and me. She truly loves you. Derek was only interested in helping you once he found out about vampires."

I wipe my tears. Derek didn't even take me seriously enough to help me until he got a phone call that added validity to what I was saying. Even he's been clinging to the idea of going to Romania.

"When you and I make a new life together, you will find so many friends who see how wonderful you are. You will make friends who won't dismiss your thoughts for the mark, only because they don't like them." He kisses the top of my head. "If Rayonne were your real friend—if she really cared about you—she wouldn't think you've lost all ability to think for yourself. She wouldn't be trying to turn you against your own mind, make you question if you can even trust yourself."

"I know," I whisper. My mind is quiet, my heart heavy. There are no rebuttals bouncing around my head. Deep down, I know it's the truth. To steer the conversation away, I say, "Your English is getting much better."

"Yes," he agrees. "It feels strange. Involuntary."

Rayonne tucks her phone into the back pocket of her rivet-covered black shorts. "That was Ziggy. He had to brag about how well Derek is doing because of him." She playfully rolls her eyes. "Want to come to the convenience store with me? We're running out of drinks. Carol wants ginger ale and I want to grab painkillers. I'm too sore to carry it all myself." Her eyes shift to Denendrius. "Can you keep an eye on Carol?"

I swallow a lump and look up at Denendrius. He smiles and nudges me. "Go on. You need some fresh air and sunlight. It'll only be a few minutes. I'll take good care of her."

At least I know Denendrius liked Carol even when he was a vampire.

I stand, heat building up in my stomach as I follow her to the front door, slip my shoes on, and shut the door behind us. My jaw locks, teeth tight, as we stroll through the parking lot and down the street.

"How's Denendrius doing?" she asks.

How casual of her. Is an interrogation the real reason she wanted me to go with her? "He's fine. Getting annoyed with all the vampires, as expected."

She sighs. "Yeah, I bet."

I can't feel the sunlight as it beats down on us, the heat of my blood alone making me sweat as I dig through Denendrius's planted words, more ideas springing up from them like they're seeds. They root themselves so deep inside me that my muscles contract and I walk stiffly with my hands curling into fists.

"I will admit, I'm going to miss the sunlight." Rayonne tilts her head back, pale face up to the sun. "I suppose it's not a terrible trade. Beautiful castle and comfortable living for the rest of eternity, versus a burning star that gives me sunburn. It sure is pretty though."

I grind my teeth together, barely getting them apart to say, "Yeah, sure, Viorel's men are coming to take us to the castle."

Her brows lift, but she quickly fixes her expression. "I don't know what to tell you, Marianna, but they're coming. It's only been a week. Word has to get to them, then they have to get on a plane and come here, then find us. I don't know how else to explain this."

"So how long?" My fists tighten, fingernails biting into my palms.

With her shrug, she may as well tell me she doesn't give a shit. "A few days. A couple weeks tops. We've already had a handful of vampires hear through the grapevine and come after us, so there's no way word is going to skip them. And you bet your ass they'll track us down as quickly as they can once they hear. They won't want to risk anyone else getting to Denendrius before them."

Bullshit. All I hear is bullshit.

I plant my feet and spin to face her, arms locked at my sides. "You want to know what I fucking think, Rayonne?"

She stares at me with wide eyes, red creeping up beneath the pale skin of her face.

"I think you don't know shit about anything. I think you're enjoying this game of keepaway with Agatha. You want revenge all right, but on her. You have absolutely no fucking idea what's going on with Viorel, and you don't give a shit about me and my life, about whether or not I can even make it to the castle. All you care about is you! If Viorel never comes, you can brush your hands clean of Denendrius whenever you want, because you already did your part."

Her jaw hangs, tongue limp.

"Am I fucking wrong?" I holler, my voice echoing through the empty street as I shake.

She closes her mouth and swallows. "Yes, you are! I know this situation isn't ideal, and I'm sorry I got us into it in the first place, but she would have killed you if it weren't for me and my rash thinking! We both would be dead."

Red pulses at the fringes of my vision. "Who fucking cares!"

I snarl. "Who cares if she would have killed me! It's not like I have anything going for me right now! I'm rotting away in that goddamn apartment, waiting for them to pick up on a rumor and come get him! I don't even know what's waiting for me after that! You can't say with certainty if I can come, and I can't exactly go off on my own when I'm going to have people trying to kill me! At least if she killed me, that would be that! Now who knows what will happen!"

"I know this is hard, Marianna." When pity shapes her face, it takes everything in me to stop from bitch slapping her. "I'm sorry. But I promise things will work out. It's really difficult being a slave to outside forces, simply hoping and waiting for things to go our way, but I'm not being naive."

My eyes burn. I pull in a deep breath through my nose and try to hold the tears back. "Viorel doesn't know." My voice cracks, and I lower it when someone across the street glances curiously at us. "He doesn't know where we are."

White surrounds her eyes. "*What?* How would you know that?"

"I met him . . . somehow. When I passed out after Paco crashed, I was in his room. It felt as real as everything else, and he seemed surprised to see me too." I twist my fingers in front of myself and shift my weight on my sore feet, the hard sidewalk only making the pain worse.

She mouths her disbelief. "I believe you, he's . . . I don't know how that's possible. But just because *he* doesn't know where we are doesn't mean his men don't. There are numerous people working for Viorel for various reasons. I doubt they're feeding him constant updates. I bet they'll find us, *then* update him."

"He wants to mark me." I shake my head, like I can stop her nonsense from getting inside it.

Her expression brightens, and she grins. "He said that? Oh my God, Marianna, you have no idea how lucky you are! So many people dream of meeting him, and he wants to *mark* you?" There's a flicker of envy in her eyes and the corner of her lip twitches. "You should be so thankful. Clearly you're getting more than an invitation."

"In what world is that lucky? He's fucking terrifying, Rayonne! He has a bed made of human bones! I don't want to be made into a fucking bedside table when he's done with me!" As Denendrius's, there's no way any good can come from Viorel wanting me. He probably wants to hurt me, like whatever vampire wants to pay a million bucks for me.

"Did he say anything about me? About Agatha?" She runs her fingers through her black curls and squints when a cloud shifts away from the sun.

I cross my arms. "No. I only talked to him for a minute before Ziggy woke me up."

She sighs, shoulders lowering. "All right." With a small smile, she says, "I know it's scary. But you can't imagine what this means for you. Viorel is *not* an evil man. You'll see once that mark is gone."

There she goes again, discounting my fears because I'm marked. Denendrius is right. Only now that I've told her about Viorel, she'll probably act like my bestie if she thinks she can get close to him.

I don't have the energy to fight or talk in circles with her, so all I say is, "Let's get our shit."

The muscles in my weak arms are on fire as I reach the apartment door. As soon as I have it open, I spot Denendrius at the table, rooting through papers and books.

"Hey—!" I drop the bags, but Denendrius is already picking up the sketch and holding it in front of his face.

His eyes tighten as he mulls it over for a long moment before he slowly puts it aside and stares at me.

Would he know what Viorel looks like? Or does he only know him by name?

He pulls in a shaky breath and shifts his weight between his feet, but there's no sign he connects any dots. "How was the walk?"

"It was fine." I shove a bag to the fridge, Rayonne coming in and setting hers on the counter. "How's Carol?"

He motions to Derek's bed, where Carol is curled up under the blanket. "Sleeping." Scratching his cheek, he glances back down at the drawing, and his chest lifts with a deep breath. "Who is that vampire?"

I press my teeth into my tongue, Viorel's name burning on its tip. "From my dream last night." I can barely manage the lie of omission.

He rubs the back of his neck as he continues to stare down at it. "You draw well. I don't like it."

I force a chuckle as I open the fridge and pile drinks on the shelf. "Why not?" I fish.

"I don't know." He flips it over and looks back up. "We have no wine left."

I put a little jug of strawberry milk up on the counter for after. "Try literally any other drink, Denendrius."

"Why? It's the most healthy drink. And modern wine tastes so nice," Denendrius says.

"Have some milk." I put the last bottle of ginger ale on the shelf and stand back to close the fridge.

Rayonne chimes in with, "Milk is probably much healthier."

He scoffs and comes over to pick up my jug of milk, lip curling back. "You two know nothing of good drinks. What are you? Barbarians."

I roll my eyes and snatch my drink from his hand.

While opening her pack of painkillers, Rayonne says, "You have milk in half the things I cook you."

He purses his lips. "Ah, well. This is okay. I like your cooking."

Denendrius's teasing mood vanishes after wandering back to look at my drawing again, Rayonne staring with astonished eyes as she soaks it in from his side. She says nothing.

After that, he's lost in deep thought for the rest of the day. He hardly speaks, and many times he needs to be asked a question twice before answering. I find myself desperate to hear the sweet lilt of his voice, how his accent makes my belly feel warm, so I resort to asking him more questions than necessary.

"What have you been thinking about?" I inquire at the end of the night when he's brushing his teeth to retire to bed early.

"Some things." He takes a sip of water and spits it into the sink.

"Like?" I lean against the counter, screwing the cap back on the tube of toothpaste for him.

Denendrius gives me a phony smile and pulls me into a bear hug. "How much I love you."

"Ghosts?" I squeeze the word out, his grip around me suffocating.

He drops me, a disturbed look in his eye. "I simply feel sick today. Finish your movie with Carol and join me in bed?"

I think of prodding more, but I know better. "Okay."

Throughout the rest of our comedy—that none of us have cracked so much as a smile to—I only think of Viorel and the look on Denendrius's face when he saw that drawing. Even if he doesn't consciously know who it's a drawing of, something inside him must.

The truth builds up in me, and I know it's going to spill out as I walk to the bedroom and shut the door behind me. Like a shadow in the dark room, Denendrius sits in bed, a loud sniffle coming from him.

"Denendrius . . . Rayonne's waiting to give you to the man in that picture." The truth tumbles over my tongue as easily as a breath. "His name's Viorel and he wants to mark me."

The nagging in my head vanishes, that guilty steel vise around me loosening.

"Yes, Marianna. I remember." There are tears mixed in the honey of his soft voice.

XXXIV

"I'm sorry." I rush to the bed and leap onto it, wrapping my arms around one of his and resting my forehead on his shoulder. "I know I shouldn't have kept anything from you, but I was scared and confused. Promise, I was going to say something soon."

His voice shakes, but there's nothing but gratitude for me in it. "Thank you for telling me now."

"What do you remember?" A little ball of anxiety lodges itself in my throat.

I wince when he pulls me away from his arm and lifts my head. He places his clammy palms on my cheeks, gently forcing me to meet his teary eyes.

"I remember not being able to find you at school and fighting vampires to get to you, that they fed me blood and how Agatha planned to take me before Rayonne turned on her."

My lips tremble, and I can't help how my voice shakes. "What about the moment before you went unconscious?"

His lips twitch into a soft smile, a tear slipping past the

corner of his mouth. "When you tried to kill me? Yes, I do. But I'm no longer angry with you, Marianna."

"Why?" I ask, placing one of my trembling hands over his.

I know I should accept his answer without question and not give him a chance to reconsider, but I need to know.

His smile drops. "I see how much you love me now . . . how deeply. Being with you without centuries of fury tainting my gaze helps me understand how unfair I've been. Witnessing your terror of me and your anger without context made me speculate about what I had done wrong. To remember how it was much worse than those speculations . . ." He drops his hands from my face and hangs his head. "I can't explain what I felt when I escaped that . . . place. I was crazed from thirst and never felt better, no matter how many years turned over. I was endlessly frustrated and on edge."

I observe his sullen face, unsure what to make of his words, though I'm thankful to hear them.

His eyes lift, peering at me through his lashes. "But I believe the cure has cleansed me of all my immortal afflictions. I am free from the anger that destroyed us. I don't feel the same emotions that my memories once brought me. Beyond Sirmium, none of them feel like mine."

His words make my breath come easier. He's sorry, isn't he? He's different now. Looking him over, I can't find lies in his eyes like I could when he made up stories to tell me when he was a vampire.

I wipe the tears from his cheeks with the sleeve of my shirt and give him a soft kiss. "Because you're not him," I console, my lips brushing against his. "He's dead now."

Denendrius shoves his lips against mine and hooks his arms around me. He makes a relieved noise as he pulls away and rests his forehead against mine. "We have to leave now."

"It's dangerous," I say, yet staying puts us in no better a position.

"We don't know that for sure. We are being attacked by vampires here because Rayonne has told every vampire in the city how to find us." He shudders. "I cannot risk Viorel taking you either, and I will not let him torture me again."

My brows stitch together, and I pull away from him to put space between us and the heavy realization that crashes down on me. "Again? What do you mean, *again*?"

The gold ouroboros bracelet is like a weight on my wrist, and I think of how Viorel erupted at the sight of it, how I was wearing it when Denendrius had flashbacks of escaping. All the pieces click together, and horror passes through me.

Wetness beads on his bottom lashes. "Sirmium is the reason Viorel wants to capture me. He wants you because I took Tatiana." A tear streaks down his face, and his gaze shifts like he's not looking at me now but through me. "I . . . I can't speak of all the ways he had his men torture me. It will be worse this time."

"I thought vampires murdered that clan?" I desperately want him to be mistaken.

"They did," he says emotionlessly. "Vampires took advantage after my escape, but I always assumed he survived. And when I heard about Viorel some centuries later . . . it was easy to fit the pieces together."

My eyes sting. It was her bracelet, wasn't it? Was she wearing it when he drowned her? "I'm so sorry I didn't tell you sooner." I wipe the wetness from his cheek again.

I was so desperate to get rid of Denendrius at first that I almost doomed myself.

"You're lucky you did." Denendrius shudders. "Because you will not find a home in that place, Marianna. *You are my love.* Do you know the things Viorel will do to you? He will not consider your innocence. I know from my own pleading. He will hurt you to hurt me, and when he's done, I won't be surprised if he throws you in the auction ring for another man who hates me. If you are alive and suffering, he knows I will be too. That will be worse than any physical punishment he can inflict on me."

"Auc—auc—" I can't force the word out, a flood of tears instant down my face.

"I heard them when I was in Sirmium. They hold them to feed the clan. They round up humans and bid on which ones to take."

"Don't lie to me." I swiftly wipe tears from my eyes. "Do you know what I went through?"

He rests his hands back on my cheeks, eyes desperate on mine. "I'm not lying. I'm telling you because I *do*, and I don't want you to experience it again. You have to know how important it is that we don't get caught. I don't want a doubt in your mind about the danger we are in."

I bite down on my bottom lip to stop it from shaking.

He wipes his own tears before ridding mine. "If perchance they capture me, you must run. Do you understand? *Run.* And if they catch you, you must fight harder than you have ever fought before. You are better off dying than being alive if he takes you. You have no concept of what never-ending suffering means until you know Viorel."

I bite back a sob, trembles infecting every muscle in my body. "Okay," I whimper.

"If my only option to escape is death, I will take that road." His wide-eyed and serious gaze burns into my eyes. "And I suggest you do the same. I know it's nothing we want to think about. But you might not have the option later, especially if they mark you."

My heart pounds in my ears. If it weren't night, I would take his hand and flee with our go bags right now. Could I kill myself in a situation like that? If it was my only choice? Suicide seemed so easy when I wanted to die . . . but when I want nothing more than to live? Yet if it is death or extreme pain, I suppose it would be much easier to make the choice.

"But that won't happen," he whispers, pulling me into his arms. "Because we will run away in the morning. I know this is my fault, but I want us to *live* without the ghosts of this place. We will go far, and I will protect you. We will be so happy and make a good life. Do you want that with me? A fresh start?"

"Yes. Do you think we can?" I close my eyes and take a second to focus on keeping my breathing in check while I listen to the frantic beat of his heart. "Without them finding us?"

"We have no option but to try." He squeezes me tighter, like I'll be ripped away if he lets go. "They are looking for us in this city and it's taking them so long. If we go, they have to start over to find us. They have not captured me for centuries. Surely we can avoid them for the rest of our short lives."

I want to believe it. My mind races with hope again. I want to forget about the darkness of our past, distance myself from my memories so I don't deprive myself of a good future. I don't want anger to destroy me like it did Denendrius.

"A fresh start," I echo, and my heart feels weightless in my chest, like the space inside me that was once full of angry beasts has now emptied. "We can be happy now."

"I love you," he whispers, lips inching closer to mine again.

I trace my tongue over my bottom lip and I'm dizzy at the feel of his warm lips and wet tongue crushing desperately against mine. My terrified trembles turn into excited twitches.

I think of his money and diamonds—more than I could ever hope to see in multiple lifetimes—and our fake identities.

A whole new life . . .

A normal-*ish* one.

Could I really have it?

I'd be crazy not to try.

If I can forgive and forget, I can have it all. *Happiness.* If I can sacrifice my past self for a peaceful future, I can erase Marianna Cortez, erase the trauma and violence, abandon the poor grades and foster kid status. I could be Marianna Sovetta, a wealthy girl who lives in a nice house with nice things, who goes to a nice school in a new city. Denendrius could hire a tutor for me, and I can graduate and go to college if I'm smart enough. I can stay human and finally have as normal a life as possible for someone in my position.

A little sacrifice, a little forgiveness. *Let it all go.* Cut myself off from my past so it doesn't drag me down again.

He pulls away, his lips tickling mine when he whispers, "Everything will be perfect."

"Where should we go?" My wide eyes are captivated by his.

"Anywhere you want," he murmurs, lying down and pulling me to his side.

"Can I go to school?" I wonder, nuzzling my head under his jaw so I can rest my cheek near his heart.

He waves his hand in the air above our heads, like he's painting a picture in the slice of moonlight cast across the ceiling. "You'll go to the best school, with the best teachers. I bet you'll be popular like the girls on TV. You'll see how intelligent you are when you're not stressed to the bone."

An image explodes in my mind. I imagine myself dressed in designer clothes, a new backpack slung over my shoulder as I enter school. There's not a security guard in sight. None of the kids look at me and see a drug-addicted throwaway. I'm intimidating, but not because of gangs and violence—because I'm confident and happy and will graduate with grades so great that I might have a chance at an Ivy League school. I'll steal a spot on the sports team, be a teacher's favorite.

But there's one thing missing from that dream.

"Am I allowed to have friends?" I whisper.

He places a gentle kiss on my lips but sounds stumped. "Why not? Everyone will want to be your friend. You can have as many friends as you like. Think of the crowd you'll bring to celebrate our real wedding one day."

I take a risk with my next question. "C-can I ever call Carol?"

His finger traces lines down my arm. "Eventually. But you can never reveal where we are."

"Okay," I agree.

His deep breath lifts my head, and I grin when he purposefully drops my head with a blissful exhale.

"Rest," he commands with a smile. "It's our big day tomorrow."

I'm too excited to even try. Instead, my mind spins fantasies like sticky webs.

We wake up right before dawn, Denendrius creeping around the apartment to collect every weapon he can find while Rayonne and Carol sleep. While he does that, I make sure we've got our go bags packed properly, leaving only one extra outfit each so we have more space for other things. I'll be loading up on fancy clothes as soon as we're in the clear.

Denendrius leaves the bag of weapons beside the wall cutout to the hidden room—after taking a few stakes and some wooden bullets for ourselves—so they can still find it to protect themselves after we leave.

I'm giddy as we empty a few old suitcases and bags and load them up with as much cash and diamonds as we can, Denendrius packing a few sentimental items from Rome and the little fireproof safe holding the cure in case we need to use it to barter with angry vampires again. We discover a set of identification for me with an even older photo behind a stack of cash too. He must have decided not to use them when he changed his plans for us. Denendrius used the same names as the other fakes, but I'm under eighteen in all of them, likely so I could finish school.

Despite having enough money for us to live lavishly for multiple lifetimes, it still hurts when he locks the safe back up with so much wealth inside. When he takes four velvet sacks of diamonds—worth at least a few million—and carries them out separately from the rest of our stuff, I'm confused until he hides two in the bottom of Carol's bag and two in the bottom of Derek's.

I give him an approving smile. Denendrius never would have done that when he was a vampire, as much as he liked Carol.

While trying to push away as much exhaustion as I can, we load ourselves up with bags and take our first trip down, throwing them in the Mustang's back seat before racing back upstairs for the rest.

My heart skips when we return to the apartment to find Rayonne texting from where she stands beside the couch—a revolver in one hand—as Carol works her way out of bed.

"Where are you going, Denendrius?" Carol demands, a sharp sternness to her voice I've never heard before. It makes my breath catch.

Rayonne looks up from her phone and lifts the gun, barrel aimed at Denendrius.

My heart lodges itself between my collarbones. "Rayonne—"

"Put it down." Denendrius steps in front of me, but I peek around him.

Rayonne scoffs. "If she needs to be protected from anyone here, it's not me."

"You're putting her in danger merely by having it aimed toward her," Denendrius scolds.

"Don't go with him," Carol pleads, her wide eyes desperate on me as she stands with her crutch.

"I'll be okay—"

She shakes her head, curls flitting around her. "No. No, you won't be, Marianna. If you leave, nobody will ever see you again. He's as dangerous now as he was before."

Rayonne tucks her cell phone back in her shorts and holds her hand out to me. "Carol is right. Come here." When I shake my head at her, she says, "I'm going to shoot Denendrius, so you need to move."

"Nobody is getting shot." Denendrius releases a breath of disbelief. "Have you both gone mad?"

Does she actually intend on using it? Or is she counting on Denendrius thinking she might? She must know how bad things will go for her—that someone will probably call the cops—if she sets off a gun in the apartment and has to deal with his pained writhing and hollering.

"Then don't leave, and I won't have to put a bullet in one of your legs," Rayonne warns.

I reach out to Denendrius when he steps away from me, but my arm falls back to my side when he nears Rayonne. "Den..."

"It's okay, Marianna," he responds softly while taking careful steps toward Rayonne.

Her grip tightens on the gun. "I will shoot you if you—"

He lunges forward and grabs the barrel of the gun, Rayonne gasping but hanging on. Denendrius forces the barrel into his own chest, his eyes locking with hers in a challenge.

"Shoot me, then," Denendrius says. "If you're so terrified for Marianna, be a good friend and keep her safe. No more games. Shoot me dead right here so I can't take her."

"You know we can't kill you, don't you?" Rayonne snaps. "You know what that means for us."

Denendrius moves Rayonne's finger to the trigger. "If you truly believe I will harm her beyond that door, you need to kill me. If you *care* about her, in any way, you will kill me. So, either you know she's safe with me and care more about exchanging me for your own immortality, or you shoot me and take whatever wrath comes to you if it means she doesn't leave with me."

She swallows and looks at me. "You know I care about you, right?"

I look down at the carpet and nod. "I know. But you also really want to be a vampire again and be a part of Viorel's clan."

Her eyes plead with mine as I look back up. "Marianna—"

"Don't point a weapon at someone if you don't intend to use it." Denendrius rips the gun from Rayonne's grip and walks backward to my side. "I won't suffer torture for crimes I cannot remember committing. There is nothing either of you can do to stop me from leaving."

Rayonne winces and rubs her hand. "I'm not buying that you don't remember."

"I've explained myself plenty. Even the few memories that have returned to me don't feel like lived experiences. I was not myself."

"Enough!" Carol's hand shakes with fury. "Marianna is trying to grapple with the heinous things you did to her and the fact you couldn't remember, and you are purposely feeding into her unhealthy coping mechanism, while knowing full well that she's still marked. *Be a man*, Denendrius. You're the one playing games."

Denendrius's lip curls. "Don't insult her only because she's no longer doing what you want her to. She *trusts me*. She knows I'll never hurt her again, that I *am not* who she knew." He holds the gun out for me to take. "She trusts me like I trust her."

I swallow a lump and take the gun, putting it my waistband before whispering, "Denendrius, come on." I don't want to stand around hearing them talk about me like I'm not here.

Carol wobbles forward. "Marianna—"

"Go back to your life, Carol," I tell her. "I love you and hate to leave you, but you've got more options than me. You'll be fine with Ziggy and Derek to protect you now."

"Yes, you have options, Marianna," Rayonne says, the false hope in her voice thickened for me. "Viorel's people will be here soon, and they'll keep you safe. I promise."

I bite my lip, my eyes stinging. "I can't go to Viorel's castle."

Rayonne stumbles over her words before spitting out, "I told you, Marianna. It will be okay. He's not as scary as he seems. Once you're there, you'll see. I wouldn't lie to you, Marianna. You're my *friend*."

Denendrius picks the last of our bags up. "Viorel is the same man who first imprisoned me, Rayonne. You would be wise to run away from him yourself."

"You really don't *know* Viorel, Rayonne. Denendrius is the only one here who has actually met him in person," I add, leaning closer to him.

She gapes at me. "Even if it's true that Viorel is the same vampire from Sirmium, you're marked, Marianna. Of course you're going to see him through Denendrius's lens. He might be the only one who has ever met Viorel, but he's also the only one here who was *imprisoned* by him. He wouldn't have anything good to say about him."

"You'll find out," Denendrius snarls. "But I won't allow you to feign friendship to Marianna. You're selfish for lying to her about the castle. Convincing her she'll get to stay human and live there so she'll help you control me? Either you are ignorant to the reality of that place, or you are being deceitful."

I wrap my arm around Denendrius when Carol takes a step toward us. "I won't be sold off to some vampire. It's not worth it to stay human. And I don't want to be a vampire either. Even the best-case scenario—which sounds like a crock of shit, to be honest—is garbage. I know everyone there will hate me and you're going to ditch me. Nobody is going to want to be my friend when they all hate Denendrius. They'd hate me by association, and we both know that would rub off on you. Any which way you look at it, the castle will not be a fulfilling life for me. I'd rather take my chances out here with spiteful vampires if it means I have a chance to be happy."

Rayonne's face twists with frustration and she shares a look with Carol. "What has he been telling you, Marianna? That is not true. None of that makes any sense—"

"Enough!" Denendrius bellows. "You two are unforgivingly selfish! All everyone has done her whole life is take, and here you two are . . . *taking* her time for a chance at more time your-selves. You don't have a clue how to get in touch with them, yet you're stringing her along for some minuscule chance that benefits you two far more than it ever could her. She could create a new life for herself right now, but she's wasting her days for your dreams. How long will you allow this to go on? How long is she expected to hang on so you can exchange me for your reward?"

I swallow and find my voice. "I can't put my life on hold forever—"

Lifting her free hand, Carol slowly shifts toward us. "Honey, remember you're blood marked—"

Denendrius tenses. "Shut it, Carol. That excuse is becoming trite. Even she knows it. You're blood marked too, and Ziggy wants Marianna, so how can we trust anything you say?" He directs his next command to Rayonne. "Tell her about the auctions, Rayonne. Tell her there are no auctions at the castle you've never been to. Tell her I didn't hear the crying, and the bidding for the humans they brought in like cattle, couldn't have tasted the blood they'd bring for me after from the ones nobody cared to spend money on."

Rayonne swallows, her mouth opening and closing.

"Go on, tell her." Denendrius smiles. "Tell her another lie."

"You were never in Romania," Rayonne counters sharply.

"No. But why would he rule that place any different from the one he ruled in Sirmium, hm?"

Wetness wells in Rayonne's eyes when they meet mine. "He

is purposefully twisting things. This is psychological warfare."

I bury my face against Denendrius's arm. She doesn't even like me. She's only crying because I'm leaving with her revenge, with her chance to be a vampire again.

Rayonne's voice shakes. "Denendrius, I know you genuinely believe that Viorel is an evil man, and that you really think Marianna is at risk. But do you not realize that not everyone has the same experience with him you do? We have no reason to bring his wrath to us."

I feel Denendrius's muscles tighten under my forehead. "Can you guarantee her safety? Can you guarantee he won't hurt her to hurt me?"

"She'd be coming with me. And she's never hurt Viorel, so why would he have any reason to take his anger for you out on her if what you say about him is even true?"

"That's not a confident answer, Rayonne. It's not good enough for me, and I don't know why you think Marianna is better off gambling her life in some castle than anywhere else in the world." He pulls in a deep breath. "I'm the only one in this room who has met him, and believe it or not, I did not deserve the extent of his cruelty back then. Perhaps you will be home there, but I will kill everyone in this room before I allow her to experience even a fraction of the vile things he allowed to happen to me down there. You idolize a man much more heinous than how you've painted me."

I peek back at Rayonne and Carol, her eyes wide and desperate on Denendrius. I wait for her to argue, for her to present more concrete evidence that Romania really is my best bet, but her lips stay trembling together.

"Let's go, Marianna," Denendrius says sweetly.

I mouth an apology to Carol as we open the apartment door and back out. I expect at least Rayonne to rush after us, but she merely pulls out her phone again while Carol stares helplessly after us.

XXXV

"Let me drive," he says as we cut through the cool morning air and find our freedom at the car. The handles are still dewy to the touch. "I remember how."

My stomach is fuzzy with hope and excitement as he drops the rest of our bags in the back seat before we buckle in. The sky glows gold with the sunrise, not a cloud in sight.

It's so calm outside that it feels like the world is going out of its way to give me a good start.

"Let's drive around for a bit in case they follow. We need to stop somewhere and check for a tracker under the car too." I kick my feet up on the dashboard, a gleeful grin on my face.

"We will. But it's okay now." His voice is so calm—sweet— that it's easy to believe him. "*Relax.*"

I inhale sharply through my nose, my heart burning. "You think so?"

He gives my thigh a gentle rub and backs out. "Yes. They won't follow. What will they do in their condition? I don't think the risk is nearly as great as Rayonne led you to believe.

Why would they have better luck when they're bound to the night? We'll be living in the day. I'll vampire-proof our home, so that stops many vampires. At worst, I can call Sergei to take care of the problem. I don't want to involve him, but it's an option."

Leaning my head back against the headrest, I close my eyes for a minute. "Okay."

"What does this light mean?" he inquires.

My eyes pop open, and thankfully we're not on a main road. "That's a fucking crosswalk light, Denendrius! You should've stopped at the line back there. I thought you remembered how to drive!"

He stutters some nonsense while motioning to the car interior. "I know how to make the car work—"

"Pull the hell over, right now," I command as I stomp my feet onto the car mat. "Before we both get arrested, hit someone, or die in a wreck."

How ironic would that be?

"Okay." His sigh is dramatic, and he teasingly rolls his eyes at me as he slows and pulls to the curb.

We get out and switch seats. "Did you not pay attention to any of us while we were driving?" I ask while buckling myself behind the wheel.

"Not really. There is so much to look at. Everything is so different." He smirks. "I will pay better attention now."

I shift the car back into drive. "Okay. So, what about all your stuff? Are we leaving the rest of it? There are a lot of valuable things there." I tell myself to be thankful for what we got out, considering it's far more than I had growing up in poverty, but the idea of it sitting there for someone else to find makes me frown.

"What stuff?" he throws me a glance.

"All the stuff in the hidden room."

He releases a burdened grunt. "I don't want any of it. It's not really mine. I have my belongings from Rome and that's all I need."

Tapping my finger against the wheel, I think of the villa he bought in Italy before he turned back—how he planned to kidnap me and take me there—and ask a perilous question. "Would you ever want to move back to Rome?"

He winces. "I'm not sure I ever want to travel there, never mind have a home there. That would be no good for my mind."

Good, he doesn't remember the villa.

"Understandable." I smile inwardly, rub my eyes, and try to get comfortable behind the wheel, but the leather is too hard for my sore bones. I gaze blissfully out the window while I drive on the calm roads, my mind pacing through the different possibilities of my future. Growing old, dying early from a vampire attack. . .what will all my years look like? How will I feel?

"What are you thinking about?" Denendrius reaches over and places his hand on my thigh.

My smile is modest, yet I feel so much weight lift away. "I don't know. The future. I'm trying to get used to the idea of a mostly vampire-free life."

There's a fervid happiness in his voice. "What about it? I want to hear your musings."

"Do you still want kids?" I ask carefully while I turn a corner at random.

His leg bounces. "Yes, eventually. When you're older. You'll have plenty of time to make friends and graduate school."

I nibble my bottom lip. I'm not completely sure I want kids, but I suppose there's no need to decide now. It'll be at least three years before I finish school. "What do I do after high school? We won't exactly need to work to survive."

Denendrius chuckles. "Oh, Marianna, you don't have to plan it all right now."

"I know." I tap my thumb against the wheel. "What are you going to do with all your free time?"

"Hm. I enjoy the idea of boxing or MMA like on TV, but I'm not really sure how much more fighting my body can do. There is also the issue that I have a hard time stopping once I start to fight. Your modern refs won't like that."

"Well, did you have other hobbies that could compare to modern ones?"

"I'm not sure." Before I think of any follow-up questions, he asks, "Where do you want to go? You look exhausted. Do you want to rest at a hotel? We should make sure we're checked in someplace before night."

I glance at the clock. We have over twelve hours before sundown. "Let's drive until we can't anymore."

He grins, his gaze so deep with admiration that my cheeks burn. "Okay. Where should we travel to live? How much driving can this car do?"

I think of driving to Canada, but he won't be able to hypnotize anybody if our passports fail us. And with no real experience visiting anywhere outside of New York State, I'm not sure what to do with my options. I think about the farthest states from ours and spend the next fifteen minutes in silence deciding on one of those. "Let's go to Washington. It's across the country, right by the Canadian border. We can cross it if we really need to. It will take us a few days to get there, but as long as we have gas, we'll be fine."

He runs his fingers up and down my thigh, his face smooth with happiness as he melts into the seat. "Only a few days to travel across the whole country? Wow. Derek showed me a map, but I cannot quite remember Washington. I trust your choice for us."

We pull over half an hour later at a gas station and fill the tank after checking for a GPS tracker and finding nothing. After loading up on energy drinks and various other drinks and snacks, we snag a handful of different maps as well and hit the highway.

The hours pass with asphalt flying under our tires and the sun beating overhead. We sit in long stretches of comfortable silence, occasionally brainstorming plans for our new life. Denendrius insists we look for a place with a pool and hot tub, not that I protest, but I tell him it has to have a fireplace and a large living room and bedroom too.

It dawns on me that *this is it*. I'm technically a grown-up now, even if I go back to high school. I'm on my own. There's no government or foster parent to manage me anymore.

I must figure out bills, how to cook *proper* meals, and do home repairs. At least Denendrius is figuring this out with me now, though unless he remembers things better, he'll have to rely on me to navigate the world until he understands it.

Luckily, we have enough money to do it all without feeling the stress of it. I probably won't even have to learn how to budget. I guess if we're living fake lives too, we don't have to deal with taxes and that whole side of adulthood.

Damn, this is going to be fun!

No calls or texts come through from Rayonne or Carol, and there's no sign of any cars following us either. It's like we've passed into another realm.

For the first time in my life, things really do feel like they'll be okay.

When it's too hard to keep my eyes open on the highway, I let Denendrius drive since it's not any more dangerous than me falling asleep at the wheel. After my short nap, we take turns driving. He does the safe stretches while I deal with driving in the busy areas.

When daylight fades, the sun dipping behind a hill, I purse my lips and say, "Should we stop in the town coming up. . .or do you think we should take the risk and drive through half the night and sleep for the other half?" Otherwise, we're going to waste time sitting around at the hotel, and I'm eager to really get started.

Besides, no vampire will have enough time once the sun sets to do the twelve hours we drove before we make it to our next stop. The only way they would know where we are by now is if Rayonne followed us and knows vampires in surrounding cities who dare get involved.

He turns the heat on a little as the temperature lowers with the sun. Leaning sideways in his seat with his elbow propped on the console, he rubs his chin and decides. "Take the risk. I want to be done with this driving."

I pull in a deep breath. It feels like a safe enough decision.

I'm unbearably sore and desperate to stand by the time we reach the next town. Needing at least a handful of minutes where I'm not driving or slumped in the passenger seat, I ask, "Want to stop for a burger before the sun completely disappears? Warm food would be nice."

"Okay." Denendrius smiles from the passenger seat.

Fifteen minutes later, we park at my favorite burger chain.

My experiences eating out with him stick close to me when we step out of the car and into the dark, but I remind myself this time will be different. I take his hand when he holds it out to me, and we stroll through the cool air into the heavy smell of greasy food.

We walk past tables to the front. People occupy most of the booths and tables with a hushed chatter over the noise of the kitchen.

Denendrius's eyes flicker over the menu when we approach the counter, and he grumbles and squints at it. Since I already know what I want, I order, and he chooses the same and pays cash.

Barely two minutes pass when they set our trays on the

counter, and we find a booth along the wall and sit on the pink upholstery.

"How does it look?" I ask as he inspects the bun and patty, a wrinkle in his nose as he picks it up and stares at it. "You look. . .kind of disgusted."

"Do you eat this often?" There's a concerned crease between his brows.

I scowl. "You're being judgmental."

"I know." He sighs and takes a bite.

Through a bite of my burger, I say, "Thoughts?"

He coughs as he swallows. "It's a unique taste. I think it's the sauce that's the most troubling part. They may as well dip my entire meal in it."

I snort. "You ate garum and you can't handle a burger?"

"At least the fish taste was *real*. Is this real beef?" Despite his complaints, he takes another massive bite.

I shrug, my grin so big it hurts. "We'll probably never know."

Denendrius reaches across the table with his free hand and takes mine, his fingers fidgeting with my ring. His eyes glimmer when he says, "You're so beautiful when you smile like that. Are you much happier now?"

I swallow a chunk of burger, and my expression smooths out. "It's nice not to be in limbo anymore, waiting for something to happen. Taking control is nice." What was I thinking, being so eager to go to a castle full of vampires? Clearly, I wasn't thinking at all. I was too busy being angry. Alaire and Edmond must have had another place in mind for me. I can't imagine they would have sent me somewhere with vampires who would have it out for me, unless they weren't as nice as I thought.

Denendrius plucks a fry from his tray. "That's good. I am— what is it?—over the moon, for us."

I grin and take another bite.

After a handful of minutes of comfortable silence, Denendrius says, "I'm beginning to appreciate the taste a bit, but I don't think my body is going to be pleased with me."

"If we go to a fancy hotel, maybe they'll have something more to your liking." I chew off another giant bite.

He nods. "Good idea. Where should we find one?"

After so many sleepless nights, the idea of being on the road all day sounds awful. I groan. "How about we stop in whatever town is closest around ten p.m.?"

He pops a fry in his mouth and smiles in approval.

I notice a woman watching me from her booth, a teenage daughter on either side of her. Her eyes shift between Denendrius and me, but her scrutiny is heavier on him, her eyes seeming to settle on our hands.

Did she hear us talking?

Though I know it's dangerous to point it out to Denendrius, the words still come out. "That lady is staring at us." I drag my hand away and move it to my lap.

When he glances sideways at her—his expression calm—she immediately looks away.

"I noticed. We'll leave in a minute," he says under his breath before taking another bite of his burger.

I frown. "I'm only half done."

In a low voice, he says, "I don't like the way she's looking at us. She looks conflicted and keeps flipping her phone open. Could she be someone who knows who I am?"

I sigh and shake my head. "No. . .but we've had reactions like this before." I swallow, thinking of the waitress who wanted to call the cops on us because she thought I was in danger.

His head tilts as his chewing slows. "We have? I can't remember. What's her problem with us, then?"

"Uh—" I put my burger down before scratching my head and wrinkling my nose. I lean into the table. "It's because we're *together*."

He clearly doesn't understand, because he tries to tease me, saying, "Are we not an attractive couple?"

Under my breath, I say, "Den, I'm obviously a teenager, and with your facial hair, you look over thirty."

He stares at me. "And?"

"It's wildly inappropriate these days. Like. . .if I was a few months younger, you would go to prison. . ." I twist my fingers in my lap. "She probably thinks I'm younger than I am and is considering calling the cops to see if I'm okay since we're talking about hotels and stuff."

Jaw setting, he scowls, a coldness infiltrating his eyes. He sets his burger down and leans back in his chair, muttering, "Ridiculous. In Rome, twelve—"

When I inhale, it sounds like a hiss, and he stops talking. "I don't ever want to hear that shit again. Fucking *ever*. Never ever, *ever* remind me you think that's normal."

He stares at me, but the hurt is clear in his eyes. "We need to go. Right now. If she calls the police, there's nothing I can do, and you'll be on your own."

She's staring at us curiously as we pack our food up and leave. Though her worry is clear, there's no sign on her face she heard our conversation.

Buckled back in the car, we drive to a gas station parking lot to finish our burgers and fill up, a tense silence between us. I ponder something to say, but I know it'll come out sounding like I'm forcing a new topic.

We hit the highway, burger joint far behind us, my lips pressed tight together as I stare at the length of yellow light from our car in front of us while he drives.

"Do you think I'm a pervert?" he asks, eyes glued to the road.

I turn in my seat and stare at him. "Is that really all you've been thinking about the last two hours?"

"Yes."

I sigh and lean my head against the window, the glass cold against my temple. "I don't want us to fight," I whisper, gazing up at the silver stars in the clear Wisconsin sky. These are supposed to be *happy times* now.

"But do you?"

My heart hammers in my chest, and my palms sweat. I piece together an answer that hopefully won't escalate things. My throat is dry when I say, "I think you were raised with ideas and values I will never understand. Those things have been different for a long time, so I don't think we will ever agree on this topic. It's a topic we should lock away and never discuss."

"Does our age difference bother you?" he asks. "Do you feel like I've preyed upon you like everyone else seems to think?"

Is he trying to start a fucking fight and ruin this?

"Denendrius," I start carefully, "our entire. . .*relationship* is built on violence and force. I'm not sure what you want me to say."

"But I'm good to you now. I've changed. You love me even with all the imperfections between us?" There's a hint of concern in his voice.

I swallow and nod. "Yes, so there's really no point digging into this. Let's be happy."

"I only want to make sure you don't feel like I've forced you to come with me."

Closing my eyes, I lean my head back against the headrest. "I want to go with you, all right? You're not forcing me to do anything. You're human now, so I'd fight you if I felt in danger."

His chuckle is quiet. "Okay. I love you, Marianna."

"I love you too."

It's much easier to bury the topic than sift through all the facts. It *is* objectively wrong we're together. No matter how good our relationship gets, nothing will change the fact that he ruined my life. It's wrong that we had a relationship in the first place.

The roots of our relationship started growing rotten, even if we're healthy from here on out. But I'd rather live like this than not at all. I don't have to be over the moon about living the rest of my life with him. I can deal with it if he doesn't hurt me, as long as I don't think about it too deeply. If I separate who he is now and who he was as a vampire, I can be happy. At least this way Viorel won't torment me endlessly.

I must accept that I might not get better than this human Denendrius, even if I could carry on without him. Besides, he's not *all* bad. We can build a good human life together, I know it. At least I know he'll ruthlessly protect me. Aside from vampires, I don't have to be afraid of anyone else.

I settle in a place of semiconsciousness, safe—at peace—for the first time in days, which might explain why I can't keep my eyes open very long now. Denendrius hums along to the radio, with brief pauses for what I assume are sips of the fruit punch I convinced him to try. Eventually, I fall into a deep sleep, just to be swiftly woken up again after what feels like three minutes.

XXXVI

"Do you know if this is a nice hotel?" he asks. "It's ten thirty."

I watch the trickle of cars and the thick collection of buildings around them. "Oh, you got into town properly. This will be perfect."

We check in without issue and bring our belongings up to our room.

Denendrius whistles when we enter the luxury room. "I like this."

My tired eyed sweep over the browns and rich greens of the room as I slip off my shoes and step onto the thin gold carpet. I inhale the clean air circulating from the air-conditioning and heating unit below the window, green drapes ruffling above it.

"That bed looks comfy as fuck," I say, thinking of nestling down on the white sheets and pulling the fluffy green duvet tight around me.

"Yes, but I'm itching for something to drink," Denendrius says. "Want to go down to the bar and celebrate?"

"Celebrate?" I press my teeth into my bottom lip, my cheeks tingling. "Yeah, okay. Let's go celebrate."

At the bar downstairs, Denendrius spends the next few hours tasting different shots while I nurse two rum and Cokes. We discover Denendrius is insanely good at playing pool before he becomes too drunk to stand and hold the cue.

The bartender cuts him off—which almost ends in an alteration fueled by Denendrius's entitlement—when he knocks his barstool over trying to sit after returning from the bathroom.

I hook my arm around Denendrius as we walk back to the elevator, his hand grabbing at my ass while we wait for it to arrive. As soon as we're inside with the doors closed, Denendrius pushes me into the elevator wall, his mouth heavy on mine, his lustful grunts sending hot quivers through me.

I can't help my giggle as I turn my face away. "You can't wait until we get to the room?"

He pulls away and adjusts the waist of his jeans. "I suppose I have to, don't I?"

For no other reason than to tease him, I twist out of his grip when we get to our floor and half-race down the hall, sticking my tongue out at him as he grips the wall while stumbling after me.

He pins me against the door as I reach for it and realize he has the key card. Giggling, he picks me up as he unlocks it, but I manage another escape when he trips over a bag and catches himself on the desk chair.

We're a mess of sloppy kisses and fumbling hands as we crawl onto the bed. He sprawls out on his back since I've got far more coordination left than him, and I straddle him while we make out. When his lips part from mine, breath changing, my eyes pop open to discover him passed out.

"Seriously?" Holding back a laugh, I roll off and pull the blanket over him before crashing into dreamland, a euphoric little smile refusing to leave my lips.

"It's all so loud and bright," Denendrius complains as we leave the hotel, pushing the luggage cart in front him.

"That's what happens when you drink so much you pass out." I glance sideways at him and smirk.

He clicks his tongue. "Yes, I'm sorry."

The morning is crisp and light like yesterday, the pavement damp with dew. I pull in a cool breath as I rake my hands through my wet hair. It's another perfect day. To be safe, we search the Mustang for a tracker before loading up and driving off.

Since we checked out early without breakfast, we take a moment to grab coffee—since Denendrius is insistent on trying it—and blueberry muffins.

"Can I have a car?" I ask him, kicking my feet up on the dashboard before burying my teeth in my muffin. "I want to drive to school instead of taking the bus this fall."

He speeds along the highway with one hand on the wheel, a half-eaten muffin in the other. "We can afford another?"

"Totally." I crush a baked blueberry between my teeth.

He shrugs. "Yes, then."

My smile is so wide it hurts, and a dozen images of cars flit through my excited mind. "Thanks."

"I love you," he says, looking at me from the corner of his eye.

When I have an idea, my heart pounds. I set my muffin on my lap and put my feet down so I can wiggle the cell phone free from my pocket. Navigating to the camera, I open it and turn sideways to record Denendrius. "Say that again," I tell him.

"I love you, Marianna." He turns his head and smiles, crumbs stuck to his lips. "Are you taking a picture?"

"Video."

He trains his eyes back on the road, the corner of his lips upturned. "I am not so interesting right now."

I shrug and hold the phone steady. "We're starting a new life. We should record it. I hardly have any pictures."

He looks back at me. "I like that idea. We can show our children."

I'm unsure of what to say, so I take a sip of my coffee and it burns all the way down.

"Hello, Adelia." He waves at the camera.

My brows lift in question.

"That is what we will name our first daughter. For my sister."

"Okay." It's not a bad name.

I curse when the phone glitches. It stops recording, and a message pops up that stops my heart.

Sergei: I drove by last night. There was quite the panic upstairs from all your friends. Good for you.

I swallow, voice shaking as I say, "Sergei messaged me. He knows we left." At least from the sound of it, they didn't follow us.

With a fond smile, he says, "What does he want?"

"I don't know—" I hold my breath as another text comes through.

Sergei: What are you doing? Where are you going?

I decide to give him some sort of answer so he doesn't get worried and hunt us down.

**Me: Starting a new life together. Not
sure where. Driving.**

Sergei's message comes through a moment after mine.

**Sergei: K. Avoid Vegas, specifically
casinos. Police want him. Many clans
around there as well.**

I scowl at my phone. "What the hell did you do in Las Vegas?"

He shrugs and picks his coffee up for a sip. "What's Las Vegas?"

Instead of asking where else we should avoid, I take a risk by hoping Sergei really wants nothing but the best for Denendrius.

Me: Thanks. Is Washington state safe?

**Sergei: As far as I know. Denendrius
likes Washington.**

Me: Yay.

**Sergei: Call me if you need me to hypno-
tize anyone.**

I smile and slide the phone between my thighs, scooping my muffin back up. "Sounds like Washington is a good pick."

He sets his coffee back in the cup holder between us and gives my leg a pat. "Wonderful."

An hour later, we stop at a gas station so I can use the bathroom.

My phone vibrates as soon as I lock the door behind me. I

expect another message from Sergei until I take it from my pocket and stare at the name on screen.

<3Ziggy Calling

My stomach churns, and I almost don't answer it, but I think of him a little more and can't help my curiosity.

"Marianna?" another British voice asks. "It's Lance. Is Denendrius in earshot?"

My throat tightens, and I grip the phone to stop it from slipping from my fingers. "No . . . is Ziggy there—"

"I'm here too," Ziggy interjects. "Rayonne told me not to contact you in case it made you panic and run farther, but I'm hoping this call is enough to change the future Patricia saw for you. Do you want to know where your desperate escape leads?"

I roll my eyes. "You're making shit up to scare me for Rayonne—"

"I would *never*," Ziggy breathes. "I'm obviously not concerned about Rayonne's wishes to take you to the castle. I can't blame you for changing your mind, though I don't agree with this either. She'll never know I called."

My heart beats at the base of my throat when I lean against the metal hand dryer and ask, "What did she see?"

"You're going to die," Ziggy says, a twinge in his low voice. "You get your normal life for about three years, we figure. There was a high school diploma on the wall, and a wedding photo, so congrats, I suppose. But one day he's in a weird daze and viciously stabs you to death in the kitchen in front of your two-year-old daughter. He slits his own throat when he snaps out of it. The government takes your kid once police find you all."

My heart hammers in my ears. I plant my free hand against the counter to stop from falling over. It feels like someone has punched a hole through me. "*What*," I rasp. It's too much to process at once.

Lance says, "I'm sorry. But that's what she showed us."

The connotations of her vision are debilitating.

"The future can change, right?" I ask. "Has it not already since you didn't blood mark me? We're not partying in Vegas. And you changed the future by keeping Lance home when you came to help us."

"Yes," Ziggy says. "I can ask her to look again now, but—"

I swallow. "Then I'll change it when the time comes. And if not, well, at least I get a few years of happiness instead of Viorel torturing me. I can't afford to dwell on that right now."

"You can't afford not to dwell on it," Ziggy says, voice cracking. "Marianna, you are likely to die by his hand, one way or another. In all Lance's and my years, we have never felt a man so *fundamentally angry*. He's in serious emotional pain, and he's incredibly good at hiding the depth of it."

I straighten and run my fingers through my hair as I shake my head. I tell myself that they're desperate—Rayonne's friends —and that they're not voicing any concerns different from anyone else's. It means nothing. "I have to go—"

"Marianna, please. I know you're at the mark's mercy but ..." Ziggy releases a hopeless breath, tears in his voice when he continues with, "You might be able to defend yourself. I don't know. But he attacks you at dinnertime while he's helping you cook, and your daughter is playing with a toy fire truck at the table. There are Christmas decorations all over, so that should give you a more specific time frame to watch out for."

"Why are you doing this?" I demand with a squeak. Why is he trying to ruin things for me? "If it's not to help Rayonne, then why?"

Ziggy's voice is thick with loss. "Because we're the best of friends in an alternate timeline. Before I chickened out on marking you, Patricia showed me how entwined all our lives would be. It would have been grand. So, we can't help but care. It feels like I've known you for years now."

I glower at myself in the mirror. "Then why did you decide not to force your blood down my throat?"

"Because it would have ruined everything for Rayonne, and she's my friend too. I didn't want that to be my fault. You would have clobbered Denendrius, and she might've lost her spot at the castle if you killed him, maybe even her life."

"That's what Patricia saw?" I ask.

"No," Ziggy mumbles. "It dawned on me when I offered my blood to you."

I grip the edge of the counter, trying not to take his words to heart.

"If you somehow kill him in self-defense and get that mark off you, or he dies some other way if we've altered the future, you call me. Marianna, I promise you would be so happy. She showed me. We would protect you."

I close my eyes and shake my head, refusing to entertain the idea.

"Okay, thank you for trying to look out for me," I whisper. "But I'm sorry, I have to go."

I hang up in the middle of their tangled protests and quickly wipe at my eyes before splashing cold water on my face. I take so long to gather myself that Denendrius comes looking for me. When he knocks on the bathroom door and inquires about my well-being, I clear the call history. Denendrius doesn't need to be burdened by their obvious manipulation. He has enough things to have nightmares over, never mind our supposed demise.

Refusing to allow the darkness of their call to follow me from the bathroom as I return to the car with Denendrius, I tell myself not to give it another thought, not to dig into what all that vision means. I refuse to spend the next three years analyzing every decision we make. For all I know, trying to change the future—if Ziggy isn't lying—is what causes it to happen.

We take turns driving for the rest of day and night and to the next morning, taking silly pictures and videos of one another between naps, snacks, and hopeful conversation. Our giddy, pure happiness is like a white aura around us, impenetrable to any outside negativity.

We fly past the Washington state sign a smidgen after nine a.m. and decide to stop at a diner in Spokane to stretch our legs and eat. Thankfully, we both managed enough sleep taking shifts.

After Denendrius and I order, I search for places to rent with the cell phone since we struggle with how to *buy* a house in our position. We search a few cities for houses that fit our list and come up with about fifteen different options in the state that are listed by their owners instead of rental companies.

There's only a handful of other families in the diner, and the kitchen is quiet, so I don't have to strain while Denendrius and I talk.

"I think the one in Bellevue is my favorite," I tell him as I flip through the pictures for the third time. "Plus, they listed it last night, it's furnished, and it's close to a good high school."

"We will try that one first," he says, touching his leg against mine under the table of our booth.

He sits back from the table as the waiter carries our food out, setting a massive waffle overloaded with whipped cream and strawberries in front of each of us.

"I haven't been sick lately," Denendrius says as he has no choice but to cut his food up with utensils since it's far too messy to eat with his hands. "I think leaving was the best choice."

"I agree." I lean forward and run my tongue across the mountain of fluffy cream before scarfing down my food so we can get back to the car to make calls.

My heart pounds as we leave the diner, and I practically run through the parking lot to clamber into the car. As soon as Denendrius is behind the wheel, I call the number listed for our top pick house.

The universe must really want this to work out for us, as the owner of the house tells us we're the first ones to call about it and that we can look after lunch.

I can't contain my excitement as we drive there, flipping back and forth through the saved pictures while babbling on about all the things I plan on filling the rooms with if we're lucky enough to convince the landlord to rent it to us on our terms.

Around two p.m., we drive into an upper-middle-class neighborhood and park in front of a gorgeous house with white stucco and a gray roof. The white garage doors—three of them —face the road with the main part of the house set back a bit to the right.

My heart palpitates with dizzying excitement as we step out of the car. I hook my arm around Denendrius's, and we amble up the gray stone walkway, past lush green bushes and teeming garden beds. We step up before white French doors.

I'm jittery as I go to knock, but the door opens before my fist reaches it.

"Charles and Maria, I'm assuming?" John asks, calling us by the names I gave him over the phone. "Come on in. Do you have questions first or should we jump straight into the tour?"

"Tour." I can't hide my grin as we step into the foyer and onto a red mat covering the honey-colored hardwood floor.

The tall walls are all the same white as the railings of the staircase that's in front of me and past the sitting room to my right. We take the stairs up, my hand gliding over the honey wood handrail until we're all the way up on the second floor that overlooks the foyer.

"Master bedroom," John says as we follow him through the open French doors closest to the top of the stairs.

My face hurts from smiling so much as I take in the room. I imagine myself jumping on the massive four-poster bed—honey wood, of course—on the far-right wall, and gazing out the long window at the trees.

"Very beautiful," Denendrius says as he looks around, his thick accent making John glance back in surprise. "Perhaps a bit more color. So much white."

"Well, I already set the place up, but there's a large storage room downstairs if you'd want to swap some of the furniture for your own," John says.

I wander through the angled French doors and find a walk-in closet to my left. Its wooden shelves match the rest of the house, and I imagine filling it with clothes, coming in every morning before school to get ready. When I spot another doorway on the other side of the room in the large mirror, I dart to it and find a white bathroom with gold accents. Next to a standing shower is a Jacuzzi tub that I imagine myself taking long bubble baths in the night before a stressful exam.

The other three upstairs bedrooms aren't as interesting. They're large and overlook the pool out back, but I can't think of anything to fill them with yet.

After touring the rest of the warm, sunlight-filled house and falling in love with every inch, I turn to Denendrius, who has said little about it unless prompted.

"I want it," I plead, hanging off Denendrius's arm as we stand back in the foyer. "Can we get it? Do you like it?"

Denendrius runs his hands through my hair. "Yes, it's really perfect. I would be happy to live here."

I feel ridiculous when I pump my fist in the air, but I can't help it.

John holds a tickled grin. "So, rent is what we discussed, but all utilities are included, as well as internet and satellite TV. No pets and no smoking of any kind. This is a quiet neighborhood, so no parties either. Pool care is on the renter."

I'm nodding along with his words. "Great. That's fine."

"If you two really want the place, we can sign some paperwork and you can move in after a background and reference check goes through in a handful of days."

My heart lodges itself in my throat, and I shoot Denendrius a desperate look before countering with, "Well, what if we pay a bit more each month, and we . . . *skip* all that checking stuff and move in *right now*? We can pay the first three months outright."

An odd scowl crosses his face—understandably so—before he purses his lips and crosses his arms. He jerks his skeptical gaze between Denendrius and me as his brows lower with deep thought.

"We won't cause any trouble, I promise." I've pictured myself doing so many things around the house already that I might actually punch myself in frustration if he says no.

"Would I have to worry about the mob poking around?" His joke falls flat, mostly because he's borderline serious.

Denendrius's head tilts, and he looks down at me. "What is . . .?"

I shake my head. "No, we're not into anything like that. We're normal people."

John's arms lower. "Ah . . . I see. He's an undocumented immigrant or something, isn't he?"

My lips purse and I scratch my neck. "Well . . ." Technically, Denendrius is.

John shrugs, but I can tell he's not fully convinced. "I know I shouldn't have asked, but that's not so bad if he is. Let me call my wife and see what she says, all right?"

I chew my nails as he walks down the hallway straight ahead and into the kitchen, only picking up half his conversation as Denendrius and I wait in silence.

From the sound of things, they really want the extra money

to pay off the house they're already living in, though the fact that he'll have trouble bringing us to court for damages if we trash the place makes him wary, which he brings up the moment he's back.

"So, there's no legal issue with me renting to you two, but if you want to rent completely off the books with cash, that creates risk for me, especially with a house like this. What brings you two here, anyway?"

I doubt I owe him anything, but if it eases some of his worries . . . "We're trying to start a new life here away from his family," I half lie.

John gives us a small smile. "All right. Well . . ." He blows a long breath from his lips and rocks on his heels, looking around pained as he considers all the expensive things in the house. "You said you wanted in today? Bring three months' worth of rent, and another month's worth as a deposit and you can have the keys. Add an extra thousand dollars to each month."

I grin and gently elbow Denendrius to go collect what we need.

When Denendrius goes out to the Mustang to gather cash, John turns to me and says, "Do you have some sort of ID you can show me with a birth date on it? I won't take a record of it."

Sweat starts in my hairline. "Why?"

He shrugs and shoves his flat hands into the pockets of his beige slacks. "Because I like to sleep at night, and I don't want to be an accessory to anything. Cover your name for all I care, I just want to see a date."

I dig my Italian one out of my pocket, cover my name with my finger, and point out the fact it says I'm eighteen. "See?"

He takes a good look before leaning away, letting out a strained laugh. "Okay, sorry. You look sixteen, is all."

When Denendrius comes back with the exact amount in cash, John counts it out and scrutinizes the bills before setting the keys to my very first home in my sweaty palm. We exchange numbers, at least, and he tells us he'll be coming back to check on the place in a few weeks.

I dangle the keys in front of my face, feeling so contented I fear for a moment that I might be dreaming.

XXXVII

"Are you so happy now?" Denendrius asks as he pushes me into the wall after dumping our bags in the foyer, his lips heavy on mine as he wraps his hands around my waist.

"So fucking happy," I whisper when our lips part, the keys clutched in my hand.

"Should we test out our new bed?" He leans down, hands trailing down my back and butt to my thighs. He hoists me up against the wall and I wrap my legs around his hips while giggling.

"We don't even have soap to shower with, or clean clothes to change into," I tell him as I hook my arms around his neck and playfully bite the air at him. "And no snacks for after. Why don't we unpack what we have and go on a shopping spree?" I glance down at the bag of money on the floor. "Maybe we should figure out how to get a safe or something too."

Denendrius groans as he leans his forehead against mine. He complains with a stretched "okay."

Since we don't have a safe yet, we hide a duffel bag of

diamonds in the dryer and a smaller one in a hallway vent before we leave, keeping my backpack full of cash with us.

Once at the grocery store, I feel like screaming with joy when Denendrius races me inside on the front of a cart. It's freeing to shop without regard to the price, and I toss in snacks and treats I was never allowed to have.

Denendrius blows out exasperated breaths as we go down row after row, but he's breathing normally again when we get to the side of the store with fresh produce, meat, and bread.

"What about real food?" Denendrius stares at me in disgusted bewilderment as he grabs packaged corn cobs from a shelf. "Real food is not rainbow."

"Fine." I set the cookies in the cart on a stack of frozen pizzas and grab a watermelon out of a cardboard bin. I roll it across the bottom of the cart and into a jug of milk like I'm bowling.

Once the cart is full of food, we realize we still need toiletries and numerous other household supplies. I snag a second cart and fill it with all the other basics—like spray bottles for garlic mix.

We fill the entire trunk and most of the back seat, and by the time we carry everything in, my arms are sore and covered in marks from loading them up with grocery bags.

I carry the last bag of groceries through the foyer and straight down the hall to the kitchen, dropping them in the dining area between me and the cooking area.

Lying down on the hardwood amongst the plastic bags to settle my heavy breaths, I grin and stare up at the ceiling and silver pot lights above the island at the end of my feet.

"I've never had so much food in my life." Or the appetite to eat it like I do now.

I feel around in a bag near my head until I find a pack of cookies. I tear it open and grab a rainbow chocolate chip cookie, eating it as I listen to the new neighborhood sounds spill in from the open French doors. The Mustang door slamming shut cuts through the chirping birds and gentle breeze.

Denendrius chuckles at me as he enters the room, going out of his way to step over me with a bag. I swat at him and sit as he sets the bag on the gray island countertop in the center of the square kitchen. He moves around it to the other end, where the stainless-steel fridge is.

"You must show me what all goes in here," he says while cracking open one door. "Get rid of that cookie."

"I'm hungry." I shove the rest of the cookie in my mouth, the muscles in my face sore from so much smiling.

He motions to the dozens of bags around me. "The food will be ruined."

I suck crumbs off my fingers and stand. "Fine."

After we're finished unloading groceries in the fridge and the white cupboards that wrap around the entire kitchen, I snatch another cookie. Hoisting myself up on the island, I admire the view of the backyard through the window above the sink.

"Why not sit in the chair beside me?" Denendrius sits down on a stool at the island and rolls three oranges back and forth between his hands.

"Because this is my house and I can sit wherever I want." I cross my legs and face him, warm sunlight hitting my back from the window.

"You might fall," he counters, tearing into an orange with his fingers.

I shrug and pluck another cookie from the pack. "It's my floor to fall on."

He laughs while popping an orange slice into his mouth.

We eat in comfortable silence, admiring the massive room. I study the kitchen table across from the doorway, and the archway with a white pillar on either side of it that leads to the sunken family room between the hall and table.

"Should we see what the mall is like before it closes?" Denendrius asks as he finishes off his third orange.

I shove the rest of my cookie in my mouth, my words muffled when I agree. Standing on the counter, I squat down in preparation to leap off. "Catch me."

"No. This is not proper behavior in the house, Marianna." He stands back with an authoritative scowl.

I roll my eyes back into my skull. "Fucking hell, Denendrius. Catch me."

He lifts his chin. "My father would have beaten me for this behavior. You have dirty shoes where we prepare food."

My lip curls. "This isn't your daddy's house, and he's not here to beat our asses, is he? You don't live with your parents anymore. This is our house and we can do whatever the fuck we want. What's the point, otherwise? I'll clean the counter later."

Denendrius's lips purse and he holds his arms out and sighs. I fling myself at him and he grunts and wraps his arms around my midsection upon collision.

I expect him to put me on my feet, but he backs me into the counter and sits me on it, his lips unrelenting on mine, his index finger hooked under my chin. I wrap my legs around his waist and search for his tongue with mine as I curl my arm around his neck and twist my fingers through his hair.

My breath is heavy as his hands wander over my body and disappear, my skin pricking with heat under his touch.

"What are you doing?" I ask when I hear his belt jingle, as if the answer isn't obvious.

With a mischievous smile, he gently sprawls me out on my back and curls his fingers around the waist of my jeans. "The counter is already dirty, yes? Let me have you here before we go again."

I bite my bottom lip, breath rapid. "Yeah, I guess it is."

Somehow, after all that, I still have energy to hop back in the car.

"You might have to push me around in a cart when we get there," I tease, my hips aching.

He blows a kiss from where he sits behind the wheel, fancy homes blurring by behind him. "You will be okay—"

"Wait, there's the high school!" I shout, pointing ahead to my right. "Can you park in the lot so I can look?"

It's around four, so the parking lot is mostly empty when we pull in. As soon as Denendrius parks, I bolt out of my seat and lean against the side of the car to get a better look at the wall of windows and all the brick. It's at least twice the size of West James High. I'm wide-eyed as I take it all in. I can tell it's a much better school than my last one, and I wish it were already September so I could walk through those doors and check it out.

I imagine myself with a nice backpack slung over my shoulder, new shoes and clothes on as I walk up the long stretch of concrete stairs from the sidewalk since it's walking distance from home. What does it look like once I get inside? What color are the lockers? Are the hallways as cramped and overcrowded as I'm used to? Is the library bigger?

The lush green sports fields behind the school are visible from where I stand. I can tell one is for football, but what else do they have that I could try out for?

I promise myself that I'm going to try my best this time. I'm going to study and do all my homework, show up to every class. If I need help, I'll ask and prove to myself that I'm capable of more than sticking a needle in my arm.

A girl walking toward me snaps me from my daydream, her black clothes and facial piercings reminding me of Ziggy and Rayonne. I think she's coming to talk to me—perhaps I shouldn't be on school property yet—but she gives me a friendly "hello" as she approaches a green car two stalls down and climbs in.

Assuming she's a student here, what are the chances she and I end up in the same grade or class together? I suppose if we don't cross paths again, there will be plenty of other people to make friends with.

But how will I explain my situation to any friends I do make? Will they think I'm weird for having an older boyfriend —or husband, I guess—and my own house? What do I do when they want to hang out or have a sleepover? What if I get invited out after dark? Do I risk it, or find an excuse why I can't? I suppose it won't be safe until I look older and don't match the description for the bounty.

I take a deep breath and decide to figure it out as it happens. Regardless, I'll be a better friend this time around. The friend Jenna, Camille, and Daina should have had from the start, before I realized my stubbornness was hurting them.

The thought of my friends back at West James High sends me into an emotional crash and my tears are instant, hot as they roll down my cheeks. They must think the worst has happened now, and here I am, fantasizing about my new life while they worry.

I wipe my cheeks and slip back into the car, hanging my head with my hair a curtain around me.

"What's wrong?" Denendrius murmurs, reaching out to tuck my hair behind my ear so he can see my face. "Did that girl say something mean to you?"

I shake my head. "No, I miss my old friends from school, is all."

"You will have new friends," he promises, slipping his hand into mine—limp—in my lap. "So many here."

My sniffle hurts my nose. "I know, but it's not the same."

His lips twist, and I can tell he struggles with my words.

What kind of friendships did he have in Rome? Did he ever have any to lose in the first place, or was he still a little more *off* than the average person back then?

I lift my head, flicking tears away from my eyes so he's not so blurry. "Do you . . . do you remember killing one of my friends?"

His eyes pop wide. "I did? Why?"

I wipe my nose with the back of my hand and swallow against the scratchiness in my throat. "I don't know. She was the only one of my friends who had a problem with our relationship," I realize, thinking about how Jenna's attitude turned when she found out how old he is. "You were convinced she was going to get in the way."

Denendrius sits back in the seat, pondering to himself as he stares out the windshield at the slow trickle of cars on the road. "I'm sorry, I cannot remember."

I pull the neck of my plain blue T-shirt up and wipe my eyes. "I'd rather you not."

He gives me a tight-lipped, penitent smile and carefully asks, "Would you still like to go shopping?"

Leaning back in the chair, I nod and close my eyes, focusing on nothing more than burying my feelings back inside me so they don't ruin the rest of my day. I refuse to allow the emotions of my past to ruin my new life.

By the time we reach the mall, I'm in good spirits again. It's difficult to be upset with the handful of money Denendrius folds up and stuffs in my pocket for clothes. I climb out of the car and head into the mall with my hand in Denendrius's, amping myself up for the shopping spree my friends and I always dreamed of.

I'm paralyzed by choices. Though I can afford any store, I realize I don't fully know where to start. I know I don't want the shops that sell clothes that are expensive for the sake of being expensive, but do I wander back into the skater shops I usually frequent, or should I try out some stores I know the "normal girls" would shop in?

My head hurts from all the questions I ask myself. I decide to go both routes and simply pick whatever I like.

Twenty minutes later, I'm stepping out of a changing room in a pleated baby-blue skirt with a white tank top tucked in. Pop music plays in the background.

"Beautiful," Denendrius says from the bench behind me. I can see him and the stack of clothes I've picked out in the mirror.

"What do you think?" the teenage store associate, Jamie, asks as she returns to check on one of the outfits she picked for me.

"I'll get it," I say, heart soaring. I look like the girls on TV.

My stomach drops when I focus on the gang tattoo on my neck for the trillionth time today. It ruins the entire outfit. It ruins *all* my outfits aside from the ones from the street wear shop. But that doesn't exactly help. I realized while picking through the shirts with brass knuckles, guns, and rappers, that I don't want to wear them anymore.

I still like them, I can't deny that, but I can't help but associate them with all the pain the street brought me. That, and I don't want anyone at school to associate me with the street either.

But then there's my gang tattoo, a dead giveaway to who I am. Covering my tattoo up with one hand, I realize I won't ever be a normal teenage girl, no matter how much I fake it. I wish I'd never gotten it.

Well, at least this new normal is much better than whatever Viorel and every other vampire want to do with me.

Jamie says, "My sister uses some special foundation to cover her tattoos up for work. I can text her and ask what it is?"

I leap at the idea and I ask her to find out, so she tells her manager that she's taking a bathroom break, and I try on the rest of my outfits while I wait.

She helps me carry up my ridiculous selection of clothes to the cash register after, and as she rings me through, she says, "Hey, what school do you go to?"

I tell her which one I'll be attending in the fall since I'm new in town, even though I'm not technically registered yet, and she grins.

"That's awesome! That's where I go." She folds a black knit sweater into a neon pink bag.

Seizing the chance to make a friend before summer even starts, I say, "Wanna swap numbers?"

Jamie's expression widens in delight, and she glances at her manager—who is off across the store helping another associate —before snagging a scrap piece of paper and scrawling her number down. She slides it into one of my shopping bags and finishes cashing us out.

"Be careful," Denendrius warns as we exit the store, arms loaded with bags. "Everybody wants to be your friend when you're rich."

"If she goes to that school, she probably lives in the same area as us," I counter.

He shrugs. "You will find out the hard way, Marianna."

I merely huff and roll my eyes.

We decide to take a detour to the car before shopping for him, but I'm running out of steam by the time I follow in Denendrius's steps into an expensive men's store.

His choice of clothes is unsurprising: dark and solid-colored sweaters, T-shirts, and silk dress shirts.

He makes a face at the jeans, but seeing as there's not many pants options, he folds them over his arm and seems relieved when he finds a table of sweatpants and comfy pajamas.

I have no complaints about his style, even now that he dresses more like Derek than he did when he was a vampire.

He doesn't even glance at the leather jackets when we walk by them, and he picks out a pair of casual dress shoes and slacks.

We make a quick stop at a makeup store for the tattoo-covering supplies Jamie recommended, and then we're done shopping for the day.

Once all entry points to the house are vampire-proofed, I spend the rest of the evening doing laundry. We're so tired from the nonstop excitement that we order food and almost fall asleep while eating it in front of the TV.

After a much-needed soak in the Jacuzzi together, we crawl into bed.

"This is all so exciting. I think this is the best decision I've ever made," I whisper, staring back at myself through the yellow lamplight in the mirror above the bed. "I've never been this happy before."

Denendrius locks eyes with mine in our reflection, and he laces his fingers through mine on the white blanket between us. "Me too, Marianna."

XXXVIII

Three weeks pass with hardly a thought of vampires. By mid-May, our closet is half-packed full of shoes and clothes, the built-in bookshelves a quarter of the way filled with books that I've actually had the mental stamina to read. We set up a pool table in the basement, and Denendrius and I splurge on finding new hobbies. Denendrius gives me more gladiator lessons since I'm so insistent, and we manage to track down a replica shield, as well as some modern training equipment.

I wake every morning afraid to open my eyes, like I'll find myself back in the apartment. But each sunny day spills through the white curtains of our bedroom, thin enough that I can see the thick green of the tall trees in our backyard. We don't hear from Carol or anyone else, though the phone stays connected, and I worry from time to time about what they're up to. Part of me believes Carol understands this is the best I've got and has let me go.

Jamie from the mall and I text often, and it's surreal the first time she comes over to hang out. Her personality is an odd mix of Camille's and Daina's, with all of Camille's maturity but with Daina's free spirit. I'm Maria to her, and though she knows Denendrius—or Charles, to her—is my fiancé, she's cool with it. Her mom's not though, and, after learning how I don't live with parents because they're "dead," bans Jamie from having sleepovers at my house but welcomes me to hers. It doesn't help that her college-aged brother comes over with her one day— her unannounced idea to give Charles an American friend— and that he later tells Jamie, who tells me, that he thinks my fiancé is a "fucking weirdo."

Regardless, my life is better than it's ever been, and I feel proud that I was brave enough to make it to this point. Everything leading up to Washington feels like nothing more than a vivid nightmare.

But the new house and town don't fix *everything*.

Denendrius jars awake most nights, sweaty and gasping for breath from nightmares of Sirmium.

He's back to normal most times after a hot shower and breakfast, though there's a few days where he's unbelievably clingy after waking and follows me around the house, and some where he flinches at every touch. I feel helpless on those days—though they aren't frequent, thankfully—because I can't think of any way to help him.

There's not enough therapy in the world to fix him, not that he even opens up to me about any of what happened to him. The only story I can get out of him is one about how they kept him in a room with moving slats to allow the sun in, off and on, for decades. That the only reason the guards stopped torturing him that way was because his body adjusted to the pain, and it took longer each time for him to burn.

I don't dare put a single real complaint out into the world, lest the universe rip this all away from me. So, I deal with his trauma, the new difficulties of our life, if it means I never have to see another vampire again.

Spanish summer pop music fills the kitchen, midafternoon sunlight illuminating the white and honey tones of the room while I sing along, stirring flour into a batch of chocolate chip cookies. Yesterday, I decided to take up baking, and Denendrius took me to buy a stack of cookbooks.

Cookies seemed like a safe place to start the journey.

I walk through a sticky patch of spilled sugar on the floor, admiring the way the light glints on the white water of the open hot tub awaiting Denendrius.

He walks into the kitchen with a towel around his waist as I do a spin to get to my bowl of beaten eggs.

"Dance with me." I reach out while I sway my hips to the beat, singing some of the Spanish lyrics at him. It sounds romantic, but the songs are about getting drunk on the beach.

He stands there rigidly, the corner of his mouth quirked in an amused smile. "You're very cute."

"Come on, dance." I sway in front of him and grab his hand, moving his arm back and forth like I can force some rhythm to pass through the rest of his body.

He laughs. "I cannot dance, Marianna."

"Can't, or won't?"

"Both." He references the towel around his hips and adds, "I do not dance, anyway."

"Why?"

"I would look silly," he says plainly. "I am made for fighting."

I roll my eyes. "How do you not dance? Do you really fight the feeling of music flowing through you?"

"I do not *feel* music," he explains, more amusement on his face. "I like the sounds, but I do not understand how it makes you want to move."

I stop dancing, my expression dropping. "What? Seriously?"

"Don't stop, I like it. *You* don't look silly."

Pouting, I ask, "What about a slow dance? A little swaying?"

He shakes his head slowly, face so serious it dampens the joy running through me.

"Oh. Okay . . . you won't even dance at prom?"

"No." There's too much force behind the word that it's like a knife in my heart.

"Okay." I grit my teeth, my scowl deep as I return to my mixing bowl with the beaten eggs, trying to hold back a tidal wave of tears. A weepy hiccup escapes me as I pour the eggs into the batter and violently smack at them with my whisk. He sighs and comes to me.

"A little dance. No crying." He holds his hand out.

I sniffle and wipe my eyes. "I don't want a pity dance. It's not that big a deal."

He stares at me with sad eyes. "I don't want to make you unhappy. If you really want one dance so bad . . ."

"Fine." The word is sharp, so I exhale my anger and rub my forehead. "But we can't slow-dance to this. Do you know a song?"

He stares past me for a long moment, thinking, before he nods and tells me what song to type in.

"This is a wartime song," I note as I select it.

"I cannot remember much else newer." He tightens the towel around his hips. "There's not exactly a recording of the songs I know from Rome."

"This is fine." I hold my hand out and he takes it.

As we sway, a girl and guy take turns singing about how it's been so long that they've been kissed by one another, that they can't believe they're together again. The brass instruments are sweet to my ears, and I can't help but smile a little.

"This is how in love with you I feel," he murmurs before humming along.

But he's so incredibly slow and out of sync—his expression

too severe—that it's hard to enjoy it. Still, I try my best since he's doing this for me.

"What's prom?" he asks.

I laugh and wipe my eyes. Of course, he doesn't remember. "It's a really important dance; a celebration. I'll get to go when I finish high school."

"Ah." He gives me a lopsided smile. "I will dance there too then."

"Thank you." I can't help but wonder what he was doing when he heard this song for the first time.

When it's over, he gives me a long kiss and steps away from me.

"How much longer until you're done baking? I want you to come relax with me."

"I have to put the cookies in the oven," I tell him. "Besides, I'm too warm for the hot tub."

He presses his lips to my forehead and steps back toward the hall. "Okay. I'm going out back to relax."

"Have fun." I step back to the mixing bowl, no desire to dance left in me for now, so I let the old songs play automatically.

No matter how human he is now, I'm not sure I'll ever get used to the fact he's had almost two thousand years' worth of experiences I'll never be able to relate to—even if he doesn't feel like the memories are really his.

When it comes time to shape the cookies into flat circles on the pan, I glance out the window and spot Denendrius settled up to his chest in foamy bubbling water.

I wave at him since he stares in my direction, but he must be lost in a daydream. He doesn't wave—or even blink—back.

Deciding to leave him be, I train my attention on my cookies as I fill three baking sheets. After popping them in the oven, I take a quick trip to the bathroom.

When I come back, Denendrius stands with blood running from his nose in the middle of the kitchen.

"Marianna—" He gags and holds his bloody hand up to catch a few drops.

I curse and rush for a dish towel, snagging one from the drawer beside the sink and returning to him to hold it against his nose. "What happened?"

"I think I hit my face on the edge of the hot tub." He swallows a mouthful of blood, and there's a dullness to his eyes that has me chewing at my cheek. "I was dizzy."

I hold the towel against his nose and pinch it, telling him to lean forward a bit. He leans but swallows another mouthful of blood, and I say, "Okay, stop that or you'll be puking."

He blinks hard, heavy gaze dragging across the room.

Worry constricts my throat. "Are you going to be okay?"

When he slurs something and shrugs away from me to stumble down the hall, my heart kicks into overdrive. I follow close behind him as he twists into the hallway bathroom and retches into the seashell-shaped white sink.

I lean back against the wall and close my eyes for a second. *Fuck.*

This hasn't been the first time since we left that he's puked, but the fact that he's not sure how he injured himself to the point of a nosebleed is . . . *not great.*

Rubbing my hand between his shoulder blades, I say, "I'm going to grab you a drink."

I rush back to the kitchen. As soon as I open a cupboard for a glass, there's a thud in the washroom.

Drink abandoned, I scramble back to the bathroom. Denendrius convulses on the floor. His eyes are rolled back, arms straight in front of him as he shakes, a raspy moan escaping from his wide mouth.

I stand above him uselessly for too many seconds before I snap myself out of my shock and drop to help him. All I know is I should turn him on his side, so I kneel and manage to roll him over with his head in my lap.

My fingers run through his wet hair and along the side of his face as tears well in my eyes. I gently shush the strangled noises he makes. A thousand horrible thoughts rip through my mind as I try to will him to stop.

Thoughts jumping to the worst—that maybe he's dying— I'm about to leave him to call for an ambulance when his jerks slow, and he goes slack.

A relieved sob escapes me and I curl over to rest my head against his.

"You're okay," I whisper.

He rouses a little, mumbling something as his hand slowly moves up to touch my leg. Neither one of us says anything as he focuses on breathing.

He asks me something in Latin, then whispers, "What happened?"

"You had a seizure."

A groan rolls in the back of his throat.

I run my fingers down his arm. "You'll be okay."

His voice is so low I strain to hear. "I think I'm dying."

A little laugh escapes me, though his words send a cold tingle through me. "You're not *dying*, Denendrius. Don't be dramatic."

He sniffles and wipes blood from his nose with the back of his hand. "I love you," he whispers. "You take such good care of me."

I smile inwardly and give his forehead a peck. "Love you too."

When he's able to move, I wipe the blood from his face before helping him to the sunken family room off the dining area of the kitchen. He lies on his side across the white couch and tucks a gold throw pillow under his head while I unfold a matching knitted blanket. A smile twitches over his lips as I drape it over his body.

I leave him to rest with the light off and return to my baking sheets.

"Marianna," he calls a handful of minutes later. There's a sliver of panic in his hoarse voice.

"Yeah?" Worry sends my tone up a pitch.

"Never mind."

I fold my arms and cross the kitchen to rest my shoulder against a white pillar, staring down into the living room at him. "What is it?"

His eyes close. "It's nothing."

Sighing, I say, "All right."

"Go bake," he orders softly, hand moving to grip the edge of the couch cushion as he squeezes his eyes closed.

Stress has me feeling sick. "You need to go to a doctor, Denendrius."

"I won't," he objects, voice low and even.

I grit my teeth. "Why not? You have plenty of fake identification, and we can afford a really good one. Obviously, something is wrong if you're puking randomly all the time. Plus, you had a fucking seizure."

He mashes his lips together, words locked behind them.

"You're *sick*, Denendrius. Stop being stubborn and get it taken care of before you . . ." My thoughts run away from me. I don't mean to entertain Ziggy's warning, but fear keeps me talking despite knowing I shouldn't question Denendrius's choice to do something like this. "Snap one day or something. What are you going to do if you have an emergency while I'm at school? If you love me, you'll go to the doctor. How am I going to survive without you if one day you don't wake up? I need you to take care of me and keep me safe."

"I will be okay," he assures me flatly.

I push myself away from the pillar when the timer beeps,

pivoting as I say, "Go to a doctor, and you'll know for sure. Who the hell knows what that vampire blood did to you?"

"Can you bring me wine?" is all he responds with. "The bottle?"

I roll my eyes, turn the timer off, and swipe the bottle he opened a few hours ago off the counter.

"It's not going to help you feel better," I grumble as I slog over to him, holding the bottle out. "Here."

He opens his eyes, squints against the light at me, and takes it. "With my mood, it will."

Thankfully, Denendrius is back to normal by dinner.

When I wake in the morning, it's to an empty and cold bed. The house is silent aside from the sound of the fridge making ice downstairs and the hiss of air from the vents.

I know before I call Denendrius's name that he's not in the house.

There's an ache in my stomach as I crawl out of bed and search around. His sandals aren't at the front door, and neither are his car keys.

There's no Mustang in the driveway, or the garage.

I gnaw on my cheek as I creep back upstairs and look for evidence of what he's been up to. My mind spins as I go to the en suite bathroom. Denendrius's towel and toothbrush are wet.

"Where the hell did he go?" I grumble while snatching my toothbrush off the counter.

Even though my mind is empty of answers, and the fact that he's gone without even waking me to tell me should be concerning—especially when he unburied a body last time he was gone—I can't bring myself to outright panic. I know I should trust him. But is he safe to be out there by himself, even if it's daytime? What could he possibly be doing that he couldn't take me along?

Regardless, I can feel it in my gut that he's safe, and that he'll be back no matter what he's up to.

Sighing, I spit a mouthful of toothpaste into the sink and brush knots from my hair.

I decide there's no point dwelling on all the possibilities when I can demand answers when he returns, so I instead take a long shower.

But lunchtime comes and goes, and soon it's two o'clock and he's been gone for at least six hours.

I result to pacing around the house—too unsettled to do anything productive—until keys scrape against the front door as it opens.

"Where the fuck did you go?" I demand as I stop mid-stroll down the stairs.

Denendrius's face widens with shock. "To the doctor . . . you said I should go."

I lean back against the railing. "I thought you'd need my help, or at least *tell me* you were going."

"Sorry, Marianna." He sets his keys down on the entryway table and bends to take his sandals off.

Well, at least he fucking went?

I hop down the last few steps as he straightens. "Why did it take so long? Is everything okay?"

His Adam's apple bobs with a hard swallow. "I don't think so."

My knees feel like jelly. "W-What do you mean?"

He scrapes his top teeth over his bottom lip, tired eyes avoiding mine as he thinks. "I have another appointment for an MRI. The doctor thinks there is an issue in my brain."

I balk. "An MRI for puking and a short seizure?" I'm not sure if that's standard or not.

"Uh . . ." He scratches his chest and looks around the room, to his feet saying, "These are symptoms of a brain tumor."

I gape at him, nothing but white in my mind. "A *brain* tumor? You told the doctor about puking and one seizure and he jumped to brain tumor?"

"I went blind for a bit yesterday too," he admits. "And that was my fourth seizure."

I lean away from him. "You haven't fucking told me any of that!"

Denendrius scratches the back of his head. "No, I do not want to worry you with all my symptoms."

"I'm already fucking worried!" I suck in a deep, burning breath and exhale. "Okay . . . a brain tumor isn't the end of the world, *if* you even have one, for fuck's sakes. That doesn't mean cancer, and even so, it's not an automatic death sentence. I bet you have a stomach issue, maybe epilepsy too?" Even to my own ears, my argument sounds desperate.

Despite furiously trying to swerve my thoughts around Patricia's vision, I collide. Did Denendrius seek treatment at all before he killed us? Perhaps I altered the future by convincing him to go, by planting the idea that he could snap. Either way, brain tumor or not, he's at least around for three more years.

I give my head a shake like I can clear the thoughts that have etched themselves there.

"I'm sorry." He gives me a small smile and closes the space between us to wrap his arms around me. I lean my head against his chest as he says, "I'm sure you're right, and all is okay. But it's true what you said, and I don't want you to worry."

I curl my arms around his back. "Thanks for going, then. But why did it take six hours? Did you go to the ER?"

"Walk-in clinic. But I already had an appointment for today as well." He twitches with an awkward chuckle and draws away from me, reaching to his back pocket and pulling out thick, folded papers.

I snatch and unfold them, jerking at their contents. "Whoa! You had a fertility appointment too? Why?"

Clearing his throat, he says, "I know you don't want babies yet, but I would rather know my health in that aspect now since I'm having all these issues. Out of all the sex I've had, it never resulted in any sort of pregnancy that I know about—so either I was lucky, I'm learning, or there's something wrong like my father."

"*Adopted* father. You've got no blood relation to him, so why would it matter?"

He shrugs. "It is still a possibility. You have an appointment for next week, too. I know things haven't been happening to you that *should* by your age."

I scowl at him. How the hell am I going to get out of that one?

XXXIX

The sticking of my clothes against me and the lack of moisture in my eyes and throat wake me in a panic that night.

Denendrius shifts against my back, and the feel of his scratchy sweater against my naked arm makes me swallow against the dryness of my throat. I peel my eyes open.

"Denendrius?" I throw my blanket back—soaked with sweat—and reach around to the side table for my glass of water. I gulp it back before asking, "Why is it so hot in here?"

"S-sorry, sweetheart. I turned the heat up. It's so cold."

The sound of his teeth chattering makes me flick the lamp on. He lies beside me, the blanket pulled tight around him as he shivers. His face and neck shine with sweat. Heat blows from the vent, and I wonder how high he cranked the furnace.

"What's wrong?" I whisper, sure I already know the answer, and that it has nothing to do with anything a doctor can help with.

"I can't get warm." He gazes up at me with bloodshot, dreary eyes.

"Are you okay?" I don't know what else to say. Maybe I want him to reassure me that everything's not falling apart.

"*No,*" he whines, sniffling. The look in his red-rimmed eyes is miserable.

I brush the hair out of his face, my heart feeling like a hummingbird with a clipped wing. "Oh, Denendrius . . ."

"*I'm so thirsty, Marianna.*"

"I know." I press my teeth into my bottom lip to stop it from quivering. "I know you are."

He squeezes his eyes closed, and the words that emanate from him are strained. "I keep dreaming about it. I can taste the blood in my dreams, feel the thirst and I wake up wanting it almost every night."

"Almost every night?" My brow furrows. "You mean, you've been having blood cravings every day? I thought everything was . . ." I thought everything was finally okay, that at most he had a few lingering issues that modern medicine might fix.

He sniffs and sits up, crossing his arms across his chest to hug himself. "Yes."

"Shit. You told me you weren't craving blood. Why did you lie?"

With gritted teeth, he inches off the bed until he's standing and slides out of his sweater. He dumps it on the carpet. "I didn't want to scare you."

I shake my head, not understanding. "Of all things, why would that scare me? Rayonne has human blood, and it helps."

Tears rush down his cheeks, his red eyes glossy. "You are right to worry about me snapping . . . I should not ignore it." His eyes bore into mine when he adds, "I killed the neighbor the night I unburied Allison."

His words slap the breath from me. "*What?*" I mouth.

Trembles run through him. "I—I woke up, and I was in her apartment with her dead at my feet." His voice rises an octave. "She was soaked with blood and so was I. It was in my mouth and nose. I ran out and down the block into the rain and remembered Allison."

I cover my mouth. How did we not hear any of it? *Is she still there?* "Oh my God. Why didn't you tell me?"

He stares at me with terror-stricken eyes. "I was petrified. I've never killed outside the arena before—" He flinches, like he's remembering, that *yes, he has.* Too many times to count.

"You can't ignore the cravings, then." I try to keep my breathing steady, hoping he'll stay calm if I do. "*You need blood. You can't ignore this. Let yourself work through it. It has to go away, eventually.*"

He crouches down. "I'm freezing. All I can think about is blood and cold."

I climb off the bed after him and I squat, resting my hand on his knee. "It's all psychological. You'll be okay."

A whine escapes him, and he shakes his head.

I tell him all the words I need to hear. "Yes, you will be. You have an addiction, okay? So you're having really shit cravings, but they'll pass. They'll get easier. You helped me get over my drug cravings, so I'll help you. It won't be like this forever. Maybe there's leftover shit making its way out of your system, right? Your brain probably hasn't fully adapted to being human again. It's only been a handful of weeks." I swallow a lump, lip quivering. "Give yourself more time. It'll get easier."

"I don't think that will help." He shudders and crosses his arms over his knees as he sits. "I think I know why I never took it."

I slip my hand out from under his. "The cure?"

"It's permanently marred me. I think I'm going to get worse." He leans his forehead on his crossed arms and groans in pain. "That's why I never got around to taking it. Every vampire I turned back only suffered."

My tone is careful. "What do you mean? Did you *force* vampires to turn human again?"

He nods against his arms. "I believe so. The results weren't good."

My mind whirs, and I think back to Rayonne's theory as to why he went after her clan. "All the vampires you supposedly kidnapped . . .?"

"Hundreds. I killed some in my frustrated search, others in my trials." He gasps for a breath. "So many young immortals died when I gave them the cure. I thought older clan leaders would have a better chance. Darkling, Child of Stars, old, young, it didn't seem to matter. I can't remember how long I took that vampire's blood and turned vampires human. Even the few that survived . . . most ended up grievously ill or mad. I can only recall a couple that were healthy enough both mentally and physically to go on as humans. And I only let them go because they remembered nothing, and I wanted to check on them later." He stares up at me with tormented eyes.

My heart beats so hard my chest hurts. "But you kept the blood?"

He sniffles. "No. I had that vampire turn another, and when I realized she produced a vampire with the same ability, I disposed of her only when the newborn's blood worked. It took a handful of tries, but the results were slightly better. I took as much blood as I could and killed her."

"That's heinous, Denendrius," I breathe.

His sobbing begins again. "I don't understand how I could do it all. I feel sick having the memory in me."

I take a deep breath. "Maybe the results do depend on which vampire they took the cure from, for whatever reason. That could explain why both you and Rayonne have similar issues, if Agatha gave her the backup blood." There's no happiness behind my paper smile. "That's good news, then . . . she's been human for a year and she's coping."

"She wants to turn back," he argues with a cry. "That doesn't make me believe she's coping well."

"She wants to turn back because she has no interest in being human," I correct. "She lived happily as a vampire. Do you *want* to be human?"

"Yes," he cries, nodding madly at me. "I do."

"Then that's the difference," I say while coaxing him back into bed.

"I have to take care of this." Denendrius sounds like he's in pain as he climbs back on the mattress.

I wrap my arms around him and rest his head against my chest, leaning us back against the plush headboard. "You'll get through it. You survived turning into a vampire, centuries of torture, turning back human . . . you can survive this too."

"I feel like I'm going crazy. *I have to take care of this.*" His tears soak my shirt.

"How? What else can you do?" The answer hangs above our heads like a guillotine.

"*I don't know.*" He shakes with sobs, hands gripping me.

"You'll be okay," I tell him while brushing my fingers through his hair, something inside me pleading with him, like I'm trying to convince him as much as I'm trying to convince myself. "You're having a bad night. The cravings will get better, and we'll go on living a normal human life and nothing bad will happen."

His cries make me wince. I clutch my arms around Denendrius like I can stop him from unraveling on my lap.

I feel a tear in my universe, a long gash down the white fabric of it. The black abyss beyond spoils the edges, and I fear this is a stain I won't be able to scrub clean. Doctors can help him with his human ailments, but what the fuck can I do about his cravings if they're so bad he already killed someone?

"You're going to be all right. I'm going to help you." I don't know how I expect my words to convince him when the panic of them is thick.

Still, I have to mend this, even if the stitch rips. All I can do is hope that more tears don't come. I know there's only so much thread on my spool.

I help him sit upright. Turning, I search for my knife in the bedside drawer. Taking it in my hand, I hold my breath as I sit back against the headboard. He lays his head on my lap, his hand clutching my leg.

"What are you doing?" Apprehension pushes his voice up an octave. "Are you worried I might hurt you? I promise I'm not going to kill more people. I didn't want to kill her."

I run my free hand over the side of his face, wetness collecting on my finger. "I'm not scared of you, Denendrius."

He rests his hand over mine.

"But maybe you need to keep tasting human blood. What it *really* tastes like. All you're doing is remembering what it tastes like from when you were a vampire. Maybe you need to keep reminding your brain about the reality of it until it gets the message."

There's not a hint of humor in his limp laugh. "I don't know if it works like that."

"You don't know. It could." My jaw sets as I rest the blade against the soft flesh of my forearm and apply pressure as I pull. I hiss in pain, red trailing after the silver blade.

"Don't hurt yourself—"

"It's too late. Drink." I curl my arm around him so the wound is mere inches from his mouth.

He whimpers. "I don't want to. What if it makes me crazier?"

"It won't. It didn't make Rayonne worse. Let's try," I plead. "I'm already bleeding all over."

"*Okay, Marianna.*" He presses his lips against the shallow and bright red slit in the meaty part of my forearm.

His tears bring my own. I let them run free, clenching my teeth against the pain as he drinks from me. When his teeth bite into my skin, I gasp and take my arm away from him.

"I'm sorry," he whispers, tears dried up. "It's reflex."

I inspect my arm and wipe my eyes. The surrounding skin is bruising, but it hardly bleeds anymore. "Did that help?"

He exhales a hot breath. "Yes."

"See," I whisper, raking my fingers through his sweaty hair and down his drenched back. "Go start the shower. I'll turn the heat down."

When the next day comes, it's like last night never happened.

I find Denendrius in the sunlit kitchen, nose buried in a cookbook as wrestling plays across the way from the living room TV.

I gasp when he looks up and shrink away from him. He's clean-shaven, his hair tied back in a low ponytail. "You shaved?"

"It was getting itchy," he explains with a grimace of a smile. "I will let it grow again, I promise. I know you like it."

There's a lump in my throat that I can't quite get down. It's been so long since I've seen him like this, I almost expect his accent to drop away and for him to scream at me.

"I'm making pancakes." He rummages through drawers, mumbling something in Latin with the word *whisk* thrown in.

"You don't usually cook. Are you sure you're feeling okay?" My steps are hesitant as I approach the island, my knees knocking together.

"I was thinking instead of sleeping last night. You take care of me so much, yet I rarely cook you anything. It's so lazy of me."

I clutch the edge of the counter, spine rigid. When he exclaims loudly upon finding the whisk, I flinch.

"What is wrong?" he asks, sweet brown eyes narrowing. "You look sick."

I stop a panicked breath before it gets all the way in. It's hard to handle him looking like this, even with his human eyes and warm skin.

With quick steps, I round the island and push his bowl of pancake mix aside.

"Kiss me," I demand, wedging myself between him and the counter while I stand on my tiptoes.

The humor drains from his face, something hungry waking up in him as his pupils expand, his breath so heavy that his chest pushes into mine. His breath is hot against my face until our lips collide.

He still tastes so human—like pancake batter.

We groan in unison, and he pushes harder against me. He rakes his fingers down my back as his mouth works against mine. I cup one hand around the back of his neck to pull him into me more and yank the tie out of his hair with the other.

The feel of his curls and waves cascading over my fingertips is so much better. Even with his lips lusting on mine, I manage a proper breath.

He breaks away and leans his cheek on the top of my head. "You were right again, Marianna. I feel so much better with blood."

I grin. "See? Maybe a little more and your brain will get the message."

"Perhaps. I love you so much, my Marianna."

"I love you too," I whisper, shoving the hair tie in my pocket.

Then, while he finishes cooking breakfast, I sneak upstairs and hide every goddamn elastic in the house.

I hide myself from the sight of him as he finishes preparing breakfast, curled up on the couch in the sitting room off the foyer, alone with nothing but my thoughts.

"Breakfast!" he calls, voice carrying down the hall. From the corner of my eye, I catch him climb the stairs. I can't bring myself to get up for breakfast yet, so I listen to him putter around upstairs, humming to himself.

"Marianna! Where are all the hair ties?" he shouts from upstairs in disbelief.

"Goblins took them!" A little smile sneaks onto my lips.

I close my eyes and listen to him rant in Latin, the honey of his lilting accent making me feel so warm.

His heavy steps sound down the stairs and he stops at the bottom and stares at me. "What are these goblins, Marianna?"

"I don't know. Why do you need a hair tie so bad?" I can hear the crack in my voice.

"For my hair." He holds his hand out expectantly.

Drawing my lips into my mouth, I try to hide the fact that my eyes are burning.

All humor vanishes from his face, and he sits down beside me. "You look so scared of me today, Marianna. Is it because of all I said last night? I don't understand why it makes you hate my hair, but I want to eat with it out of my face."

"You look like him," I whisper. "When you were a vampire."

He slouches as he forces out a sigh. "Ah. Well, same body. You will get used to it."

Tears collect on my bottom lashes, emotion so thick in my throat all I can do is nod. A few droplets shake free and run down my cheeks. I rub them away.

"Yes, it's ridiculous," I whisper. "It just . . . makes my heart hurt."

He lets out another breath and scoops my hand up. "No matter how I look, I will never hurt you. I will always be me, right now."

"I know," I whisper, leaning my head against his shoulder.

"I hope so," he says, giving my hand a squeeze. "Because I will love you forever."

After we eat fluffy, thick pancakes soaked in butter and syrup, we spend the rest of the morning locked in the bedroom together and hanging out around the house after. He follows me around like a needy puppy for the rest of the day, and when the next morning repeats similarly, I decide I need at least an hour without his hand touching some part of my body.

I ask if Jamie can come over after school in hopes it'll force him to do something by himself, and he reluctantly agrees to a few hours.

"She went home now," I tell him once I find him in the wine cellar sitting on the cold floor with an open bottle of wine in hand.

His gaze climbs me. "Good. I have you to myself again."

I scratch behind my ear. "Why don't you, I don't know, see you if you can make some friends too? That way you won't be lonely when I'm at school."

He smiles widely. "I won't be lonely. I will wait for you."

That's not healthy. "You need at least one friend, Denendrius." He opens his mouth and I add, "Not including me."

He grunts. "I have a friend, technically. Sergei."

I roll my eyes. "We don't even talk to him."

"Still counts—"

"No, it doesn't." I walk over and sit next to him, swiping the bottle of wine for a long sip. "Did you not have close friends in Rome?"

He purses his lips. "Eh . . . some friends, but not close, no."

"But you did when you were a vampire," I note, thinking of the vampire who saved him centuries ago when he tried to kill himself.

He puts a hand on my knee. "I don't want so many friends, Marianna. One at a time is best for me. It is not as easy for me to make friends like you can."

I sigh. "Fine. What are you doing down here, anyway?"

He motions to the walls of wine. "Admiring my collection."

I walk my fingers down his thigh and give him a peck on his cheek. "Well, get up, let's have dinner."

We order seafood, and Denendrius focuses intently on his salmon as we sit at the dining table across from one another with a glass of wine each.

With the candles our only light, short flames flickering at the top of the red pillars, the brown of his eyes looks black. Every time I look up from my food, my heart skips a beat. We've been so busy eating we haven't said much.

Sensing my stare, his eyes meet mine and he smiles. "What's wrong?"

I shake my head. "Nothing. I was thinking."

He wipes his mouth with his cloth napkin. "What about?"

I press the prongs of my fork into my bottom lip. "If you grew your facial hair out, you'd probably be less recognizable to vampires. Don't you think?"

"You miss it so much?" Denendrius smirks.

I shrug and set my fork down. "It's sexy. And, hey, if I cut my hair short, I won't be as recognizable either."

He gapes at me like I said I wanted to shave my hair and eyebrows off. The hardened look flashing through his eyes is far from playful. "Absolutely not. You are not to cut your hair!" he snarls.

My heart lodges itself in my throat. "I-I wasn't planning on it. I was joking."

He throws his napkin down. "That is not funny. Promise me you will not do anything so stupid to yourself."

"I promise." I hadn't even planned on it since I like my hair long. It was a random thought. "Sorry."

He takes a sip of his wine and blows a breath out. "Good. I would be *furious* with you."

There's no doubt in my mind that he would be.

I try to lighten the mood. "You're not allowed to cut your hair either, then," I say with a playful smile.

He rubs his chest, like he's recovering from a heart attack

over the very idea of me altering my appearance. "I will not, don't worry."

"Okay, so no haircut, but Jamie's mom wants to take us to get our nails done tomorrow after lunch. What are your thoughts on that?"

He takes a bite of fish, chewing as he stares at me and thinks. "Like how?"

"A little color. Some nail polish. I don't want fake nails." I bat my eyelashes a little.

"That would be pretty." His eyes crinkle in the corners when he smiles, butterflies fluttering in my stomach. "I think Jamie is a good friend for you."

"Thanks." His approval sets me at ease. I straighten in my chair and pick my fork back up, sliding some lettuce around my half-empty plate.

He's cheery again, and after dinner we curl up on the couch together, fireplace flickering below the romantic thriller we watch. We're halfway through when there's a knock on the door.

Denendrius's entire body tenses against mine, and his eyes drop to his lap.

XL

"Open it for me." His demand is gentle, and he takes a shuddery breath in.

"It's . . . it's nighttime. What's going on?" I'm so nauseous I almost gag.

He looks weighted to the couch, every part of him stiff aside from his chest. It lifts and lowers in heavy breaths. "Please, Marianna. Give me a moment."

I'm jittery as I leap off the couch and race to the door. My hand shakes as I open it, and I break out in a cold sweat at the sight of Sergei.

"What the fuck is Sergei doing here?" I holler, my voice cracking.

He buries his hands in the pockets of his bomber jacket as he comes and looks at me with utter pity. "Oh my." Sergei heaves out a breath. "I'm sorry. You must talk to him about this."

It feels like my heart falls through me to the floor, the

strings of it tangling around my legs and almost pulling me down with it. I catch myself on the wall. "*No.*"

He's here to turn Denendrius back, isn't he?

Denendrius emerges from the hallway with heavy steps. "Go upstairs, Marianna."

"You've had days to tell her, Denendrius—"

"Upstairs!" Denendrius barks.

I spin around and race up them, my sight so blurred I almost trip. Denendrius follows me into the bedroom.

The door shuts, and I twist to face him, tears soaking my cheeks. "*Days?*"

He holds his hand out, like he can stop the flood ready to crash out of me. "Marianna—"

I clasp my hands together in front of me and hold them tight against my chest to stop my heart from falling out and shattering on the floor. "You can't do this, Denendrius. Stay human, like you always wanted, like you killed *hundreds* for. Don't turn back into *him*. I'll do anything if you don't bring him back."

"I'll still be like this," he promises. "Everything will be the same. You will go to school, have your friends—nothing will change."

I shake my head, tears cascading down my cheeks. "You can't promise that. You will remember every little thing again like it happened to you. If you turn back, *everything* changes. Don't bring him back. Please don't do that to me."

"I'm not asking your permission for this, Marianna. I have decided," he says sternly.

"You can't do this to me!" I shriek, slamming my fists into his chest. "You *can't*! You were supposed to give me my life back, pay me back for all the shit you did with something better!" I grab fistfuls of his shirt as he looks across the room, his eyes wide with a wet sheen over them. "Look at me," I wail. "You fucking look at me!"

He drops his eyes instead, staring right through my hands. "I'm sorry," he mumbles.

I unclench my hand from his shirt, wind up, and slap him in the side of his head.

He flinches and grabs my hand, holding it in his fist. "Marianna, I love you—"

I tear my hand away from him, emotion clogging my throat as I fight to get words out. "If you love me, you won't do this. You are breaking my heart all over again. What do I have to do to make you *stay*?"

"I'm not going anywhere, Marianna," he says. "The only thing that will change is my mortality."

"Don't you understand? That alone changes everything." I wrap my arms around myself, face scrunching as I pull in a strangled breath. "You're a fucking monster," I cry. "You're a monster if you bring him back."

"I'll still be me—"

I whip my head side to side. "No, you won't. Denendrius, you can't handle vampirism. You'll lose yourself all over again, I know it. You're damning yourself as much as you are me if you turn back. You practically *killed* me to get this"—I reference the room, our *life*—"and now that we're here, it's not good enough for you?" I pull in a breath and shriek, "You are such a selfish prick!"

"You are not the one suffering right now, Marianna!" he snarls, pointing a finger in my face.

"No," I whisper. "I'm not. But if you do this, I will be."

He lowers his hand, fists balling up at his sides. "I can't you give you the world if I'm not in it, Marianna. I might die."

My lip curls. "I don't believe this is about your physical health for one second. You haven't even had an MRI yet. Nothing says you're dying. You'd be a coward to turn back before at least allowing medical intervention. You're a fucking *addict*, and you can't get your fix. That's what all this is about—"

He shakes his head roughly as I speak. "No."

My entire body burns with fury. "You gave me shit for over-dosing, and here you are! Literally off to *kill yourself* so you can get your high. You are a goddamn fucking hypocrite."

Denendrius's lips tremble, his head falling forward as his shoulders shake. "I can't stop it," he cries. "The thoughts torment me. I killed the neighbor for blood, Marianna, and I can hardly remember doing it. What if one day that's you? Or our children? I am worsening as the days pass."

"You think it was any better when you were a vampire?" A sick chuckle rolls out of me. "Denendrius, it was *worse.* Can you not remember? It was so bad you were drinking vampire blood! You threw a hissy fit and stabbed me, used to beat me blue for having a bad attitude!"

He rubs the back of his neck as he sniffles. "It will be different this time. Fresh."

"You're a blood fiend," I spit. "And you want to be a newborn again? How exactly is this going to work?"

"It will be okay," he whispers to the floor. "We will figure it out."

I scoff. "That's if you even survive turning back. Have you considered that yet?"

"I'll survive. Sergei and I have a strong connection. The odds are in my favor."

"This is impulsive," I tell him. "You—"

"Stop trying to convince me! No more questioning me!" he bellows. "I marked you. You should not be meeting me with such defiance!"

How dare he. I spit at his feet, and he takes a step back, face contorting with disgusted fury.

"You want to pull that card?" I growl. "If Rayonne knows anything, then the mark is the whole reason for this fight. I'm simply trying to protect you from yourself. I *know* that this is a massive fucking mistake!"

He takes a step back toward me, the anger melting from his brown eyes. "I'm sorry." Wetness wells on his bottom lashes. "I truly am. But I have only so many choices. We are safe now, Marianna, and Sergei will help me. You are scared, is all. I am too. But all will be okay. I will *never* hurt you again, no matter if I am human or not."

"What do you want?" I sob.

He tilts his head, not understanding.

"You want a baby? Will that change your mind? You want me to go to that appointment? Move it to tomorrow." I bite down on my bottom lip, tears dripping down to my chin. Being an unwilling mother is far less terrifying than what could wait for me if he turns back.

He holds my face in his hands, and I memorize the warmth of them. "We will still have our own babies, Marianna. I have taken care of that."

"I don't care. Don't go back downstairs." I move my hands to the belt of his jeans. "You're not going back downstairs."

He doesn't resist as I undo his belt. It's like a switch, I see it in his eyes. He's completely entranced by that hungry monster inside him.

His breath turns frantic, eyes locking on mine as his hands fall from my face and to his sides.

"If you turn back," I say while unzipping his pants, "you won't get to touch me without hurting me for so long."

I grab his hand and lure him back toward the bed. He gives me a gentle shove and I land with my butt on the mattress. Denendrius climbs on after me. His lips are vicious on mine as he crawls over me. I hook my arms around his neck as he yanks my pants off, his heavy panting making me quiver.

He holds my legs apart and pulls his pants down enough to uncover himself. I bite down on my lip as he starts, his breath and motions frenetic as he rocks his hips into mine. His hand is feverish against the sweaty dread layered on my skin, and he holds my face. With desperate lips on mine, it's like he's taking every last kiss he can get.

Tears form a constant stream from my eyes, something sharp constricting my heart with each beat.

My arms are vises around him, muscles hot. "Please don't do this to me," I choke through a sob.

"I love you," he breathes against my lips.

My breath staggers, voice higher as I repeat, "Don't do this."

Denendrius pushes sweaty hair out of my face and kisses away salty tears that are quickly replaced. "I love you, Marianna."

"*Please.*"

My body aches with grief, and even as we touch it feels as though this is already a memory.

I continue to beg, clutching at him and hoping I can screw his head back on straight.

He's finished too soon, kissing me as he pulls my pants back up, then his.

I grip fistfuls of his shirt as he climbs off the bed. "Stay, please. I'm fucking begging you."

"I'm sorry," he whispers, fingers gliding over my cheekbone before he pries my fingers off his shirt. "But I've made up my mind. I'm doing this for us."

"No." I lock my fingers around another section of his shirt. "You're doing this for you."

Instead of trying to wrench free from my grip, he hooks his arm around my waist and hoists me off the bed. I thrash uselessly under his arm as he carries me out of the room against his side.

"Where are you taking me!" I screech as he hauls me down the stairs, unbothered by my efforts.

Sergei gets off the couch in the sitting room as we come down, and I kick at him as he nears.

"Don't change him back!" I beg as Denendrius carries me

into the laundry room and to the basement stairs, kicking at the walls as we descend them, so hard that Denendrius has to catch himself on the railing. Sergei's boots thud down the stairs behind us. "Don't do it, you compliant piece of shit! Would you suck him off too if he asked you? You're a fucking vampire, what's wrong with you!"

I try to grab hold of the handrail, but Denendrius slaps my fingers away from it.

"Marianna, stop," Denendrius begs. "There is no reason to act like this."

When he turns toward the wine cellar past the pool table, my heart leaps. "You better not lock me in there!" I screech, wriggling harder.

Sergei opens the wrought-iron door for him, and Denendrius swings me through it and roughly places me on a makeshift bed of blankets at the end of the stone room. He grabs an open bottle of wine waiting by the pillow before I can straighten and, with a firm grip under my jaw, gives me a long kiss that I don't even get to enjoy before he tilts my head back and forces wine down my throat.

The taste of garlic cuts through the wine, and I gag. It burns over my tongue and down to my stomach. He doesn't let me go as I fight and fail to twist my head out of his grip, though he slows the flow of the vomit-inducing concoction.

"Swallow it," Denendrius coaxes. "It will help deter me from biting you when I wake."

I try to pry his hand off my face until his fingers tighten. Tears run into my ears as I gulp the wine back, half choking on it.

When he pulls it away, I fall forward, gasping for breath with stinging wine dripping from my lips. I wipe my mouth with the back of my hand and cough.

He takes a spray bottle from where it's stuffed beside a bottle of wine and shuffles back a step. When he aims the bottle at my head, I squeeze my eyes shut for a moment as wetness and the thick stench of garlic settle over my hair.

"Ugh!" I grit my teeth and smack at him, flinching when I feel moisture on my neck and collarbones, my bare arms soaked next.

"It needs to hurt me if I touch you," he explains, heavy sadness in his eyes. "There needs to be something to stop me."

"Kiss me now, then." I wrap my fingers around his arm, nails digging into his hot skin. He tears out of my grip before the rivers of garlic water running down my wrists can make it to him. "I want one more. The last one wasn't enough."

"I can't," he whispers, though his tongue runs over his bottom lip like he wishes he could taste me once more too. "I don't want garlic on me when I wake up."

I move my face toward his, and he jerks back. The pain in his eyes makes tears form in my own.

"This is going to hurt horribly, Marianna," he starts as he stands up and steps away from me. "You're going to hear things. Please don't break out of here. This is the safest place for you right now."

"Tell me you love me," I beg, refusing to blink so I can collect one more second of those sweet brown eyes on me.

"I love you," he murmurs, and I memorize the cadence of his voice.

Will he still speak this way when he's a vampire? Or will his accent dampen with the return of his memories?

"Tell me again," I cry as he backs up and hooks his fingers on a wrought-iron vine in the door's design.

"*I love you.*"

"Now, please, act like it," I whisper, biting down on my bottom lip.

The door clangs into place and I whimper.

"Forever," he promises from the other side. "I will love you forever, *amica mea.*"

When his warm hand drops to his side, he stares at me for an excruciating moment before standing back to let Sergei spray the bars down with garlic water as he coughs.

"Please," I whisper. "Denendrius . . ."

But he walks away.

Every hope and dream I thought I had for Denendrius and me dies along with him.

I mourn harder than I ever have before—for the past I despised, for the human future I wanted to salvage—and for that, I want to hate him as much as I hate myself.

I should have done more to convince him. I failed him.

Shoving the pillow into my face, I let a scream out from the deepest parts of me. I kick against the floor with my bare feet, shrieking until my lungs are burning and my brain feels like it's going to scramble.

The only thing that halts my shrieks is *his*.

My muscles are as frozen as the breath in my throat. I listen to the wails of anguish that echo through the house as the venom tears through him, my heart pounding in my ears. There are sporadic thuds against the floor above, and I can't help but imagine the blood that must run from Denendrius as he thrashes.

Time stretches on forever, and Sergei must have to gag him to keep him from waking the entire neighborhood, as his Latin pleading turns muffled.

My ears ring when silence crashes over the house. The room spins with a sharp pain through my head, and I feel the hard floor catch me as my vision leaves.

Sergei leans over me and jostles me back into consciousness.

"It's done," he informs me. "He will wake up."

There's not enough spools of thread to mend this rip in my universe.

I press the heel of my hand against my forehead, nothing left in me to cry. "I know." And I do, I can sense he's alive as easily as I know I am. "I think I blacked out."

"You did. I heard your head thud against the floor the moment after his heart stopped."

A thought crosses my mind. "Wait . . . he died?"

Sergei must know where my thoughts are leading as he says, "Yes, and you're still marked."

I waver as I sit and rub my sore eyes. "Can I come out now?" My voice is hoarse.

"No. I only came to check on you. I don't know when he'll wake up, so it's best you stay here."

I frown. "When can I come out? Do I have to stay in here until he's not so . . . newborn-y?"

Sergei's pout is almost mocking. "You will stay here until he wakes, and at least until he's fed a bit. I'll live here with you two until I know you're safe."

"Can I at least go pee and get a snack to bring back?" I push my bottom lip out.

His jaw sets and he inhales sharply. "Be quick."

The room spins when I stand and he holds a hesitant hand ready to catch me. My feet feel leaden as I drag them across the wine cellar.

"Can I see him?" I ask as we climb the stairs. "*Please?*"

He looks over his shoulder at me, eyes hard stones. "As we walk by."

My sore lungs force rapid breaths in and out of me, my heart bruised from slamming against my aching ribs. I can't feel my legs—it's like I'm floating—as I follow Sergei out of the laundry room and to the foyer.

My eyes immediately land on Denendrius in the sitting room. He lies across the couch on his side, his crimson eyes lifeless and bloody as he stares blankly across the room. A limp arm hangs off the couch with his open hand on the floor. Waves of brown hair cascade across his cheek. Blood trails from the corners of his closed mouth and from his ears. There's a patch of blood on the carpet where he must have been lying at some point.

The image brands itself into my brain. He still looks like my Denendrius.

I can't help the urge to run to him, to wipe the blood from his soft lips. I want to tangle my fingers in the silky curls and waves of his hair. Would he still be warm for now? My foot lifts off the ground, but Sergei grabs my elbow.

"You can't touch him," he warns. "You're covered in garlic."

I hang my head as he pushes me along down the hall and stands outside the open bathroom door while I pee. Afterward, he lets me pick a couple snacks and a drink before walking me back down the hall.

"Do you want a book, or something?" he asks.

I shake my head and give Denendrius another long look, waiting for a twitch of his lip so I can see if he has fangs too.

"Go on, I'll take care of him," Sergei says, nudging me along while coughing at the smell of me.

My legs are so weak that I barely make it back to the wine cellar. I collapse on the pile of blankets as he locks the door again.

"I would keep you company," he starts, "but I have to stay beside Denendrius for when he wakes."

"Okay." I don't want his company anyway.

I lay on the thick blankets. Through the dim light, I trace my gaze over the wrought-iron leaves and vines making up the door.

I feel tangled in a nightmare with no way out.

I have no way to quantify the time that passes as I sit through the silence that weighs on the house.

Sergei comes down in a moment when he must think I'm sleeping and sets a glass on the other side of the door within reach. I grab it once I scrounge up the effort to move, no thought in my mind to what it could be until I find myself staring down into a small portion of blood.

My eyes flutter when I lift it to my nose. It's Denendrius's.

I gulp it back and feel my nerves ignite at the familiar taste of his blood. In that moment, with the taste of him flowing over the back of my tongue, I decide to continue loving Denendrius. I believe his promise to stay the same.

It's not as if I have another option.

Soon, I'm straining to hear the pained groans and desperate cries that carry downstairs from Denendrius. But I can't make out a word between them.

"*No!*" Sergei calls frantically. "Denendrius, no! You'll kill her!"

There's a scuffle, and—

Denendrius stands on the other side of the door, staring at me with unblinking, blistering red eyes. He falls into a squat with an exhale.

"Denendrius?" I squeak, pushing myself back against the wall.

Tears trail down his bloodied cheeks from his tormented eyes. "You were right," he rasps, his accent still intact. "This is so much worse. I had forgotten."

"It'll be—"

He nods and flinches as Sergei appears beside him. "Yes, we'll figure it out." His teeth chatter, fangs out, as he shudders with emotion and thirst. "But I think I'm going to regret this forever."

I choke on a sob, and he's gone in a blink, more frantic chaos ensuing upstairs.

XLI

The hours pass, but there's no way to tell how many. There's no sun, no proper change in temperature. The wine cellar feels like it's cut off from the rest of the world. It doesn't help either that a bulb burns out.

My eyes snap open, heart rocketing from the pit of my stomach and imploding inside my chest when the wine cellar door creaks open.

I see his brown hair through the blur of tears in my eyes and bound across the space between us, no weight in the thought that he could rip my throat open. "*Denendrius!*"

When I throw myself against him, I realize my mistake instantly. Instead of my head landing square in the center of his chest, short facial hair scrapes against my temple.

Jolting back like I've received a shock of electricity, I swiftly scrub the tears from my eyes and take in the stranger. His deep brown hair is wavy, stopping at his shoulders, a black bandana tied around his head like some pirate. His beard and mustache are trimmed short, his thick eyebrows low above his black and wary eyes.

Tripping backward, I catch myself on a wooden section of the wall of wine. "You're not Denendrius."

His hands—a gold or silver ring on every other finger—lift tentatively, like he's ready to grab me if I make a sudden move.

"It's okay, Marianna. My name's Mateo," he says, a Spanish accent I'm not used to hearing lingering on his words.

"Denendrius is coming back for me," I warn. "He's a vampire now."

His chest lowers as he exhales and nods. "Good. We'll all wait."

"All of who?" I breathe.

As he takes a careful step toward me, his hesitant hands inch closer. "We're not here to hurt you—"

"Wait, how did you find us?" I squeak, cringing away from him.

His head tilts. "Do you not remember? You contacted two bounty hunters through a forum post claiming to know them and asking for help. All the information led us to your friends in the apartment you mentioned."

I feel the heat drain from my face and the room swims. "Alaire's alive?" Two waves—happiness and dread—collide against one another inside me.

"No." He swallows, a flash of loss in his dark eyes. "But they had a fail-safe system set up. When their system went inactive with a tip logged—yours, of course—it was rerouted to a third party who transferred the message to us in Romania. Don't worry, your friends are safe. We brought them too."

"Romania? V-Viorel?" My hearing sounds like TV static. The whole room tilts.

"*Yes, Marianna, I'm one of his most trusted men.*"

I did this.

This is all my fault.

I'm detached from my body, everything a hazy blur as he walks me up the stairs. There's no use fighting him. I know I won't win.

Wetness spills over my cheeks, regret bubbling like acid in my stomach.

I'm blind with panic by the time I reach the top of the stairs. It's amazing I don't trip down them considering I can't feel my body.

There's a flurry around me as we reach the laundry room. I can hear Carol's frantic voice while Derek reassures her, under the hum of what sounds like a dozen men.

Rayonne's voice cuts through it all. *"I'm so sorry, Marianna. You were right to question me. Viorel's men didn't even know who Agatha was. She and her higher-ups lied to recruit people—"*

My brain shuts down. There's so many streams of thought in my head that they all collide into one torrential flood that pulls me under.

I gasp and half-shriek when cold water washes over my head, and I snap to. I made it to the master bathroom somehow to where I stand now, drenched in my clothes in the shower.

Mateo stands outside the shower. "I'm sorry, Marianna, but I told you if you didn't undress I would have to put you in fully clothed. I can't have you around my men reeking of garlic, impairing them when they have to deal with Denendrius. And we certainly can't bring you on a plane to the castle like this."

I clutch my arms around myself and shudder.

"Is it too cold?" he asks.

"Yes, it's too fucking cold!" I screech, the temperature cutting through my clothes.

He points to the tap and glides the glazed shower door closed. "You'll have to adjust it yourself. Take your clothes off, please, and thoroughly wash your hair and body."

After cranking the heat higher, I peel my garlic-tainted clothes off. I can't bring myself to take issue with the fact it's a man in here forcing me to bathe when it feels like the whole world is ending.

My whole body vibrates with terror as I scrub myself head to toe.

"I'm done." I hiccup a sob.

Mateo clears his throat. "No, you're not. I can still smell it on your skin. Wash properly this time."

I wipe tears with the back of my wet hand and add more soap to my loofah. My scrubbing is so vigorous that my skin is sore to the touch.

"How many men are there downstairs?" I choke out.

"Eight of us, not including Derek."

A sob rolls out of me.

Denendrius doesn't stand a chance.

"You need eight men for Denendrius? He left there human." Bubbles trail down my sore flesh.

"He's a trained fighter with a screw loose, Marianna," he says matter-of-fact. "I've seen him fight with a sword firsthand before I sank his ship, and we had to assume the worst would happen."

I drop my loofah aside and pick up my shampoo again. "How did you find us here?"

There's a long silence in the bathroom, the droning sounds of chatter downstairs carrying up.

The words *steel coffin* from one man downstairs have my heart hammering so hard again that I have to grasp the shower wall with one hand.

Mateo sighs. "There's an active police case on you, Marianna. You're a missing person, and someone called a tip hotline after suspecting they saw you in a liquor store last week in this area. The photo they provided was undoubtedly you and Denendrius. Rich area . . . makes sense for him. We were keeping tabs on the case, of course, and thought it wise to check this city. Plus, he made quite a mess tonight in his newborn frenzy. Cleared out three houses down the block and tried to cover his tracks with arson. We heard it on our police scanner. It wasn't too difficult to narrow it down to this house with your scent. Whoever turned him back and lost control of him is going to be very sorry. Not as sorry as whoever turned him human in the first place, though."

My knees buckle, my foot slipping against the tile floor of the shower.

Why didn't I hear sirens? How could Sergei let this happen?

Everything was supposed to be perfect.

I may as well be dead now.

"Blood aside, you smell fine now," Mateo says.

My fingers are numb when I turn the shower off and catch the towel he throws on me. Once I'm dry, I swap the towel for a clean pair of clothes brought in by someone with heavy boots.

Climbing out of the shower, I stare at Denendrius's straight razor on the counter two feet away and think about how Denendrius said we're better off killing ourselves if we're captured than suffering through what waits for us in Romania. My fingers twitch, the sight of it entrancing me.

It's a far less terrifying option than belonging to Viorel.

Mateo snatches the blade and sets it on the top shelf in the closet.

"This one is on suicide watch!" he calls down.

"That far gone?" a man responds from somewhere in the house.

Mateo stares at me. "Is that his plan? Murder-suicide?"

I can't manage a word through my breathlessness.

Mateo shadows my every move as we step into the bedroom, like he thinks I'm going to grab the nearest object and plunge it into my brain.

But I know nothing can get me out of this situation. I can't run, and they're full of venom to bring me back from whatever painful escape I attempt.

"Thank God you're okay," Carol says. She's free from her casts already somehow, and her green eyes are bright as she hovers close to me with an empty bag in one hand. "Let's get you packed. We're all going to Romania together, honey. You're safe now. What do you want to bring? There's enough room for a few bags."

She doesn't have a clue. I suppose I can't blame her for her naivety. It must be simpler than accepting your niece is about to be taken by a powerful vampire king, and that you'll be eaten.

Hopefully, her blood mark saves her. Would Viorel respect another vampire's mark, so long as they weren't someone like Denendrius?

"Carol, I've been okay, I promise. Denendrius just had a little trouble." A shaky breath leaves me. "I signed up for the school down the street—" My voice cracks and my tears spill over. I can't get a breath in.

It's all over. *My life is over.*

At least I tried.

"Oh, honey . . ." Carol murmurs.

As she takes a step toward me, Mateo puts his hand out to stop her from coming closer and gives her a warning look like he thinks I might attack them.

"I'm not leaving," I sob.

"You are," Mateo says gently, "But you can either come with some of your belongings or have nothing at all."

"Do you want us to pack for you?" Carol tries to step around Mateo's outstretched arm.

"Don't touch my fucking stuff!" I shriek. "I'm not going anywhere!"

Carol tries to bypass Mateo again as Rayonne rushes in—black lace dress flitting around her—and grabs her arm to pull her back.

He huffs and stands between Carol and me. "You must stop

trying to interfere. We went over this many times on the way here."

"She's my niece," Carol argues. "She's not going to hurt me. It's bad enough none of you let me try contacting her."

"Enough. Don't doubt it for one more second," he tells her, taking the bag from her and holding it out to me. "Go on, take some things. You will wish you had later."

I wipe at my eyes, not sure what they expect of me. They want to rip me out of my home and expect me not to get violent?

A tall blond-haired man in his fifties pauses in front of the room and in Spanish says, "Should I get an update to him now?"

They must not expect me to understand them, as Mateo responds in Spanish with, "Please. Tell him he might not want to waste time prepping his chamber. She's so far gone it'll be like locking a feral animal down there with him. See if they dealt with who's all making wagers so she can go into general population."

The blond man laughs and, again in Spanish, says, "Who are you more worried about? Him, or her? I'm sure he has enough patience left for her."

"Are you talking about Viorel?" I demand, a quiver in my voice shaking loose a sob. "You're all fucking evil," I yank the bag from Mateo. "I didn't do anything and you're going to hand me over to Viorel to be tortured because he's got a hate hard-on for Denendrius."

Mateo blinks at me. "Nothing gets by you, yeah?"

"What's he been telling you?" Carol says before Mateo can get another word in. "Whatever it was, it's all lies. You're going to be perfectly safe, Marianna."

"No. Denendrius warned me all about Viorel," I spit. "He's *trying to protect me*. He loves me and doesn't want me to suffer."

"Denendrius has a skewed perception of Viorel," is all Mateo says.

Carol gives me a small smile before her lips part to speak.

"You are dumb for trusting all these vampires," I interrupt.

"Pack, *now*," she demands, sounding much more like a parent than I'm used to.

I grit my teeth and humor them. "Yeah, sure! Let me pack like we're off to fucking Enchanted Land!"

Storming to the closet—Mateo practically up my ass still—I shove my favorite tracksuit in the bag with a handful of random tops and pants. I dump my entire drawer of expensive lacy underwear into the bag for dramatic effect.

"Is this packed good enough for you?" I punt my bag out of the closet.

"Don't take it personally," Rayonne whispers to Carol. "It's the mark. I'm sure she'll apologize later."

"Like how you tried to apologize for messing everything up!" I screech at her. "What was that shit back there about Agatha having no connection to Viorel?"

Her blink is slow as she exhales and shakes her head. "I'll discuss it with you once you're *you* again."

I angrily zip my bag as the rest of the vampires monitor the tense house. Derek's voice drifts up from downstairs—they must have cleaned the garlic off one of the doorways to let him in—but I can't see how he'll be any help to them.

"I can't leave without that." I point to a small wooden chest that peeks out from under the bed.

Inside it are all the sentimental items I've collected and a few strategically hidden diamonds. It's full of pictures and videos of Denendrius and me over the past few weeks, and all the ones of us when I was a child as well.

Mateo calls for another vampire, who whisks my stuff away.

Will I ever really have a use for any of it? Maybe I will, if Viorel plans on keeping me locked in his room like a pet.

Mateo guides me back downstairs to the sitting room and forces me to sit on the far side of the couch. He crosses his legs beside me, angling his body a tad in front of me as he wraps a cold arm around my back to keep me in place, his leg jutting out in front of mine. Carol and Rayonne sit on the couch across from us on the far side of Derek.

He looks so normal as he sits there with concerned eyes wandering over me. If I didn't know better, I'd have no idea Ziggy turned him. Part of me wants to ask him how he's coping, but since they're all here to ruin my life, I keep my inquiries about his to myself.

Derek says nothing to me either, but by the way his lips keep parting, I can tell he has plenty on his mind. I don't want to hear any of it.

My tears are endless and I've got such a horrible headache that it only fuels them. I clutch the sides of my head in my hands, the sounds of the house muffled.

All I can hope is that Denendrius doesn't come back as much as I want him to rescue me. He once said he'd never risk his life for mine, that if it came down to him or me, he'd choose himself. But he came to rescue me before he was turned back, so maybe that was a lie to make me feel bad too.

Would he risk endless suffering for me?

I want to be important enough for the answer to be yes despite it being such a selfish wish.

"Think he'll show up in the next few hours?" a man says from the foyer.

From upstairs, another says, "She's in so much distress I'm surprised he hasn't already—"

Glass shatters in one of the spare rooms upstairs.

He's come back for me.

I'm torn between the grief of that truth, and the warmth of the fact that he's risking torture to protect me.

He must really love me.

Too much happens far too quickly for my brain to register it all. Mateo's hand locks around my mouth as vampires vanish from the room. I can't scream to warn him of anything.

There are echoing thuds, pained outcries and furious snarls.

Then, Mateo's hand is wrapped around the blade of a knife as its tip sticks through my shirt.

I don't feel the prick. My whole body is numb at the sight of Denendrius standing in the opening of the room, his bloody fingers clutched around the handle of a blade buried deep in his own heart.

Despair seeps from his crimson eyes as they lock with mine. There's more terror in them than I thought a man like him could ever harbor. His rapid, desperate breath passes through his bloodied, fanged teeth as I watch him accept his fate.

The blade never reached my heart, yet it splits in two.

"I tried, I'm sorry. I can't let them take you without me." His voice cracks, so much pain rolling out of him. He rips the blade out of his chest, dark crimson soaking his green shirt. His hand vibrates as he lowers his arm to his side and drops the knife on the hardwood in surrender.

I blink, and he's thrashing on the hardwood beneath four vampires, his pleading words leaving him through whines. Denendrius's pained shriek makes me grit my teeth when they jam a soaked cloth in his mouth to silence him, his lips blistering on contact.

They're a tangle of hasty limbs. I can't get a grasp of who's doing what to who through their speed, just that Denendrius is failing his fight for freedom.

He's a newborn now, weaker than all of them.

"Come on now, you sick fuck. Quit fighting." The vampire half laughs as they drag him to the stairs with his arms bent behind his back, getting him up them despite how he kicks at each step.

My eyes are unblinking as I stare at what few bottom steps I can see, my ears hyperfocused on every grunt and wail that leaves Denendrius while they haul him to the second floor.

"Wouldn't it be easier to stake him?" Derek says.

Mateo holds me tighter, like he can anticipate all the thoughts I'm having about grabbing a gladius from where Denendrius mounted them above the fireplace to cut through everyone.

"No," he says. "They're going to bleed him until he's too weak to get loose. Viorel wants him conscious for everything. He was appalled to hear someone turned him human in the first place. He's wanted him for a long time, but he's never been desperate enough for a risky move like that."

I suck in a breath, my exhale a shrill scream. *"Denendrius!"*

Mateo clamps his hand over my mouth again.

"Hold him still already so I can slit his throat," someone says upstairs. Flesh hits flesh and then, *"Quit fucking moving!"*

There's clanging against the floor and the Jacuzzi upstairs. A long and muffled shriek comes from Denendrius before it's abruptly cut off by the sound of gushing liquid against the bottom of the tub.

There's laughter from the men upstairs, so many jeering words I can't distinguish anything else.

An image of Denendrius bent over the Jacuzzi conjures up in my brain. He's completely at the mercy of the men around him as they slit his throat and fill the bottom with red, his legs kicking out against the floor.

My eyes flutter and if it weren't for Mateo's hold on me, I'd slip onto the floor. Tears stream from my eyes and land on his hand.

"I know it's hard for you," Mateo murmurs in my ear. "But this is what he deserves. The world will be a much better place if he's not free."

When I hear a gurgle, I gasp against Mateo's palm. My ears

ring, my blood pressure plummeting so hard it's a miracle I stay conscious.

I wish I wouldn't though. I wish I was blind to it all when two men come down the stairs, blood splatter across their shirts and wicked smiles on their lips. They're out the front door and back in mere seconds, dragging in a steel box—a rectangular coffin, really—through the foyer and slamming the door.

They unlatch massive locks down its side, metal hinges groaning as they open it. They gag and wince, and even my eyes burn from the stench of garlic wafting from the box. The metal inside has a wet sheen over it.

"Hurry up!" one of the men holding the steel lid hollers up the stairs, his black eyes squinting against the fumes.

"Jesus Christ," Derek breathes, wide eyes glued to the stairway. He's got a much better view from where he sits than I do. "Marianna, don't look."

I can't help it. I have to see him.

Shoes thud down the steps as they carry Denendrius's limp body down. My stomach turns at the sight of him.

There's a deep and gory gash in his throat, up his wrists, and through various other arteries. His red eyes are half-lidded and staring into the abyss. There's no sign he's breathing, that he knows what's happening around him.

He doesn't fight them—though I'm not sure he could—as they lay him in the box and kick the lid closed before latching it again.

"All right," Mateo says. "Let's hit the road, yeah?"

I writhe as Mateo pulls me from my seat, biting and kicking at him until he's tucking me under his arm and clamping his hand painfully tight over my mouth.

He carries me out into the empty air of the night behind Viorel's men as they move the steel box to the back of a large van waiting in front of the house. Five of them disappear into it, the rest moving with us to another parked in front of it.

There's nothing I could do to save Denendrius or me, even if I managed to tear free.

Still, I fight so viciously when Mateo tries loading me onto a gray seat next to another vampire—Carol, Derek, and Rayonne climbing onto a bench between the front and back one without a second thought—that I knock myself unconscious on the metal door frame.

My tears are endless, my body wedged between two vampires in the back seat of the van as we barrel down the highway. A plane awaits us. It's so dark outside the heavily tinted windows it's like we're traveling through a suffocating void.

I lean against Mateo's side, trying to keep air between me and the vampire to my right, who sits rigidly beside me. I can't help but think he wants to tear my throat out.

"I hate all of you," I whisper while I stare at the headlights of the vehicle carrying Denendrius in the rearview mirror visible between Carol and Rayonne's heads.

All three bodies in the seat ahead twist to face me.

Derek sighs and says, "You're going to be so proud of yourself when Viorel breaks Denendrius's mark, Marianna. You saved yourself and you can't even see it. The fact you could even write for help like that . . ."

Rayonne chimes in with, "He's going away forever. You are the reason we captured one of the most sought-after vampires. *You* did that. I know it seems like a bad thing right now, but you have no idea."

Everything in me screams. If I had the energy left, I might lash out again, but I don't even have it in me to cry. "I did this to him." My strained voice barely makes it out of me. "He loves me, and I did this to him."

If I had never written that tip, how much more time would we have gotten together?

Carol gapes at me. "Marianna, he tried to *kill you* back there. If Mateo had been a fraction of a second slower, you would be dead."

I would be better off dead than barreling toward whatever hell waits for me in Romania.

"Denendrius did this to himself," Derek says. "We already knew you were in Bellevue—it was only a matter of time before we tracked down the right house. Maybe, if he didn't drink through three families, he wouldn't have gotten himself caught so quickly." Derek shakes his head. "He doesn't love you, Marianna. He would rather you die with him than live happy without him."

"Denendrius loves me," I hiccup. "I had a normal life because of him, and he's been so good to me. He loves me, I know he does. He has to."

"Maybe he feels some sort of love for you," Derek whispers. "But however much, it's not enough."

"Marianna, of course he's been nicer to you," Carol says with a slow shake of her head. "You've probably been giving him everything he wants."

"He tried to save me," I say, like it'll make any difference to them. They don't know him like I do. "He loves me so much he knows I'm better off dead than with Viorel."

Carol throws a desperate glance to Mateo. "Tell her Viorel won't hurt her. That he has the best intentions."

"It doesn't matter what I tell her. She won't believe it," he says gently from beside me.

I squeeze my eyes shut and pull my knees up to my chest, bare feet sticking to the leather seat beneath me as I lean my head on my knees.

"Twenty more minutes," a husky voice says from the front.

"Everyone needs to stay out of the way when we get there. They're loading Denendrius up first."

Those twenty minutes feel like an eternity, and I can't imagine how excruciating and painfully slow the rest of my life will be now.

I don't dare lift my head when I hear how we've arrived at the hangar. I try to will myself to wake up from this nightmare, to wake up in my sunny bedroom with Denendrius sleeping soundly beside me. But reality doesn't shift for me no matter how hard I try to force it.

"It's time to go now, honey," Carol whispers, her voice drifting from her seat.

"*No*," I gasp.

Mateo's voice is tender as he says, "No more fighting now. You've got a whole new world waiting for you. I can't imagine what you're feeling right now, but hang on a little longer."

Cold hands gently pull my arms from where they're wrapped around my legs. I don't resist.

"I want to go home," I cry as I lift my head when the vehicle door opens, and a cold gust of wind reaches in to beckon me. "Please, I want everything to go back to how it was a few days ago. He's so different human." I think of the cure back at the house. Would Denendrius survive if he took it again? Would I be able to convince him to?

Mateo holds my face in his hands as he stands outside the door, his rings cold against my flushed cheeks. "Denendrius is a very sick man, Marianna. This is what he does. He's stuck in a loop, and I don't think he could stop himself even if he really wanted to."

My bottom lip trembles. "Maybe someone should have helped him when he really needed it, then. Viorel broke him in Sirmium, and now he's going to break him again." A tear darts from my eye, and he rubs it away with his thumb.

"I know nothing about that, Marianna. Now come on, we

have to board the plane." Mateo's lips form a tight line, and his hands lower.

I hug myself and shake my head, then tense as he picks me off the seat like I'm a small child and rounds the front of the van.

A large white jet waits on the runway, red and green lights illuminating the shadowed men busy around it. Wind assaults my ears, and I squeeze my eyes shut and will it to blow me out of Mateo's arms and back home.

I feel like I'm falling through time. The wind disappears, the sound of a TV filling the surrounding space. My eyes pop open as my body presses into something soft.

I'm in the jet, lying on the beige leather seat of a couch across from a large TV in the plane's wall. A colorful animated film plays on screen. My mind is too numb to focus on it.

"Where's Denendrius?" I whisper, looking around the light beige tones of the interior seats and walls for the steel coffin.

"Don't worry about him anymore, Marianna," Mateo says as he sits on the couch next to my head. "There's a movie here for you to focus on. My wife thought it might make the flight more bearable for you."

"Can he hear me?" I whisper. He must be able to if he's on board, if he's really aware of everything.

"Asil, pass me a blanket from the cupboard, will you?" Mateo asks instead of answering my question.

Asil, a tall man with a thick beard, nods as he appears through the plane door beside the couch next to the TV. A dark, star-speckled sky is beyond it.

A fraction of a second later, soft fabric is cascading over me.

"How's she doing?" Asil asks Mateo as he moves aside for Carol, Derek, and Rayonne as they come up the steps.

I answer the stupid question myself. "How do you think? I'm being kidnapped."

A low chuckle escapes Mateo and he adjusts the blanket on

me. "The thing about my world is that I don't have to ask your permission to save you."

Asil gives me a thoughtful smile. "Don't you worry, once your head is clear, you'll be so happy to be there. The castle is a beautiful place."

I doubt it when it's run by an evil man like Viorel.

When the plane door closes, it seals the fate of my future. I'll never see my friends again, never know if I'm smart enough to pass tenth grade this time, never know what it's like to go to prom or hold a diploma. I'll never know if Denendrius would have been okay if I had done a better job at convincing him to stay human.

My chance for any type of normal human life takes off when we do. I can feel in the marrow of my bones that nothing will ever be the same. Everything is truly different now, and I've never been more terrified.

READY TO READ THE NEXT INSTALLMENT?

Head over to www.beronikakeres.com to keep up with the action.

If you'd like to sign up for my newsletter while you're there, you'll get to stay in the loop about upcoming releases and other fun stuff!

ABOUT THE AUTHOR

Beronika Keres is a fantasy, thriller, and horror writer. After deciding in the second grade that she was destined to be an author, she has spent her life honing her craft and pursuing her dream. Fueled by coffee, she can often be found chasing plot bunnies and writing books.

When she isn't writing, she can be found spending time with her family and enjoying the forests, mountains, and lakes of where she resides in British Columbia, Canada.

www.beronikakeres.com

facebook.com/AuthorBeronikaKeres

instagram.com/beronikakeres